Jᴇꜱꜱᴇ ꜱᴛᴏᴏᴅ near the back of the crowd of well-wishers and listened as first Beck made a toast, followed by one given by Dallas, then another by Grant. His mind began drifting back to that moment earlier when he'd crossed Cherry Street at the top of the block just as Brooke began to park the car. He'd just made it to Vanessa's driveway when Brooke stumbled and fell forward and the tower of white boxes began to shift. If he'd been two steps sooner, he'd have been able to prevent the top boxes from toppling.

The look on Brooke's face had been sheer panic and total devastation when those three boxes hit the ground. He understood what it meant to need to make a great first impression, how sometimes the direction of your life could depend on it. He was glad that he had been the one there to lend a hand and to help put a smile back on her face.

It was a beautiful smile, and a heart-stoppingly beautiful face. Hadn't his own heart all but stopped when she'd walked up to him and called his name a few minutes ago? Through the crowd he could see her, and he was finding it hard to look away.

By Mariah Stewart

Almost Home
Home Again
Coming Home
Hometown Girl

Acts of Mercy
Cry Mercy
Mercy Street

Last Breath
Last Words
Last Look

Final Truth
Dark Truth
Hard Truth
Cold Truth

Dead End
Dead Even
Dead Certain
Dead Wrong

Forgotten
Until Dark
The President's Daughter

Hometown Girl

The Chesapeake Diaries Book 4

Mariah Stewart

BALLANTINE BOOKS • NEW YORK

A Ballantine Books Mass Market Original

Copyright © 2011 by Marti Robb
Excerpt from *Home Again* copyright © 2010 by Marti Robb
Excerpt from *Almost Home* copyright © 2011 by Marti Robb

Published in the United States by Ballantine Books, an imprint of The Random House Publishing Group, a division of Random House, Inc., New York.

BALLANTINE and colophon are trademarks of Random House, Inc.

ISBN 978-0-345-53121-6
eBook ISBN 978-0-345-53146-9

Cover illustration: Chris Cocoazza/Artworks

Printed in the United States of America

www.ballantinebooks.com

9 8 7 6 5 4 3 2 1

Ballantine Books mass market edition: October 2011

For Sweet Baby James Delvescovo—
keep on fighting, little buddy

ACKNOWLEDGMENTS

Once again, my thanks to the fabulous team at Ballantine Books who work so hard to make my books the best they can be: Kate Collins, Linda Marrow, Scott Shannon, Libby McGuire, Kim Hovey, Gina Wachtel, Junessa Viloria, Scott Biel (those glorious covers!), Kristin Fassler, and Katie O'Callaghan. Thanks to Andrea Sheriden, The Decimater, for doing what she does, and doing it so well.

Thanks as always to my agent, Loretta Barrett, and the crew at Barrett Books.

Many thanks to the booksellers who have been hand-selling the books in the Chesapeake Diaries series. Bless every one of you.

Thanks to my FB buddies who start and end the day with me.

Recently it occurred to me that *Hometown Girl* is my thirtieth book. Thirty books! The number stuns and amazes me and gives me chills. So I must say thank you from the bottom of my heart to those readers who have been with me since *Moments in Time* was published in 1995. This has been one wild and crazy ride!

To my friends who have made this journey with me—especially Helen Egner and Chery Griffin . . . thanks and love.

And of course, much love and thanks to my beautiful family—Bill, Becca, Katie, and Mike.

Diary ~

Is there anything quite like a brisk morning in late October? The blood moves a bit quicker, the heart beats a little faster, and the step is just a little livelier than in summer when the heat and humidity bear down mercilessly. But I do have to confess that I do not like this daylight savings time moving into early fall the way it has these past few years. It's bad enough that the days are starting to grow shorter on their own, without imposing an earlier "fall behind" on us all!

There. Rant over!

I love all the merriness of the season as much now as I did when I was a child—the scarecrows that suddenly appear on the front porches and lawns, their straw-filled flannel shirts and old jeans held up by corn shocks or lampposts that seem to be everywhere. And the pumpkins! Oh my, the pumpkins, with faces like grinning demons, lit from within, or painted to look like clowns. Oh, and the ever-popular cat silhouettes, their tails straight up in the air as they shriek silently at some passing fright—ah, I have to admit, I love it all! I have always loved Halloween—especially here in St. Dennis, where we do the holiday justice.

Just last month, I sat in on the planning committee for this year's Halloween Parade, and I have to say it's going to be glorious fun! We're going to close down Charles

Street and have the children parade right through the center of town to the marina, where we'll give out prizes for the best costumes and award all the participants with ice cream made especially for the occasion by Steffie at Scoop and apples from Madison's Orchards. All the merchants in town have contributed something to the festivities—mostly in the form of prizes—and I love that the entire community is involved. We have selected our Halloween queen, as we do every year, but of course, my lips are sealed, as it's a huge no-no to reveal her identity until the day of the parade. As far as I know, no one has ever let that cat out of the bag prematurely. It would simply take away the fun of it all. But I will say that this year's selection is especially fitting, and will be met with universal approval, I believe. Then, later, there's the traditional trick or treat for the children, and later still, a bonfire on the square.

It seems like only yesterday I was dressing my children in their costumes and shepherding them into town for the parade. Dan would take the three of them—Daniel, Lucy, and Ford—trick or treating among the friends and neighbors and family in town, and bring them home hours later, exhausted and dragging pillowcases stuffed with enough treats to last for weeks. No thoughts of razor blades or poisoned candy bars back then, although one year someone did slip a couple of dog biscuits into Ford's bag, much to his dismay.

Those were indeed good old days. My Dan was still alive and we were all together, all five of us, under the same roof every night. When I closed my eyes to fall asleep, I knew where all three of my precious children were. That's a claim I haven't been able to make in many years, much to my sorrow. Ah, well—perhaps someday . . .

~ Grace ~

Chapter 1

AT the moment the moon began its descent and the sun started to rise, the back door of the old farmhouse opened and a petite woman with a long strawberry-blond ponytail stepped out onto the porch. Brooke Madison Bowers hesitated for a moment before walking on bare feet through the cool dew-covered grass that was a week overdue for a mowing. When she reached the small fence-enclosed garden, she pushed aside the squeaky gate and headed for the stone bench, where she sat alone in the soft shadows and the hush of the new day until the dawn began to break in earnest.

The backs of her thighs drew the chill from the damp stone despite the sweatpants she wore, and she shifted uncomfortably. She pulled up her legs and wrapped her arms around them and wished she'd grabbed a jacket on her way through the kitchen. Shoes would have been nice, too. Goose bumps rose on her arms under her sweatshirt, and she thought it would be especially nice if the sun, just now nudging over the smallest of the three barns, would move just a little faster.

Light silently fanned out across fields she'd played in once upon a time. The memory of chasing their dogs through the rows of corn was so fresh, so real, she had to stop and mentally tally just how many years it had been since she'd been a child.

That many? Really?

The dogs were long gone, and her life had taken many an unexpected road since they'd romped together. It was hard to believe that the onetime Miss Blue Claw and Miss Eastern Shore—the golden girl, the beauty queen, the girl most likely to succeed—was once again living on her family farm, sleeping under the familiar red roof with her mother down the hall to the left in the room she'd shared with Brooke's father for forty-two years, and her brother two doors down to the right. Déjà vu all over again. Except that it wasn't.

For one thing, her father had passed away two years ago. For another, the room next to Brooke now belonged to her son. The biggest change of all was that the once happy-go-lucky girl was now a not-so-merry widow.

"Brooke? You out there?" her brother called to her as he crossed the yard. She'd been so lost in thought she'd heard neither the back door nor his footsteps.

"Here, Clay. In the herb garden."

He pushed through the gate, telling her, "I've got coffee."

"You're a good brother."

"The best." He handed her a mug of coffee and took a seat next to her on the bench.

"Thanks."

"Sure." Clay stretched his long legs out in front of him and took a deep breath. "Everything okay? How are your finances holding up?"

"Fine. Between Eric's benefits and the life insurance and some investments, I'm fine."

"You know if you needed anything . . ."

"I do know. And I thank you."

"You're welcome."

"Beautiful sunrise," she observed, mostly to change the subject.

"Nothing like early morning. Watching the light spread across the orchard like that . . . I never get tired of it." He raised his mug in a sort of salute in the direction of the apple trees that formed the property line beyond the garden.

"Old Clay Madison had a farm," she sang under her breath. "Do I have to add the 'E-I, E-I-O'?"

Clay laughed. "Hey, it's all old Clay Madison ever really wanted." After a pause, he asked, "What about you, Brooke? What do you want?"

"Today?" She sighed. "I just want to get through today without going off the deep end. I keep going back and forth between feeling just plain sad and just plain pissed off."

"Please accept my apologies in advance for being an insensitive ass, but what's today? Other than Logan's birthday."

"That's it. Logan's eight years old today."

"And that makes you sad and angry?"

"Because Eric isn't here for it, and he'll never be here for any of Logan's birthdays." She paused. "Actually, Eric hasn't been around for any of his birthdays. He was in Iraq for the first four, and these past few years, he's been gone."

"Damn," he said softly. "Has it been three years?"

"Two and a half since my husband was blown up in Iraq and my life blew up in my face." She cleared her throat and tried to keep her voice from quivering.

She glanced at her brother and could tell he was struggling to find something—the right something—to say.

"It's okay," she assured him. "I mean, what do you say? 'I'm sorry Eric didn't live to see his son grow up and I'm still sorry that he died'?"

"I am still sorry that Eric died. He was a hell of a guy."

She turned her back on him and rested against his shoulder.

"Did I say the wrong thing?"

"No, you said exactly the right thing. I just want to lean," she said. "'Member when we were kids and we sat out here at night and tried to count the stars?"

"Yeah. I think the most I ever counted was a hundred and fifty-three before I gave up." He turned and faced the opposite direction so that she could rest her back squarely against his. "Better?"

"Much. Thanks."

They sat in silence and drank their coffee while the day unfolded around them.

"I guess I should go in and see if Logan—"

"Brooke, I know how hard the past few years have been for you. I know it's *still* hard. But . . ." Clay hesitated, as if not sure he wanted to continue.

"But . . . ?" She waited.

"But maybe . . . well, maybe it might be time to try to start to rebuild your life."

"I *am* rebuilding my life. By December, I'll have my degree and I'm starting my own business. I'd call that rebuilding."

He nodded. "It is. You are. Of course you are. And I'm really proud of you for doing all those things. A lot of people wouldn't have bothered to take those last courses for their B.S., and I know you've put a lot of time into starting up this business of yours, but . . ."

"But . . . ?" She swung her legs around and plunked her bare feet on the ground. Her toes curled up against the cold.

"But maybe it's time for you to, you know, get out a little more."

"I get out. I get out plenty. Last night I went with Dallas to look for her wedding dress. Tomorrow night I'm going over to Vanessa's to help get things ready for the engagement party she's hosting this weekend for Steffie and Wade."

"That's not exactly what I meant. I meant, like, with a guy."

"You mean dating?" She frowned. "I've gone on dates. I've gone on *lots* of dates."

"You've gone on lots of *first* dates."

"What's your point?" Brooke loved her brother but knew where he was heading and she didn't really want to go there.

"My point is that sooner or later you're going to run out of guys to have first dates with." His voice was gentle, and she gave him points for the effort. "I'm just a little concerned that you never seem to give anyone a real chance."

She stared at him.

"What's that supposed to mean?"

"It means that you flirt with a guy, you go out with him, then . . . nothing. I mean, every guy on the Eastern Shore can't be a dud. There are a lot of nice guys in town."

"I know." Mentally she took back the points she'd just given him. "I've gone out with several nice guys."

"Once. You go out with them once, then find a reason to never go out with the same guy again."

"No chemistry."

"I think the truth is that you don't want there to be any chemistry. You like the company, you like the attention, and I know you well enough to know that you like getting dressed up and looking gorgeous and going out. But the bottom line? You don't really want a relationship with anyone." He took her hand. "You're too young to give up, toots. You're beautiful and fun and you deserve to have a beautiful, fun life with someone who adores you."

"I had that." She pulled her hand away. "Now I don't. End of story."

"Doesn't mean that it's the end of your story."

"Yes, it does. You get one soul mate, Clay. I had mine." Her eyes filled with tears. "I loved Eric so much. We had the best plans for the best life you could possibly imagine. We were going to have more kids, he was going to go back into the business he started with his brother, we were . . ." She swallowed back the lump in her throat. "We were going to grow old together. Raise our kids and spoil our grandkids. Buy a boat and travel the Intercoastal Waterway, then retire on a beach somewhere. Then *bam!* Gone."

"Brooke, the human heart . . ." Clay struggled to voice his thoughts, as if speaking them aloud for the first time. "There aren't limits on how many people we can love."

"Oh, I know that. But I could never replace him."

"It's not about *replacing*. Of course you can't. You're always going to love him, and you should. But that doesn't mean you can't find someone else to love, too." Before she could protest, he added, "Loving someone else doesn't mean you're replacing Eric, honey. It's not a betrayal. And sooner or later, you're going to have to move on."

"Why?" She knew she sounded pathetic but didn't really care.

"Because the last thing Eric would have wanted would be for you to not live—really live—the rest of your life. You're really young, you know. There's someone else for you to love somewhere."

"You know, there was a time, after Eric died, I wanted to die, too, so I could be with him. But there was Logan, and I couldn't leave our son alone like that." She shook her head. "I don't want to love anyone like that ever again. I'll never risk that kind of pain again." She looked up at Clay. "I appreciate that you care, I really do. But I have no interest in falling in love or anything that complicates my life. Thus the occasional first date suits me just fine."

Clay nodded, his way of conceding the argument.

"Would it be rude of me to mention that I don't recall the last time you were involved with anyone for any length of time?" She thought she'd throw that out there. Tit for tat, as it were.

"I haven't found the right girl." He looked away.

"The difference between you and me is that I'm looking. You're not looking."

"You're right. I'm not."

"Brooke. Life goes on. It has to."

Because she didn't know how to reply to that, she stood and drained the last drops of coffee from her mug. "You coming in?" she asked, signaling that the discussion was over.

"I'll be along. I want to do a little watering out here first. Won't be too much longer before we get frost. I want to keep the herbs going for as long as I can."

"I'll see you inside." Brooke pushed the gate open, but before she stepped through it, she turned back. "Clay, I do appreciate that you're concerned. I know that you care. It means a lot to me that you do."

He nodded and handed her his mug to take back to the house. "You're the only sister I've got. I want you to be happy."

"I'm happy," she assured him. "Just not in the way I used to be."

Halfway to the house she called back to him. "You need to cut the grass, bucko."

"It's on the list," he called back.

Brooke tiptoed on cold feet into the quiet farmhouse. The ticking of the ancient grandfather clock in the front hall was the only sound. She made a brief stop in the kitchen to refill her mug before going upstairs to wake her son for school.

Logan had been a baby when Eric first deployed. Brooke could count on the fingers of one hand the number of times father and son had been together. She knew that Logan had no real memories of his father, and that in itself was enough to break her heart.

Eric had been thrilled when Logan was born and had looked forward to watching him grow. Brooke took every opportunity to talk about Eric, to make him a real person to Logan, but she couldn't help but wonder how her son really felt.

She pushed open his bedroom door and found him already up and looking out the window.

"Whatcha doing?" She tried to force a light tone to her voice.

"Uncle Clay is out in the garden," he told her without turning around. "He's watering the stuff that we planted out there. We checked last night. Some of the stuff is still growing, but he said the season is almost over."

"That's what happens. You plant the seeds, you water them, they grow. Then one season comes to an end, and the next begins." She sat on the corner of his bed.

"Today is my birthday," he told her.

"That's right. Happy birthday. You're a big eight years old today."

He went to his desk and picked up the calendar where he'd marked off days with a big X and where he'd printed important reminders in his awkward second-grade hand. Softball practice. A class trip. The Halloween parade. His soccer games.

"See?" He pointed to today's date and read, " 'My birthday.' "

"I see."

He put the calendar back on his desk.

"Let me give you a birthday hug." She motioned for him to come to her and she put her arms around him.

He permitted a quick one before running off to the bathroom. Seconds later, he stuck his head back out through the door. "Can I still go to softball after school even though it's my birthday?"

"Sure. It's your day and we're not having your party till Friday afternoon. So definitely, you can go to softball."

Logan ducked back into the bathroom and closed the door.

After breakfast, while Logan was packing his schoolbag, Brooke noticed that he'd removed the old catcher's mitt—Eric's old glove—and replaced it with the new one he'd gotten last Christmas.

"Don't you want to use your dad's glove?" she asked.

"No," he replied, and continued on packing his things.

"Why not?" She picked up Eric's worn mitt and slipped her hand inside, tracing the path his fingers had once taken with her own.

"Sometimes the gloves get mixed up and kids take the wrong stuff home with them."

She understood. Eric's glove was too precious to risk to a possible switch.

"Wait till I get something on my feet and I'll walk you to the bus stop," she said.

"You don't have to."

"I'd like to." She searched for the flip-flops she knew she'd left downstairs the night before. "If it's okay . . ."

"It's okay."

"Great." She located her sandals under the kitchen table and slipped her feet into them. "Let's do it."

They were almost to the end of the lane when Logan asked, "Can I have a dog?"

"What kind of dog?"

"A nice dog. I don't care what kind." He shifted his shoulders to distribute the weight of the book bag. "A dog would make a really cool birthday present."

"I thought you wanted a new bike," she said, thinking of the new three-speed that Clay had hidden in the barn.

"I do. But a dog would be even cooler."

"I guess you like playing with Cody's dog." Cody was his best friend and the proud owner of a bichon frise named Fleur that he'd gotten from the rescue shelter run by the town vet.

"Yeah." He nodded. "But I saw a thing on TV about what happens to dogs if no one rescues them and it was awful. They said lots of good dogs were waiting for their new owners." His face darkened, and when he looked up, his eyes told the whole story. "What if there's a dog waiting for me? What if it was waiting and I didn't come for it?"

She started to speak, but he continued what sounded like a well-rehearsed argument.

"You and Uncle Clay had dogs when you were little. I saw their pictures. And Daddy had a dog, too. It was in one of the pictures in that book you have."

Brooke remembered.

"I'll have to talk to Uncle Clay," she told him. "After all, it's his house now, not ours."

"How come it's his and not yours?" At the sound of the approaching school bus, Logan leaned toward the road, craning his neck as if he could see around the curve.

"Because he's the farmer in the family, and Grampa was happy to pass the farm on to someone who loved it and who'd work it."

"How come you didn't want it?"

The yellow bus slowed as it came around the bend and came to a stop on the opposite side of the road. Several small boys hung out the windows, calling Logan's name.

"'Cause I'm a baker, not a farmer."

She started to reach for him to kiss the top of his head, but he was already on his way across the road, yelling to his friends. He disappeared for a second or two as he rounded the front of the bus, but once on board, reappeared bounding down the aisle to join the other kids. The bus driver waved as she pulled away, and Brooke waved back. She shoved her hands in the pockets of her khaki shorts and watched the bus take the first curve in the road. When she could no longer hear its groaning engine, she started back up the lane to the farmhouse.

"Hey, Brooke!"

She turned at the sound of her name just as a sleek little sports car, its top down, stopped at the end of the drive.

"Hi, Jesse." She smiled and strolled over and leaned on the passenger-side door. "What's up?"

"Not much. Just taking the long way to the office this morning." Jesse Enright had arrived in St. Dennis several months ago to help out his grandfather in the family law firm. As far as Brooke could see, he wasn't in any hurry to leave.

"If I had one of these little babies, I'd be taking the

long way everywhere." She ran an appreciative hand along the side of the car.

"Hop in. I'll take you for a ride."

Jesse's smile was enticing—there was no way of getting around that, but she glanced at her watch and knew she was already off her self-imposed schedule.

"I'd love to, but I have some things that need tending to this morning," she said, not without some small degree of regret. It had been a long time since she'd tossed her "must-do's" aside and started off the day with the wind in her hair.

"Another time, then." He revved the engine. "By the way, when are you coming in to talk about your will?"

"I'll call your office and make that appointment soon."

"Ask for Liz. Tell her I said to fit you in at the first available. Not that we expect anything to happen to you, but—"

"No, you're absolutely right. First I have to dig up Eric's will and the one we made together."

"Just bring them in and we'll take care of it."

"Thanks, Jesse. I appreciate that."

"Sure." He put the car in gear. "See you around."

"See you around." She stepped back and watched him turn the car around and head off into town. He waved without looking back, and she returned the wave even though she doubted he'd seen her. She made a mental note to call his office as soon as she got into the house. Jesse was right. She needed to have her will updated. What if something did happen to her? Logan's interests needed to be protected, and she felt she could trust Jesse to know the best way to do that.

There was something about him that was solid and strong, and the times she'd been in his company, she'd found him to be funny and smart. She'd tried to put her finger on the ways he was different from most of the guys she'd dated in the past but wasn't really sure she could define it.

And okay, yes—the guy was hot, there was no point in denying, but that had absolutely nothing to do with it.

Her mother's car was heading down the lane, the old Subaru swerving to avoid several large potholes in the dirt drive. It slowed as it approached Brooke.

"Clay's going to have to do something about these damned potholes," Hannah Madison called out the window, barely pausing. "I'm off to meet the girls at the marina for our morning walk, then I'm going into the shop. I'll see you later."

"Have fun." Brooke waved as the car rolled by. It occurred to her that her mother might be handling her widow's status better than she. A lifelong resident of St. Dennis—except for the three years of retirement she and Brooke's dad had had in Myrtle Beach before his fatal heart attack—Hannah Madison had many friends and her shop, Bow Wows and Meows, where she sold fun items for pampered pets.

So what does it say about you if your sixty-eight-year-old mother has a more fulfilling social life than you do?

Brooke told her inner voice to shut up and she went into the house. She stopped to refill her mug before going into the small den her father had used as an office. Clay had commandeered the room when he took over the farm, but Brooke had carved out a corner for herself when she decided to start up her cupcake business.

She sat on the window-seat cushion, turned on her laptop, and waited for her screen saver to appear.

When the big cupcake with the pink frosting filled the screen, she smiled, and opened the file titled *Cupcake*.

She scrolled through the list of things to do and realized that she'd already accomplished so much.

On the current day's list there were three items:

1. Test lemon recipe (try fondant flowers).
2. Need van.
3. Make appointments for next week to take samples to Lola's, Scoop, and Cuppachino.

She was sure the test batch of cupcakes would be good. She'd been playing around with the recipe for the past few days, and thought she had it nailed now. Finding a van to take her cupcake business mobile the way she'd planned might not be as difficult as she'd originally thought. There was that old white van in one of the barns. Clay didn't seem to be using it, and with an appropriate paint job and a little bit of a tune-up, it could be just the thing. Visiting the three most popular establishments in town was never a hardship: she had friends in each place, and felt fairly certain that no one would turn down her offer for them to sell her amazingly good confections. Another week or so and she'd be ready. "Cupcake" would be off and running.

She couldn't help but think how proud Eric would have been.

Chapter 2

BROOKE fussed more than she'd intended when she began arranging her cupcakes on the round silver tray she found in the sideboard that had stood in the dining room for as long as she could remember. The tray was black with age and she suspected it had last been polished when she was still in her teens. But under the tarnish were roses that wound completely around the tray, and once she started polishing, she couldn't stop. By the time she finished, the roses gleamed and the fancy scripted monogram in the middle—*MJG*—was visible.

She carried the tray to the back porch, where her mother was drinking her after-dinner coffee and watching the sun set.

"Mom, who was MJG?" Brooke asked from the doorway.

"Who was who?"

Brooke stepped out onto the porch and held up the tray.

"MJG, see the monogram right here?"

Hannah peered more closely, thought about it for a moment, then shook her head. "I have no idea. Must have been someone on your father's side. It's lovely, though. Where did you find it?"

"In the sideboard. I was looking for something pretty to put cupcakes on to take over to Vanessa's." Brooke sat on the porch railing. "I'm debuting my rose-garden cupcakes tonight. This tray is perfect for displaying them."

"Make sure you take some pictures for your portfolio before you leave. Those fancy little cakes are beautiful."

"I hope Steffie thinks so. They're for her engagement party."

"I'm sure they'll be a big hit. You haven't had a miss yet. Of course, your brother and I are packing on the pounds, with all the sampling we've been doing." Hannah hastened to add, "Not that I'm complaining. I can't deny that I love a little sweet something after dinner."

Brooke smiled. "You've both been such good sports about having to be my guinea pigs." She leaned over to kiss her mother on the forehead. "I left a few on the counter. Don't let Logan have more than one, and make sure his homework is finished before he has his snack. I'll try to be back before his bedtime. And tell Clay not to eat all the cupcakes at one sitting."

"I'll pass that on, but I have no control over your brother. Not that I ever did."

Brooke laughed and went back into the house. She found the white paper doilies in the pantry and selected one that would fit the inside of the tray. She placed the cupcakes in concentric circles on the doily, then added a tiny bit of sparkly sugar crystals to the frosting.

"Too cute," she murmured.

She took half a dozen shots with her digital camera, grabbed a sweater and the tray, and set out for Vanessa Keaton's house on Cherry Street. Brooke was the last of the party-planning group to arrive, and she sailed into Vanessa's kitchen and placed the tray on the counter.

"So, what do you think?" Brooke's friends gathered like staring vultures and peered over her shoulder.

"Oh, dear Lord." Vanessa crossed both hands over the center of her chest. "Are they real? They're too pretty to be real."

"Gorgeous." Steffie Wyler leaned closer. "They look like flowers. Perfect little flowers." She looked up at Brooke. "How could anyone eat one of those pretty little things?"

"Like this." Dallas MacGregor, Brooke's closest friend and Steffie's soon-to-be sister-in-law, scooped up a cupcake that looked like a pale pink rose and took a bite. "I happen to know from experience that these little numbers are perfection."

"Keep scarfing them down and we'll be ordering your wedding dress two sizes up," Stef warned.

Dallas licked frosting from the corner of her mouth. "Then there'd be more of me for your brother to love."

Steffie rolled her eyes.

"Stef's right." Brooke nodded. "I don't want to be known as the woman who ruined Dallas MacGregor's film career by pushing an extra thirty pounds onto her previously flawless body."

"I have no immediate plans to return to the big screen. For the time being, I'm happier behind the scenes." Dallas took another bite and smiled. "This is heaven."

Vanessa studied the array of goodies, then reached for the yellow rose cupcake, muttering, "No will-power. None at all."

"Dallas, how's your new screenplay coming along?" Brooke asked, knowing that Dallas was dying to talk about her new project.

"It's finished. Finished and fabulous, if I do say so myself. I can't wait until we complete the casting and start shooting the film."

As teenagers, Dallas and Brooke had been rivals for Grant Wyler's affection. On her way to becoming a big screen star, Dallas had left St. Dennis and Grant behind. But since she'd moved to St. Dennis following a divorce, Hollywood style, Dallas and Grant had fallen in love all over again, and she and Brooke had become best friends in spite of their history.

"I think it's so cool that you're building a studio right here in St. Dennis." Vanessa peeled the paper from her cupcake.

Dallas shrugged. "Those old warehouses were just sitting there, waiting for someone to come up with a good use for them. I was lucky to buy them before someone else did. The renovation work is coming along quite nicely, by the way. The contractors have promised that everything will be finished by spring."

"Grant said some Hollywood types would be in town next week to look over your progress." Steffie looked from Dallas to Vanessa, who were obviously enjoying their treats. "I can't be the only holdout here. It would be wrong."

She glanced up at Brooke as she lifted her choice, chocolate with ganache rosettes. "But I do think you should pick up the tab for the alterations on the dress I was planning on wearing to the party."

"Brooke did not force you to commit . . ." Vanessa paused and appeared to ponder. "Now, would over-indulging in cupcakes be considered gluttony or lust?"

"Both," Brooke told her.

"In for a dime, in for a dollar." Dallas grinned and surveyed the remaining cupcakes as if debating with herself. "I really shouldn't have a second."

"No, you shouldn't," Steffie replied. "A moment on the lips, forever on the hips."

Dallas backed away from the tray and sat on one of the stools that were lined up in front of the counter.

"I think it's nerves. There's so much going on right now that some days I don't know what to do first," she confessed. "It's the wedding and starting my business—just trying to decide who to invite to the one and who to hire for the other is making me crazy."

"Understandable." Brooke nodded. "But the answer isn't in food."

"Where is it?" Dallas asked.

"We could have consulted the Ouija board," Stef told her, "but Ness gave hers to Grace Sinclair. Maybe I should buy one. I wonder if it would work as well . . ."

"Yoga." Brooke ignored Steffie. "It's amazing how calming it is."

"I've done yoga for years and I'm still running on fumes right now," Dallas told her.

"In that case, I'd go for the cupcake," Stef told her. "But I do highly recommend yoga."

"You're having the wedding at the inn and they have a wedding planner, right?" Brooke said, referring to the Inn at Sinclair's Point, St. Dennis's renowned historic inn where more and more weddings were being booked. "Don't they take care of everything? Shouldn't their wedding planner be worrying about all the stuff that's making you crazy?"

"One would think. But apparently the new person isn't accustomed to an event on the scale Grant and I are having," Dallas replied.

"I thought you were going low-key. Small wedding party, not a lot of fuss," Brooke noted.

"That was before we started making up the guest list and found we weren't able to leave anyone out. We are still sticking to just the few attendants," Dallas told her. "The three of you plus one old friend for me, Wade, Beck, and Cameron for Grant. And of course, my soon-to-be stepdaughter, Paige, will be my junior bridesmaid and Cody will be a junior usher."

"Did you make a decision on who will walk with you down the aisle, Dallas?" Vanessa asked.

"Wade is the only person I want to make that walk with."

"Will your mother be there?" Stef asked, knowing that Dallas and Wade's mother hadn't been a big part of their lives for a long time.

Dallas shrugged but made no comment.

"You should talk to Grace." Brooke was still thinking about the logistics of the actual wedding and the reception. "You know that her daughter, Lucy, is an event planner in California, right? Maybe some of your Hollywood friends have even used her. I heard she's really popular."

"If she's really good, she'll be busy out there," Dallas said. "Grace did say she's been trying to get Lucy to come back to St. Dennis and take over the wedding part of the business, but Lucy isn't interested."

"Lucy and my brother, Clay, went all through school together," Brooke recalled. "They used to be good friends, but I don't think they keep in touch anymore."

"Well, it would be nice if the inn had someone who didn't seem to be overwhelmed every time I called her." Dallas took the stool next to Brooke. "Madeline seems to be in a perpetual state of confusion."

"So have you and Wade set a date yet?" Brooke turned to Steffie. "Or will you be saving that bit of info to make an announcement at your engagement party?"

Steffie shook her head. "We can't decide on a date."

"What's the problem?" Dallas asked.

"We just have different ideas, that's all," Steffie explained.

"Like what?" Dallas persisted.

"Like just stuff."

"Talk, Stephanie."

"I can't." Steffie shook her head.

"Why not?"

"Because she doesn't want to upset you, that's why," Vanessa chimed in.

Dallas glanced from Vanessa to Steffie. "One of you will have to tell me."

"Steffie always wanted a winter wedding." Vanessa

blurted it out. "But since you're getting married in December, she feels like she can't."

"Ness." Stef turned to her friend. "Shut. Up."

"I don't understand." Dallas frowned.

"It's all about asking people to make the trip twice, you know, one wedding right after the other . . ." Stef began to fidget. She turned to Vanessa. "Did someone say there would be wine?"

Vanessa took a bottle of Chardonnay from the refrigerator. "Who besides Stef?" she asked.

Brooke and Dallas both raised their hands.

"If you always dreamed of a winter wedding, you should have a winter wedding," Dallas told her. "Grant and I can wait till spring."

"No. You have dibs," Stef protested. "You got engaged first. And you already reserved the date at the inn."

"So you and Wade take the date," Dallas offered.

Steffie shook her head. "All along you've been saying that you wanted the wedding behind you before spring because you're going to be tied up with your movie."

"Well, that part is true, but—"

"I have the solution." Brooke pinged a fingertip against the side of her wineglass to get their attention. "You both get married in December at the inn. On the same day."

"What?" Steffie frowned.

"Wow, that could be very cool," Vanessa said. "If, of course, you'd both be all right with that."

"Interesting idea." Dallas considered. "We'd be inviting a lot of the same people, so they would only have to make the trip once. We could reserve the inn for the entire day, and—"

"Your wedding is going to be much bigger than ours. We're small town. You're Hollywood."

"Hollywood *and* small town," Dallas reminded her. "I like to think we're both."

"Your Hollywood friends won't care a fig about seeing Wade and me married," Stef continued.

"Why don't you have one ceremony in the afternoon, and the other in the evening?" Brooke suggested. "Cocktail hour in between ceremonies. Big blowout reception after the second one."

"We've already decided that what we really want is a big party. After all, this is the second wedding for both Grant and me," Dallas reminded them. "But having both on the same day could be fun. What do you think, Stef?"

"I think you're all bat-shit crazy if you think I'm going to set myself up to be compared to Dallas MacGregor on my wedding day."

"What are you talking about?" Dallas frowned.

"You're going to be the most beautiful bride that ever was." Stef replied. "I'm—"

"You're the woman my brother fell in love with," Dallas told her gently, "and you will be a drop-dead, stunningly magnificent bride."

Steffie sniffed and Vanessa went for the tissues.

"That's so nice of you to say, but . . ." Steffie held out a hand and Vanessa handed her a tissue.

"No *buts*. Let's look at the bottom line. You're right to consider that some members of your family will have to travel a distance to get here. I know I'll need to talk to Grant—and of course you'll discuss it with Wade—but as far as I'm concerned, I would love to share my wedding day with you and Wade. It's up to you, of course, but that's my two cents."

"It could be really fun, Stef. A big family affair. Brother and sister marrying brother and sister." Vanessa refilled everyone's wineglass. "Why don't you think it over and talk to Wade?"

"I haven't even started looking for a dress," Steffie reminded them.

"We'll go to Annapolis tomorrow," Dallas told her. "And if they can't accommodate you there, we'll go to New York. We will find the dress of your dreams and it will be ready by December."

"This will really throw Madeline for a loop. If she's having trouble with just one wedding for that date, how do you think she'll handle two?" Brooke glanced from friend to friend.

"Probably not very well," Dallas conceded.

"Which means we have to work on Grace to get Lucy back here, even if it's just for your wedding." Brooke thought it over for a moment. "Maybe you need to remind Grace that this is Dallas MacGregor. This wedding will draw a lot of attention to the inn. It could be great publicity for them, especially since they're actively trying to build up their reputation as a wedding destination."

"Grace isn't the problem, it's Lucy. She's the one who hasn't wanted to come back here," Vanessa reminded them. "But someone should point out to Grace that if they are trying to establish the Inn at Sinclair's Point as the go-to place on the Eastern Shore, they need to hire someone who can handle anything that's being thrown at them. Madeline's a sweet girl, but she doesn't seem to have much confidence in herself."

"I have the feeling she doesn't have a lot of experience," Dallas added. "I wonder why Grace hired her."

"It wasn't Grace," Brooke told her, "it was Daniel. He knew he was in over his head when he realized the number of weddings he had booked and he knows he doesn't have the temperament or the background to handle anything but small weddings. He mentioned once that he doesn't even really like doing those. Said he's an innkeeper, not an event planner, doesn't like dealing with all the little details, which is why he put the ad out for a professional. Madeline was the first person to respond to the ad and I think she caught him at a moment when he was feeling overwhelmed and desperate."

"You're right, of course. I'll talk to Grace," Dallas said. "I'll tell her that things are going to get much more complicated with two weddings back-to-back. She won't have a choice but to talk to Daniel. And with luck, between the two of them, they can convince Lucy to come back, even if it's only for us for that one day. For Lucy to stay in business for any length of time out in L.A., she has to be good, and she has to have experience with long guest lists and big affairs."

"Maybe Daniel will have more luck with his sister than his mother did," Brooke noted.

"One can hope." Vanessa pulled up a stool and sat. "Now, to get back to the business at hand, that being the party we're supposed to be planning. Though we all know this 'meeting' was merely an excuse for the four of us to get together, drink wine, and eat delicious cupcakes."

"The cupcakes will be ready for Saturday," Brooke told them. "Assuming, of course, that you like what you sampled, Stef."

"I feel I can't really make a decision without trying one of each." Stef smiled. "Or at the very least, one of the fruity ones. Perhaps the lemon. Or maybe the strawberry . . ."

"I can attest to the fabulosity of the lemon," Vanessa said.

"The strawberry is equally fabulous," Dallas assured her.

"But of course, if you feel you must . . ." Brooke moved the tray of cupcakes closer to Stef.

"I had one. I'll resist the temptation to have another." Steffie sighed. "But, Brooke, I think you should be selling these in my shop. What's more wonderful together than ice cream and cake?"

"Well, I admit, I had thought of asking you about that," Brooke replied.

"I get requests all the time for cakes to go with the ice cream I sell for kids' parties and showers," Stef continued. "It would be great if you had some samples right there in the shop so customers could try them out. And after school I am deluged with hungry kids. Maybe we could work out a cupcake-and-one-scoop special."

"Whenever you say, I'll bring down a tray." Brooke's heart danced in her chest. She'd been wanting to approach Steffie about selling her cupcakes from the very popular ice-cream shop for the past couple of weeks, but wasn't sure how Stef would feel about it. "Just give me a call."

"Whenever you have—let's say, a dozen, dozen and a half—bring them down. You don't need an invitation. Just pack them up and bring them. And hope that I and my staff are able to resist eating them before we can sell them. If you have more of those"—Stef pointed to the tray—"at home, you can bring them down tomorrow." She picked up one of the cupcakes and turned it around. "These would be darling for a shower. Baby or bridal."

"I actually have other designs in mind for showers. Some, I might add, are quite adorable," Brooke said modestly.

"You should make up a few and we'll put them on the counter under a glass dome," Steffie told her. "And bring your business cards down so that everyone knows that they're yours. St. Dennis loves to support its own, you know."

"Thank you, Stef." Brooke smiled. "I appreciate it."

"Don't mention it." Stef turned to Vanessa. "So what else do we have to discuss tonight?"

"Just the ice cream for the party . . ."

"Which I am taking care of myself," Stef reminded her.

"What kind are you making?" Brooke asked.

"It'll be a surprise, but it will be something really, really good," Stef assured her.

"It won't be beer flavored, will it?" Vanessa frowned.

"Why would I make ice cream that tastes like beer?" Stef stared at Vanessa.

"Well, you know, because Wade owned a brewery. Beer is his life," Vanessa explained.

Stef rolled her eyes. "Remind me to consult with you the next time I'm stumped for a new and exciting flavor."

Dallas pulled a pen and a small notebook from her bag and opened it.

"So the cupcakes are under control, as is the ice cream." She crossed two items off her list. "And the caterer has the final count?"

"I'll give it to them on Thursday morning," Vanessa told her. "I don't know that there will be any changes, though. Anyone?"

The other three women shook their heads.

"Petals and Posies will bring the flowers over on Saturday morning," Vanessa continued, "and that's about it for the party. Except, of course, to add that if you're looking for something new and gorgeous to wear, I just took a delivery this afternoon of some stunning little numbers. Nice discount if any of you are interested." Vanessa's shop, Bling, carried upscale clothes and accessories, and she was always generous in offering discounts to her friends.

"Thanks, Ness, but I'm set," Steffie told her.

"Me, too." Dallas closed the notebook and dropped it into her bag along with the pen.

"I might take you up on that," Brooke said. "It's been a while since I bought something new."

"I have just the perfect dress for you. Gorgeous shade of green to set off your eyes."

"I'll be in to take a look."

"Are you bringing a date?" Steffie drained the wine from her glass.

"Me? Nah." Brooke brushed off the question.

"You're welcome to bring someone if you like." Steffie stood and stretched. "You know that, right?"

Brooke nodded. "Thanks, but I'm good."

"If you want, I can have Grant bring that new vet that just moved to Ballard . . ." Dallas offered.

"No, thanks. I'm okay going stag."

"It's not like there aren't any guys in St. Dennis who wouldn't be more than happy to be your date for the evening," Steffie noted.

"Stop. You're starting to sound like my brother," Brooke griped. "And I don't mean that in a good way."

"I just wanted you to know that you were welcome to bring someone," Vanessa said, and Stef nodded in agreement.

"I appreciate that, but no thank you. Besides, anyone I asked would think that I was interested and I'd never get rid of him."

"And besides, too, every eligible guy in town has asked her out at one time or another," Stef reminded them, "and she's sent them all packing."

Not quite everyone, Brooke could have told them. One eligible guy had noticeably *not* asked her out.

"I haven't met anyone I wanted to spend any time with."

Brooke took a few flat white boxes from her bag and began to assemble them.

"What are they for?" Dallas asked.

"So you all can take the leftovers home. I know that your aunt Berry has a fierce sweet tooth," she told Dallas.

"That's so nice." Dallas kissed her on the cheek. "Thanks so much."

"Don't mention it." Brooke split the little cakes equally between the three boxes and left them on the counter. "I should get going. I want to see Logan before he falls asleep. I'll see you all on Saturday."

"Thanks for the bringing the refreshments."

"You're welcome, Ness." Brooke opened the front door. The wind had picked up since she arrived earlier, and a cool shot of air hit her in the face. She lowered her head as she headed out.

"Wait up," Steffie called just as Brooke was about to close the door behind her. "I'll walk out with you."

"Brr, it's getting chillier every day." Brooke huddled inside her sweater and watched a small tornado of leaves spin across the front lawn.

"I know. We both should have worn jackets." Steffie followed Brooke down the sidewalk.

Brooke stepped into the street and stopped in front of her car. "Stef, I really do appreciate your offer to sell my cupcakes at Scoop. I want you to think about what percent of the sales you want."

"What are you talking about? You mean charge you?" Steffie frowned. "I'm not going to charge you for bringing them in."

"But you'll be taking your time . . ."

Steffie rolled her eyes. "Yeah, as much time as it takes for me to say, 'Would you like a cupcake with your ice cream?' and 'Which flavor?'"

"Still, I think I should . . ."

"And I think you shouldn't. If you want to do anything at all, just pay it forward someday when you get the chance."

"That's very nice of you."

"People were very kind to me when I first started Scoop, gave me breaks that I didn't expect. It's my turn now. Someday it'll be yours."

"Thanks, Stef." Brooke unlocked the car with the remote.

"You're welcome. I'll see you sometime tomorrow, right?" Stef called over her shoulder as she hurried against the wind to her car.

"Right. See you then." Brooke opened the driver's-side door and slid behind the wheel of her old Toyota. She took her time getting her seat belt on and the key into the ignition. Stef's unexpected kindness had almost brought tears to her eyes. Not that Stef would have made very much off a few dozen cupcakes, but still, it was the gesture that mattered.

Brooke shifted into gear and headed toward the farm, the game plan for her business running through her head. She really believed that if you visualized what you wanted often enough, sooner or later it would become reality. So in her mind's eye, she saw her cupcakes displayed on a tiered stand on the counter at Scoop. Then she visualized the stand empty after all the little cakes had been sold. She saw them in the front case at Cuppachino, the coffee shop where the local merchants met early in the morning before they opened their respective establishments and stopped in for a quick bite at lunchtime. She saw them on the dessert cart at Café Lola, St. Dennis's upscale dining spot. She saw herself making her deliveries—and for a while, even selling down in the municipal parking lot—from a pink van with a big pink-frosted cupcake on the side. Lastly, she saw

them in the window of her own shop on Charles
Street, right in the very heart of the business district.
There'd be an old-fashioned striped awning and fancy
letters spelling out the name: CUPCAKE.

Every journey begins with a single step, she reminded herself. Tonight, she'd taken hers. Feeling
better about things than she had all day, she drove
slowly up the long drive to the farmhouse, envision-
ing herself behind the wheel of her van, then eventually, turning the sign in the window of her shop from
CLOSED to OPEN.

She parked the car near the back gate and got out,
pausing for a moment to look up for a star to wish
on. It didn't occur to her until much later that, for the
first time in a very long time, her wish had been all
about her and her plans for the future—*I wish this
could work out for me*—and not about her past.

Chapter 3

"Wow, they look great." Clay reached a hand out just as Brooke began to arrange cupcakes in the covered carrier she would use to transport her carefully crafted creations to Scoop.

"Keep your mitts off, bro." She moved the tray out of his way. "None for you this time around."

"Who are they for?"

"I'm taking them to Scoop. Stef offered to sell them in her shop, so I made a few batches when I got home last night." She added the last two cakes to the carrier.

"Nice of Stef." He watched her snap on the lid.

"It really is. And she won't even take a percentage of the sales."

"That's a good friend."

"Don't I know it. I need to get my business up and running as soon as humanly possible so that I can cash in on the coming holiday season, then hopefully build it up through to next year's wedding season. A lot of brides are replacing the traditional wedding cake with special cupcakes. Dallas serving my cupcakes at her birthday party last month did a lot to call

attention to me, but now I have to capitalize on that."
Brooke looked through her bag for her car keys. "I
want to stop at Lola's and Cuppachino this morning
and see if they'll let me sell there as well."

"You're going to be baking around the clock if
everyone says yes," Clay pointed out. "Which I fully
expect they will. The last time I was in Cuppachino at
lunchtime, the only baked stuff they had were the
muffins left over from the early-morning delivery, and
to tell you the truth, they weren't all that good. Maybe
you could take over the muffins, too."

"That's up to Carlo. Meanwhile, I have to get moving. I have a class at one." She glanced at the clock as
she gathered her things. "By the way, that old van in
the garage?"

"What about it?"

"Are you using it for anything?"

"Not at present."

"Could I use it?" She paused in the doorway.

Clay frowned. "Something wrong with your car?"

"No, but it's too small. I could use the van to deliver my cupcakes and I could sell out of it, sort of like
a hot-dog vendor."

"The van needs a lot of work, sis. For one thing, it
has some body cancer. Rust. For another"—he poured
himself a glass of water and took a long drink—"it
doesn't have a backseat. I took it out so I could transport stuff."

"What kind of stuff?"

"You know, stuff. Bushels of apples. Buckets of
herbs. Stuff for the restaurants that we supply during
the summer months."

"Can I clean it up? Paint it?"

"Sure. Do whatever you want." Clay shrugged. "I'm not using it."

"Great! Thanks!" Brooke blew past him on the way to the back door.

Brooke mentally checked off *van* from her list of things she needed to keep her plan moving forward. There was a place in town that painted cars. Over the weekend, she'd drive the van out and get an estimate. Maybe they could do something about the body rust, too. And she'd need to see about having some advertising painted on the side of the van as well. She knew exactly how she wanted it to look.

The flagman for the road repair crew held up a hand for her to slow, then motioned for her to detour from Charles Street onto Elgin. She waved to acknowledge the instruction then turned left. She made a four-block loop before taking a right onto Old St. Mary's Church Road and around the square, the heart of the historic district. A tall, lanky dark-haired man crossed diagonally at the intersection ahead of her, and she stopped at the stop sign to let him pass. He wore a light blue button-down shirt with the sleeves rolled to the elbow and khakis. Brooke smiled as she rolled down the driver's-side window. He certainly did justice to those khakis.

"Looks like casual Friday," she called to him.

"No court today." Jesse walked over to the car. "No tie, no jacket."

She made a point of looking at her watch. "I've heard of banker's hours, but I didn't know lawyers had them, too."

"I'll have you know I was at my desk before seven

this morning." He held up a brown paper bag. "I just ran up to Cuppachino for a midmorning snack."

"Let me guess." She closed her eyes and pretended to go into a trance. "I see . . . a cranberry-orange muffin."

"Not even close. Walnut-apple muffin for me, a strawberry scone for Liz—she's my paralegal—'cause she has to put up with Mrs. Finneran."

"Violet Finneran? Your grandfather's secretary?"

"The one and only."

"She's been there forever," Brooke said. "She has to be . . . jeez, about a million years old by now."

"Close enough." Jesse nodded. "My granddad expected her to retire when he did, but she wasn't ready. She only comes in three times a week, but when she's there, she makes her presence known."

"Bless her for her fortitude."

"I'm not sure it's fortitude that keeps her coming in," he said drily. "I think she's afraid I'll bring the firm to ruin if no one keeps an eye on me."

"Now why would she think that?"

"Who knows?" Jesse shrugged. "Probably because I'm not my grandfather and I'm not my uncle Mike."

"She taught us Sunday school one year," Brooke recalled. "She can be a bit formidable."

"That's one way of putting it."

"So here's a hot tip. You're the first to know." She lowered her voice as if she were about to share a secret. He leaned in closer, close enough for her to see that his brown eyes were flecked with gold. Nice. "As of today, you'll be able to get one of my amazingly fantastic cupcakes at Scoop. Cupcake—that's what I'm calling my business—is ready to roll."

"Congratulations. That's great." She couldn't help but notice that he had the kind of smile that went all the way to his eyes. "I love cupcakes. I'll stop down later and pick up a few. Is Scoop going to be your exclusive outlet?"

"I hope not. I'm stopping at Cuppachino and Lola's this morning to see if they're interested."

He held up the brown bag. "You mean after today I could be picking up cupcakes instead of muffins in the morning?"

"I don't know that cupcakes could be considered part of a nutritious breakfast."

A car rolled to a stop behind her and the driver laid on the horn.

"Oops! That would be for me."

"I'll see you at Vanessa's on Saturday night?" he asked.

"Sure thing."

Jesse stepped back from Brooke's car, and waved amicably at the impatient driver who'd just hit his horn for the second time.

"See you," Brooke called as she hit the gas.

Seconds later, her eyes drifted to the rearview mirror. She was surprised to see Jesse standing on the corner, watching her drive away. At least, she thought maybe he was, since he seemed to be looking after her car. She glanced out both side windows, but nope, there was nothing happening on either side of the street. When she stopped at the next stop sign and checked her mirror again, he was gone.

Seeing him reminded her that she still hadn't made the appointment with him to have her will redone. It was time to take Eric out and put Logan in—past time, really. She knew that. She just hated having to do it, as if she were officially erasing Eric from her life.

Brooke made a left onto Charles, then a few blocks farther, a right onto Kelly's Point Road, which led to the municipal parking lot, the town hall—the administration building that housed the police department as well—and the marina. Kelly's Point ended in a tee at the boardwalk that ran along the Bay. To the right of the tee and past the marina was a well-regarded seafood restaurant, Captain Walt's, and to the left Steffie's ice cream shop, One Scoop or Two, known as Scoop to the locals.

Brooke parked in the municipal lot, swung her bag over her shoulder, and grabbed the carrier holding the cupcakes. It was still early in the day, but already she could see that Steffie had customers inside the shop. A tinny bell rang when Brooke opened the door and Stef looked up from whatever concoction she was preparing behind the counter.

"Hey, Brooke," Steffie called to her.

"Hi." Brooke pushed the door closed with the toe of her shoe. "Brought you a little something."

"Yum. I can hardly wait to see." Stef smiled at her customer and handed over a triple-scoop cone. "Are you sure you don't want to take a dish? Just in case?"

"Maybe I should." The man who appeared to be all of twenty had justifiable second thoughts.

"You eat all that, you might want to come back for a cupcake." Stef handed him a dish, a spoon, and a pile of napkins.

"Brooke, bring your goodies right here." Stef pointed

to the counter, where she was handing change to the three-scoop patron.

"I left the display stand in the car," Brooke told her. "I'll be right back."

Minutes later Brooke was setting up her stand, which resembled a Christmas tree in shape, with arms that had little metal cups to hold the cupcakes. She carefully placed the cupcakes onto the stand.

"Don't they look magnificent?" Steffie's hands were on her hips as she admired Brooke's production. "I'll have these sold by two this afternoon. If they last that long."

"You're optimistic." Brooke smiled.

"I know my clientele," she said confidently, then turned to her customer, who was still trying to get his change into his wallet. "What do you think? Don't they look delicious?"

"Yeah, they do." His tongue took a swipe at the top scoop on his cone while he surveyed the display. "They're for sale, right?"

"Absolutely," Stef assured him. "Made right here in St. Dennis by my lovely friend Brooke."

"What kind is that one?" He pointed to a chocolate-frosted cake.

"That one is mocha with fudge frosting." Brooke gave him a smile.

"I'll buy that one. How much are they?"

Brooke and Steffie exchanged a glance. They hadn't discussed pricing.

"Tell you what," Brooke said. "Since you're the first customer I've had, yours is on me. But if you like it, you have to tell everyone you know to come down and buy one."

"Deal," he readily agreed.

Stef put the cupcake on a napkin and handed it to him. "Sorry I don't have any paper plates . . ."

"I don't need a plate," he said as he walked to one of the tables.

"I'll drop some off," Brooke told Steffie. "I should have thought of that. And I should get some plastic forks, too."

"Not to worry. Most of the customers I'll have this afternoon will be kids and they won't care what it's on or whether or not there's a fork to eat it with."

Stef nudged Brooke with her elbow and tilted her head in the direction of the young man at the table. "What'd I tell you? Does he look like he needs a fork?"

The cupcake was almost gone.

"But we do need to decide on a selling price," Stef reminded her.

After a few moments of discussion, they came to an agreement.

"I really appreciate this," Brooke said as she snapped the lid back onto her empty carrier.

"Don't mention it." Stef waved her off. "I think it's great for my shop to offer a little nibble with the ice cream. I've been thinking about bringing in coffee and tea for the after-dinner crowd. Of course, now that the weather has cooled, I'm closing at seven at night, so there won't be too many of those."

"How was it?" Brooke asked the young man at the table who'd just finished his cupcake.

"It really kicked." He nodded appreciatively. "Seriously good stuff."

"Great. Glad you liked it." Brooke grinned. "Now go tell your friends."

"Sure thing," he told her, "but I think I'll take a few to go. Maybe one of those pretty ones with the flower on it for my girlfriend. The pink one. And maybe another chocolate one."

"Whenever you're ready, I'll bag them for you." Stef turned to Brooke and whispered, "What did I tell you?"

"You do know your people," Brooke agreed, and made a mental note to order some small boxes. She had ordered the larger ones, some to hold a half dozen and bigger ones that could contain a dozen, but smaller ones, for individual sales, would be nice. And she'd have to come up with a logo for the top of the boxes.

She noted the time on the clock over the door. "I need to get going. I was going to stop at Lola's and at Cuppachino to see if either would be interested in putting my cupcakes on their menu."

"I'm betting they will. Lola hasn't had a really good pastry chef since Renée left, and Carlo is getting his muffins from some commercial bakery and he's never really been totally happy with them."

"Well, then, I'm on my way." Brooke nabbed her shoulder bag by the strap. "Wish me luck."

"Of course." Stef leaned against the counter.

Brooke waved good-bye to the young man at the table and took off for her car. She was running a little later than she'd planned, but if she hurried—and didn't stop to talk to anyone else—she'd be able to make all her stops and still get to school on time.

She moved her car to Charles Street and, as she

feared, found no empty parking places, forcing her to park on one of the side streets. She grabbed one container of her samples and dashed to the corner, crossed at the light, and stepped into the elegance of Lola's Café, where the lunch crowd was just beginning to trickle in.

"Hi, Jimmy," Brooke greeted the host.

"Hello, Brooke. Nice to see you." The elderly gentleman had worked for Lola for thirty years and knew everyone who'd ever passed through their doors.

"Jimmy, is Lola here, by any chance?" Brooke scanned the room for the owner, a woman in her nineties, who still ran the business, and from all indications, ran it well.

"She'll be a little late getting in today," he told her. "Would you like to leave a message for her?"

Brooke held up the container and explained the reason for her stop. She popped off the lid to show off her wares.

"My, they do look luscious." Jimmy's eyes lit up and he reached for the container. "Now, you just leave them here with me. I'll be sure to pass them on to the boss."

"Can I trust you not to eat all of them?" Brooke teased.

"I promise I will not eat them all. I cannot promise not to sample one. Or two."

"Go for it." Brooke handed him the container. "Enjoy."

"I imagine I will." With a smile, he patted the container. "I'm sure you'll be hearing from Lola before too long." He paused before adding, "That woman has a fierce sweet tooth, you know that, right?"

"That's what I'm counting on." Brooke waved and stepped aside to allow a small group of diners to enter before she went out through the door. Once outside, she hurried back to her car to pick up the remaining container of cupcakes and practically ran back to Charles Street with them. She again crossed the street and went directly to Cuppachino, where she noted a group of local merchants seated at a large table facing the picture window that looked out onto Charles.

"Hi, guys," she called to the locals.

"Hey, Brooke," several voices responded.

Brooke looked around the coffee shop for Carlo, the owner. Locating him near the very end of the counter, she waved as she approached him.

"Carlo," she greeted. "Do you have a minute."

"A minute, yes," he told her. "I'm short a person on the counter today."

"I'm sorry. Maybe I should come back . . ."

"You're here now. There was something you wanted to see me about?" He gestured for her to get to the point.

She did.

"So show me what you got," he said impatiently.

Carlo's eyebrows rose when she removed the lid from her carrying case. He scanned the contents.

"What have we here?" he asked.

Brooke told him.

He picked a cupcake from the container, peeled back its paper cup, and took a bite.

"Uh-huh. Very nice flavor. Uh-huh. Very nice." He nodded. "You made these?"

"Yes."

"How many of these can you make for me?"

"How many would you need?"

"First week, probably three, four dozen to start. Maybe a dozen, dozen and a half every other day."

"I can do that."

"Good, good." Carlo grabbed a napkin from the counter and touched it to the corners of his mouth. "On second thought, bring me two dozen for to-morrow, let's see how they go. Have them here by seven A.M. Do something to mark them so we know the flavors. What are we charging?"

She told him what Steffie was charging, and he nod-ded. "That's a fair price."

"And you can let me know what you'd like to keep for carrying them," she said.

"You just starting?" he asked. "You're planning on making a business, right?"

"Right."

"I know what it's like to start a business, get a break here and there. We'll sell these for you and give you a break, turn over whatever we take in, okay? Maybe someday you'll name a cupcake after me. The Carlo." He winked at her.

"Carlo, that's very nice of you, but—"

"No *buts*. I gotta get back to work. Go home, start baking. I'll look for you in the morning." He grabbed one more cupcake off the tray, then called to one of his employees. "Rachel, I want you to put these cup-cakes in the front case and then give Brooke back her container."

Without another word, Carlo turned his back and went into his kitchen through a swinging door.

Brooke popped the lid back on the case and turned to go, and walked right into Grace Sinclair.

"Oh, Miss Grace!" she exclaimed. "I'm sorry, I didn't see you."

"My fault, dear," Grace said. "I came up behind you without paying attention to how close I was. I had my eye on that tray of goodies Rachel just put into the display case." Grace got a little closer to the glass. "Of course, they're yours. You made something similar for Dallas's party. They were certainly delicious. And you're selling them here now?"

Brooke quickly explained the arrangement and tried not to look at the clock. She knew she'd be late for class if she didn't leave now, but she couldn't bring herself to be rude to Grace, who was everyone's favorite seventysomething lady in town.

"Well, you're certain to be a success. We haven't had a decent bakery here in town since . . ." Grace paused and appeared to think. "Frankly, I don't think we ever had a really good baker in St. Dennis. That new place doesn't do it for me. And frankly"—she leaned closer to Brooke—"I don't think they're going to make it. Apparently they aren't doing it for anyone else around here either. So the field is wide open, dear. Now's a good time to make your move."

"From your lips, Miss Grace."

"Yes, well, after you get a few weeks under your belt, we'll do an interview for my paper. Get some customer feedback to go along with it. Nothing like word of mouth." Grace patted Brooke on the arm. "And speaking of which, I think I'll try one with my tea. Which do you recommend?"

"All of them," Brooke replied. "But I know you're partial to fruity things, so you might try either the lemon, the strawberry, or the pineapple coconut."

"Oh, the lemon." Grace motioned to Rachel. "I think we need to put some little index cards out here, pass them out with the cupcakes so people can leave their comments."

"Grace, that's an excellent idea. I wish I'd thought to do that."

"Like I said, dear, nothing like word of mouth." Grace searched her bag for her wallet.

Seeing an opening, Brooke smiled and said, "I'm off to class now. Enjoy your cupcake."

"I loved the ones you had at Dallas's," Grace told her. "I'm sure this will be just as good."

"I hope you think so." Brooke bolted toward the door, and hurried across the street.

Vanessa stepped out from Bling's front door and waved. "Hey, Brooke. I put a few dresses aside that I think you might like for Saturday."

"No time now. I'll be back later," Brooke called back. "I have to get to class."

"I'll be here," Vanessa assured her.

Back in her car, Brooke took a deep breath. She didn't dare stop to compute how many cupcakes she'd have to bake, frost, and decorate by tomorrow morning. She'd worry about that later. Right now she just wanted to savor the feeling that someone—*several* someones—had agreed to sell her cupcakes. She'd taken her first orders. The cupcakes she'd made for Dallas's party had been a gift and therefore didn't count. These cupcakes—the ones she'd make for Steffie and for Carlo and hopefully for Lola—were stepping-stones that would, hopefully, in time, lead to that little shop she'd been dreaming of.

Next stop, school. After class, she'd stop at Bling,

try on the dresses Vanessa had put aside for her for the party, then she'd run home, help Logan with his homework, and once he was settled, she'd start baking.

Tomorrow, after she made her deliveries, she'd take Clay's old van out to Krauser's Auto Body and see what Frank could do to pretty it up. It was time for her to get her show on the road. Literally.

Chapter 4

WHEN he realized that he'd just read the same case notes for the third time, Jesse gave up and closed the file. To say he was agitated would be an understatement. He'd been on edge since he'd spoken to his sister, Sophie, and as much as he tried to tell himself that he wasn't going to be affected by anything their father did, his inner self apparently wasn't listening. The call from Sophie had been unexpected but not particularly surprising, given their father's track record.

Then again, pretty much everything associated with his father turned out to have a downside.

"Mom doesn't know that I'm calling, so if she calls, don't let on that I gave you a heads-up." Sophie had opened the call on an ominous note.

"What's the matter?" Jesse had been deep in notes for a trial that was scheduled to start the following week.

"It's Dad." Heavy sigh from Sophie.

"Isn't it always?" Jesse had muttered. "What is it this time?"

"He's left Pammie and he's living with this woman

he met at a casino in Atlantic City. He says she's his soul mate." If an eye roll had a voice, it would sound exactly like Sophie's. "Say something, Jess."

"I'm trying to decide who I feel sorrier for, Pammie or the soul mate." Whenever Jesse was angry or tense but needed to maintain control, he drew little concentric circles on whatever paper was available. He picked up a pen and started to draw on the back of an envelope on his desk, and wondered what it said about his personality that the more tense or angry he became, the smaller the circles he drew.

"Yeah, poor Pammie, right? And yes, I did remind her that Dad left Mom for her, and that once upon a time, she was the other woman."

"Payback's a bitch, Pammie."

"Oh, so true," Sophie agreed. "I have to admit to feeling a certain amount of satisfaction on that score. I'm petty that way."

"Karma can be a good thing." Jesse knew exactly what his sister meant. He was fifteen when his father left them for Pammie, who at the time was twenty-four. "Does she still call herself Pammie?"

"Yeah."

"So what happened? She just called you out of the blue?"

"First she called Mom, and I guess when it dawned on her that she wasn't going to get any sympathy from Mom, she called me."

"Bad move on both counts." Jesse's circles grew smaller.

"Duh."

"Another day, another Craig Enright scandal."

"Dad doesn't even scandalize anymore. Everyone just pretty much ignores him, Jess."

"Which is exactly what I think we need to do. Ignore it. He'll either crawl back to Pammie or he'll take off with . . . what's this one's name?"

"Tish something. And Jess?" Sophie paused. "She's thirty-three. Younger than you but older than me."

Jesse's circles continued to shrink.

"Well, like I said, just ignore it, all of it. It's not like we haven't been down this road with him before."

"Easy for you to say from down there in that cozy, idyllic little town. How are things, by the way?"

"Cozy and idyllic."

"I swear, if I didn't have so much going on here, I'd be studying up to take the Maryland bar."

"That's not a bad idea. Maybe you should think about it."

"I did, but Jonathan wasn't wild about the idea."

Count to ten, Jess, he told himself. For some reason, his sister's boyfriend always brought out the snark in Jesse. When they hung up a few minutes later, he was still trying to figure out what Sophie saw in Jonathan.

Or what Tish saw in his father, for that matter. Was she aware of his track record? That he'd had three children with wife number one—none of whom he'd had contact with in years; two children with wife number two, that would be Lainie, Jesse and Sophie's mother. And now he was apparently leaving wife number three; at least he'd refrained from reproducing again. It was enough to make your head spin.

Jesse tossed the doodled envelope into the trash can and got up from his chair to pace. He went first to the front window, from where he could see Old St. Mary's Church Square—known to the locals as just the square—and the narrow streets that led to it. This was the most historic section of a historic town, the house in which he now stood one of the oldest. The oldest section of the Oliver Shallcross House had been built in 1702, and was purchased in 1820 by Peter Enright, Jesse's great-great-great-grandfather, and Enright and Enright was established the following year. Ever since, there'd been at least one Enright to provide legal counsel to the residents of St. Dennis and the surrounding communities. But even with this legacy, Jesse wondered if he'd ever feel like he'd earned the right to walk up that cobbled path and to call St. Dennis his home.

He had his grandfather, Curtis Enright, to thank in no small part for his uncertainty.

Jesse went into the small kitchen at the end of the hall and poured himself a cup of coffee. He never walked past the steps leading to the second floor without remembering his first visit here.

He'd heard through the family grapevine that his grandfather was retiring due to age and ill health, and that his uncle Mike—his dad's brother—was taking a leave to care for his terminally ill wife, Andrea. Jesse had been practicing law in Ohio, where he'd grown up and where his mother and sister still lived, but from day one, he'd been under the shadow cast by his father. When the idea of relocating to St. Dennis first occurred to him, Jesse arranged to take the Maryland bar exam so that if he was successful in repairing the damage his father had caused, and was able to convince his grandfather to take him into the firm, Jesse would be ready to go.

He hadn't been aware of just how devastating the damage had been.

Just something else to thank you for, Dad.

Curtis Enright had been cordial when Jesse showed up in St. Dennis and asked to see him. When he realized that Jesse had come, not for a visit, but for an interview for a position with the firm, Curtis's cordiality turned decidedly cool.

"Can we speak frankly?" Curtis's eyes had narrowed almost to the point of slits. He didn't wait for a response. "Your father was a great disappointment to me. How do I know the apple hasn't fallen too close to the tree?"

"You don't, unless you're willing to take me at my word that I am nothing like my father," Jesse had replied calmly. He'd expected some resistance, but not this chilly a reaction. "Something tells me you're not willing to do that, so why not give me a trial? Test me. Let me work for you for six months."

"Anyone can pretend to be anything they want for six months." Curtis had waved away the proposal.

"Then make it a year." Suddenly Jesse had wanted this job more than he'd realized. Maybe it had been the chance to prove to his family that he was a better man than his father, that he was more worthy to inherit a position with Enright and Enright than his dad had been. "A year with you looking over my shoulder."

His grandfather had fallen silent, and for a moment, Jesse had thought he was thinking over the offer he'd just made.

"I had high hopes for all my children, but Craig was my first son, and God, he was so bright! Had so much promise. Just shows how astute I am when it comes to judging character," Curtis had grumbled. "They say it's a wise man who knows his own child." He'd shaken his head almost imperceptibly. "Obviously, I wasn't very wise. Craig was a screwup from the time he hit his teens until"—he paused to glance at his watch—"two-twenty this afternoon."

Curtis had turned slightly to gaze out the window. When he'd turned back to Jesse, it was to ask, "Is there something in your background I should know about?"

"Excuse me?" Jesse had asked.

"DUIs? Been kicked out of college? Annulled marriage to a Vegas stripper? Embezzlement?"

The last one had struck home hard and fast. Jesse had stared at the old man seated behind the desk for a long moment, then stood.

"I'm sorry," he'd said as he walked toward the door. "This was a waste of time for both of us."

He'd paused in the doorway. "I know better than anyone the kind of man my father is. I've had to deal with his antics all my life. If I said it hasn't affected me, I'd be lying. But I hope it never affects me the way it's affected you. I'm really sorry that your expectations of me are so low."

Jesse'd left his grandfather's second-floor office, wishing that he'd listened to his mother when she told him that coming here, hoping for an offer to join the family firm, was a really bad idea, that the trip could only end in disappointment. Well, she'd had that right.

He'd walked out the front door and down the cobbled path to the sidewalk, oblivious to the simple
beauty of the square he cut across on his way back to
the bed-and-breakfast where he'd been staying. The
pain he'd carried inside was so sharp, so fierce, it
seemed to burn right into his heart. Back in his room,
he'd sat in quiet mourning for all the pieces of his life
that had scattered: for the man his father might have
been; for the dream he'd had of being accepted into
the fold here, and for the place he'd hoped to carve
for himself in St. Dennis, away from the scandals
and the taint on his name that had nothing to do
with him.

Well, they say you can't pick your family. Except
for his mother and his sister, the rest of them could all
go rot for all he cared.

Jesse'd sat by a window and stewed until it grew
dark and his stomach reminded him that he hadn't
eaten in hours. The innkeeper had suggested a place
for dinner, and Jesse had followed the directions
to a restaurant several blocks away on the main
street that went through the town. He'd been two
storefronts from the restaurant when his cell phone
rang.

"You've got one year." Curtis hadn't bothered with
pleasantries nor had he identified himself. "Let me
know when you've passed the Maryland bar."

"I already have," Jesse had replied with as much
warmth as his grandfather offered.

"Pretty damned sure of yourself, aren't you?"

"I just always like to have my ducks in a row."

"In that case, you can start the first of next month.

I'll be looking over your shoulder. Don't ever forget it."

"Don't you want to check my references?" Jesse had asked.

"Already did that." Curtis had paused, then added, "I like to have my ducks in a row, too."

That had been eight months ago, and while those first two months had been hell—with Curtis initially micromanaging to the point that he demanded to see every one of Jesse's letters before they were mailed—by the six-month mark, Curtis rarely questioned Jesse's judgment and had stopped shadowing him in court. They'd entered into a quiet truce based on growing mutual respect, but there was still a bit of unease between them.

Jesse took his coffee outside to the small courtyard off the kitchen. The day that had started out with the promise of sunshine had grown overcast and he could smell the coming rain. The leaves that had dropped since the beginning of the week formed a deep carpet of red and gold and brown across the yard. He set his coffee next to some potted plants on a table near the back door and went to the shed at the rear of the property. He found a rake and began to rake the leaves into a big pile near the driveway. He was so engrossed in what he was doing that he didn't hear the back door open.

"I hope you're not thinking about jumping into that pile." Violet Finneran folded her arms across her ample chest. "Your granddaddy has someone to do that."

"I know. I just felt like I needed a little fresh air and exercise."

"Well, while you were playing maintenance man, you had a few calls. Lou MacGruder wants to change the settlement conference on the Jackson case from Monday afternoon to Tuesday morning, which of course will remove the trial from Monday's calendar if you're agreeable, which I told him you would be. He'll take care of the motions. Liz apologized but she wasn't able to come back in after lunch because she got a call from the elementary school to come pick up her sick daughter." Violet counted off the calls on the fingers of her right hand. "And Brooke Bowers called to make an appointment to have her will drawn up."

"Why didn't you tell me she called?"

"Did you tell me you were coming out here? If I hadn't gone into the kitchen to make a cup of tea, we wouldn't even be having this conversation now."

"Touché."

"Indeed."

"So did you give Brooke an appointment?" he asked.

"I gave her the Monday slot that would have been the settlement conference."

"Good. Thank you." Jesse went back to raking leaves. He could feel Violet's eyes burning through his shirt. He and his grandfather may have come to an understanding, but clearly, the jury was still out as far as Violet Finneran was concerned.

He glanced over his shoulder and found her still standing in the doorway.

"What else?" he asked.

"I've known Brooke since she was a child."

"Nice lady." He made an attempt at sounding non-committal but wasn't sure he succeeded.

"Well, she is now but she wasn't back then." Violet paused. "When she was a child, that is. She was a bit of a brat for a while there."

"Okay." Jesse stopped raking and waited to see where she was headed with this.

"This firm has served as legal counsel for that family going back over a hundred years."

"And . . ." He gestured for her to continue.

"And the girl needs her interests looked after." She stared a hole right through the center of his face. "Don't screw it up."

She went back into the building, the door slamming behind her. It was almost a full minute before Jesse was able to pull his jaw off the ground and follow her.

"What makes you think I'd do anything to screw up Brooke's will?"

"It's not just her will. She needs solid counsel."

"Why do you think I'm not capable of giving her good legal counsel, Violet?" He stared her down. For a moment he felt as if he was staring into the face of a dragon.

"Law of averages, sonny. I've known your grandparents all my life, went to school with your grandmother. So I knew your father. I know what he did to this family. How all his nonsense broke his mother's heart. Sooner or later, blood will tell."

"My grandfather is satisfied with everything I've done since day one. If he had any complaints, I imagine he'd have let me know, but hey, I'm still here." He paused. "And don't call me 'sonny.'"

"Right now Curtis doesn't have anyone else, what with Mike having to take care of poor Andrea day and night. He's just waiting for the other shoe to drop." A mean little smile crossed her face. "We're all just waiting for the other shoe to drop. Sooner or later, it will."

She started into her office near the front door.

"Violet, I'm not my father," Jesse said softly.

"Like I said, blood will tell." Violet went into her office and started to close the door in his face. At the last minute, she added, "And don't think I didn't see you flirting with Brooke, standing out there in the middle of the square, holding up traffic."

"I wasn't flirting; she stopped at the stop sign and called me over." *Why,* he asked himself, *am I bothering to defend myself to this old shrew?* "And even if I had been, what business is it of yours?"

"Like I said, I've known her all her life. Her grandmother and I were best friends all through school," Violet said, as if that explained her interest. "We watch out for each other here."

Jesse nodded slowly. "This is your way of letting me know I am now, and always will be, an outsider, right?"

"Take it as you see it." She sniffed pointedly and closed the door.

He went back into his office and closed the file, making a note that the trial would be postponed at the request of defense counsel and that a settlement conference would be held on Tuesday morning. All of which was fine with Jesse, but he would have appreciated it if Violet had given him the opportunity to have had a say in the change. Apparently, over the years, Curtis had given her a certain amount of responsibility when it came to such things, and she assumed that she still had the authority he'd granted her. Jesse's first reaction had been to remind her that things had changed and that he wasn't his grandfather, though he knew she was all too aware of that. Violet kept his calendar much as she had kept his grandfather's. Was that really such a bad thing? Hadn't he given the same authority to his secretary back in Ohio?

And just this morning, when he stopped at Cuppachino, hadn't Grace Sinclair patted him on the back for keeping Violet on, telling him how the older woman had devoted her life to the firm and his grandfather, how she'd lived for her job and taken such pride in being Curtis Enright's right hand?

Jesse sighed. There was no graceful way to get rid of Violet, and apparently no way to make her like him, or to convince her that he had the right to be there, or to accept him as Curtis's successor. He understood that none of those things were likely to happen. Which, in itself, was okay; he could be mature and reasonable about the situation, even if Violet couldn't. After Sophie's call that morning, he was ready to put a big black X on the entire day.

But there'd been those few unexpected moments with Brooke that morning, he reminded himself, so the day hadn't been a complete wash. There was something about that woman that made him smile, inside and out, and had since the first time he noticed her.

Well, she was hard to miss. To his eye, she was drop-dead gorgeous.

It had been months before that they'd been introduced by Steffie one night at Captain Walt's. He'd gone there for dinner with Stef and her family, at her mother's invitation, and on the way out, Brooke, her

brother, Clay, and Wade MacGregor were seated at
the bar. It had been obvious to Jesse that there was a
strong undercurrent between Stef and Wade, and he
hadn't been at all surprised when the two of them left
together, leaving Jesse at the bar in conversation with
Brooke. That first conversation, which had started
with her asking his advice about her will, had lasted
for almost two hours, during which they'd covered
everything from sailing (she did, he didn't) to rock
climbing (he did, she didn't) and the best place in
St. Dennis to hear live music (Captain Walt's on Friday
nights). Over the course of those few hours, it was apparent that she was more than just a pretty face. When
she spoke, she looked directly into his eyes. When he
spoke, she listened, as if what he was saying mattered
to her. And she had a knockout laugh. Brooke wasn't
one of those women who covered their mouth when
they laughed. Nothing was more irresistible than a
beautiful woman with a good sense of humor, and
he'd wanted to see more of her.

There had been many times since that first meeting
when he'd thought about asking her out, but the word
around town was that Brooke had yet to be willing to
go on a second date with anyone, and that just didn't
fit into Jesse's plans. She was the only woman he'd
met since he'd been here that he really wanted to get
to know—not to just take out occasionally, but to
spend time with, see what there could be. Jesse had
never been a love-'em-and-leave-'em kind of guy. Life
with his father had taught him all he needed to know
about playing the field, and he wanted none of it.
Since coming to St. Dennis and making a place for

himself there, more and more, he was starting to feel like it might be time to start to settle down.

Jesse knew from that first meeting that he wasn't interested in being one of Brooke's onetime dates, that he was going to have to wait it out until she was ready. The same instinct that told him that the time was right for him to come to St. Dennis had been telling him that Brooke was worth waiting for, and at first, he'd been okay with that. Now, however, might be the time to try to speed things up a bit.

Timing, he'd long since come to understand, in life and in love, was everything.

Chapter 5

BE careful what you wish for. Don't bite off more than you can chew. Know your limitations," Brooke muttered as she lined up several dozen cupcakes on the kitchen counter. "Then again, we could counter with 'Opportunity seldom knocks twice. Opportunities are often disguised as hard work. Luck is the intersection of opportunity and preparation'—or however that one went."

"Talking to ourselves, now, are we?" Clay leaned upon the doorjamb. "Is this what it's come to?"

Brooke nodded. "I've been reduced to mumbling strings of platitudes."

"Must be all that flour you've been inhaling this week." He came into the room and surveyed the lines of cupcakes. "How many of these did you make, anyway?"

"Don't ask me to add numbers together." She shook her head. "The effort might break me."

"Should I count them for you?"

"I don't really want to know. I just want to know when I'm finished." She measured butter into a bowl, followed it with confectioners' sugar.

"These can't all be for the engagement party."

"These are for Lola's." Brooke pointed to the first two dozen on the counter. "And these are for Cuppachino." She pointed to the pans she'd placed on cooling racks near the stove. "And those are for Scoop."

"I thought you took cupcakes to Scoop on Wednesday," he noted.

"They sold out." She paused and smiled. "The same day. Actually, everyone sold out. Lola, Carlo . . ."

"Nice." Clay nodded. "A very nice start to your business."

"I'm not complaining. I swear I am not. But if I'd had any sense at all, I'd have waited until next week to solicit orders from the local businesses." She picked up her zester and ran an unpeeled lemon over the top, then tapped the zester on the side of the bowl, sending the little scraps of peel into the butter-and-sugar mix.

"Because of the party." Clay pulled up a chair at the kitchen table.

"Right. Because of the eight thousand cupcakes I have to make for the party."

"I thought you said you agreed to make twelve dozen."

"Right now it seems more like eight thousand. If this keeps up, I'm going to need to buy another oven."

"Anything I can do to help?"

Brooke considered for a moment. "No, but thanks. I like to do things in order, you know? Frost all the lemons, then the strawberries, and so on for the frostings. Then I like to go back along the lines and decorate. All the twists of lemon peel, all the bits of coconut, all the little fondant flowers."

"Yeah, my fondant flowers would never stand up to yours."

"Go away." Brooke laughed and picked up her hand mixer. "Anything else before I turn it on?"

"No, I'm good." He snatched an unfrosted cupcake from the counter and headed for the back door.

"If you hadn't grabbed one, I'd have thought there was something seriously wrong with you." She turned on the mixer and drowned out his reply. "Which is why I always bake an extra dozen. I'll leave them in the fridge. Logan can have one after lunch. You're still on to bring him home from soccer in the morning?"

"I've cleared my schedule for the entire day. I'm at his beck and call, at least until Mom takes over when I leave for the party."

"Great. Thanks, Clay. I appreciate it."

"Hey, he's my favorite kid. We'll have a great day."

She frosted and decorated a dozen of each of three flavors—lemon, raspberry, and chocolate—for each of her new local clients. After tucking them into the white pastry boxes she'd picked up that afternoon, she turned her attention to the cupcakes for the party. They were cool enough to frost, but she wanted to wait until tomorrow to add all the finishing touches, so she packed them into a series of large white boxes and left them on the counter.

"Crap," she said aloud after a glance at the clock. It was almost two A.M. Logan had soccer in the morning and she had three delivery stops to make—one before seven. Any thought she'd had of studying tonight was dismissed.

"Tomorrow is another day," she reminded herself.

She checked the back door to make sure it was locked, pausing for a moment to push aside the curtain to look up at the sky. Wisps of clouds, remnants of the day's earlier rainstorm, hung low over the back fields, but the moon was visible over the barn, its pale light more dim than luminous. She left the light on over the back porch—her mother was convinced that that alone kept burglars from breaking in at night—and turned off the lights in the kitchen.

She was so tired that she skipped her usual nightly routine and fell face-first onto her bed, so tired that she would be asleep in minutes. Exhaustion directly into sleep was her new game plan to avoid lying awake and thinking about things she didn't want to think about. Most nights it worked. She figured any morning she woke up and knew she hadn't spent half the night asking questions that had no answers was going to be a good morning.

I can't believe how late I am. Brooke parked in front of Vanessa's house a full fifteen minutes later than the caterer had told her to be there. *Way to make an impression.*

Deanna Clark was the Eastern Shore's most sought-after caterer, and she never—but *never*—contracted out any portion of an event. She hadn't been pleased when she learned that the desserts for this party would be provided by someone other than herself. But since the party was for Dallas MacGregor's brother and his fiancée, and Dallas personally had given Deanna the news, there'd been no discussion. At least, that was what Dallas told Brooke, who wondered just how gracious Deanna actually had been. All that really mattered to Brooke was that she'd make the most spectacular array of cupcakes she could, and hoped that Deanna was impressed—if not enough to ask her to work with her on occasion in the future, maybe enough to send a little business to her from time to time. It was a long shot, Brooke knew, but she was back to that opportunity mantra again: *Luck is where opportunity and preparation meet.*

She got out of the car and waved to Jesse, who was jogging on the opposite side of the street. She smoothed her skirt, then opened the hatch of the back of the SUV she'd borrowed from Clay. She slid the large white pastry boxes forward and hesitated, debating on whether or not to stack the smaller ones atop the pile.

Reminding herself that she was late, she piled on the small boxes and took a few steps back. There was no way she could get the hatch closed, but she'd have to come back out for the boxes of trays and cake stands and display racks. Leaving the back of the car open, she stepped up onto the curb, and tripped on the raised root of a nearby oak tree. She lurched forward, but was able to maintain her balance enough that she did not fall, but not enough to keep the three smaller boxes from slipping from the top of the pile and hitting the pavement. The other boxes shifted in her hands.

"Shit!" she yelled.

"Whoa, hold on there." Jesse grabbed the bottom of the stack to stabilize it.

"Shit. Shit. Shit," was all Brooke could think to say.

"At least you didn't drop them all." Jesse steadied the rest of the boxes.

"I can't believe this." Brooke all but wept. "*Damn* it. I knew I shouldn't have tried to carry them all at the same time."

She blew out a long frustrated breath, then looked up at Jesse.

"Thank you," she said. "If you hadn't grabbed onto the box on the bottom when you did, I might have lost all of them. And then I'd really be screwed."

"Cupcakes, right?" He gestured toward the boxes on the ground.

She nodded. "They're probably mush now. Orange mush. Yum." She couldn't believe this was happening.

He leaned over and lifted the lid of a box at his feet. "These don't look too bad. You might have lost one or two, but you can salvage most of them." He closed the lid and looked into the next box. "These, too." He looked up at Brooke. "When you get inside you can touch them up and no one will be the wiser."

"She'll know," Brooke told him. "She'll know and she'll be feeling really really smug about the fact that I screwed up."

"I thought you guys were all friends."

"I meant Deanna. She's the caterer. She has the reputation for only serving things she's prepared herself when she does a job, but Dallas told her they wanted me to do the desserts, so she had to let me. I spoke with her on the phone a few days ago and she has a major attitude toward me, like she's sure my cupcakes couldn't possibly live up to her standards. I, of course, assured her that they would." Brooke tried unsuccessfully to blow an errant strand of hair from her forehead. "Now I have a mess and I'm late on top of it."

Jesse picked up one of the boxes from the sidewalk and opened it, held it so she could look inside.

"You don't think you could salvage any of these?" he asked.

She peered into the box.

"Maybe a few," she conceded, "but I don't have time to go all the way back to the farm and then back here again."

"What would you need to fix them?"

"A knife, for starters." She looked into the box again. "Maybe some orange rind."

He picked up the other boxes and stacked them neatly, then lifted them carefully. "You go on inside with those, I'll take these with me. You tell the caterer you have more and you'll be back in a minute with the rest. Then you run around the corner to my house—"

"You live around the corner?" she asked.

"I'm renting a house on Hudson. Three houses down from the corner here. You drop those off—"

"Please. Not the D-word."

"Sorry. Take a deep breath, take the cupcakes inside, then come over and do whatever repair job you need to do, then bring them back. No one needs to know."

"It could work," she said thoughtfully. "I could at least fix up a few of them." She nodded as if convincing herself. "There's a bag in the back of the car with some fruit that I brought to use in the presentation. Maybe I could—"

"You can. Of course you can." He walked backward for a few steps in the direction of the corner. "Four twenty-nine Hudson."

"Thanks, Jesse. I don't know how to thank you."

"The front door will be open." He turned and jogged off.

Ten minutes later, having been chastised for her tardiness by the caterer from hell, Brooke all but ran up the steps at 429 Hudson Street. The door, as promised, was open.

"Jesse?" she called.

He stepped into the narrow foyer through an arched doorway. "Come on back."

"I cannot believe what a bitch that woman is." Brooke stripped off her jacket on the way to the kitchen. "You'd think we were serving dessert first instead of last. And she was still arranging the canapés, so it's not as if she's ready either."

"Got chewed out, did you?"

"A little." Brooke looked around the kitchen of Jesse's rented house. Wooden cabinets, walls, old Formica counters—all in the same shade of dull green. "Wow. Haven't seen this much green since, I dunno, maybe never."

"It's depressing if you stare at it too long," he agreed, and handed her a butter knife. She noticed then that he'd taken all the cupcakes out of their boxes and placed them on the table. "I thought it would save you time if you could see all the patients before you started to operate."

"Thanks, Jesse." Brooke took a quick inventory of the damages. "You're right. I can do this. Maybe not every one of them. But a good many . . ."

She started with the cupcakes closest to her and began to remove their decorations. "I can't use these pretty little flowers. They're too messy." She glanced up at Jesse. "Do you have a really sharp, small knife?"

"Maybe. The cutlery's all in this drawer, if you want to take a look." He opened the drawer and stood aside. "Anything I can do?"

"Thanks, but no. I'm going to have to figure this out as I go along." She smoothed the smooshed frosting on all the cupcakes that had bits of orange rind on them before rinsing the knife, drying it, and starting over with the lemon.

"If you don't need me, I'm going to run upstairs and grab a shower and get dressed. Just close the front door when you leave."

"Jesse, I can't thank you enough."

He smiled. "I'll see you at Vanessa's."

She looked up to see him leave the room on long tanned legs, then took a second look. The lawyer looked damned good in shorts. How had she not noticed?

The story around St. Dennis was that the previous occupant of the house Vanessa Keaton shared with her guy, Grady Shields, was still in residence—in spirit only, of course, Alice Ridgeway having passed from this life about two years ago. Brooke was one of the skeptics, however, so when the chatter at Steffie and Wade's engagement party turned to a possible unseen guest, she excused herself from the conversation and took the opportunity to slip into the kitchen.

"I was just going to send someone to look for you." Deanna, the caterer, glanced up from the counter when Brooke entered the room. "We're going to start cleaning up from the dinner buffet. Start getting your desserts ready."

"Good timing," Brooke replied. Hoping to ingratiate herself with Deanna, she added an honest compliment. "By the way, everything was delicious. You guys earned an A-plus in my book."

"Thanks."

Deanna passed a stack of empty plates to one of her helpers.

Vanessa swept into the room in a tea-length rose chiffon dress. "How are we doing in here?"

"We're doing fine. I'm just getting the desserts ready. The party is fabulous," Brooke told her.

"The party *is* fabulous, thank you. Deanna, the food was everything you promised. Everyone's raving about the Asian beef and the roasted vegetables."

Deanna's "thank you" was overlooked as Vanessa paused to watch Brooke stack cupcakes on one of several three-tiered displays she'd brought with her. "Oh, look. These match my dress." She pointed to a trio of dark rose cupcakes that were still in the box.

"That one's raspberry," Brooke told her. "It has a little bit of ganache inside as a little surprise."

"Oh, yum." Vanessa picked one out and peeled the paper back. "Sorry. I can't wait." She took a bite. "So delicious. So . . . oh, man, that ganache just blends perfectly with the raspberry in the frosting. Wow, Brooke. Just . . . wow."

Deanna's head lifted and her eyes shifted to the cupcakes.

"Glad you're enjoying it." Brooke's smile was sheer satisfaction. She'd worked for several hours to ensure that the flavors of the ganache and the frosting balanced each other. The look on Vanessa's face told her she'd succeeded. "Ness, you have frosting on the right side of your mouth."

"I'm so happy that everything worked out just right tonight." Vanessa grabbed a napkin and touched it to the spot. "Did I get it?"

Brooke nodded. "Everything looks beautiful. I love the decorations."

Deanna's head came up again and she sighed heavily, as if disturbed by the chatter.

"Steffie loves those little white fairy lights. She says she's going to have her entire wedding reception built around them." Vanessa rolled her eyes. "As long as she doesn't set them all to 'blink' at the same time, it should be fine."

"Speaking of which, Dallas just told me that she and Steffie have agreed to have their weddings on the same day at the inn." Brooke went back to stacking the cupcakes.

"I saw her speaking with Grace in the foyer a few minutes ago. I wonder if she's told her about needing a more experienced wedding planner."

"She did and Grace agreed." Steffie came in through the door that led into the dining room and deposited an empty champagne bottle in Vanessa's recycling bin. "Deanna, everything is to die for. Your reputation is well earned."

"Thank you," Deanna replied somewhat stiffly. "I'm glad you're satisfied."

"Totally," Steffie assured her.

"So Grace is going to talk to Lucy?" Vanessa asked.

Steffie shook her head. "Grace suggested that Dallas call Lucy directly. She thinks it will have more of an impact if Dallas asks her, and she's probably right."

"How does an event planner say no when Dallas MacGregor asks her to do her wedding?" Brooke nodded. "Makes sense to me."

"Right. So Dallas is going to give her a call tomorrow." Steffie watched Brooke open another white box of cupcakes. "Can I have that white one? The one with all the coconut on top?"

Brooke handed it to her.

"I love vanilla. It's my favorite flavor," Steffie told them.

"I thought lemon was your favorite," Vanessa reminded her.

"That, too." Steffie bit into the small cake. "This is too delicious for words. I want these for my wedding."

"Since I understand that's going to be a shared event, you might want to discuss it with your future sister-in-law," Brooke pointed out. "She might have other ideas."

"We already talked about it. We're having wedding cake *and* cupcakes." Steffie took another bite. "Everything frosty white, like snow, since it's going to be winter. Except you guys are all going to wear plaid."

"Plaid?" Vanessa and Brooke asked at the same time.

"Uh-huh." Steffie took the last bite, then wiped her hands on a napkin. "The MacGregor tartan. You'll love it."

"Does this mean Wade is going to wear a kilt?"

"Brooke, what a great idea." Steffie nodded. "I like it." Steffie turned as one of the waitstaff carried a tray in and set it on the counter near the sink.

Vanessa opened the refrigerator. "We need more champagne for the toast."

"I'll take care of it," Deanna told her. "You just go on back out there and enjoy your party."

"Oh. Well, in that case, sure." Vanessa took Steffie's arm. "Come on, guest of honor. Let's find your guy and get ready for some toasting."

"You, too, Brooke," Steffie told her.

"I'll be out in just a minute." Brooke finished setting up the tiered displays and stepped back to admire her work. "Nice," she said to herself.

"We'll take it from here, Brooke." Deanna held the door open as her staff filed in, carrying the plates and bowls and trays they'd removed from the dining room. "If you're finished . . . ?"

"I have a few trays to do, but you can go on and put those displays out as soon as the dining room table is clear." Brooke arranged cupcakes on silver trays along with some chocolate-covered strawberries and champagne truffles she'd picked up at the gourmet shop on her way over. From a cooler, she selected several white orchid blossoms and used them to decorate the all-white cupcakes that she'd placed on the white doilies on one tray, and added purple orchids to the tray of chocolate cupcakes. Pleased with the finished product, she stepped back and told Deanna, "They're all yours."

Deanna's gaze went from tray to tray. Finally, she said, "They're beautiful. I love orchids. They add such an elegant touch. Usually I like to put the desserts together myself, but I couldn't do a better job than you did. You really do have a knack for this."

"Thank you. That's really nice of you to say." A startled Brooke removed the apron and hung it in Vanessa's pantry.

"Oh, I'm not being nice," Deanna assured her. "I'm impressed. Any chance I could talk you into doing some work for me over the holidays? I have a lot of parties on the calendar, and after seeing what you've done here, I'd love to be able to include your cupcakes in the portfolio when I meet with my customers."

"We can talk about it. Sure." Brooke nodded.

"Great. I'll give you a call." Deanna popped open several bottles of champagne.

Brooke drifted into the foyer, a small smile on her lips. It was all she could do not to pump her fist in the air and shout "YES!" If Deanna Clark contracted some work for her this winter . . . well, she could almost smell her success.

Feeling more optimistic and more relaxed than she had for days, she stood in the living room doorway. From there, she could see into the dining room and the small sitting room in the front of the house. *Standing room only,* she mused.

"Is there anyone in St. Dennis who isn't here tonight?" Jesse Enright appeared at her elbow.

"I was just thinking the same thing." She glanced from room to room. "And I can't think of anyone. Steffie probably should have held this at Wade's aunt's house over on River Road. It's much larger and has more rooms than Vanessa's bungalow."

"I've been past that place," he said. "Berry Eberle's place, right? The big house on the point right where the river hits the Bay?"

Brooke nodded. "But I understand why Vanessa wanted to be the one to host the party. She and Stef are best friends."

One of the waiters approached carrying a tray of champagne flutes. Jesse took two and handed one to Brooke.

"I'm guessing you could probably use this," he said.

"More than you know." She took a sip. "Thanks. I mean, thanks for everything. For coming to my aid earlier, for all the help. I was so rattled when those boxes fell, I don't know that I would have had the presence of mind to have done anything but toss the fallen cupcakes and cry."

"Nah, you'd have figured it out," Jesse assured her.

"I don't know. When I say I was rattled, I mean, my mind turned into a big black void."

"How's the dragon lady?" Jesse nodded toward the kitchen.

"Deanna? She was pretty testy there for a while, but once she saw my pretty little cupcakes and saw how Vanessa and Steffie reacted to them, she took a closer look and decided she liked what she saw." Brooke leaned a little closer to Jesse and added, "She wants to talk to me about possibly working with her on a few holiday parties."

Jesse touched the rim of his glass to hers. "To your success, then."

"I will most certainly drink to that."

Brooke raised the glass to her lips, but before she

could take a sip, Gabriel Beck, Vanessa's half brother and the town's chief of police, known to everyone as simply Beck, called everyone to the dining room for the congratulatory toasts to the engaged couple. The overflow of guests filled the foyer.

"We'd like the members of the wedding party to come in here," Beck said when the noise level began to die down.

"Excuse me," Brooke said to Jesse. "That would include me."

She made her way through the crowd to the dining room, looking back once to see that Jesse's eyes followed her every step of the way.

Jesse stood near the back of the crowd of well-wishers and listened as first Beck made a toast, followed by one given by Dallas, then another by Grant. His mind began drifting back to that moment earlier when he'd crossed Cherry Street at the top of the block just as Brooke began to park the car. He'd just made it to Vanessa's driveway when Brooke stumbled and fell forward and the tower of white boxes began to shift. If he'd been two steps sooner, he'd have been able to prevent the top boxes from toppling.

The look on Brooke's face had been sheer panic and total devastation when those three boxes hit the ground. He understood what it meant to need to make a great first impression, how sometimes the direction of your life could depend on it. He was glad that he had been there to lend a hand and to help put a smile back on her face.

It was a beautiful smile, and a heart-stoppingly beautiful face. Hadn't his own heart all but stopped when she'd walked up to him and called his name a few minutes ago? Through the crowd he could see her, and he was finding it hard to look away.

"Enright." Clay appeared at his elbow.

"How's it going?" Jesse whispered so as not to be heard over the toasts that were still being made.

"Good. You?"

"Can't complain."

"Heard what you did for Brooke this afternoon. Thanks for helping her out. She says you saved the day for her."

Jesse nodded, his eyes still on Brooke.

"You . . . ah . . . interested? In my sister, I mean?" Clay asked.

"Might be." Jesse's gaze remained straight ahead.

"You want a tip?" Clay leaned in closer. "Don't let her know. Let her think you only want to be her friend, and for God's sake, don't ask her out."

"Sounds like something a big brother would say when he thinks someone wants to date his sister," Jesse muttered. "Actually, sounds like something I did say when my little sister—"

"No, I'm serious. And for the record, she's older." Clay took a few steps back toward the foyer, to the very edge of the crowd, and he gestured for Jesse to follow. "Look, if you ask her out, she'll go out with you one time, and after that, she'll be busy every time you call her."

"So you're saying that if she thinks I'm interested in her—should I be, that is—"

"She'll turn you off like a light switch."

Jesse just stared. It was a novel way of scaring off a potential suitor for your sister. He might try it some-

time. It was too late to work on Jonathan, he reasoned, but if Sophie ever came to her senses and
dropped that jerk, maybe the opportunity might arise
at some point in the future.

"Look, I've been watching guys make fools of
themselves over Brooke since I was a kid, but she's
always been picky. Now, since Eric, she's even worse.
You can ask any single guy in St. Dennis, since most
of them have asked her out. And she's gone out with
most of them. Once." Clay pointed across the room
to a tall blond guy. "One time. And see the guy in the
navy sport jacket? One date." He pointed throughout
the crowd and repeated, "One date. One date . . . and
oh, yeah, there's Owen Petrie. One date. Go ahead.
Ask any one of them."

Clay lowered his voice even more. "If you're really
into Brooke, don't let her know."

It wasn't anything Jesse hadn't heard from other
people, but it was interesting to hear Clay's take on
the situation.

"So how do I get to know her? That is, if I
wanted to."

"You run into her here and there, you talk, you
make nice, you let her know that you like her but let
her think it's only friendship. But don't ask her out. I
mean it. Every guy in town has tried. With Brooke,
it's one and done. If you don't want to be done, just
be her friend until she decides she wants it to be something else."

"And if she never does?"

"Then you're no worse off than you were before."
Clay paused. "My sister's had a rough time these past
few years."

"I heard about her husband."

"I've tried talking to her, told her she needs to start to make a life for herself, but she just can't seem to get past it."

"Could you?"

Clay thought it over for a moment. "I think losing someone you love puts a hole inside you that's bigger than anything you can imagine—bigger than anything I can imagine, anyway. But I also think that sooner or later, you're going to have to start filling that hole in. Brooke's been in mourning for more than two years now. It's not that I think she should forget about Eric. He was one hell of a guy and she loved him. He's the father of her son. But she's very young—much too young—to . . . well, to give up on life."

"Why are you telling me this?" Jesse asked.

"What you did for her today was pretty decent. And it's obvious that you're interested in her."

"So you're giving me the inside word as a thank-you?"

Clay shrugged. "I guess you could put it that way."

"Then when do I get to go out with her?" He added, "Assuming, of course, that I wanted to."

"You'll probably have to wait until she asks you."

"How many guys has she asked out?"

"None that I know of," Clay told him, "but you could be the first if you play your cards right."

Clay slapped him on the back and headed for the waiter who appeared with another tray of champagne. He took a glass and raised it in Jesse's direction.

"A word to the wise," Clay said before turning back to the toasts that were still being given.

"Thanks," Jesse muttered, and wondered if he was being played.

He looked around the room at the other guys Clay claimed had never gotten a second date with Brooke. They all looked like nice enough guys to him. He'd met Owen Petrie a couple of times, and thought he seemed like a good guy.

He was going to have to do a little research among some of the guys Clay claimed Brooke had gone out with once and then promptly crossed off the list, Jesse told himself, because he wasn't about to give up on getting to know her better. Every conversation he had with her seemed to end too soon, and any time he spent with her had never been long enough.

From across the room, Jesse watched Owen, who was hard to miss because he topped six feet by about another six inches and was almost the tallest guy in the room. Maybe he could chat him up a bit, see what he had to say.

Jesse emptied his glass and returned it to a passing tray. If Owen and a few others corroborated Clay's story, Jesse was just going to have to come up with a plan that no one else had thought of. What that plan might be, he had no idea, but he figured he could learn from their mistakes. He made his way through the crowd to Owen Petrie, who had just been joined by the tall blond fellow Clay had pointed out as a victim of Brooke's "one-and-done."

Of course, Jesse was going to have to be subtle—no guy likes to admit he's been dumped by a girl he likes—but he could do subtle. As a trial lawyer, he'd gotten witnesses to admit to things on the stand that no one had foreseen—no one on the other side, that is. He knew how to phrase things to get people to open up. He cleared his throat, and smiled as he caught Owen's eye and raised a hand in greeting.

Let the interrogation of the witnesses begin.

Chapter 6

JESSE had always been proud of his analytical skills, so he was pretty pleased with himself as he walked to work the next morning with what he thought sounded like a reasonable plan: if pursuing a relationship with Brooke was destined to result in a door closed in his face, he was just going to have to make *her* want to pursue a relationship with *him*. Unfortunately, he wasn't sure of how best to get from concept to reality, since he'd adopted subtlety as his motto. His plan was admittedly sketchy, a work in progress. Some things were going to have to be played by ear.

He began when he arrived at the office by having Liz call Brooke and ask if she could change her appointment and come into the office at eleven thirty, rather than later in the afternoon, to go over her will. It was quite brilliant, Jesse thought, because they'd be forced to work through the lunch hour, and well, then he'd have to feed her, wouldn't he? If he arranged to have food delivered at twelve-fifteen, when she'd surely still be there, he could invite her to join him. While they ate, maybe they could put business aside for a few minutes. Almost like a lunch date, he reasoned. If he'd kept the appointment for four o'clock, however, she'd most likely want to leave to have dinner with her son, and she'd be out of his office by five.

Subtle. Mentally he patted himself on the back.

At eleven-twenty, he heard the front door open and close. He loosened his tie to achieve that hard-at-work, rumpled look, and spread the contents of a file across his desk as if he'd been working diligently all morning instead of popping up to look out the window every time he heard a car door slam.

"Brooke Bowers is here, Jesse," Liz buzzed in to tell him.

"Great." Jesse got up from his desk, tugged his shirtsleeves up just a bit more, and opened his office door. "Brooke." He greeted her with a friendly smile. "Come on in."

"Hi, Jesse." Brooke smiled back as she walked toward him, and he felt his heart flip.

He held the door for her, then after she entered his office, closed it behind her. He moved one of the leather side chairs a little closer to his desk. Would a guy tell a woman *friend* how great she looked in yoga pants and a casual, loose top? Would he say "great"? "Nice"? He wouldn't say "hot," though, right? He wasn't sure, so he let it go.

"Sorry to be a little early, but I dropped off cupcakes at Scoop and at Cuppachino, and thought maybe I'd read if you were busy." Brooke pulled a paperback out of her bag, held it up, then dropped it back in. "I told Liz I didn't want to inconvenience you if you weren't ready to see me . . ."

Jesse brushed off her concern with a wave of his hand.

"I can get back to this later." He returned all the papers to the file on his desk and set it aside. "Besides, I can always make time for a friend."

"Thanks, Jesse." She sat and opened her bag again, this time removing a fat envelope. "I know I should have done all this sooner, but it's just been so hard to deal with—"

"No need to explain," he replied. "I can only imagine how difficult these past few years have been for you."

"I really appreciate that you're so understanding." Her shoulders relaxed a bit. "I want to make sure that Logan's interests are protected should anything happen to me. And there's this matter of the business Eric had started with his brother . . ."

"We can take care of everything for you," Jesse assured her. "One thing at a time. Now, did you bring your existing will with you?"

"I have the one Eric and I made after Logan was born, and I have the one he made right before he left the last time." She opened the folder and sorted through the papers. "You must think I'm an airhead. I apologize for not having these papers in better order."

"I don't think anything of the sort. Take your time." He glanced at the clock. He could easily drag this out until lunch was delivered.

"This is the one Eric and I made together." She handed him a folded sheaf of papers with her right hand, and with her left, passed him a file. "And this is the one Eric made on his own."

"Thanks. Give me a minute or two to look these over."

"Of course."

From the corner of his eye, he could see her looking around his office, and he wished he'd spent a little time adding some personal touches to the decor. He wondered what she thought that portrait of his great-great-grandfather hanging over the corner fireplace said about him.

Then again, since he wasn't sure how long he'd be staying in St. Dennis—his employment being dependent on the whims of his grandfather—he hadn't spent much time thinking about decorating the office.

"This is all pretty standard." Jesse held up the joint will. "You leave everything to each other, and in the case that you are both deceased, the estate goes to Logan."

Brooke nodded.

"I don't see anything about a business, though." Jesse frowned and searched for a possible codicil.

"That's all in Eric's last will," Brooke told him. "He and his brother had agreed to go into business when Eric came home before his last deployment. His brother started up the business while he was gone, but Eric provided half the funding. It's all in there." She pointed to the file he was opening.

"Let's see what we have here . . ." Jesse began to read. When he got to the end, he looked up at Brooke. "So your husband and his brother agreed to go fifty-fifty on this business, with the brother actually running it until Eric left the service."

"Right."

"What kind of business are we talking about?"

"Landscaping. His brother has a degree in landscape architecture, and wanted to start his own business. Eric totally supported him in that, and was going to work with him when he retired from the military."

"What contact have you had with"—Jesse scannned the will for the name—"Jason Bowers since Eric's death?"

"Jace was at the funeral, of course," Brooke replied. "And he always remembers to send Logan presents on his birthday and at Christmas. We talk on the phone once in a while—less and less as time goes on, though."

"And what does he have to say about this business?"

"Not a whole lot. He says he's busy and that things are going well."

"He never asked if you wanted him to buy you out or pay you back for the money Eric invested? Has he ever referred to the financial arrangement he had with his brother?"

"He did broach the subject right after the funeral, but I sort of waved it off. I told him I thought that was all between him and Eric." She looked a little sheepish. "I probably should have pursued it, shouldn't I? At the time I just wasn't up to having that conversation."

"Obviously, you were distraught back then. We can touch base with him and find out the particulars. You're certainly entitled to know how the business is doing. If nothing else, you want to know if it's profitable or if it's operating at a loss."

"I don't really want to be involved with it," she was quick to add. "I mean, that was his and Eric's thing, you know? I don't want him to think I want to be involved or that I'm somehow threatening him."

Jesse held up a hand to stop her from continuing.

"There's no need to threaten him or to put him on the defensive in any way. But since your husband put up half the money, and owned half of the business, Jason should be more than willing to let you know how things are going, since Eric's half is now your half."

"I don't want half of the business," she explained. "But I do want to make sure that whatever Eric invested in that business is secured for my son."

"Would you feel better contacting him yourself?"

When she hesitated and appeared uncertain, he added, "Or I could write a quick letter letting him know I'm the family attorney and as such, I'm looking into any assets Eric might have had that might go into a trust for Logan."

"Could you do that?" Her face brightened. "Could you do it in a way that doesn't make him think I've gone all lawyer on him?"

When she realized what she'd said, she laughed self-consciously. "Not that there's anything wrong with lawyers."

Jesse smiled. "Yes, I can do it in a way that doesn't sound like you're suspicious of him. I'm assuming that's what you meant?"

Brooke nodded. "That's exactly what I meant. I'm not even questioning why he hasn't sent me a status report from time to time. But I would like to know if he's still in business . . . well, according to Google, he is. And if anyone's to blame for failing to follow up, it's me."

"Don't give it a second thought." Jesse made some notes on a pad of paper. "I'll take care of it. Now, we need to work on a new will, and I'm guessing you're going to want—"

"Jesse, excuse me, but lunch just arrived." Liz announced over the intercom. "Do you want me to take it into the back?"

Jesse pretended to be surprised, and looked down at his watch as if unable to believe it was already past noon.

"No, I'll come out for it."

"I'm heading out for lunch now, unless you need me for something," Liz told him.

"No, go ahead. Take your time." Jesse turned to Brooke as he hung up the phone. "Excuse me for a minute."

"Jesse, we can reschedule to finish this up if this is an inopportune time . . ." Brooke began.

"Not at all. Sit tight." Jesse went into the front room, where Liz sat, and picked up the box from the Checkered Cloth, a relatively new take-out place that had quickly established a reputation for fine food. He came back into the office, this time leaving the door open, and placed the box on his desk.

"Don't you love getting takeout from this place?" Jesse moved things around on his desk to make room. "They make the best stuff." He looked up at Brooke. "I hope you don't have plans for lunch. I took the liberty of ordering for both of us since I figured we'd be working straight through an hour or so."

He removed a few wrapped items and peeled back the foil. "Chicken salad." He peered into the box. "Tossed salads, éclairs. And two bottles of water."

Next he unpacked napkins and plastic cutlery. "We

can talk about your new will while we eat. One stone. Two birds."

"Thank you, Jesse. This is very thoughtful of you. And eating now will save me time. I have a two o'clock class."

"Perfect. We'll be done before then and you'll make it to class without having to talk yourself out of a quick run through the golden arches." He unpacked the entire box and passed a sandwich, salad, dessert, and water across the desk to Brooke. "One of your cupcakes would make this the perfect lunch."

"Their éclairs are sinful, though," Brooke told him as she unwrapped the sandwich. "Clay brought some home a week or so ago. Chloe does a great job on everything."

"True enough. Without her and a few other establishments in town, I'd starve to death."

"Not a cook?" she asked.

"Not much of one," he admitted. "I always say I'm going to get a few good cookbooks and teach myself some basic things, but I haven't had time."

"You only need one really good cookbook. Something sort of basic but not idiot-basic. Something that gives you recipes that are easy and fast and good."

"That's exactly what I need."

"I'll find a good one for you. I have a lot of cookbooks at the farm. Between Clay and me, I'll bet we have fifty or sixty of them. I'll see if I can find one that might work for you."

"I'd appreciate that. Thanks." He took a bite of his sandwich, but barely tasted it. All he could think was, *Yes!* His subtle plan was working!

Then, to keep the conversation on the personal side, he asked, "Does Clay do a lot of cooking?"

Brooke rolled her eyes. "He thinks he's, I don't know, one of those guys on Food TV. Takes his food very seriously these days. It's hard to believe, but he's become a better cook than Mom ever was. He was like you, I guess, after Mom and Dad turned the farm over to him and moved to Myrtle Beach. He knew some basics, but he had a lot to learn if he didn't want to eat out twice a day. Which he wouldn't want to do, because he's so into food—assuming, of course, that it's organic and locally grown. He's become almost militant about what he eats, but he's got quite a repertoire of recipes."

"I guess a farmer—one who grows all the vegetables and fruits that Clay grows—would have to believe in what he's doing."

"That's exactly what he says." She put down her sandwich. "Clay has never wanted to do anything but farm, and he's always looked for ways to grow his crops without using pesticides. He's been way ahead of the popular movement in that respect. My dad was, too."

"Clay and Wade MacGregor were talking about starting a brewery together." Jesse started on his salad, taking his time. "Is that off the table now?"

"Oh, no." Brooke shook her head. "They're both totally into the whole concept of brewing organic beer. They've already found organic seed for the hops and barley they want to plant in the spring. I heard Clay on the phone the other day talking to someone about organic rye seed." She grinned. "But I predict that, for Wade, the actual growing part is going to be a life-changing experience."

"How so?"

"He's never grown anything before. Never operated farm equipment. It's not the same as being the brewer. When Wade was in Texas, everything that went into his beer was delivered to him. Growing it all from scratch, that's a whole 'nother thing. There's a lot of physical work that goes into getting the fields ready. Planting. Fertilizing. Irrigating. And those are just the things you can control."

"Oh." Jesse nodded. "I think I'll stick with law."

"Yeah, farming's not my cup of tea either." She opened her container of salad. "I hated it growing up. All the chores, you know? But I'm so grateful that Clay is who he is. It would break my heart to see the farm sold, maybe have a bunch of town houses slapped up. It's been in our family for so many generations. It's comforting to think it will be intact for Logan and any kids that Clay might have one day."

"Like this place," Jesse said. "My great-great-great-grandfather started this firm. An Enright has been in practice here every generation since."

"Handling legal matters for the Madisons, did you know?"

"I think my grandfather may have mentioned that." Actually, Jesse'd found the old files of many a St. Dennis family in the attic and had gone through them when he first moved to St. Dennis, before his grandfather was spending more than a few cursory hours each week with him.

"Are you the last lawyer in your family? I know your uncle Mike has his generation covered."

"My sister Sophie is a lawyer."

"How did your father manage to break away from the family tradition and avoid law school?"

"He didn't." He paused to tamp down the snap that was about to rise in his voice. She had no way of knowing who and what his father was. "He went to law school."

"How was he able to avoid getting roped into the family firm?"

By being a crook and a womanizer and a total screwup.

"He followed another path," Jesse said simply, and prayed she'd let it go at that.

"How is your aunt? I know everyone's been worried about her."

"My uncle stopped in for a few minutes last week, and he said she's hanging in there but she's still very ill and isn't expected to recover."

"That is so sad." Brooke twisted the cap off her water bottle. "Andrea has always been such a sweet and cheery woman, you know?"

"To tell you the truth, I don't really know her or my uncle well at all." There was no point in trying to explain to her why.

"Oh." She drank from the bottle for a moment. "Well, I can tell you they're both pretty terrific people."

"So I've heard." *From just about everyone in St. Dennis,* he could have added. Everyone in town seemed to know his relatives better than he did.

His uncle Mike just happened to stop into the office the first week Jesse started there. Jesse knew the man had come to look him over, afraid, no doubt, that Jesse was too much his father's son and therefore was

unworthy to tread the hallowed halls of Enright and
Enright. The memory of his uncle's unconcealed
scrutiny—the skepticism in Mike Enright's eyes as he
openly evaluated Jesse and obviously found him
lacking—still rankled. Even though Jesse knew he'd
proven himself over and over since that day, and even
though his uncle had come around and actually seemed
to like him, that first meeting, where he'd been dismissed as nothing more than a chip off of Craig Enright's block, someone who'd come to St. Dennis with
some sense of entitlement toward the family firm, still
rankled.

Then again, who better to know Craig's character
than his brother?

"Why did you decide to come to St. Dennis?" she
asked.

"Why?" He thought for a moment. "My grandfather was retiring, my uncle wasn't in a position to
take over for him, so it just seemed like the thing
to do."

"Will you stay on when Mike comes back? After
Andrea . . . you know." She obviously couldn't bring
herself to say, *After Andrea passes.*

"We'll see." He hadn't wanted to think about his
uncle Mike coming back and wanting to head up the
firm, but he was aware that he might have to deal
with that at some point. For now, he was keeping
things afloat here and doing a damned good job of it,
and that's all Jesse was focusing on. "I don't know
what my uncle's plans are."

"Well, we're all hoping for a miracle." Brooke finished both her salad and her sandwich and looked
for a place to dispose of the wrappings. Jesse slid the

box toward her side of the desk and she tossed everything in.

"I can't believe I ate all that," she told him. "I guess I was hungrier than I realized."

"Sounds like you've been burning the midnight oil."

Brooke nodded. "I have been baking every minute of every day for the past week. The only exceptions are when I'm sleeping or in class. The rest of the time, I'm either whipping something up to put in the oven, or waiting for something to finish baking."

"Do you count little cupcakes to help you fall asleep at night?"

"Believe me, I have no trouble falling asleep these days." Brooke laughed. "Though I do make these minicupcakes that look like little lambs. I suppose if need be, I could envision them being tossed over a fence and count them as they flew by."

"Sounds like your business is really taking off."

"It's starting to. I need to streamline my game plan so that things flow a little smoother, but all in all, I have no complaints. Tomorrow I have an appointment with Frank over at Krauser's to see about having this old van of Clay's fixed up so I can use it for deliveries." She rested her chin in her hand, and a lock of strawberry blond hair fell over her forehead. She eased it behind her ear. "I'm going to try to use the van to sell from for a while, until I can make enough to get a storefront in town. I used to think I just wanted to sell from the van, but I changed my mind after being around Scoop and Bling. There's a permanance about them that I hadn't realized I wanted until I started hanging around with Steffie and Vanessa. Even Dallas is going for a permanent home for her film business here in St. Dennis. It just got me thinking . . ." Her voice trailed away.

"Thinking about what?"

"About how maybe it was time to set roots." She grew quiet for a moment. "I never thought about moving back here, but I'm glad I did."

"So am I," he couldn't help but add.

"Well, I'm glad you're here, too." She glanced at her watch. "I'm happy to have someone my own age to share my legal issues with. This way, I won't have to worry about breaking in a new lawyer when you decide to retire, the way so many people in town have had to switch from your grandfather . . ." She stopped and shook her head. "I don't mean that to sound in a negative way."

"I didn't take it in a negative way. I've tried to accommodate my grandfather's older clients and reassure them that they'll continue to have the same fine representation they've always had. For the most part, I think I've done okay, holding on to the old-timers' business. We lost a few during the transition, but I think they would have moved their business anyway. Most of the clients have been willing to give me a chance."

"That's St. Dennis for you." She smiled and gathered her things. "Is there anything else we need to do right now? I should get going if I'm going to make it to class on time."

"I think we're fine for now. I'll write the letter to Jason Bowers and copy you on that. We will have to schedule another appointment to go over what you want in your new will."

Brooke stood. "I want everything to go to Logan if something happens to me."

"By everything, I'm guessing you mean whatever cash, life insurance, property . . . do you have an interest in the farm, or is that all in Clay's name?"

She frowned. "There was some mention of some portion of it being retained for Logan if the farm is sold in the future, but I don't remember the percentage."

"We can talk about that next time." He stood to walk her to the door. "I can have Liz give you a call and set up another appointment."

"That would be great. Thanks so much, Jesse." She walked with him to the front door. "You don't know how much it means to me to have someone help me sort all this out, to make sure that Logan is taken care of should something happen to me."

"That's what I'm here for." He opened the door and stepped outside. The sun had disappeared completely and the sky was turning dark.

"Really. I can't thank you enough." She touched his arm. "I feel so much better knowing there's someone I can depend on for legal advice."

"Always," he told her. "I'm always here for you, Brooke. Besides, what are friends for?"

"Are you going to watch the Halloween Parade?" she asked when they reached the end of the walk. "The kids are so excited about it. Cody and Logan are going as dueling pirates."

"Dueling pirates?"

"They plan to duel with each other—with cardboard swords—as they pass the judges' stand."

"Well, I certainly can't miss that."

"I'll see you there, then."

He waved as she got into her car, and after she'd driven away, he went back into the office, a smile on his face, thinking that subtlety was, in fact, the right way to go. After all, wasn't it slow and steady that won the race?

Chapter 7

BROOKE balanced the container holding her cupcakes in one hand while pushing open the door to Cuppachino with the other. Once inside the coffee shop, quiet at barely seven in the morning, she waved to Carlo and placed the container on the counter.

"Be with you in a moment," Carlo called to her. "Want a cup of coffee?"

Brooke started to decline when a voice from across the room called back, "Of course she does. And she wants to come sit with me while she drinks it."

Brooke turned and smiled at the older woman. "Good morning, Miss Grace."

"Good morning, dear. You're up and out early," Grace replied.

"Places to go, people to see. Cupcakes to deliver."

"Half decaf, half regular. Light, one sweetener," Carlo recited to the counter girl while he unpacked the cupcakes and arranged them on a tray. "Give it to Brooke . . . there you go, Brooke. Here's your carrier. The cupcakes are a huge hit. Keep 'em coming." His voice trailed away as he went back into the kitchen.

The young girl working the counter finished making Brooke's coffee as per her boss's instructions and passed the mug to Brooke, who carried it to the table near the front window where Grace sat watching the morning traffic and making notes in a small notebook.

"Working on your column for your newspaper?" Brooke asked as she took a seat across from Grace.

"Just doodling." Grace closed the notebook and dropped it into the huge shoulder bag she always had with her.

"You're up early today yourself," Brooke noted.

"I've been up since five," Grace told her. "Not by choice, I might add. But I thought as long as I was up, I'd get an early start on the day. We go to press this afternoon, so I do have a lot to do between now and then."

"Lots of news this week?"

"Pictures from Steffie's engagement party. The route for the Halloween Parade. The dates for leaf pickup. The usual."

"The party was terrific, wasn't it?" To Brooke's eye, Grace appeared a little subdued.

"Oh, my, yes." The woman perked up a bit. "The cupcakes were scrumptious. And combined with the ice cream Steffie made for the occasion . . . well, one has to wonder what you'll both come up with for the wedding."

"I'm glad you liked the cupcakes, and yes, the Blueberry Bliss ice cream was delicious. As for what will be served at the wedding . . . we're still working on that. They're having cupcakes and wedding cakes, so we need to coordinate things. And of course, the brides need to decide on a date."

"Oh, they've already done that." Grace waved a hand. "Tentatively, that is. It all depends on whether or not Lucy will agree to come back to take charge of the affair. You may have heard that Dallas called Lucy and got her to agree to come home next week to talk about what Dallas and Steffie want."

"No, I hadn't heard, but that's wonderful!" Brooke exclaimed. "For them and for you."

Grace nodded. "When I spoke with Lucy last night, she reminded me that she's only coming home to talk, to see if it's something she might be interested in doing." She rolled her eyes. "As if any event planner—especially one whose business is based in Los Angeles—is going to turn down what is certain to be a huge celebrity event. The publicity is going to be priceless. So I feel comfortable in saying that Lucy will most likely take the job. I'll be very surprised if she says no."

"You miss her terribly, don't you?" Brooke placed a hand on the older woman's arm.

"I do. I miss her as much as I miss Ford. Maybe more, since she's my only daughter," Grace admitted. "You know, I had three children, but only one of them chose to stay here in St. Dennis. It makes me wonder if something I'd done—perhaps when Lucy and Ford were younger—made them want to move away and stay away."

"Grace, I'm willing to bet that you were a terrific mother. I think it's probably just circumstances, you know? Lucy went into business with someone who was based on the West Coast. Ford's job is always going to have him running around the world. It isn't unusual to want to see more of the world than the place where you grew up."

"This is no world for a young man like him to be running around in. It's dangerous."

Brooke nodded. How many times had she had that conversation with Eric? How many times had she asked him to make *this* trip his last one?

"I'm so sorry, dear. How insensitive of me." Grace's eyes clouded with concern. "I know you've suffered a terrible loss."

"It's all right, Grace. And of course I understand why you'd be worried about your son. Who wouldn't be?"

"Ford's been lucky so far, but I'm afraid that one of these days, he's going to run out of luck. He's always in the midst of things, it seems."

"That's his job," Brooke reminded her, painfully aware of just what such a job demanded. "The UN Peacekeepers go where they're most needed, and that's always going to be right smack in the middle of, well, *things*."

"I worry about that boy every day," Grace said softly. "He always ends up in the most godforsaken places. It's always where there are civil wars and up-risings . . ." Her voice trailed off.

"He's doing what he believes in, though, right? Doing something important, something that can have a lasting effect for the good of the lives of people he doesn't even know. I'd have to think that you were a very good mother to have produced a son who is so selfless that he's willing to put his own comfort aside for the sake of other people." At the last minute, Brooke had stopped herself from adding, *And of course he's putting his own life on the line*. She was sure

Grace knew that part and didn't need to be reminded. No more than she had needed to be reminded when Eric was in Iraq. Brooke, more than most, understood what dangers lurked in those "godforsaken places."

"Ford was always a thoughtful boy."

"And now he's a thoughtful man and you can be proud of him." Brooke finished her coffee, thinking about how she'd feel if it were Logan. She knew she'd be on the border of Lost It and Crazy every day.

"I *am* proud of him. I'm proud of all my children. I just wish I could have them all together for a while."

"Well, maybe one of these days that will happen." Brooke pushed back her chair and stood. "Maybe someday Ford will quit and come home and Lucy will decide to give up her L.A. job and take over at the inn."

"A mother can dream." Grace looked up. "Thank you, dear."

"Don't mention it."

"Now, where are you running off to? Do you have class this morning?"

"No. I'm meeting Frank at Krauser's to go over the estimate for some work I'm having done on my brother's old van. He said I could use it for my business, but it needs a tune-up and tires and God knows what all else. Plus, I'm having it painted." Brooke reached into her bag. "Here's how I want it to look."

She laid her sketch on the table in front of Grace.

"Oh, my. Clay's van, you say?" Grace's glasses slid forward as she leaned over the drawing. "Does he know you're doing this?"

"He said I could paint it however I wanted." Brooke grinned. "That's what I want."

"Well, I can't wait to see it." Grace folded the paper and handed it back to Brooke. "I'm sure it's going to be the talk of the town . . ."

"Mom, thanks for picking me up. It would have been a long walk home. Not that I couldn't use the exercise," Brooke hastened to add as she slid onto the passenger's seat of her mother's car. Brooke had driven the van to Krauser's and left it there.

"You and me both," her mother, Hannah, replied. "All those cupcakes we've been forced to sample." She sighed heavily. "I suppose someone has to do it, though."

"If you're worried about your waistline, you could always let Clay do the sampling."

"A mother never sends her children someplace she herself would not go," Hannah said archly before breaking into a grin. "Besides, if you think I'm going to let him have all the fun, you're crazy."

"Glad you don't mind pitching in."

"Wouldn't miss it." Hannah put on her left turn signal and checked her mirrors before turning. "So when does Frank think the van will be ready?"

"He thought probably by Tuesday. I can't wait to see it when he's finished." Brooke glanced out the window. "Mom, you missed the turn."

"We're not going right home."

"Where are we going?"

"I want to show you something," Hannah told her.

"Animal, vegetable, or mineral?"

"You'll see in just a moment."

After another left turn, a right, and another quick left, Hannah stopped the car in front of a short row of newly constructed town houses. The Realtor's sign that stood on the newly sodded front lawn of the end unit boldly announced that the house had been sold.

Hannah turned to Brooke. "Let's go inside for a quick tour."

Without waiting for her daughter to reply, Hannah jumped out and waited for Brooke to join her on the sidewalk in front of the "Sold" sign. Puzzled, Brooke followed her to the front door, where Hannah took a key from her pocket and fitted it into the lock.

"Mom, why do you have the key? Are you going to sell real estate again? 'Cause if you are, you might note that this one has been sold."

"I have the key because I bought it." Hannah pushed the front door open and gestured for Brooke to enter.

Brooke remained frozen to the spot. "You bought it? You mean, you bought this house?"

Looking pleased with herself, Hannah nodded. "I did."

"So it's what, an investment? You're going to rent it out? Maybe to tourists?" Brooke stepped inside and looked around. "Oh, nice. I like the way the bookshelves go all the way to the ceiling on either side of the fireplace."

"No," her mother said.

"You don't like the bookcases?" Brooke frowned. "I suppose you could have them taken out, but—"

"No, I mean I didn't buy it as an investment. I bought it to live in."

"Live in? You mean you—"

"Don't you love this kitchen?" Hannah's voice trailed down the hall as she walked to the back of the house. "Look at the view of the Bay from back here. Do you know I've lived in St. Dennis all my life and I've never been able to see the Bay from my house? My bedroom upstairs has a wall of windows with this view."

"You mean you're moving out?" Brooke frowned. "Why would you move out? The farm is your home—"

"No, sweetheart, the farm is *Clay's* home." Hannah brushed sawdust from a counter and leaned on it. "It belongs to him."

"Did he say something that made you feel that you weren't welcome there?"

"Of course not. He's been as generous letting me stay there as he has been with you and Logan."

"Then I don't understand."

"Your father and I would have been married forty-five years come March, did you know that?" Hannah walked to the French doors that overlooked the back-yard and opened and closed first one, then the other.

"I knew it was fortysomething coming up, yes." Brooke wondered where this was going.

"I lived every day of my married life on that farm with him, until we retired and moved to Myrtle Beach, which, in retrospect, was probably not a good idea. I don't think your father ever really adjusted to life off the farm. It was all he ever knew."

"I thought he liked playing golf and the boating and all the other activities he got involved in."

"He said he did, but I really think those activities were just a substitute for what he missed. It was merely a means to keep moving. I don't think he ever saw any of it as particularly useful." Her mother re-locked the doors and began to stroll around the kitchen, opening and closing the cabinets. "I've never had a new kitchen before. Or new bathrooms, for that matter. Oh, we did remodel a bit over the years, but I never lived in a new house, one where I got to pick out everything myself. I think I'm going to like it."

Hannah opened a pair of louvered doors. "Pantry," she told Brooke. "And there's a laundry room right back—"

"I'm not following why you can't stay at the farm. Is it just because you wanted a brand-new house?"

"I can't live there without your father, Brooke. I see him everywhere I look. I hear Clay coming down the steps, and I think it's Dave. Funny how Clay's foot-falls on the stairs sound so much like his father's." She turned to her daughter with tears in her eyes. "I just can't live in that house, sweetie. After your dad died, and I stayed in Myrtle Beach for a few months alone, before you and Logan came to stay with me, I missed him terribly. But nothing like I do when I'm at the farm. He's everywhere there. Our life together is everywhere." She shook her head. "I just can't live there without him, honey."

"And here, in this new house . . ." Brooke went to her mother and took her hands.

"There's no sound of him here. No memories ex-cept the ones I bring with me. The first time I walked in the front door I realized there was nothing of Dave here. In many ways, that saddened me more than I can say. But in others, it was a relief."

"You think you'll be all right with that? Alone here?"

"I think I will." She looked around at the kitchen that would be all hers, then into the dining room, where the contractor had yet to hang the light fixture she'd picked out. "I'm hoping I'll be able to sleep a little better at night, anyway." She smiled wanly. "I figured it's worth a try."

"If it doesn't work out—"

"Then I can rent it and move back to the farm, but I hope it doesn't come to that. Clay is such a good sport, and he'd never say anything, but it has to be hell, living with his mother at his age. It has to be cramping his style something fierce."

"Clay's like Dad. All he thinks about is the farm. Besides, he's lived there all this time, even when you and Dad lived there, and it didn't bother him."

"When your father was alive, before he retired and we moved, Clay lived in the tenant house. He lived there from the time he graduated from college until we turned the farm over to him. He didn't move into the main house until we moved out. And I don't expect Clay to be single forever."

"He isn't even dating anyone right now."

"Hopefully, once I move out, he'll be more inclined to find someone." Hannah gave Brooke's hands one last squeeze.

"I'm sorry. I never realized how hard it must be for you." Brooke shook her head. "I, of all people, should have known . . ."

"Don't be silly." Hannah smoothed the hair back from her daughter's forehead. "I don't expect either of you to be a mind reader."

"Still, we should have—"

"No, you shouldn't."

"Does Clay know? About this house?" Brooke asked.

"I told him at lunchtime."

"What did he say?"

"Pretty much everything that you just said."

"Are you sure that this is what you want?"

"This is exactly what I want. More importantly, it's exactly what I need." Hannah put an arm around Brooke. "Moving back to the farm was really just an attempt on my part to hold on to my old life. That really hasn't worked out so well." She shrugged. "So I figure it's time to make a new life for myself. By myself."

"When are you going to move?"

"As soon as the contractors finish up a few details and the Realtor gets the place cleaned. Probably no more than a week."

"You're sure you're okay with this?"

"I'm more than okay. I'm looking forward to it." Hannah took Brooke by the hand. "Come on, let me show you the upstairs. Wait till you see my bath . . ."

Her mother's new bath was gorgeous. Her bedroom was everything anyone could want, with a huge walk-in closet and double doors leading to a small porch that looked out over the Bay. Hannah had opened the doors and a crisp breeze floated in, and Brooke had had to concede that the house was darned near perfect.

Hannah dropped Brooke off at the farm before heading off to her shop, which she had confided to Brooke she would probably be selling.

"I bought it because I was bored and wanted something to do. Buying this new place for myself has energized me and I don't feel I need to think up ways to keep myself busy anymore," Hannah had said. "Know anyone who wants to buy a shop that sells fun things for pets?"

Brooke stood at the kitchen window in the farmhouse and watched Clay, who was out near the barn working on a tractor that was having engine trouble. The conversation she'd had with her mother was still in her head, and it was forcing Brooke to reflect on her own circumstances.

It occurred to Brooke that her mother was much braver than she, to take on a new house, to start this next part of her life with her head up and her eyes looking to the future. Of course, Hannah was lucky to be able to afford to live on her own, her husband's life insurance policies having been ample; the sale of the Myrtle Beach house combined with their retirement investments assured that she needn't be dependent on her children.

Of course, Brooke reminded herself, her mother didn't have a small child to consider. Because Logan had never gotten to know his father, Brooke felt it was important that he have a strong male role model in his life, and Clay certainly fit the bill. Besides, Clay loved his nephew and spent part of every day with him. Brooke definitely believed that raising Logan in close proximity to her brother was in Logan's best interests. And Logan did love living on the farm. He loved having his friends over, loved having the fields and the orchards for a backyard, and the pond behind the orchard was one of his favorite places. Last spring and summer, Logan had spent countless hours with his buddies roaming the woods. If she were to move into town, he'd lose all that. Of course, if they moved he could come back and visit, but it wasn't the same as living there and being part of the day-to-day rhythm of the farm.

On the other hand, though he'd probably never admit it, Clay was certainly hamstrung socially with his mother, sister, and eight-year-old nephew living under the same roof with him. Her mother had been right about that. Even if Clay did meet someone, it could be awkward explaining that they couldn't hang out at his place because his mother and sister were there.

Brooke walked out the back door thinking that Clay could well be the last man on the face of the earth whose maturity or masculinity would be threatened by the fact that his mother lived with him.

Still—it was the mother, not the sister, who was moving out, partly to give Clay the space he might not even know he needed.

Brooke walked across the yard and around the corner of the barn, where Clay was tinkering with the tractor.

"How's it going?" she asked.

"Right now, it isn't going at all. However"—he looked up and smiled—"once I get this engine back together, it should be going just fine. How's it going with you?"

She nodded. "Okay."

"You don't seem sure about that."

"Mom just took me to see her new house."

"What's it like?"

"Very nice. Everything's brand spanking new, of course. It's not real big, but it's more than enough room for her and her things. I certainly wouldn't mind having a place like that someday."

"Did she say anything about . . . well, about anything I might have said that may have made her feel unwelcome?" He stopped working and looked at her over the partially dismantled engine.

Brooke shook her head. "That's not why she's moving. She said it's just too hard for her to live here without Dad."

"Yeah, she told me that, too. I just wanted to make sure that maybe somehow I didn't make her think I didn't want her here."

"I think she would have said something if that were the case." Brooke climbed up onto the tractor seat. "I believe she means what she said. That it's too hard for her after all those years she and Dad lived here, and I understand that."

"Do you think she's sorry she didn't stay in Myrtle Beach?"

"I don't think she was ever really happy there. I think she agreed to go with Dad because he thought he'd be happy, but I don't think he was either. After he was gone, there was nothing to keep her there. She wanted the comfort of her old friends and the familiarity of her hometown. I felt the same way. I needed to come home, too."

"Do you think she'll be happy in her new place, living by herself? She hasn't ever really lived alone, you know."

"I think she'll be very happy once she gets settled in."

"I hope so." Clay stopped working and straightened up. "I hope you don't feel like you have to leave just because she's moving."

"I don't."

"Good. This is your home, too, you know. Yours and Logan's. I know that my name's on the deed, but this will always be your home."

Brooke nodded her thanks, not trusting herself to speak for a moment, her throat having tightened with emotion. She did love the farm, it was as much a part of her as it was of her mother and Clay, and she loved her brother for understanding that.

Still . . .

From her seat atop the tractor she could see clear across the fields to the woods on one side and the orchard on the other. Clay was engrossed in his task again, so she hopped down and started off across the fields that weeks ago had been harvested of their grain and corn. She surprised a flock of geese that were feasting on the remnants of the corn shocks, and they headed off noisily toward the pond. Brooke found herself following them, and minutes later, stood on the bank, thinking how small the pond looked to her adult eyes. When she'd been a child, it appeared almost as big as the Bay.

The red-winged blackbirds scolded her from the dried cattails and the geese continued to grumble as if her sole purpose for being there was to spy on them. The red-and-yellow maple trees were reflected in the water, and as Brooke walked around the pond she startled a great blue heron that flew off indignantly, its territory invaded.

When she turned toward the orchard and the ten-

ant house that stood at its edge, she realized that it
had been her destination all along. She followed the
well-worn path to the front porch, which was almost
flush to the ground and held up by two thin pillars.
The window in the door was caked with dust, and she
brushed it away so that she could look inside, but the
sun was low in the sky behind her, creating a glare on
the glass. Almost as an afterthought, she tried the
door, and was surprised to find it unlocked. She
pushed it open and stepped into the still, stale air of
the large front room.

The light was poor, so she found the switch on the
wall near the door and turned it on. She went from
window to window, pulling up the shades to let in the
afternoon sun, all the while brushing away the dried
dead flies and bees from the sills to the floor. She suspected that the rooms had not been aired out since
Clay left.

Her footsteps echoing on the wide plank floorboards, Brooke went into the kitchen. The room was
a large rectangle with plenty of room for a table and
chairs near the windows that looked out on what
might have been a garden many years ago. The appli-
ances were so old she couldn't even venture a guess as
to when they'd been purchased or by whom. She
turned on the faucet and watched the rust-colored
water spew out in fits and starts before settling into a
steady stream and finally running clear. There was
only one real counter, which she guessed was added
sometime in the 1950s judging by its Formica top.
The porcelain farm sink was attached to the wall and
held up by two scrawny legs, and the stove was a
light-it-yourself gas job. The windowsills and the

stove top were a study in dust and mouse droppings. She backed out of the kitchen and made her way upstairs.

There were three bedrooms, one large one in the front and two in the back, each with dormer windows and alcoves. She would have bet money that the bath would contain a claw-foot tub, but it turned out that it had been replaced with a small porcelain one. Brooke didn't bother to turn the water on. She was pretty sure she knew what color it would be. Before going back down the wide stairway, she glanced out all the upstairs windows, which offered views of the farm in every direction. The back bedrooms looked out directly onto the pond, and the front one, into the orchard. If nothing else, this old place had beautiful views, she noted.

Once back downstairs, she went through a small room that divided the two main living areas. There was a stone fireplace on one wall in the front room, but other than that, it was just one big empty space. It could be nice, she thought, cleaned up and painted and with some nice furniture. She went back into the kitchen and took a long hard look. One old stove, one ridiculously old refrigerator. One worn and badly scratched counter. A sparse row of wooden cabinets on one wall and linoleum that had probably been installed back around the time of the Second World War.

But there was so much room, room for more than one big stove and a second oven. Room for more cabinets and counters and a baking center with a marble top. A new sink and dishwasher. It needed a new floor, and paint would be a necessity, but maybe the windows were okay. She tried them, one by one, but almost all of them would need to be replaced.

She wondered how much all that would cost.

It was unlikely that the electric wiring had been updated and the plumbing system would most likely need to be replaced as well.

But still . . . the possibilities taunted her as she walked around the house, seeing it with an eye toward what it could be.

A room off the kitchen could be divided and made into a powder room and a laundry room. The small room between the kitchen and the living room could be an office. There was enough space upstairs to add another bath and some decent closets.

"It could work," she said aloud as she stood in the middle of the living room floor. "It could work . . ."

Taking one last look around, she went out and closed the door tightly behind her. She stepped back to assess the outside, and even though she knew she'd have her hands full, her mind was buzzing. Yes, it needed paint and the shutters needed repair. It needed a new front door. The porch needed shoring up. She walked around the house through the tall weeds, and tried to be realistic about what it would take to make this a home for her and Logan.

"A lot of hard work and a fair amount of cash," she muttered. But still, it wasn't impossible. She did have Eric's life insurance and there was still money in an account from an inheritance from her paternal grandmother, who'd left each of her three granddaughters a lump sum so they'd never have to be dependent on anyone. Brooke didn't know how her two cousins had spent or invested theirs, but she'd invested every penny of hers with an eye toward the down payment on a house someday. She couldn't think of a better way to spend some of it than to spiff up this little place.

Brooke headed back toward the farmhouse thinking how she'd approach her brother. The tenant house, like the fields and the barns and the equipment and the main house, belonged to Clay now. She was pretty sure he'd have no objection to her sprucing it up so that she and Logan could move in. He seemed sincere when he said he liked having her and Logan there at the farm. Well, this way, she would say, you can have your cake . . . make that *cupcake* . . . and eat it, too. You can have your nephew here, and you can have the farmhouse to yourself. You can have a social life, she'd say. You could even have a date over for dinner and—well, what you do after dinner is your business, she'd say.

She checked her watch and noted that it was almost time for the school bus and Logan's birthday party down at Scoop, so she took a shortcut around the side of the farmhouse and walked down the lane. Logan could still take the same bus to and from school and she'd still walk down to meet him at the same place. There'd be no real disruption to their schedule. The only real difference would be that they'd be in their own house again, just the two of them, like they were when Eric was overseas.

In retrospect, she knew that she'd been stronger, back then, than she was now. But Eric had still been alive, and the path before her had seemed so clear and sure, there'd been no reason for weakness, no cause for doubt. Now her steps were more tentative because she no longer knew where they were leading, and her dreams were as muddled and confused as her future. And somewhere deep inside she knew that the longer she put off taking those first steps to put her life back together—however small those steps might be—the more likely it was that she'd still be here, living under her brother's roof, in the house she grew up in, until she passed from this life into the next.

Watching her mother take those first steps had made Brooke think about things she really hadn't wanted to face. Moving away from her comfort zone, even if that move only took her from the farmhouse as far as the orchard, was still a move in the right direction. The tenant house was close enough that Logan could still see Clay every day, but separate enough to give Clay his privacy. It seemed like the right solution at the right time.

Now she just had to figure out what it would take to make the old neglected house livable once again . . . and sell the idea to Clay.

Chapter 8

You know, I'd thought about asking if you wanted me to fix up the tenant house for you, but I didn't want you to think I was trying to get rid of you." Clay leaned against the kitchen doorjamb.

"Was this before or after Mom told you she was moving?" Brooke emptied the dishwasher of the implements she needed for frosting and decorating her cupcakes for the following day. Logan's birthday party had been a big success—as any child's party at Scoop was sure to be—but she'd lost several hours of work time that now had to be made up. Not that she minded. Besides making her son happy, the few hours off had given Brooke a few hours of socializing with the mothers of Logan's friends.

"Before. Actually, I've been thinking about it for a couple of months. I thought maybe it was hard for you, living with Mom and me again after having been on your own and having your own place for so long. But I didn't know how to bring it up without making you feel like I was kicking you out. You know I like having you around, but I gotta be truthful, Brooke. I really love having the kid here." He grinned. "Logan gives me an excuse to be a kid again."

"When did you stop being a kid?" their mother asked as she came into the kitchen.

"I keep the kid in me around for Logan. He needs a playmate," Clay replied.

"A shoddy excuse, that." Hannah tapped Clay on the back of the head with a rolled-up newspaper as she passed on her way to the paper recycling bin.

"Brooke's thinking she might want to spruce up the tenant house and move down there," Clay told her.

"Oh?" Hannah dropped the paper into the bin, then came back to the table where her son sat watching her daughter frost cupcakes. "Are they all going to be for sale?"

Brooke nodded. "Everyone wants three times as many because of the Halloween Parade tomorrow. At this rate I'm going to be baking until dawn."

"So is that supposed to be a spiderweb?" Clay pointed to the thin black lines crisscrossing the top of one cupcake.

Brooke nodded. "That's the prototype." She picked up a cutting board and a package of black licorice. "Here. Make yourself useful. Cut the licorice as thinly as humanly possible."

"Where's the spider?" Hannah asked.

"I'm still working on that," Brooke admitted. She looked toward the ceiling at the sound of running feet. Logan and his friend Cody were on the move. "That's right, boys, run off all that sugar," she muttered.

"While you're working you can tell me about moving into the tenant house." Hannah pulled out a chair and sat.

"It just occurred to me that now would be a good time to start to move on." Brooke looked up at her mother. "You know, like you're doing."

"Honey, I'm going because I have to," Hannah said softly. "You don't have to."

"No, but I want to." Brooke turned her back and began to measure the ingredients for another batch of frosting.

"Well, that place is going to need a considerable amount of work," Hannah said.

"Besides painting inside and out, it looks like it needs everything: a kitchen and bath update and new wiring and plumbing."

"The electric and plumbing were updated about ten years ago when I was living there," Clay told her. "I got tired of blowing fuses every time I turned on the TV and the coffeepot at the same time."

"Really?" Brooke turned around, a smile on her face. "Then it's just the other things. Mostly the kitchen remodeling and new bath and some cosmetic stuff. I figured I could use some of the money Gramma Madison left me."

"You still have some of that?" Hannah asked.

"Every last dime."

"I'll help you out where I can," Clay told her.

"You don't have to," Brooke said. "Especially since you already took care of two of the biggies in the wiring and the plumbing. We just need to decide on a fair rent."

"If you're going to pay to upgrade the house, you shouldn't pay rent." Clay swiped a finger into the bowl of frosting Brooke had left on the table. "Not if you're spending your money to improve my property."

"We can work something out." Brooke turned on the mixer. Whatever Clay said as he left the room was lost, so she turned off the appliance and called to him to repeat what he'd said.

"I said, I'll call Cameron O'Connor and make an appointment for him to come out and look the place over, give us an estimate for the work. If you're going to do this, let's see if we can get it done before the weather turns cold."

"That would be great, Clay, thanks. I can't think of any reason to put off the work." She paused. "How was the heater?"

"The heater worked fine. That was replaced, too," he told her. "But there's no air-conditioning."

"I'll worry about that next summer."

"You might want to have Cam look at the duct work. It might be easier to have everything done at the same time. Less disruption."

"Good point."

Logan and his friend Cody ran through the kitchen on their way to the backyard. Still wound up from Logan's birthday party, the two of them were falling all over each other laughing at something only eight-year-old boys could understand. They dashed through the kitchen, then stopped at the back door.

"Mom, did you make our swords for Halloween?" Logan hung on the doorjamb.

"Not yet, sweetie. But I will, as soon as I finish these cupcakes."

"Hey, I thought I got to make the swords." Clay

came down the back steps from the second floor. "I make way better swords than your mother does."

"You think," Brooke challenged him.

"I know," he tossed back then turned to the boys. "We'll let the guys decide. Who would you rather make your swords, me or your mom?"

"You!" both boys cried.

"Sorry, sis." Clay looked smug as he ushered the boys out the back door.

"I bow before your superior sword-making ability," Brooke called as the back door slammed behind him. She glanced at the clock then counted the number of cupcakes she'd finished and figured out how many more she had to make. She groaned and promised herself that the new kitchen in the tenant house would have that second oven for sure.

"Isn't Halloween the coolest holiday *ever*?" Logan slid his eye patch over his head and covered his right eye. He swung his cardboard aluminum-foil-covered sword as he dashed through the kitchen, his free hand curved over his head. "Uncle Clay taught me and Cody how to duel. You do it like this." He demonstrated his newly learned technique.

"Quite impressive." Brooke nodded as she stacked the unused pastry boxes and put them into the pantry, remembering the previous weekend's debacle in front of Vanessa's house. Thinking about those bouncing boxes of cupcakes made her think of Jesse. Twice this week when she went into Cuppachino in the morning, Grace mentioned that he'd just left.

She wondered if she'd run into him at the parade later this morning. He did say he'd be going.

"We practiced with our swords a lot last night," Logan was saying. "We showed Cody's mom when Uncle Clay drove Cody home from my birthday party. Cody's mom was impressed, too. So was his aunt Berry. She said we looked like real swashbucklers." He paused. "What's a swashbuckler?"

"A pirate who knows how to duel really really well," she told him.

Logan nodded. "That's us. And she said we looked just like Earl . . . I don't know, Earl somebody."

"Errol Flynn?"

"Maybe." Logan shrugged. "Can we go now?"

"Yes. Just give me a minute to brush my hair and maybe put a little makeup on." She pulled the elastic from her ponytail.

"You don't need makeup, Mom. You're beautiful just the way you are."

"Who told you to say that?"

"Uncle Clay."

Brooke laughed and ran up the steps, taking them two at a time. She washed her face and ran a brush through her hair, then got out the mascara. No need for eye shadow or blush, just maybe a little color to the lips. She stood in front of the mirror and took a good look. When had she started to look so tired? Where had those circles under her eyes come from? She started to look for concealer, but it had been so long since she'd bothered, she couldn't remember where she might have put it.

"Mom!" Logan called up the steps. "I think we should go now."

"I'll be right down." Brooke took a second look, decided that it was going to take more than a little concealer, and said the hell with it. She pulled off the T-shirt she'd been working in all morning and tossed it in the direction of her overflowing hamper. She'd been so busy with her cupcakes all week that she hadn't gotten to her laundry. She rummaged through the pile for a sweatshirt, found one she'd worn a few days ago, then went into the bathroom and ran cold water, hoping to remove the little bit of chocolate frosting that she'd gotten on one sleeve.

"Brooke, the parade starts at eleven," Clay called to her as he passed by her room. "We need to leave now if you want to ride up with me."

"Coming, coming." She grabbed a ribbon from the top drawer of her dresser and sat on the edge of her bed to put on her walking shoes. On her way down the steps, she tied the ribbon around her ponytail and grabbed a jacket she'd left on the newel post in case it got cooler later in the afternoon.

"Here I am," she announced as she came into the kitchen.

"Let's go. Move it." Clay attempted to hustle her toward the door.

"Wait! I want to get my camera so I can take some pictures of the boys in their costumes," Brooke called to her brother.

"I have mine." Hannah came into the kitchen behind her. "Go."

"All right. Everyone's in such a damned hurry this morning," Brooke grumbled.

"Brooke, are you sure you want to wear that sweatshirt?" her mother asked. "Perhaps you should change—"

"We're only going to a parade." Brooke frowned.

"Besides, everyone's been hustling me along for the past ten minutes. We don't have time for me to change. Anyway, I haven't done laundry in a week and I don't think I have anything else to wear."

"She doesn't have time to change," Clay called from the back porch. "She looks fine."

"You know there's chocolate on the sleeve . . ." Hannah held the door and waited till Brooke went past her before closing it.

"What's the big deal?" Brooke climbed into the backseat of Clay's SUV and sat next to Logan, who was busy strapping himself in.

"As soon as we get to town, we can line up for the parade, right?" Logan asked. "I'm supposed to meet Cody right by Scoop."

"How convenient," Brooke muttered. "No ice cream until after the parade."

"What if we get boiling hot? What if we get so hot we start to sweat?"

"You can drink some water." Brooke helped straighten Logan's eye patch. "Steffie always has cold water."

"Maybe after the parade we can have ice cream?"

"You betcha," Brooke told him. "But only after. You would not want to dribble ice cream on that very cool pirate shirt."

Logan looked down at the bright red shirt. "No, I would not want to do that."

They had to circumvent the center of town because of the parade route and park on a side street several blocks away.

"Good thing you made your deliveries earlier," Hannah noted as they walked to Charles Street. "Those boxes of cupcakes would be getting mighty heavy right about now."

"It's almost eleven," Brooke replied. "I'll bet half of those cupcakes have been sold by now. Carlo says they never last past noon at Cuppachino."

"Then maybe you're not making enough," Clay told her.

"I think once school is over for me in December, I'll have more time to bake. And by then I should be able to assess how many I need to make in a week." *And by then, with luck, I should have that second oven,* she reminded herself.

The streets of St. Dennis were crowded with every manner of ghoul and ghost, vampire and werewolf, witch and warlock. And pirate. Logan was distressed to count seven pirates on their way to registering for the parade.

"I thought me and Cody would be the only pirates," he grumbled.

"Pirates are very popular this time of year." Jesse walked up behind Brooke. "It's been a favorite costume for years."

"Logan, do you remember Mr. Enright?"

"Uh-huh." Logan nodded. "Were you ever a pirate?"

"Actually, I was a pirate once. But I didn't have an eye patch like you have." Jesse smiled at Brooke. "Nice touch."

"You and Cody will be the only pirates with perfect swords," Clay noted.

Logan stopped dead in his tracks and his face went white.

"My sword! I don't have my sword!" he wailed.

"Where did you leave it?" Brooke asked.

"In the car!"

"I'll run back and get it. You stay right here. I won't have time to go looking for you." Clay turned and took off.

Cody ran up to meet Logan, who continued to wail about his missing sword.

"But Clay went to get it for you," Brooke reminded him. She waved at Dallas, who'd stopped to chat with one of the parents from the boys' class.

"What if he doesn't get back in time?" Logan continued.

"He'll be back," she assured him. "He's pretty darned fast."

Brooke turned to Jesse. "This is what passes for excitement in St. Dennis."

"Hey, I love a little drama before a good parade," he replied. "Check out those little ones dressed up like pumpkins in the wheelbarrow."

"Looks like a perfect pumpkin patch to me." Brooke smiled at the man who was pushing the wheelbarrow. "Are they all yours?" She pointed to the children who were all dressed exactly alike, in puffy orange costumes.

"Three are mine, the rest are neighbors'," the man replied as he headed toward the registration table.

"Mom, we have to do that, too." Logan tugged on her sleeve. "We have to sign up."

"We'll do that when Clay gets back. I think we need to wait right here. This is where he'll be looking for us."

"What if we're too late and they don't let us in the

parade?" He pointed to the three sports cars at the head of the parade, their drivers looking ready to roll.

"I keep trying to get Dallas's attention but she's deep in conversation," Brooke said. "She could sign the boys up while I wait for Clay. I don't think she realizes that the parade will be starting soon."

"How 'bout I take the boys over to the registration table while you wait here for Clay," Jesse suggested. "He'll be looking for you in the crowd, not me."

"Do you mind? They can sign themselves up. I just don't like them wandering around alone in a crowd this large."

"I don't mind at all." Jesse turned to the boys. "Let's go, guys. I bet by the time we get back, Clay will be here with Logan's sword and you'll be good to go."

"We practiced dueling last night and you know what . . ." Logan's voice trailed off as Jesse shepherded the two boys to the registration table.

Brooke folded her arms over her chest and scanned the crowd for her brother. The municipal parking lot was crowded as more and more parade entrants began to gather. The sun was warm on the back of Brooke's neck, and she slipped off the denim jacket. She frowned at the smear of chocolate she'd been in too much of a hurry to wash out completely. She twisted the sleeve slightly, hoping it would be less noticeable. She turned toward the registration area in time to see Jesse making his way through the crowd with the boys. He was, she noted wryly, much better dressed than she was. Khakis and a rust-colored cotton crewneck sweater, dark glasses . . . did noticing just how very good he looked make her shallow?

By the time she spotted Clay jogging through the crowd, Jesse and the two boys had just caught up to her.

"Perfect timing," she told him.

"Don't put it down someplace and leave it." Clay handed over the sword to Logan, then leaned over, his hands on his knees, to catch his breath. "Hi, Jesse."

"Hey, Clay." Jesse stood next to Brooke and watched the boys show off their sword-fighting skills. "Nice job, guys."

"Everyone's starting to line up." Logan pointed to the crowd that was starting to ease in the direction of the lead cars.

"Let's go!" Cody started off, dragging Logan with him.

"Cody, hold up." Brooke addressed both boys. "Wait for me."

"You don't have to go with them, Brooke." Clay straightened up. "I'm going to tag along."

"You're going to be in the parade, too?" Cody asked.

"No. I'm going to be on the sidelines and I'll bring you back to Scoop when it's over." Clay turned to Brooke. "I ran into Grant up on Charles Street. He and I will watch the boys over the course of the parade route. Why don't you just stroll on up to the judges' stand? That's going to be the only really good view because the crowd is so large this year. You'll probably see Dallas up there. Grant said Berry was reserving some seats. Besides, someone needs to show Jesse the ropes. I'll bet he hasn't been to one of our Halloween Parades."

Clay glanced at Jesse as if for confirmation.

Jesse nodded. "This is my first."

"See? He's going to need someone to interpret some of our St. Dennis traditions. So you don't need to play eagle eye with the boys. Go on, the kids and I will meet you after the parade."

"Okay, thanks, if you're sure . . ." she began, but Clay was already off with the kids.

"Think we'll be able to make it through this crowd to Charles Street in time to see the parade?" Jesse asked.

"We'll miss a good part of it." Brooke touched his arm. "I know a great shortcut. Follow me . . ."

They made their way around the back of the crowd to a worn dirt path that led up a slight hill.

"I used to walk home from school this way," she told him as they started up the incline.

"After a stop at Scoop?"

"Scoop wasn't even a twinkle in Stef's eye back then. Her building used to be a crabber's shack that was owned by someone in her family. Uncle, grandfather, I forget which. Stef always knew she wanted her own ice-cream shop one day, and when there was talk about tearing the shack down, she asked if she could have it." She stopped for a moment to search her bag for her sunglasses, slid them on, then resumed the climb. "She totally renovated it, mostly by herself."

"That sounds like one determined woman."

"I'll say. That was all she ever wanted, and she made it happen. I admire her for that."

"How's her story so different from yours?"

"What do you mean?" Brooke was grateful they were nearing the top of the path. She was getting out of breath and starting to sweat in the strong October sun.

"Steffie had a vision for owning her own business. So do you. I see you both working for what you want."

"I haven't succeeded yet," she reminded him.

"I don't know." He took her arm at the end of the path as if to help her up the bit of last slope. "I seem to see those cupcakes of yours everywhere I go in St. Dennis. And I have to say that the ones I sampled were pretty darned good."

"You bought them?"

"Of course I bought them. I had two at Vanessa's party last week and got hooked on them. I've had to add time to my workouts just so that I don't have to cut back on my consumption of cupcakes."

Jesse followed Brooke through a parking area behind the stores that faced Charles Street.

"Which reminds me. My grandfather is going to be eighty-five in two weeks, and I'm thinking it might be nice to have a little party for him. I think he'd rather have cupcakes than a cake. Would you be interested in doing the baking?"

"That's a really nice idea and I'd be happy to take on the job. How many people are you thinking about inviting?"

"Ahhh . . . I don't know."

"So what's his favorite flavor? Chocolate? Yellow cake? White?"

"Ahhh . . . I'm not sure."

"Well, we can always make several kinds. I can e-mail you with a list of the different flavors I make and you can pick a few you think he might like if you don't want to ask him outright."

"That sounds like a good idea. Thanks."

"But you'll have to let me know how many people you'll be serving." They reached Charles Street and turned to the left where the judging stand and bleachers had been erected on the side of the road. "You do have a guest list, right?"

"Not exactly." Jesse looked mildly uncomfortable. "I thought I'd ask my uncle Mike for some suggestions, but he's taken my aunt down to Baltimore for some tests and I didn't want to bother him."

"Maybe I can give you a hand with that," she told him as she took his hand and led him toward the bleachers. "Berry has been a client of your grandfather's forever and is a contemporary of his, so she might know. And there's always Violet."

"You had to bring her up." Jesse grimaced. "And the day was going so well, too . . ."

Brooke laughed. "It was just a suggestion. She probably knows better than anyone who your granddad's friends are."

"Probably." He was still grimacing.

"Besides, maybe she'll be nicer to you if she knows you're doing something nice for Curtis. They've known each other forever, remember. And she was a close friend of your grandmother's."

"She did mention that."

"Did she mention that my grandmother Hallie Simpson was one of her good buddies as well?"

"No, she left out that part." For a moment Jesse looked as if he wanted to say something else. Brooke waited, but when he didn't continue, she said, "They all grew up together and went all through school together. They started at that one-room schoolhouse out on White Oak Road."

"I didn't know there was a one-room schoolhouse here."

Brooke scanned the bleachers, looking for Dallas. Finding her in the crowd, she waved.

"Come up here and join us," Dallas called to her. "We can make room."

"Want to?" Brooke asked Jesse.

"Sure."

She led him up the bleacher seats until they reached Dallas, who was sitting with her great-aunt, Berry Eberle, and Berry's gentleman friend, Archer Callahan. Brooke and Jesse took the seats next to Archer, a retired judge, who after being introduced to Jesse, noted that Curtis Enright had tried many a case in his courtroom.

"A fine attorney," Archer said. "As is Mike Enright." The judge frowned for a moment. "I think there was another boy as well . . ."

"My father." Jesse's back had stiffened slightly at the admission and Brooke thought his jaw set just a little tighter.

"Ah, yes." Archer nodded as if he had recalled something about Jesse's father but wasn't quite sure exactly what it was.

"Oh, here comes the parade." Brooke elbowed Jesse. "Now the entertainment begins."

"So what's the protocol here?" Jesse asked.

"This is where the action is." Brooke gestured to the opposite side of the road, where spectators had set up folding lawn chairs. "Just about everyone in town comes to see the costumes. The marchers are lined up according to their age group. When your group is called, everyone gets a chance to pass the judges' stand, and if there's some sort of performance that goes along with your costume, that's when you do it. Like, see, that first group, the little ballerinas?"

The entire crowd ooh'd and aah'd as six little girls in pink tutus danced around in front of the judges.

"That has to rate pretty high on the cuteness scale," Jesse noted.

"They are adorable," she agreed.

Next came a threesome of clowns on two-wheelers, the training wheels of which were still attached.

"More cuteness," she noted.

"So are there winners?" Jesse asked.

Brooke nodded. "Winners, prizes, trophies, pictures in the local paper, and of course, these days, online at St. Dennis's Web site well."

"Who are the judges?"

"The mayor, the chief of police, the librarian, and a couple of the shop owners."

"But don't they know everyone?"

"They know everyone in the parade and there's more than one relative of each of them, I'd imagine."

"How can you be objective if you're judging your niece or a cousin?" Jesse frowned.

"Who said anything about objectivity?" Brooke shrugged. "But I think they somehow manage to choose the best costumes and the best performances in spite of themselves."

"So, okay, we have the parade and then they announce the winners. Then what?"

"They don't announce the winners now. That doesn't happen until later, at the ball."

"They have a ball? A Halloween ball? Seriously?"

"Seriously. They've been doing it for almost one hundred years."

"So do you have to be in costume?"

"Only if you think you're going to win."

"Anything else I should know?" he asked.

"There's a queen, and—"

"A queen?" His eyes danced with amusement. "A Halloween queen?"

"Yes, indeed."

"Were you ever the Halloween queen?"

"No." She shook her head. "That's one I missed."

Jesse stared blankly at her.

"When I was younger, I was in a few pageants," she explained, feeling the embarrassment she always felt when she looked back on the girl she'd once been. "It was all a long time ago."

Thinking about those days brought up a lot of old feelings that Brooke would just as soon forget. Back then, she hadn't been the person she was now, but there were a lot of people in St. Dennis with long memories who didn't know that. She'd been snubbed on more than one occasion since moving back home by women who, back in their younger days, had been the target of the mean girl that Brooke used to be. She could crawl into a hole and just die every time she looked back on her old self.

"So what if they announce who the queen is and she isn't there?"

"Oh, that's part of the fun. They send people to get you, to find you in the crowd. The queen doesn't know she's the queen until the committee comes for her, and it's strictly come-as-you-are. In other words, you don't get to go home to change. Which is why"— she lowered her voice—"there are so many women dressed just a little too well for a parade. They think this might be their year, so they dress up just enough to look good in the pictures, but not so much that they'd look foolish when the crown is handed to someone else."

"And if you aren't in the crowd?"

"They'll go to your house," she told him. "We take our traditions very seriously here in St. Dennis."

"Look." He gestured to the right. "The boys are starting their duel."

"How serious they are." She leaned forward and watched as the two boys parried and thrust their swords as they made their way across the street and past the judges' stand. Just as they reached the opposite side, they pretended to run each other through, then both dropped dramatically to the ground to resounding applause.

"It would appear that the duel ended in a draw." Berry beamed and clapped wildly.

"Oh my God." Brooke laughed. "Did you ever see anything so funny?"

The crowd was on their feet after the two boys stood up and grinned.

"What timing," Berry said proudly. "What showmanship."

"You can tell that Cody spent his formative years in Hollywood"—Dallas leaned halfway across Berry to tell Brooke—"but Logan is just a natural."

"That's going to be a hard act to follow," Jesse agreed.

"Here come the jugglers." Berry pointed to the street below. "I do believe they're Nita's grandsons."

"Nita owns the antique shop across the street from Cuppachino," Brooke told Jesse.

"Which sort of proves my point about everyone knowing everyone here," he leaned over to whisper in her ear.

She tilted her head slightly so that his lips were dangerously close to the side of her face. For a moment she met his eyes, and her heart thumped inside her chest.

Stop it, she commanded herself. *Just . . . stop it.*

Jesse was so easy to be with, such fun to be with, because all he wanted from her was her friendship. Hadn't he made that clear? He hadn't asked her out, hadn't called the house like some love-struck teenager the way some others had. And she did like him— a lot—but since she wasn't looking for a relationship, she appreciated the fact that he hadn't put her in an awkward position by trying to be something more. Which would ruin their friendship, she reasoned, and that would put an end to days like today, when she'd totally forgotten herself and simply enjoyed his company without feeling any pressure to be anything else. Besides, he wasn't attracted to her in the way other guys were, or he'd have pursued something other than friendship, right? So it was a good thing that they could just be friends, wasn't it?

Wasn't it?

An hour later, when the last of the parade participants had passed the judges' stand, Brooke stood and stretched.

"So will we see you at the ball tonight, Jesse?" she asked.

"Are you going?"

"Sure." She pointed to the crowd of costumed children. "There could be a prize in someone's future. No way I'm going to get out of attending."

"Where do they hold it?"

"In the old Grange Hall on Harbor Road. It usually starts around eight, it's over by ten. Not a real 'ball' in the traditional sense. Though I suppose it was at one time." She turned to Berry, who was slow to get up and grumbling about having stayed in one position for too long. "I'll bet Berry would know."

"What's that, dear?" Berry leaned on Archer's arm.

"Didn't there used to be a real ball on Halloween night? With fancy costumes and a band and champagne at midnight?"

"Oh, my, yes." She nodded enthusiastically. "Back before Halloween became such a big holiday for children."

"Back before members of our generation started dying or moving away," Archer added.

"True enough, dear. There aren't quite so many of us former queens left in town."

"You were a Halloween queen, Berry?" Dallas turned to her great-aunt in surprise. "You never said."

"You never asked." Berry sniffed and started down the bleachers to the street below.

"She was magnificent," Archer told them over his shoulder as he accompanied her.

"Of course I was," she said grandly.

"The woman never changes." Dallas shook her head, and followed the elderly couple. "And may she never . . ."

"She was quite the thing back in the . . . what, thirties, forties, fifties?" Jesse took Brooke's arm to steady her as they made their way through the crowd. "She was a real film star, right?"

Brooke nodded. "She was the most famous person ever to come out of St. Dennis. Well, until Dallas, but Dallas wasn't born here. She and Wade started coming to stay for the summers after their father died. He'd been Berry's only nephew, and they were very close."

Jesse appeared to be about to speak, but they were distracted by the small group of three who started to climb the bleachers toward them. Brooke's first thought was that it was strange that anyone would be coming up the bleachers when everyone else was going down. Until she saw Grace Sinclair's beaming face—and the sparkling shiny thing Grace held in her hand.

Oh, no, no, no. Please no. Not me. Not me. Anyone but me . . .

Chapter 9

OVERHEAD, gulls were circling and squawking, and a breeze had kicked up off the Bay. Jesse had just taken Brooke's arm so that she wouldn't stumble on the somewhat unstable bleachers, and he was thinking that so far today, he must have scored some serious points, when she stiffened and her entire demeanor changed. Her face had lost its color and her eyes had widened as if in terror. And frankly, the grip she had on his arm sure did feel like real fear to him. She'd stood motionless and mute as Grace Sinclair and two people Jesse recognized but didn't know approached her with a sparkly crown.

"Brooke Madison Bowers, we're happy to say that you've been unanimously selected as queen of this year's Halloween festivities," Grace had said. She leaned forward and added softly, "We're all so proud of you. Your acts of kindness have not gone unnoticed."

"Congratulations, Brooke," the two men had said with much enthusiasm.

Brooke had appeared to be in a daze. When she finally snapped out of it, she'd said something like, "I don't think . . . that is, maybe someone else . . ."

"No, no, dear. We all agreed that you were the perfect choice." Grace had stepped behind her and placed the crown on her head. "Hold still now. We're going to have to secure this with some pins."

Grace had pulled some bobby pins from her pocket and proceeded to affix the crown to the unsmiling Brooke's head. The look she'd shot Jesse had been sheer misery.

"Now come along so we can make our announcement." Grace had started toward the street, leaving Jesse to descend with Brooke.

"What's wrong?" Jesse had whispered. "What's the problem?"

"I don't want to do this."

"Are you nervous because there's a large crowd?"

"I just don't want to be queen, Jesse."

"You said you'd been in pageants before, right?" She'd nodded.

"Did you win any?"

"Yes."

"So what's the difference? Pretend this is just another pageant win."

"You don't understand." There'd been panic in her eyes when she looked up at him. "I'm not that person anymore."

"Which person is—was—that?" he'd asked, somewhat confused.

"The person who enters pageants to win, the one who wants to stand out all the time." She'd looked close to tears. "People are going to hate me all over again."

"What are you talking about? No one hates you."
He'd almost laughed at the absurdity of the thought.
How could anyone hate Brooke?

"Look, you didn't know me before. When I was
younger, I . . . I wasn't always a very nice person. Actually, most of the time I wasn't very nice at all. I was
the girl who always got everyone to gang up on people she didn't like. I was Miss Perfect. I was more
concerned about how I looked than how I acted."
Her sigh had been full of regret. "I put the *mean* in
mean girl."

"Well, like you just said. You're not that person
anymore."

"I haven't been back here long enough for most
people to figure that out. There are a lot of women
here"—she'd indicated the crowd—"who I picked on
when we were kids."

"I think you're doing yourself a disservice. I think
people like you just fine," he'd said softly.

"Everyone is going to see this as just one more time
when Brooke won." She tapped her foot nervously on
the seat she was standing on.

When he started to protest again, she said, "Look,
you didn't grow up here, so you wouldn't know, but
I was Miss Everything. Miss Eastern Shore. Miss Regatta. Holly Ball Queen. May Queen. I was Memorial
Day Poppy Princess an unprecedented *three* times."
She looked up at Jesse and explained, "My dad and
granddad were both vets."

"Do you really think that's what everyone here is
going to be remembering?"

"I think they're going to be remembering that under

my picture in the yearbook, they wrote 'Princess' as my middle name."

"What is your middle name?"

"Diana."

"Nice."

She smiled weakly at his attempt to lighten the mood.

"Look, maybe this is a good opportunity for you to show people who you've grown up to be," he said.

"Since Logan and I moved back to St. Dennis, I did everything I could think of to live it all down. I joined the PTA and volunteered for every job no one else wanted to do. Last year, I was homeroom mother and chaperoned every single class outing. I teach English as a second language at the library two nights a week and I go to the senior home every Sunday afternoon to read to the residents. And still this." She pointed to the crown.

"Maybe it's because of all those things that they wanted you to have it"—Jesse pointed to the crown just as she had—"this year."

Brooke had gone quiet then.

"Didn't Grace say something about your acts of kindness not going unnoticed?" Jesse straightened the crown on her head. "Maybe it's not because of who you were, but who you are. Hasn't that occurred to you?"

She shook her head.

"You think people think you're Miss Perfect? That you're only interested in appearances?" He'd tugged at the sleeve of her sweatshirt. "Would Miss Perfect appear in public with . . . what is that on your shirt, anyway?"

"Chocolate frosting."

"There you go. Not so perfect after all." He'd stepped down to the seats below and held out his hand. "Put your head up and smile and act like you're as happy about this as Grace seems to be."

She'd nodded then, taken his hand, and made her way down the bleachers with him. He stood aside as the hoopla began, and before he realized what had happened, Brooke had been whisked away in a convertible as the parade was led back through town the way it came. She'd looked back frantically as she was escorted from the judges' stand and he'd been pretty certain she'd been looking for him, but there was no way she'd have found him. He stepped back and let her have her moment, then fell in with the crowd and followed the parade to the marina, and to Scoop. But there, too, there'd been a crowd, and he'd been unable to get close to her.

He left the festivities and walked to his office, where he reread some files, wrote a few letters, and made some notes for an upcoming settlement conference. He finished one last letter, then walked back to his rented house, where he ate leftover spaghetti for dinner, then watched the tail end of a college football game while he waited for seven o'clock.

The conversation with Brooke had baffled him. He couldn't imagine anyone not liking Brooke. Okay, so maybe she hadn't been as nice back when as she was now. Do people really hold grudges for that long? Well, except for the Enrights, that is.

Yeah, he supposed a lot of people did, but he honestly hadn't seen any evidence of that as they'd walked through the crowd earlier in the day. People had smiled at Brooke and greeted her like, well, like an old friend. He wondered if she noticed that no one had made a hex sign when she approached.

It was sort of endearing that she'd been so contrite about her school-age self, and it was clear to him if not to her that she'd tried really hard to redeem herself in the eyes of her hometown. It was hard to believe that she'd ever been as bad as she said she was, though. From the first time he'd met her, one thing that had attracted Jesse to Brooke was her sweet nature.

That and her mane of curly pale reddish blond hair that had a sassy swing to it when pulled back in a ponytail, the way it tumbled around her face when it wasn't. Heart-shaped face, pale green eyes, a mouth that was quick to smile and widen in a laugh.

And then, there was her body. Brooke was petite, but perfectly proportioned.

Best not to go there, he thought, while they were still on the friendship track.

He wondered how long he was going to have to pretend to be her best buddy before she started to think of him as something more than a friend. And what if she never did? What if she thought this BFF thing was just swell? What if Clay had been wrong when he'd suggested that the only way to make Jesse stand out in the pack was to treat her differently than everyone else had?

If she never saw him in any other way, he'd have to accept that. He wasn't a fatal attraction kind of guy. Something was better than nothing, and at least they'd still be friends—real friends—which was more than those other guys could say. Besides, he was finding that the more time he spent with her, the more he genuinely liked her. He couldn't remember the last time he'd dated someone that he hadn't gotten to know *while* they were dating, instead of *before*.

Practicing law had taught Jesse patience, and he'd long since learned that some things couldn't be rushed. But he had to admit that he was getting a little antsy waiting for Brooke to realize that he had so much more to offer than friendship.

Then again, considering the alternative, he figured he could practice patience for a little longer. What did he have to lose?

The Grange Hall in St. Dennis had been built in 1878 by the farmers who grew corn and wheat and barley in the fields that lay east of the town limits. What had been started as a social organization had grown political when Midwestern farmers organized to protest the high transport prices set by the railroads. Years later, the conflict resolved, the Grangers, as the members were called, went back to being a social organization.

The hall was constructed of clapboard, had one large main room inside the big double front doors, and was painted white inside and out. There was a stage area that spanned the width of the building, and a few smaller storage rooms behind the stage. In keeping with their autumnal theme, the committee had decorated the room with bales of hay, shocks of corn, and stacks of pumpkins. Jesse's first thought when he walked in was that he'd somehow landed back at his eighth-grade dance. Even the music was from the late 1980s. He looked around for a table where ladies dressed as witches served punch and cookies—and yep, there it was across the room. How did he know?

He wandered over and took a paper cup of punch, more for something to do than anything else, and stood to one side as other residents—some in costume—arrived. He greeted those he knew and smiled at those he didn't, though it occurred to him that he seemed to know almost everyone. He waved at Clay when he came in with the boys, and figured Brooke couldn't be too far behind.

"Hey, Mr. Enright." Logan waved his sword back and forth. A loose strip of foil fluttered from the handle. "Do you think me and Cody will win a prize? We think we'll win a prize."

"I think there's a very good chance that you could." Jesse nodded. "You were far and away the best pirates I saw all day."

"I told you." Cody gave Logan a whack on the arm with his sword, the blade of which had apparently given a few too many such whacks, as evidenced by the fact that hardly any foil remained to cover the cardboard. Neither boy appeared to notice.

"Cody, your mom and Grant just came in," Clay told him. "Why don't you go over and let them know that we're here?"

The two boys took off across the room, dodging a few senior citizens who looked askance at their antics.

"Oh, to be eight again, and to be at the Halloween ball," Clay said.

"Were the refreshments any better when you were a kid?" Jesse asked.

Clay shook his head. "Same punch recipe since the place was founded. I think there's a clause in the contract that says it has to be served at every event held here. And the cookies all have to be burned on the bottom. Another tradition," he explained.

"Looks like tradition's safe for another year."

"So Brooke tells me you're writing a letter to Jason Bowers about that business Eric bankrolled."

"Already sent it."

"Jace reply yet?"

"Too soon," Jesse told him. "It was only mailed on Thursday. You know him?"

Clay nodded. "Sure. He was Eric's brother."

"What's he like?"

"Good guy. I'm surprised he hasn't kept Brooke in the loop a little better, but I don't think he'd cheat her or Logan out of anything."

"That's pretty much what she said. She told me he had broached the subject after her husband died and she brushed him off because it was something else she couldn't deal with."

"It was a bad time for everyone," Clay said simply.

"Anyway, I kept the letter pretty light, more of a gentle inquiry."

"That's good. Glad you're helping her. She needs to get all that straightened out for Logan's sake."

The two boys came racing back, swords in one hand, paper cups of punch in the other.

"Slow down," Clay told them. "And watch so that the punch doesn't spill."

The boys immediately stopped running and took very small, slow steps.

"Do you have kids of your own?" Jesse asked.

Clay shook his head. "Logan's the only kid I've ever been around all that much. I'm going to miss him like crazy when he and Brooke move."

"They're moving?" Jesse felt stunned. "Brooke is moving? Away from St. Dennis?"

"Relax," Clay told him. "They're moving into a small house on the farm." He studied Jesse's face for a moment, then said, "Don't let her see that."

"See what?"

"What I just saw in your face when you thought she might be leaving town."

"It's that obvious?"

Clay nodded. "Keep it under wraps, my friend."

"Hello, boys." Grace buzzed into the room and paused on her way to the stage, where, Jesse assumed, she might be looking for photos for her newspaper.

"Miss Grace, I heard a rumor that Lucy might be coming back in a few days," Clay said.

"Yes, indeed, she is. She'll be consulting with Dallas and Steffie about their big wedding plans. With any luck, they'll convince her to come back to handle the entire day. Should keep her home for a while, anyway." Grace smiled. "One can hope."

"Did she say how long she'd be staying?" To Jesse's eye, Clay appeared to be acting a little too nonchalant. "Would you tell her I said hi? And ask her to give me a call if she gets a few minutes?"

"I certainly will, dear. Now, I must hustle if I'm to get the photos I want. They've brought the queen in through the back door and they're going to introduce her soon."

"Who's Lucy?" Jesse asked after Grace had scurried away.

"Grace's daughter. We went all through school together, from kindergarten right through senior year of high school. We used to be best friends."

"What happened?" Jesse thought back on Clay's previous advice about Brooke. "Let me guess. You asked her out and the minute she thought you were interested she shut you out."

Clay seemed oblivious to the reference. He shook his head and said, "Nah. I guess we just grew apart."

"Maybe you'll see her next week."

"That would be awkward. We haven't seen each other since the week after we graduated from high school. She went on some summer study thing to London, came back, and left for college in Colorado. Went into business in L.A. I heard she was home from time to time but never for more than a few days."

"So maybe she'll call when she's here," Jesse told him.

"To tell you the truth—"

The mayor walked across the stage, tested the microphone, and called for everyone's attention. The crowd that had hugged the sides of the room all drifted forward and to the middle as introductions were made. The various committees were thanked, the merchants who had donated prizes and who had closed their shops for the morning to permit the festivities to close off the main street for three blocks were thanked, and it seemed to Jesse at one point that everyone had been thanked except Clay and him. And then Clay was thanked for donating the apples for the apple bobbing.

It was hard not to smile, Jesse was thinking, when you realized that some of those small-town clichés had become clichés for a reason.

Next, it was announced that Brooke had been crowned this year's queen, and still wearing her jeans and sweatshirt—the chocolate stain seemed to have disappeared—Brooke joined the mayor on the stage to applause. A litany of all her volunteer work was read off, followed by a moment of silence to honor the service of her husband and all of the men and women from the Eastern Shore who had served their country.

"And now, for her first official duty, our Halloween queen will present the prizes for the best costumes and the best performances from this morning's parade." Mayor Christina Pratt handed the microphone to Brooke, who took it with one hand while balancing a handful of large index cards in the other. There was much laughter and applause as one after another winner was brought to the stage and presented with a small trophy, even when the queen's son and his friend were announced. The two boys ran onto the stage, said polite thank-yous, then grabbed their trophies gleefully and ran back off.

"Uncle Clay! Look! We won!" Logan headed for Clay and Cody took off for his mother.

"I am not surprised. You two did a great job. Now go find your grandmother and show her your very cool trophy. She's over there by the punch table with Mrs. Engle."

Cody dashed off, his trophy held high.

"Hey, Clay." A pretty dark-haired woman strolled by and slowed down to smile at Clay.

"Hi, Mary Ellen," Clay replied.

"What's this I'm hearing about you starting up a brewery? Are you finished with farming?" she asked.

"No, I'm doing both . . ."

Jesse drifted closer to the stage, his hands in his pants pockets. In spite of her initial reluctance, it appeared that Brooke had taken to her role and was performing her obligations with a smile.

"And now, for her second official duty, our queen will lead off the first dance." Mayor Pratt turned to Brooke. "Who's your partner, honey? You want to dance with your brother?"

"No, I think I want to dance with . . ." Brooke looked over the crowd, until her eyes met Jesse's. "I think I want to dance with my lawyer tonight. Jesse Enright."

"Jesse Enright it is . . . assuming he's here."

"Oh, he's here." Brooke smiled and came down off the stage, and Jesse met her halfway.

She slipped into his arms as the recorded music began to play a slowed-down version of "I Put a Spell on You."

"I guess this is what passes for Halloween music in St. Dennis," he said as he pulled her close.

"It was this or 'Monster Mash.'" She shrugged. "Which you'll hear later if you hang around long enough. I saw the playlist."

Jesse chuckled. "That's a tough tune to slow-dance to."

"Which is why I asked for this one." She sighed and leaned into him, her cheek resting comfortably against the side of his jaw.

"You know, I never danced with a queen before."

"First time for everything."

"So, what should I call you now?"

"Hmm. Good question." Her head tilted back and she looked into his eyes. "I am now royalty, and you . . . well, you are not. So I'm thinking you should probably address me as . . . Brooke."

Holding her had felt so right to him that he hadn't realized the song had ended and was followed immediately by "Thriller." She broke their hold and stepped away, but kept her hand on his arm.

"Sorry," she said. "I cannot do that 'Thriller' dance."

"So how are you feeling about all this now?" he asked to keep her close.

"I feel a lot better. Jesse, I can't thank you enough for the pep talk you gave me. What you said stayed with me all afternoon. I looked for you at Scoop but there were so many people there."

"I did follow the rest of the crowd down there but it was impossible to get near the place."

"So what did you do?"

"I went home, watched the Alabama-Florida game and ate leftover spaghetti."

"Warm or cold?"

"Cold," he admitted.

"Then I owe you dinner." She edged a little bit closer. "As a thank-you."

Jesse's heart began to race. Was she flirting with him?

"Hey, Brooke." Clay appeared with Logan who held up his trophy for Jesse to admire. "I'm taking the kid home. He's getting a little crazy now."

Brooke looked up at the clock over the front door.

"I guess he is. It's almost nine, past his bedtime." She looked hesitant. "I think it's too soon for me to go, though. I think I need to stay until ten."

"You're right. You're still queen for another hour. But he"—Clay pointed to Logan, who was trying to balance his trophy on the top of his head—"isn't going to last."

"I can probably get a ride home with Mom," she said.

Clay shook his head. "She's going to Captain Walt's for drinks with her girlfriends."

Brooke grabbed the trophy as it was about to topple.

"I'll drive you home," Jesse offered casually, as if he hadn't been waiting all day to be alone with her.

"Are you sure you don't mind?" Brooke asked.

"Not at all," he assured her.

"Well, then, come here, Logan, and give me a hug." Brooke stepped around Jesse and opened her arms to her son. While she was giving him instructions—"Don't give Uncle Clay a hard time. Brush your teeth super-long tonight because you ate a lot of sugary things today"—Clay leaned over and said from the corner of his mouth, "Be strong, buddy. From where I'm standing, it looks like you've got her on the ropes. I think she's interested. But don't give in yet. Let her make the first move. Stick to the plan, like I told you."

"Clay, she's your sister. I don't think we should be discussing—"

"Trust me. You gotta turn the tables on her."

". . . and you can have popcorn if your uncle feels like making it." Brooke kissed Logan on the top of his head and stood up. "It's up to him."

"Can we make popcorn when we get home?" Logan jumped up and down.

"Maybe." Clay put his hand on his nephew's shoulder and steered him toward the door. "See you later. And thanks, Jesse, for offering to bring Brooke home."

Jesse nodded and watched Clay make his way to the door.

The next hour passed in a blur. Brooke's hand remained resting on his arm as they made their way around the room. Brooke introduced Jesse to some of her old classmates, most of whom seemed to bear no animosity to her. Well, there were a few women whose smiles hadn't seemed totally genuine, and whose "We really need to get together's" didn't sound all that sincere. But for the most part, Jesse thought that Brooke's earlier fears had been unwarranted, and she said as much on the way home.

"You were right, you know? About everything." Brooke had curled up in the passenger seat and turned so that she was facing him. "For the most part, everyone was really, really nice." She made a face. "Except for Angela Lampisi and Courtney Mason. Apparently neither of them has gotten over high school. And I say, if Dallas MacGregor can get over it, they should be able to, too."

"Were you mean to Dallas when you were kids?"

"Every chance I got. We were both in love with Grant. He was in love with her, but she left at the end of the summer and the rest of us threw ourselves on him all through the school year. Then summer would come and Dallas would come back, and Grant—and half of the guys in St. Dennis—would be deaf and blind to the rest of us girls."

"You seem to be good friends now," he observed.

"The best. We've made our peace," she told him. "But Dallas grew up and some of the others don't seem to have."

"But all in all, it was a good day and night for you."

"All in all, it was terrific."

"I'm glad."

He put on his right turn signal and pulled into the lane leading up to the Madison farmhouse.

"Clay mentioned that you were moving," he said to keep the conversation going.

"Just to the tenant house back there by the orchard, and not until we get some work done. I think it'll be perfect. The views are beautiful from every window. The orchard, the woods, the fields, the pond . . ."

"There's a pond back there?" He parked near the side of the house.

Brooke nodded. "You can't see it from the road and it's not real big, but it's there. I'll take you back and show you sometime."

He nodded. "Sure. I'd like that."

There was a moment of silence, which he had to fill. He didn't want to think about what he wanted to be doing with her in the front seat of his little sports car.

"I noticed you gave the crown back to Grace before you left."

"That's the tradition. You return it and it goes back into some locked box until the following year." Brooke laughed softly. "You'd think it was part of the crown jewels or something. It's not worth anything except to the people in St. Dennis. The same one has been used forever."

"Where'd it come from?"

"Someone in Dan Sinclair's family." She shrugged, then added, "Dan was Grace's husband. He died years ago and she's kept the inn going. Well, her son has. She's devoted more of her time to the newspaper. Her grandfather started the *Gazette* a long time ago."

"It seems like everyone in St. Dennis has connections that go back 'a long time ago,'" he observed.

"True enough. Much like yourself," she reminded him. "Your family's been a part of the town forever, too."

When he didn't respond, she said, "You know that, right? That you're part of all this, too?"

"I don't feel as if I am," he admitted. "I feel like an observer more than a participant."

"That's because you haven't been here all that long. I give you another year." She touched his arm. "You'll be as much at home here as anyone."

"Maybe," he said, not wanting to tell her that the jury might still be out, as far as his grandfather was concerned. The year he'd been given was almost up, and he was hoping to make it through to the end of that year without anything going wrong.

"Jesse?" Brooke waved her hand in front of his face.

"Sorry. I was just thinking about something at the office."

"Oh." She grinned. "That's flattering."

"I didn't mean . . ." Jesse shook his head. What a dolt. "You know how sometimes something just pops into your head for a moment."

"Something important?"

"Not really." He could feel her eyes on him, and he knew the moment of truth was almost upon him. *Be strong, buddy,* Clay had said.

But Clay had no idea of just how strong the attraction was, or how badly Jesse wanted to take her in his arms and kiss her. And how did he know whether or not Clay knew what he was talking about? *Trust me. I know my sister.*

Jesse sighed and opened his car door. "I guess I'd better let you go. I'm sure you're tired, what with all the baking you've been doing and the parade and everything . . ."

He got out of the car as she opened her door and got out as well.

" . . . and Logan mentioned when we were signing up for the parade that he'd had a birthday party yesterday."

"He did. Thank God, I'd had the presence of mind to book Scoop for the party. No way I'd have survived all that madness in the house." She looped her hand through his arm as they went up the front steps. When they got to the porch, she looked up at him and said, "Did you want to come in for a few minutes?"

Yes, damn it! Yes! his inner self shouted.

Cool Jesse merely smiled. "Thanks, but it's been a long day for me, too. Maybe another time."

"All right." She sighed quietly.

Had that sigh been one of disappointment?

"Well, thanks again for bringing me home," she continued. "But thanks most of all for everything you did for me today. I don't know that I would have made it through if you hadn't given me that little kick in the butt."

Her hand had taken his and she'd moved a little closer.

Here is the big test, he told himself. *This is the moment that could make or break you. Are you man enough to buck the trend, or are you going to cave?*

Could he really succeed where so many others had failed?

"Hey, that's what friends are for, right?" He gave her hand a little squeeze, and hesitated. Would one little kiss throw off his game completely, ruin his chances forever?

Before he could decide, she'd turned just slightly, enough so that her upturned face was positioned just perfectly, and he couldn't resist. He lowered his mouth and brushed his lips over hers. For a moment he was tempted to dive in, to sacrifice the long-term possibilities for this moment. Her lips were soft and warm, and tasted of the fruity punch they'd had at the Grange Hall. He wanted nothing more than to plunder that mouth and taste all of her.

His hands on her shoulders, he slowly eased himself from her, put distance between them that he really didn't want.

The lawyer in him kicked in, even while his head was still buzzing. His lips still felt the pressure of the kiss, and he backed toward the steps.

"'Night, Jess," she said.

"'Night, Brooke." Then, "Oh," he said as if just remembering. "I wrote to your brother-in-law. You'll probably be hearing from him."

She walked to the porch railing. "I got the copy of the letter yesterday. Thank you."

"Oh. Right. Okay, well, I guess I'll see you this week to finish that will we started last week." He backed toward the car, tossing his keys from one hand to the other.

"I'll call Liz on Monday."

"Good idea. Well, good night." He walked backward around the car, unable to take his eyes off her. The light of the moon surrounded her like a soft white halo, and for a moment she looked too ethereal to be real, and he was mesmerized. He somehow managed to get the car door open and slid behind the wheel before exhaling a very long breath.

"Shoot me now," he muttered as he turned on the ignition, made a quick K-turn, and waved out the window. He felt her eyes on him as he drove past.

"I cannot believe I just did that," he groaned, and for the next few blocks, he tried not to think about what could have been . . . what? A few hot kisses in the moonlight on the Madisons' front porch? Would that have counted toward the *one and done* that Clay had warned about?

Or would it have opened the door for something more?

If Clay was right and Brooke was interested—and Jesse had to admit that he'd sensed back there that she was—then right now Brooke was back there wondering why he didn't kiss her.

If Clay is right—he may be the best friend I ever had.
But if he was wrong . . . I just might have to kill him.

Chapter 10

Brooke stood on the porch and watched Jesse's taillights fade down the lane, and tried to figure out what had just happened. One minute Jesse'd been kissing her, and the next, gone. Just like that. As if he wasn't really all that interested in kissing her. Thanks, Brooke, but no thanks.

Could it be that she'd misread him?

Unlikely. She'd felt that spark, and she knew damned well he'd felt it, too. There was moonlight, there'd been a day when she'd shared things about herself and he'd been supportive and had said all the right things. There'd been the way they moved together on the dance floor, and the light in his eyes when he looked at her. She went back over all the things he'd said and the things he'd done, the way he looked.

The way he looked at *her*.

No. She hadn't been wrong about that. This certainly wasn't the way she'd thought the night would end, nor was it the way she'd wanted it to.

And wasn't that, right there, the main reason she felt so damned confused? She'd wanted something from

Jesse that she hadn't been used to wanting lately, and he'd walked away.

Perhaps Jesse was just a little bit confused himself. Hadn't he said "That's what friends are for" right before he kissed her? So who was he trying hardest to convince that they were just friends?

The night was turning cooler and she turned the collar up on her jacket, but she wasn't ready to go inside just yet. When her mind started to clear, she realized there was more than one issue here. One was why didn't Jesse want to kiss her when she knew he was attracted to her. The other was why she'd wanted to kiss him in the first place.

Brooke had always known when a guy was attracted to her. She'd had plenty of practice. Guys had been falling over her since she was in junior high. It wasn't that she'd expected it to be that way—she'd just always known that it was. Things hadn't changed since she'd returned to St. Dennis. There was still any number of men who were ready, willing, and able to jump through any hoops she might ask them to, if only she'd give them a chance. Though she'd denied it to Clay, she really hadn't been interested in giving anyone the chance.

There were a lot of reasons why. Some she knew were valid, and some she admitted were a little weak. But it all came down to the fact that she'd loved her husband with all her heart and had believed they'd be together for a very long time. That whole till-death-do-us-part thing had been only words at the time they'd exchanged their vows. Neither she nor Eric really believed that either of them would die young . . . not even given the fact that Eric was a soldier who'd gone back into combat again and again, that he'd had friends and comrades who didn't make it home. Does anyone ever really think it would happen to them? Doesn't everyone secretly believe that the worst can only happen to someone else?

What woman planned on being a widow before she turned thirty-five?

And yet Eric had died, and she had become a widow, and replacing him with another man had seemed obscene to her. Clay had been right when he'd said that she never went out with a guy more than one time. One date was enough to know whether or not the man she was with understood that she wasn't coming off a breakup or a love affair that had turned bad, but that she'd *buried* the man she loved. Even some of the nicest guys she knew expected her to be "over it."

Jesse was the first man who hadn't made her feel like she was foolish for not being over it. Like when she was in his office last week and said that she knew she should have listened to Jason when he wanted to talk about the business after Eric died but she'd felt like she wasn't ready for that conversation. Jesse had understood that she'd been distraught and hadn't made her feel like an idiot for not following up with Jace sooner. He'd seemed to understand how she felt about a lot of things besides Eric—her need to start her own business, her insecurities, the way she felt about the person she used to be.

No, she definitely hadn't misread him. It seemed more likely that he was misreading her. She'd obviously sent him the message that *she* wasn't interested. And since she was just realizing herself how she felt, she couldn't blame him for not recognizing the signs. There hadn't been any.

It was a curious place to find herself, she had to admit. Respect for Eric's memory was only part of the reason she had no interest in finding someone else. When he died, the pain had been intense and unending and unlike anything she'd ever experienced. There was no way she was going to set herself up ever again to feel that kind of pain, that soul-shattering loss. Over the past few years, she'd learned to shield herself from any relationships that might eventually bring her to grief, and she could count the number of people she truly loved on one hand. For a long time, she'd believed there wasn't room in her heart for anyone else. Now she was wondering why she was spending so much time out here in the cold second-guessing herself about why Jesse had pulled away from her— and why it mattered so much.

It took a few more moments before she could admit, even to herself, that it mattered because she really liked him. There was something about Jesse that drew her to him. She'd poured her heart out to him earlier that day and he'd listened, heard every word without judging or patronizing her. He'd understood and he'd helped her to believe that the person she used to be didn't matter anymore. He'd put his arms around her and drawn her in and held her close when they danced and she'd felt as if she belonged there. He'd kissed her one time and she'd wanted him to kiss her again—and friendship was the least of what she wanted from him.

There, she'd said it, if only to herself.

A star fell suddenly, a brief shining trail of light

streaking across the late October sky. When she and Clay were kids, they used to sit outside and watch for shooting stars. The rule had been that you had to call the star and make your wish before the star disappeared or your wish wouldn't come true.

"Well, too late for that one," she murmured as she watched the star's light fade away. Too confused to even know what she would have wished for, Brooke went inside, turned off the porch light, and slowly climbed the stairs to bed.

Halloween fell on the Monday night after the Halloween ball, and since her mother and Clay were at the farmhouse handing out treats to the few trick-or-treaters who ventured so far out of town, Brooke took Logan into St. Dennis for an hour of knocking on doors and collecting treats. In the past, when they'd lived in Kentucky and South Carolina, she'd only permitted him to ring doorbells of those people they knew, which greatly limited Logan's haul. But in St. Dennis, where she knew just about everyone, choices had to be made or they'd be out all night. They'd mapped out their route over a quick dinner of pizza and headed out for some Halloween fun.

The first stop was at Dallas's aunt's home, the stately Victorian mansion on River Road. Logan had been disappointed to find that Cody had left a half hour before Logan arrived, which to him meant only that Cody had thirty minutes head start on him. The two dogs—Cody's Fleur and Berry's Ally—danced around the visitors in the foyer.

"You boys make such dashing pirates," Berry had

said, one hand over her heart. "I can't remember when I feared walking the plank more."

"Miz Berry, we would never make you walk the plank," Logan had said with all sincerity, causing Berry to plant a kiss on the top of his head and earning him extra candy.

"Thanks, Miz Berry." Logan watched her drop a few more candy bars into his trick-or-treat bag, hugged each of the dogs, then took off across the porch and down the steps.

"Thanks, Berry." Brooke hastened to catch up with her son as a crowd of seven or eight children made their way to the front door.

"Now, who do we have here . . ." Berry's voice drifted across the drive.

Logan waited for his mother at the entrance to Berry's driveway. "Where do we go next?"

"We're going to get in the car and drive up to the center of town and park there. We know a lot of people who live in the neighborhood behind the shops. But remember, just one hour, and then we have to go home. You have school in the morning."

"I know, but this is special, right? I heard you tell Gramma that."

"Being 'special' doesn't mean we throw out all the rules. You know that this is usually the time we set aside for homework. The only reason you're getting out tonight is because you have no homework." Using the remote, Brooke unlocked the car as they approached.

"Uh-uh, we do." Logan opened the back door and climbed in. "We're supposed to write a story about the best part of trick or treat and it can't be about candy."

"You have to do that tonight?" Brooke frowned as she started the car and, careful to watch for other trick-or-treaters, proceeded toward the stop sign at the end of River Road.

"No, tomorrow morning in school. We're just supposed to *think* about it tonight."

"So what's the best part of trick-or-treating if it isn't the treats?"

"I haven't decided yet. We only went to one house so far."

Brooke watched in the rearview mirror as Logan folded his arms across his chest the same way both she and Clay did when they were thinking about something, and the gesture made her smile.

"Mom, aren't Fleur and Ally the best dogs ever?" he asked.

"They are both pretty terrific dogs," she agreed, no doubt in her mind where this would lead.

"Mom, did you ask Uncle Clay if I could have a dog?"

"No, I didn't."

"How come?"

"I haven't gotten around to it." Actually, Brooke had thought about it, and had decided that they'd take a look at the dogs in Grant Wyler's shelter after they moved into the tenant house. She hadn't wanted to tell Logan until they got the report back from the contractor, in case there was something terribly wrong that would prevent them from moving in. She didn't expect that to be the case, but better to wait on good news rather than have to take it back.

"Could you get around to it sometime?"

"Sometime I will."

"Sometime soon?"

"We'll see."

"I wish you'd just say yes."

At the corner of Charles and Cherry streets, Brooke made a left and parked the car halfway up the block. The sidewalks here were jammed with kids in costumes accompanied by parents—mostly fathers—who called for their offspring to "slow down and wait up." Brooke recalled her mother shouting the same orders when she and Clay were of the age. Some things never change, she mused as she and Logan got out of the car. He saw a friend from school and took off, but not before she called out to him to wait right where he was. She let him blend in with a small group to ring doorbells while she and the other parents remained on the sidewalk making small talk.

Every once in a while, Brooke would get a flashback from her own trick-or-treat days when she and Clay had run up the same sidewalks and rung the same doorbells of the houses Logan and his friends were approaching. Different families lived in them back then, she reminded herself. The house the children now converged on had once been owned by the Clintons. Their daughter, Patti, had been two years ahead of Brooke in school. She'd died in an auto accident her junior year of high school, and the family had moved away shortly after. Brooke wondered if anyone knew where they'd gone. She'd never heard.

She wondered, too, if any of her companions who'd grown up here were thinking about Patti as their chil-

dren ran back down the sidewalk toward the next
house.

Eventually they made their way to the end of the
block, where the children waited to be crossed. Logan
and his group of friends crossed the street with someone's dad serving as crossing guard and started up the
other side. When they reached Vanessa's and she appeared in the doorway to give out her treats, there
was a whoop from the pack of kids, and Logan ran
back to his mother waving a card.

"Hey, Mom, look what Vanessa gave us!"

"What have you got?" Brooke asked.

"A card that says I can take it to Scoop for an ice-
cream cone anytime I want!" Logan handed the card
to his mother. "You hold it so it doesn't get lost,
okay?"

"I'll put it right in here and you can have it when
we get home." She tucked it into her shoulder bag
and followed the group, which was starting to thin
out, to the corner. The cross street was Hudson, and
three houses down on the left was Jesse's house. She
stood on the corner, her hand on Logan's shoulder,
and wondered if Jesse was doing the trick-or-treat
thing. A lot of single guys she knew didn't bother.

Logan and his friends went up the walk to the first
house on Hudson. By the time they reached the second, Brooke saw that a large group of older kids was
parading up the walk at number 429, just one house
away. The front door opened and Jesse stepped out
onto the porch. He must have been handing out
something because the kids all converged on him momentarily before they turned back to the sidewalk,
their calls of "thank you" drifting through the night.

Logan's group shuffled through the fallen leaves to Jesse's house, and Brooke followed along. She stood on the lawn near the walk while Jesse, who hadn't bothered to go back inside after the last group, greeted the kids and invited them to select a treat from a large bowl that he held in both hands.

"Hey, there's my favorite pirate," Brooke heard Jesse say when he saw Logan.

Her son responded, but Brooke couldn't hear what he said. She hoped it contained "thank you." Jesse looked beyond the group to where Brooke was standing, and waved.

Brooke waved back, and without thinking, walked toward him. Jesse came down the steps, the bowl still in his hand.

"Candy bar?" He held the bowl out to her.

"No, but I'll take that bowl off your hands anytime you want to part with it," she said, relieved to have something to say besides a lame hello, and something to talk about besides last Saturday night. "I love yellow ware."

"Is that what this is?" Jesse held up the bowl as if inspecting it. "I picked it up at that flea market off Route 50 when I moved in last year. I just thought it was a nice bowl for pasta." He tilted the bowl in her direction. "Or Halloween candy."

"It's a beauty."

The silence that followed hung between them for one beat too long before they both tried to fill it at the same time.

"By the way, I . . ."

"Liz told me . . ."

Brooke smiled and nodded. "So you know that I

did follow up and called your office to set up my appointment."

"Late Thursday afternoon. I hope that doesn't interfere with picking up Logan after school."

She shook her head. "The bus usually brings him home, but on Thursdays, Clay picks him up for soccer. Logan's playing with one of the Boys Club teams at Packer Park, so I'm good for a few hours."

"Great." His eyes met hers and held them for a long moment before they were both distracted by the next round of trick-or-treaters. "I guess I'll see you then."

"Right. See you then." She headed toward the street, searching for her son, who, she realized, was waiting for her on the sidewalk.

"Brooke," Jesse called to her, and she turned around. "Maybe this time we should plan on dinner."

"All right." She nodded. "Great. See you on Thursday."

She caught up to Logan, a smile still on her face.

"Mom, why are you having dinner with Mr. Enright?" Logan asked.

"He's doing some paperwork for me," she told him, "and it might run into the dinner hour, so we'll eat while we work."

"Oh." He opened his bag and held it up so she could look inside. "I have a lot of candy, see?"

Brooke peered into the bag, then groaned. "No way can you eat all that."

"I know. But we got a note at school that said we could bring in some of our candy to Dr. Hess's office this week."

"Why would the dentist want all that candy?" she wondered aloud.

"He's going to send it to soldiers in places where they don't trick-or-treat. Like Iraq." His voice was increasingly softer. "Like where my dad was a soldier when he died. I told my teacher that and she said he must have been a brave soldier and I told her that he was. Right, Mom?"

"Right, sweetie. Your dad was a very brave soldier." She ran her hand over his hair, smoothing the spots where the night breeze had lifted it. "I think I'm ready to go home now. How 'bout you?"

"I think I am, too."

Logan took her hand and they walked back around the corner and down the block to the car.

"Did you have fun tonight?" Brooke asked as she drove home.

"I guess."

She glanced in the rearview. "Something bothering you?"

In the dark interior of the car, she barely saw his shrug.

"Was that a no?" she asked.

"I guess."

"Anything you want to talk about?"

"No." A few seconds later, he amended his response to, "No, thank you."

"Okay," she said, "but if you feel like talking to me about something, you know you can come to me about anything, right?"

"I guess."

He said very little the rest of the way home, but

while she was tucking him into bed, he asked, "Was my dad ever a pirate for Halloween?"

"I don't know." She bit her bottom lip thoughtfully. "I don't remember him ever talking about it. But when we talk to your uncle Jason sometime, we can ask him."

"When will that be?" Logan's eyes closed slowly, and though he reopened them again, he was fighting a battle he was clearly going to lose.

"I don't know. But I am hoping to talk to him soon."

"Good." Logan yawned and turned his head toward the pillow. "I like Uncle Jace . . ."

Brooke turned off the lamp on Logan's dresser and closed the door halfway when she left the room. She took the steps quietly and went to the kitchen. Before they left for trick-or-treating, she'd taken butter and eggs from the refrigerator to warm so they'd be ready for her baking when she arrived home. She rolled up her shirtsleeves, turned on the oven, and proceeded to bake. Once she got the first batch into the oven, she could work on that paper that was due on Friday for her business accounting class. It was satisfying to know she only had a few more weeks before final exams, and then she'd have her degree and several hours more each week in which to bake.

She was happy to be over the Halloween theme—she'd had enough of spiders and bats and witches' hats over the past few weeks. For the next two weeks she'd concentrate on autumn themes—pumpkins rather than jack-o'-lanterns, colored leaves, and cupcakes that looked like apples with red frosting and fondant stems. After that would come the Thanksgiving cupcakes, with turkeys and cornucopias, before she turned her attention to Christmas. She had a dozen or more different ideas for that holiday, and already she'd agreed to bake for several private parties, three company parties, and three buffets with Deanna. St. Dennis being a small town, there was no way she could serve the same cupcakes for similar events, which meant she needed to play with the fondant a little more.

"Right," she muttered. "In my spare time I'll figure out how to make little Christmas trees for the top of the cupcakes. And of course, people will expect those trees to have lights that actually blink."

Okay, that was an exaggeration, but not by much. It seemed the better you got at something, the better people expected you to be.

She picked up her recipe cards and debated which to make first. Since she'd been delivering to the three places in town every day, it made the most sense to make triple batches of three varieties, and give each of the establishments some from each batch so they'd have a variety to offer their customers. Tonight she was too tired to be inventive, so she settled on an apple spice, a chocolate peanut butter, and a plain yellow cupcake with chocolate frosting. She returned all the cards to the box except the one for chocolate ganache. She'd make them on Wednesday night so she could take a few with her to Jesse's. He could order dinner, but she was bringing dessert.

The first batch in the oven, she settled at the kitchen table and resumed writing. She couldn't wait until her classes were finished. There'd be that many more hours each week to bake, to experiment, and eventually, to sell her cupcakes directly to the public. Frank from Krauser's had left a message for her earlier in the evening that the van was finished and she could pick it up first thing in the morning. She couldn't wait to see it.

Around noon the following day, Clay appeared in the kitchen. He walked to the window that overlooked the drive and pointed outside.

"That van out there," he said. "The one in the driveway . . ."

"I just picked it up a little while ago from Frank." Brooke was all smiles.

"Please tell me that's not my van."

"That's the van you said I could use." Brooke looked up from the little leaves she was tracing onto fondant and smiled happily. "Isn't it glorious?"

"It's pink," he said. "Why is my van pink?"

"You said I could paint it however I wanted," she reminded him.

Clay continued to stare out the window. "And there's a great big cupcake with bright pink frosting painted on the side."

"The color is called hot raspberry."

"It says 'Cupcake' in big letters." He turned around and looked at her. "Brooke, I can't drive around St. Dennis in a van with a big pink freaking cupcake on the side."

"I asked you if I could have the van painted to use for my business and you said you didn't care what I did."

"Sorry, but it never occurred to me to specify any color other than pink and nix the cupcake."

"I'm sorry, Clay. But you said *you didn't care.*"

"I have an orchard full of apples to deliver this week. I can't deliver all those apples in a pink girlie-van, Brooke."

"Afraid your masculine image will suffer?"

"Damn right."

Brooke lowered her head and resumed working on the fondant and tried not to laugh. Clay had looked so bewildered when he looked out the window. He'd been blinking as if to clear his vision. Finally, when she couldn't hold it in any longer, she began to chuckle.

"I wish you could have seen your face." She sat on the closest chair. "You looked . . . stunned."

"I was stunned," he told her. "I'm still stunned."

"Look, if you load the apples in the van and give me a list of who gets how much, I'll deliver them this week when I take my cupcakes into town."

"Seriously, Brooke, whatever possessed you to do that?" Clay laughed in spite of himself.

"I wanted something that would make a statement."

"No problem there."

The back door opened and Hannah came in, her arms filled with grocery bags.

"I just saw the van in the driveway," she said. "Brooke, it's darling."

"Clay thinks so, too," Brooke deadpanned. "He can't wait to drive it into town. He's not afraid to show off his feminine side."

"I'll get that list for you." Clay shook his head and left the room. "You can make the first delivery this afternoon."

Hannah looked from Brooke to the fleeing image of her son. "Was it something I said?"

"Clay thinks the van is going to hurt his image." Brooke got up and checked the timer on her cupcakes. "I told him I'd deliver the apples for him."

"Oh, for heaven's sake." Hannah rolled her eyes. "He can borrow my van for his deliveries if it really bothers him. He can take out that last row of seats."

"He'll get over it," Brooke said confidently. "When he sees what a chick magnet that big pink cupcake is, he'll be thanking me."

Chapter 11

JESSE turned up his collar and walked into the wind that blew up the street, scattering leaves in its wake. It was six forty-five in the morning and facing down the wind was his current best reason for investing in a new coffeemaker to replace the one in his kitchen that had rolled over and died a few weeks back. For now, and at least until winter set in and it turned really cold, there was Cuppachino, his first stop every morning.

It was warm and fragrant inside the coffee shop and he went right to the counter, where the pretty young girl who worked the early shift took down his mug, the one Carlo's wife, Elisa, had made for him. She was a potter, and from their earliest days in the shop, Elisa made personal mugs for every one of the morning regulars. Grace's said EDITOR, ST. DENNIS GAZETTE. Steffie's said SCOOP; Vanessa's, BLING. Jesse's said EN-RIGHT, ESQ. But to Jesse, it said that someone recognized him as one of them, that he belonged. He was inordinately proud of it.

He was early, so he took a seat near the front window where he could watch St. Dennis come to life on

Charles Street. Observing life in a small town never failed to fascinate him, now that he was living in one. He turned at the sound of the door being opened and closed, and he waved to Clay, who waved back on his way to the counter, where he placed his order. When his mug was filled, he added cream and sugar—raw— and made his way around the tables to Jesse. He plunked down his mug—MADISON'S ORGANICS—and pulled up a chair.

"You ever play soccer, Enright?" Clay asked as he sat.

Jesse nodded. "High school, then club ball in college."

"Got a few hours each week you wouldn't mind sparing?"

"Maybe. Why?"

Clay came right to the point. "I just started coaching my nephew's Boys Club team. The assistant quit and I need a replacement fast." He took a sip of his coffee. "You interested?"

"How fast?"

"Now."

"What's the schedule?"

"Thursday afternoons from about three fifteen till four forty-five. Saturday mornings from nine till eleven. Pizza night once a month on Fridays. Party at the end of the season, win or lose." He took another sip. "You in?"

"Sure. I'll have to leave a little early this Thursday, though." Jesse didn't want anything to cut into his time with Brooke.

"That's okay. I'm grateful that you said you'd do it. By the way, we practice and play on the same field, the one in the park off Charles Street. One light down from Kelly's Point Drive."

"I'll find it."

"Great. Thanks. I . . ."

The door opened and Grace entered with a woman whose red hair was twisted at the back of her neck. She wore a black pencil skirt with a matching jacket and four-inch black leather heels. Clay's jaw dropped and Jesse was tempted to reach across the table and shut his friend's mouth for him. Fortunately, Clay came to his senses and closed it on his own.

"Good morning, boys," Grace called to them.

"Morning, Miss Grace," they both replied.

The woman in the black suit turned and gave them both the once-over, said something to Grace, then walked to their table.

"Hello, Clay." Her voice was just a little on the raspy side. "Nice to see you."

Jesse couldn't decide whether or not she really thought it was nice to see Clay, but Clay didn't seem to care.

"Lucy." Clay stood. "I heard you might be around this week."

"Big doings at the inn." She nodded in Grace's direction. "Celebrity wedding, St. Dennis style."

Grace started toward the table.

"I see you called in the big guns for Dallas and Steffie," Clay called to her.

"We're doing our best to talk her into it," Grace replied. She handed a to-go cup to the redhead and turned to Jesse. "Jesse, this is my daughter, Lucy Sinclair. Lucy, Jesse Enright. Mike's nephew. He's taking over the practice."

"Mom told me about Andrea's illness," Lucy told him. "I'm so sorry."

"Thank you," Jesse said. No reason to tell a stranger that he'd yet to meet his aunt.

"Please give Mike and Andrea my best when you see them," she continued.

"I'll be sure to do that. Thanks."

Lucy took a quick look at her watch. "I'm going to be late if I don't leave now. Thanks for the coffee, Mom." She leaned over and kissed Grace on the cheek.

"I'm leaving with you, dear. I have about three hundred photos from the Halloween Parade to go through before the paper goes to press and I want to get an early start." Grace patted Jesse on the shoulder. "You're in quite a few of them, by the way."

"Lucy, it was nice to meet you," Jesse told her.

"You as well." She nodded.

"Lulu." Clay touched her arm.

Her smile was faint, and to Jesse's eye, a bit sad. "No one ever got away with calling me that but you," she said softly.

"How long are you . . . ?"

Before he could finish, she told him, "I'm leaving in the morning. I just flew in to speak with Dallas and Steffie because Dallas wanted me to." She shrugged and forced a smile. "How do you say no to Dallas MacGregor?"

"I guess if you're a wedding planner, and she's getting married, you don't."

"Right. Well, it was good seeing you, Clay."

"Come back when you can stay a little longer," he said as she walked away.

"If I take this job, I'll be doing just that." She waved and went to the door, opened it, held it for her mother, then closed it behind them.

"So that's Lucy Sinclair," Jesse said.

Clay nodded and sat back down.

"Aren't you going to say anything?" Jesse asked him.

Clay shook his head from side to side.

"She just smoked every last one of your brain cells, didn't she," an amused Jesse said.

"She grew up real good," was all Clay said. He took a few sips of his coffee. "Sorry. I haven't seen her in a long time."

"How long?"

"Since we graduated from high school."

"Where's she been?"

"College, then she went straight out to California."

"Doesn't she ever come back to see her family?" Jesse asked.

"She does. Holidays and such, but she mostly stays at the inn. She's always gone before anyone even knows she's been here."

"That's odd, don't you think? Kind of slipping in and out of town as if she didn't want anyone to notice?" Jesse frowned. "Considering that she grew up here and all?"

"She didn't used to be that way." Clay picked up a wooden stirrer and tapped it on the side of his mug. "We used to be best friends, like, the very best of friends. From kindergarten right on through till about sophomore year in high school."

"What happened?" Jesse asked.

"Damned if I know," Clay replied. "One day we

were crabbing out near Culver's Cove, the next, she wouldn't even come to the phone when I called her. We never did anything together after that, hardly even spoke. It was like she had some switch in her head, and she'd turned it off."

"No explanation, no 'Clay you just piss me off and I don't want to be your friend anymore' . . . ?"

"Nothing."

"Are you sure she hadn't found a new best friend to hang out with and—"

"No. That's the thing. Like I told you before, she didn't hang around with anyone. None of the girls, none of the guys. She wasn't dating anyone, didn't go to any of the proms. Dropped off the field-hockey team. I mean, she just . . ." Clay shrugged as if he had no more words for whatever it was that Lucy had done.

"It still bothers you," Jesse said.

"Nah. It was a long time ago." Clay finished his coffee and stood. "I was just sayin'."

Jesse nodded as if he understood, and he did. Twenty years later, Clay was still bothered at having been dumped by a friend in high school—not a *girl*friend, but his *best* friend. Jesse knew that sometimes friendship went deeper than high school lust, and apparently it had for Clay. Despite his denial, he was still bothered by the unexplained loss of a friendship that obviously had meant a great deal to him.

"Well, I guess it's time for me to go and get my daily dose of humility." Clay pushed in his chair.

Jesse looked at him quizzically.

"My sister didn't tell you what she did to my van?"

"No," Jesse replied.

"It's parked outside." Clay gestured for Jesse to follow him. "You have to see it to believe it . . ."

Jesse was still smiling about the pink van with the big hot-pink cupcake painted on the side when he arrived at his office. Liz wasn't at her desk, so he left her muffin there for her. And because he'd decided that someone had to take the first step, he'd bought one for Violet as well. He saw her coat hanging on the freestanding brass rack in the reception area, but she wasn't at her desk either. Jesse left the muffin in its bag and went into his own office, the door of which was already open.

Curtis Enright sat at Jesse's desk, in Jesse's chair, which had been turned sideways. Violet sat in one of the visitors' seats, a happy smile on her face. The smile visibly faded when she saw Jesse enter the room.

"Good morning," Jesse said. "Pop, this is an unexpected pleasure." He extended his hand and his grandfather began to rise. "No, no, stay there. I can sit here next to Violet."

He patted Violet on the shoulder as he stepped around her to take the other visitors' chair. Violet flinched imperceptibly, and Jesse smiled. He still wasn't sure what her problem was, but he wasn't about to acknowledge it to his grandfather, who apparently thought enough of the woman to keep her on the payroll.

"I stopped at Cuppachino and got you a muffin," he told her. "Carlo said you're partial to the pumpkin walnut."

"Thank you." She managed a smile.

"You're welcome." Jesse turned to his grandfather. "If I'd known you were stopping in, I'd have brought something for you. As it is . . ." He placed the small white bag with the Cuppachino logo onto the desk. "I'm more than happy to share." He met his grandfather's eyes. "It's blueberry pecan."

"No, thanks. I'm watching my . . ." Curtis paused as Jesse unwrapped the muffin. "Oh, hell, go get a knife."

"I'll get it, Curtis." Violet rose as if she'd been waiting for an opportunity to leave.

"Thank you." Curtis turned back to Jesse. "I heard you were one to come in early every day. Did the same thing, when I first started."

"I've always been an early riser. Makes sense to get a good start on the day." Jesse leaned back in his chair and wondered what had brought his grandfather in this morning. Was he checking up on him? Or was he just bored with his newly sedentary life?

"Exactly." Curtis nodded his agreement.

Violet appeared with a knife, two small plates, several napkins, and a cup of coffee, which she set down in front of her old boss.

"Thank you, Violet. I don't know how anyone functions without someone like you to run their office." Curtis smiled. Violet turned as if about to take her seat again when he said, "I'd appreciate a few moments with my grandson, Violet."

"Oh." She appeared startled, and almost insulted at having been asked, however gently, to leave. "Of course."

She closed the door softly as she left, her offended sensibilities trailing behind her.

"Sure you don't want your seat back?" Curtis asked.

Jesse shook his head and said, "Keep it as long as you like."

"I ran into Steve Duffy this morning." Curtis leaned forward on the desk, and for a moment, avoided making eye contact with Jesse, who figured out real fast where this was going and why his grandfather stopped in. "You know that this firm has been representing the Duffys for longer than I've been around."

"I believe Violet may have mentioned that."

"Then you probably know that after you turned down his son's case, he called me. Actually, he called from his cell phone as he was walking out the door." Curtis pushed back from the desk and stood, walked to the windows, and looked out. "Put me in a bit of a bind there, son. I would have appreciated a heads-up."

"I'm sorry. I didn't think—"

"Didn't think he'd call me, or didn't think I'd care?"

"I figured that sooner or later he'd get around to complaining to you. But did he tell you—?"

Curtis held up a hand to stop Jesse from saying anything further.

"For the record: you should assume that every time you meet with someone who'd once been a client of mine, that person is going to call me. Whether that person is pleased or pissed off." Curtis sat again, and this time, looked Jesse in the eye. "Mostly I've heard from people who have been happy with you. Steve Duffy was pissed off."

"I imagine he was." Jesse stifled the urge to add "sir," as if this were a military interrogation, which is what it felt like. He wasn't used to having his judgment second-guessed.

"I'd like to know why you turned down the request for legal counsel from an old client of ours, Jesse." Before Jesse could open his mouth, Curtis added, "I should probably add that Steve's father was a close friend of mine."

Jesse nodded slowly. "I wasn't aware that before I turned down a case, I was supposed to clear it with you."

His grandfather merely gestured for Jesse to get on with it.

"I wasn't aware of all the circumstances when Steve first came in and asked if I'd help his son with some legal problems. What he'd told me was that his former daughter-in-law had made up some story about Kyle abusing her to extort more child support from him, that she'd threatened to call the police and have him arrested. When Kyle refused to increase the payments, the daughter-in-law, Amber, followed through and called the cops, who arrived at her house and arrested Kyle."

"And . . ."

"And I said I'd look into it. Which I did." Jesse got up and started to pace. He wasn't going to be bullied into representing someone he didn't want to argue for, and didn't appreciate being asked to explain himself, but having reminded himself of his position with the firm, he proceeded to do exactly that. "I walked down to the police station and got a copy of the police report. I also spoke with Beck. These weren't trumped-up charges. I saw the photos of that girl after Kyle Duffy had unloaded on her face. According to Beck, it wasn't the first time Kyle had done that and it wasn't the first time that she'd called 911. But it was the first time that Kyle wasn't able to talk Amber into dropping the charges."

The expression on Curtis's face was unreadable. He sat behind the desk, sipping his coffee but saying nothing.

"There were two reasons why I didn't want to take the case. One, because I have no respect for any man who has to solve his relationship problems with his fists, and two, because I felt that this firm stood for more than that."

Jesse leaned back against the windowsill and summed it all up by saying, "I didn't want to go into court and argue a lie when I knew it was a lie."

Curtis drained his coffee cup and pushed back from the desk. He barely paused as he patted Jesse on the shoulder.

"I'd appreciate a heads-up next time."

"I understand," Jesse replied.

In the doorway, Curtis turned and looked back at his grandson. "Steve Duffy's father was a saint of a man. I can't say as much for his grandson. And for the record, I'd have done the same thing."

From across the hall, Jesse could hear Curtis speaking to Violet in the reception area.

"I hope you drove today, Violet," he was saying. "It's no day for a stroll. That wind has some teeth to it."

Jesse couldn't hear Violet's response, though he was certain she'd had one. He stepped into the hallway as his grandfather was buttoning up his overcoat.

"Thanks for stopping in," Jesse told him. "It was good to see you."

"Good to see you, too, son. Let's try to get together for dinner one night soon."

Jesse surprised them both by saying, "How 'bout Sunday?"

"Sunday'll be just fine, thank you." Curtis reached for the knob on the front door but Jesse beat him to it. "I'm already looking forward to it."

In spite of the wind, Jesse stood in the doorway and watched his grandfather amble to his car, an old Cadillac Seville in mint condition that had been pampered and would have looked brand new if the style hadn't changed so much.

"Your grandmother always loved a Cadillac." Violet had come up behind him quietly. "Never drove anything else. I think Curtis would dearly love one of those fancy German cars, but it would make him feel disloyal to Rose."

After the old Caddy was around the corner and out of sight, Jesse closed the door, and Violet started toward her desk.

"Violet, I'd like your advice on something."

She turned to face him, one eyebrow raised skeptically.

"My grandfather is going to be eighty-five in a few weeks," he said.

"I'm well aware of that," she said archly.

Ignoring her tone, he continued. "I'd like to have a surprise party for him, and I'd like to invite as many of his old friends and clients as are still around. I'd like your help in figuring out whom to invite."

She continued on to her desk and took her seat

without comment. Finally, as he was beginning to think she was just going to flat-out ignore him, she said, "That's very thoughtful of you. I'm sure I can be of assistance."

"Great. Thank you, Violet. I appreciate it, and I'm sure my grandfather will appreciate it, too."

He went back into his office and made some phone calls, typed up a brief on his computer, and made dinner reservations at Café Lola for Sunday at six. A few hours later, there was a tap on his door, though it was open.

"I'm calling that new sandwich shop to place an order. They deliver and they have excellent soups." Violet took a deep breath and added, "Could I order something for you?"

"Thank you, yes, that would be great. What would you recommend?"

"The crab bisque is delicious." Violet almost smiled. "The girl who makes it comes from a long line of watermen. The recipe she uses has been handed down in her family over the years."

"You've sold me. I'd love some."

"I'll call them now."

"Thank you," he said simply.

"Of course," she said as she went back across the hall.

Jesse had felt the tension rise and fade into nothingness when he'd asked Violet for her help with Curtis's birthday party. He wasn't sure how long the truce would last, but he'd take it for as long as he could get it.

Later in the afternoon, when Jesse had gone into the kitchen looking for coffee, she followed him in.

"Let me do that," she told him as he started to measure coffee into the paper filter. "I can always tell when you've made coffee because you make a mess every time."

"Guilty," he'd acknowledged, and sat at the table to see where this conversation was headed.

"I put Liz's muffin in the refrigerator," she said. "I think you forgot that she was off today."

"You're right. I did."

Violet tended to the coffeemaker in silence for a few moments. After she poured in the water and set the machine to "brew," she turned to him and said, "I have the list of friends and clients completed. I'll print it out for you."

"Thanks, Violet. I really want this to be a great time for him. I want him to have everyone there he cares about."

"Will that include your father?" she asked.

Jesse paused. "I don't know how much he cares about my father."

"To tell you the truth, neither do I." Violet took the chair opposite Jesse. "They always had a tumultuous relationship. Craig always seemed to have a chip on his shoulder, and no one could ever figure out why. The things that boy did when he was growing up . . ."

"I don't think I want to know."

"I wasn't going to tell you." Violet got up, taking the sugar bowl with her to the counter. She opened a cabinet and proceeded to refill the bowl with packets of the artificial sweetener that Liz preferred and the sugar that she favored. "But how Curtis feels now . . ." She shook her head. "I don't really know for certain."

"If it makes you feel better, I hadn't planned on inviting him."

"You'd leave your father off the guest list?"

Jesse shrugged. "It's not my party." He paused, then added, "I don't know if I'd invite him to a party for me either."

"That brings me to the next quandary. Whether or not to invite the others."

"What others?"

She took a deep breath. "You are aware that your father was married to someone else before he married your mother."

"He was married to Delia Enright, the novelist."

"Did you know that he had three children with her?"

"I know he had them, but I never met them. Apparently the divorce was not a friendly one." He smiled wanly. "Neither of my father's divorces were all that friendly, to tell you the truth. I'm thinking the next one won't be, either."

"Delia was a lovely woman. Your grandparents adored her. Craig's split from her was the last straw as far as Rose and Curtis were concerned. They'd doted on their grandchildren, and were distraught when Delia cut them off completely."

"She did?" Jesse frowned. "I thought Pop just didn't want to have anything to do with them."

"Rose confided in me once that she'd called on Delia in person and asked her to let her spend some time with the children, but she said that Delia told her that she didn't think it would be a good idea since their father had rejected them."

"That's the word she used, *rejected*?"

"Her exact words. When Rose asked Delia what she meant, she told her to ask Craig, but when Rose pressed her son, he refused to talk about it."

"So all this time, there's been no contact between Curtis and Delia's children?"

"Not as far as I'm aware."

Not that Jesse was especially surprised. Curtis hadn't had much contact with Jesse or his sister since Jesse's parents' divorce. There'd been Christmas cards, but the birthday presents had stopped when his grandmother Rose passed away.

"I was wondering if I should add them to the list," Violet was saying.

"You know their names? You know where they are?"

Violet nodded. "Your half brother's name is Nick. He's a marine biologist in New Jersey. Your half sisters are Zoey and Georgia. Zoey is a host on one of those TV shopping channels, and at one time Georgia danced with the Baltimore Harbor Ballet Company. She's retired now, lives on a farm over toward the western part of the state. They're all married and have young families."

For reasons he might never understand, Jesse's throat tightened. He had siblings—a brother and two sisters he'd never met—well, half siblings. He repeated their names inside his head, and couldn't wait to share them with Sophie.

"I've long suspected that Curtis has regretted having cut himself off from them, particularly after Rose died and he started losing touch with you and your sister. He never said, but I think he'd like to establish something while there's still time. I'm just not sure . . ." Her voice trailed away.

"You're not sure if we should be the ones to decide that for him." Jesse pondered the situation. "It could be a wonderful reunion and he could be very happy. Or"—he met Violet's eyes across the table—"it could go very badly and he'd be really angry."

"Exactly."

The coffeemaker beeped to signal it had completed brewing, and Violet rose and took two mugs from the cabinet. She filled them both and sat one in front of Jesse.

"I suggest we both think long and hard before we send out those three invitations," she told him.

"Agreed."

Jesse got up to get the half-and-half from the refrigerator and handed the carton to Violet to use first. When she finished and returned it to him, she thanked him and left the room.

But a moment later, she reappeared and stuck her head through the doorway.

"By the way, I saw you dancing with our Halloween queen on Saturday. She's a lovely girl, Jesse. It looked to me that she just might be crazy about you . . ."

Chapter 12

VIOLET backed up the file she'd named *Curtis's 85th,* saved it, and turned off the computer. She wasn't so very far from her own eighty-fifth, she reminded herself. Today she was feeling every bit her age.

It had certainly been a day for surprises. It started when Curtis had shown up at seven forty-five that morning. In the old days, he'd always walked through the door at that same time, never earlier, never later. Rose used to say that Curtis had a clock in his head and it was set to do certain things at certain times. He definitely was a creature of habit, and he'd made one out of Violet as well. She'd unlocked the office door at seven thirty every morning for almost sixty years, went straight back to the kitchen, and got the coffee ready. Curtis always said knowing she'd have a perfect cup waiting for him when he arrived made up for the fact that Rose had never learned to brew a decent pot. Even now, on those days when she was scheduled to work, she still arrived at the same time.

No one should follow the same routine for sixty years, she admonished herself. If she were wise, she'd follow her boss's lead and retire this year.

Old habits indeed died hard.

That morning, when Curtis came through the front door, she had a déjà vu moment. For just a flash, she remembered how it used to be, and she got up from her desk apologizing for not having his coffee ready. Now she was trying to be honest with herself—had it been memory, or confusion, that had caused her to hurry into the kitchen and begin to fill the pot with water?

Maybe it was time to retire. She rolled her eyes at the thought. Who in their right mind wanted to be working at her age?

And since she was being honest with herself, she had to admit that the real reason—the only reason—she insisted on coming in was to keep an eye on Jesse Enright.

When he arrived in St. Dennis that first time, she'd been convinced that he was up to no good. After all, hadn't she known his father from the day he was born until the day he cut ties with his family? She knew the havoc he'd caused. Havoc and heartbreak, that was Craig. He'd been such a sweet little boy, she recalled. Up until he entered his teens, that is. She'd watched along with his family as a sort of restlessness had begun to take over the boy. What had caused it, she'd never known, and she suspected no one else did either. Maybe not even Craig.

The real sin of it all, in Violet's eyes, was Rose dying so suddenly before she had a chance to reconcile with her son. Oh, they'd tried to track Craig down, but hadn't been able to locate him until his mother was already buried. By then, Curtis had nothing left to say to his firstborn, and he'd never forgiven him. All ties were severed, and had stayed severed, until Jesse showed up in St. Dennis that morning about ten months ago.

Violet sighed at the memory. She'd assumed a lot of things about Jesse that had turned out to be so wrong. She'd thought he was a clever gold digger from the time he arrived until just that morning, when she'd seen the genuine affection and respect in Jesse's eyes when he came into his office and found his grandfather waiting for him.

And then there was this matter of a surprise party for Curtis. Jesse would have no way of knowing that his grandfather hated surprises.

Which put Violet right in the middle. Jesse had confided his plans in her, but there was a real possibility that Curtis might not react the way Jesse thought he would. And then there was the question of Craig's other children. What to do about them? It was one thing not knowing how Curtis would feel about being surprised, but where those three were concerned, might he not feel he'd been blindsided? On the other hand, perhaps he'd see this as an opportunity to become reacquainted while still allowing him to save face.

"Well, there is only one way to deal with this," she murmured. She grabbed her handbag, put on her coat, and turned out all but the hall light. It was time to pay a visit to the boss.

There had been a time when she'd been a regular visitor at the big house at the end of Old St. Mary's Church Road. Back in the day, she and her Allan and Rose and Curtis had been such close friends. It had been Rose who'd helped them to make the arrangements to bury their daughter, Amelia, who'd fallen off the bridge linking St. Dennis to Cannonball Island, and Rose who'd convinced her that Curtis needed assistance in the office, someone he could trust implicitly. It had taken Violet several years to figure out that offering the job was Rose's way of helping Violet move on after Amelia's death, but she'd never regretted one day she spent working for Enright and Enright.

Ringing the doorbell brought back more than a few memories. Seeing an aged Curtis open the door brought her back to the present.

"Violet." He smiled. "Twice in one day after not seeing you in weeks. Come in, come in. It's too cold for either of us to be standing in that wind."

He ushered her into the sitting room that looked exactly the way it had when Rose was alive, and gestured for her to have a seat.

"Can I take your coat?"

"No, I'm not going to be staying that long."

"What brings you by? Did I leave my glasses at the office again?" He patted his shirt pocket. "Nope, there they are."

"I just wanted to have a chat with you, Curtis. Something's bothering me." She took off her gloves and held them on her lap. "It's about Jesse."

Violet watched the color drain from Curtis's face as he slowly sat on the chair that faced hers.

"What about Jesse?"

"Oh, nothing like that," she assured him when she realized he was expecting something really bad. "No, no, he's a fine young man, Curtis. It's something quite good, actually, but it's something I feel I need to discuss with you."

Curtis visibly relaxed. "Go on, Vi."

"First you need to promise that you won't tell him that we had this conversation."

"All right. I promise." Curtis looked wary, so she decided to just throw it out there.

"Jesse wants to throw a party for your birthday. A surprise party."

It took a moment for her words to sink in.

"Oh," Curtis finally said. "That's . . . that's very . . . *thoughtful* of him."

"You can't let on that you know, Curtis. You promised. And he took me into his confidence. He's trusting me." Violet paused. "You may not have noticed, but we—Jesse and I—haven't always gotten along."

Curtis nodded. He'd noticed.

"Well, it's entirely my fault. I didn't give him a chance. I'm not proud of that, but there it is. But he's won me over."

"Good. I was hoping—"

"—that I'd judge him on his own merits, not permit the sins of the father . . . oh, all that."

"I'd harbored a lot of the same prejudices, Violet. We all did. Even Mike has come around."

"So. The party. Jesse has asked me to help with the guest list. Which of course, I'm happy to do."

"No one better," Curtis agreed. "You know everyone—friends, clients, family. The nieces and the nephews and the grandchildren."

"Yes, well, that's part of the reason I'm here. It's about inviting your grandchildren."

"Well, of course, Jesse will invite his sister. And

there are Mike's kids, you know how to get in touch with them." Curtis stared at her for a moment. "What's the problem, Violet? Out with it."

"It's the other ones I'm not sure about."

"The other . . ." She was several feet away, but she heard the soft intake of his breath as he realized who "the other ones" were. "Delia's children."

Interesting, Violet thought. Not Craig's children with Delia, or Craig's children with his first wife, but Delia's children.

"What about them?" he asked gruffly.

"How would you feel about inviting them?"

The silence was almost overwhelming.

"They're your grandchildren, just as much as the others, Curtis," she reminded him.

"I'm aware of that."

They stared at each other for a long time, until Violet began to think that this time she'd really overstepped. But finally, Curtis said, "I haven't seen those children since they were . . . well, children. Delia's choice, not ours, Violet. God knows that Rose and I tried, but Delia's a stubborn cuss. She wanted nothing to do with us after Craig walked out on them."

He got up and began to pace back and forth across the room. Funny, she thought, how Jesse had the same habit when something was bothering him and he was searching for a solution.

"I don't know them, Vi."

"Then I suppose you'll need to decide if you want to know them. If you do, now's your chance." She smiled. "And Jesse inviting them even lets you save face."

"What if Jesse invites them and they won't come?"

"Then you're no worse off than you are right now."

Curtis rubbed his chin. "What if it just opens up a lot of old wounds? For them, I mean, and for their mother."

"They're adults, Curtis. I suspect they can deal with it, if they haven't already."

"May I think it over?" he asked.

"Of course," she assured him. "It is your surprise party."

"Jesse is a thoughtful boy," he said. "He's smart and he's a very good lawyer. I respect his judgment. I respect him as a man. I've grown very fond of him. He's everything we'd hoped that . . ." He left the sentence unfinished, but Vi knew what he meant.

Jesse was everything they'd hoped Craig would have been.

"Well, maybe we'll find out that Nicky has grown up to be a good man, too, Vi, and that his sisters take after their mother, not their father."

"That was my thinking, as well."

"I wish that one of them—Jesse or one of Mike's kids—would settle down here in St. Dennis. Do you think that would ever happen?"

"Oh, I'd bet on it." Violet smiled.

"Do you know something I don't know?"

"I know that Jesse and Brooke Madison . . . that would be, Brooke Bowers now . . . seem to have eyes for one another."

"Really?" Curtis smiled, too.

"Just my observation, of course."

"You're usually right about such things, Violet. I relied on that intuition of yours many times in the past, and I never regretted it."

"Thank you, Curtis." Violet stood. Her work here was done.

"You think we should invite Delia's three, don't you?"

"I do, Curtis. I think it's the right thing to do." She added, "I think it's what Rose would want you to do."

"You're right, of course." He nodded. "Tell Jesse that you thought it over and you think it might not be a bad idea to invite those half siblings of his. Who knows how many more birthdays any of us will have? It's time we tried to put this family back together again." He paused and looked at her from across the room. "Let's hope it isn't too late . . ."

Diary ~

Had a lovely visit with Lucy, though all too short, as always. But she will be back soon—perhaps several times between now and the big wedding, which could be even more exciting and star-studded than Dallas's birthday party, though I could be wrong about that. I only hope that dreamy Sidney Warren is invited back. I'll even let him have my room at the inn if we're sold out (down, Gracie!). Just kidding, of course.

I just happened to be driving past Curtis Enright's grand old house last night and who did I see marching up the front walk but Violet Finneran. Mustn't read anything into that—they've been friends forever and a day. And of course, Violet was such a close friend of Rose's. I remember my mother telling me once that when they were girls, they were known as the Three Blossoms. That would have been, of course, with Lilly Ryder as the third. Anyway, it took me back to the days when the Enrights had such parties in that house. There was a cook and for a time, Mother said, a real butler, if one could imagine such a thing in St. Dennis! Of course, thinking about the family reminded me that Mike and Andrea are having such a terrible time with her illness. I must not forget to keep them both in my nightly prayers. And young Jesse, too—what a dear boy he is. You'd never believe he's Craig's son. I swear I don't see a trace of his father in him, which leads me to think that Jesse's mother must be a lovely woman. I did hear that Craig divorced her some years ago. Anyway—I think the boy is going to work out just fine here. I also think I see something developing between him and Brooke, which would please everyone so much. She's grown up to be a lovely girl, one who deserves another chance at happiness. I watched them dance at the Halloween ball—she was our unanimous choice for queen this year—I couldn't have been the only one who thought they looked so right together.

I'm wondering if I dare get out Alice's books to see if I could help that along somewhat . . .

No, no, of course not. I wouldn't dream of such a thing. I have sworn off magic and have retired my book of spells. Besides, who knows if any of that was real? Sometimes, in retrospect, I think that it may have been just a way to pass the time for Alice, who was so lonely, and a bunch of young girls who were curious and easily influenced and who so much wanted to believe . . .

~ Grace ~

Chapter 13

Brooke finished frosting the last of the chocolate ganache cupcakes and stepped back to assess their appearance. There was more than a little ganache left over. Would little truffles adorning the tops of the cupcakes be overkill?

Maybe. But she decided to go with them anyway. If she made the truffles small enough, she might have enough ganache for all three batches. She rolled the ganache into little balls then rolled them in powdered cocoa. When she was finished, she packed them into their designated boxes: one for Scoop, one for Cuppachino, one for Lola's.

The remaining six cupcakes were to be packed into a box of their own. She was just placing them inside when her mother came into the kitchen, her bag over her shoulder. She was clearly headed out, but she stopped to inspect her daughter's handiwork.

"Those look delicious," Hannah told Brooke. "Aren't you late getting these out?"

"Stef and Carlo both wanted to test the waters for afternoon and evening sales, since the morning batches are selling out by lunch. So I said I'd make an extra dozen and drop them off on my way to school."

Hannah glanced at the three marked boxes. "Who are these for?"

"I made extra to take to Jesse's office. I have an appointment later this afternoon to rewrite my will. We're going to try to get it finished today."

"You're paying him in cupcakes?" Hannah appeared amused. "I knew the firm would be accommodating since we're clients from way back, but really . . ."

"I'm taking them because the appointment will most likely run through the dinner hour and Jesse suggested we plan on eating there at the office. I thought I'd bring dessert."

"Oh?"

"It seemed a good time to take care of this once and for all, since Clay will be bringing Logan home from soccer and they usually stop somewhere on the way home to eat. We almost never eat dinner with them on Thursday anyway." Brooke cut a length of string from a nearby spool. "Does this leave you on your own? Do you mind?"

"Not at all. I'd be just as happy to pick up soup or something light and go right over to the new house and start unpacking some of the boxes in the kitchen. Clay dropped some things off for me this morning after he finished making his apple deliveries."

"Oh, then it's good timing all the way around." Brooke wrapped the string around the box and tied it off.

"That must be some will that could take several

hours to write." Hannah opened her bag and looked for her keys.

"We're rewriting the one that Eric and I had drawn up when we were first married," Brooke explained. "A lot has changed since then."

Hannah rubbed Brooke's back for a few seconds before swiping her finger through the leftover ganache in the bowl on her way to the back door.

"Delicious." She licked her finger clean. "I have an early appointment with the decorator at my house in about twenty minutes, so I guess I won't see you until later this evening. Have fun at school and at . . . the lawyer's office." She smiled and added, "No one can say that my girl doesn't know how to have a good time."

Brooke laughed and reached for the phone as it rang.

"Hey, Dallas," she said when she saw the caller ID. "What's up?"

"I was hoping to catch you at home so I could bring you up-to-date on the latest," Dallas told her. "Got a minute?"

"Sure."

"Steffie and I met with Lucy yesterday and she's agreed to do our weddings—both on the same date if we could work that out with the inn, which we've done. So December tenth it is."

"Terrific. So you're all set." Brooke quietly ran the water in the sink to rinse out the ganache bowl. "Congratulations."

"Thanks. It will be crazy to get everything done that we both want, pull it all together so it all works, but Lucy said she loves a challenge. So I'm taking Stef to New York tomorrow to see about getting a gown for her and I thought you might want to come along, since we'll be looking at the gowns for attendants at the same time. I did call ahead to the designer—I'm going with Teresa Kearney—who, after she finished having a heart attack, assured me that she could do anything we wanted and she promised to have it all done on time. She even agreed to come to St. Dennis personally with her seamstress to do the fittings."

"Of course she did." Brooke snorted. "As if anyone would be nuts enough to turn you down. Anyone without your clout wouldn't have been given the time of day."

"This is one of those times when I was glad to have a little clout. So what do you say? Can you come along?"

"I would love to," Brooke admitted. "I haven't been to New York in so long, and I've never in my life been anywhere near the studio of a famous fashion designer like Teresa Kearney. But I have a paper due by eleven tomorrow morning and it isn't finished. It's the last one before the final, so it has to be good."

"I understand. And I realize it's last-minute notice, but I was just this morning able to get through to Teresa to confirm that she could see us." Dallas sighed. "All of a sudden there's so much to do. I can't wait to go over all the details with you. Lucy had some amazing ideas, but between you and me, if she can pull this off, she's a genius. Just thinking about what it's going to take to coordinate what Stef wants with what I want gives me a headache."

"So don't think about it. Let Lucy worry. That's what you hired her to do, right?"

"Right. You're right." Dallas sounded relieved. "I wish you were coming with us tomorrow."

Brooke wished she were, too, she assured her friend, but they agreed to get together on Sunday night so that Dallas and Steffie could share their newly made wedding plans. A glance at the clock reminded Brooke that she had two stops to make on her way to class. She opened the refrigerator and put the box of cupcakes she was taking to Jesse's office on the top shelf and closed the door, then paused. She took a piece of paper from the stack near the house phone and a pen from the desk.

DO NOT EVEN THINK ABOUT TOUCHING THIS BOX, she printed in large letters. THIS MEANS YOU, CLAY MADISON.

She taped the note to the top of the box, gathered her bag, slung it over her right shoulder, and picked up the boxes for Stef and Carlo. Her phone conversation with Dallas had left her with just enough time to make her deliveries, but no time to stop and chat.

It was almost dark when Brooke arrived at Jesse's office. She'd gotten home from class earlier than she'd expected, and took a few minutes to freshen her makeup and change into something a little nicer than what she'd worn to school. Added a little jewelry. Brushed out her hair and let it fall over her shoulders instead of pulling it back into her usual ponytail. As she descended the steps, she caught a glimpse of herself in the mirror at the foot of the stairs, and stopped to take a look.

I look like a woman who's going on a date, she reflected.

It wasn't so much in what she wore—though she clearly hadn't been thinking about "going to see her lawyer" as much as she was thinking about seeing Jesse—but it was there in her eyes, in her expression. She was going to see a man she was interested in, someone she hoped was interested in her as well. How it was all going to play out, well, that was anyone's guess. But for the first time in a very long time, she was going to give herself the freedom to go with the flow and see where it led.

She'd spent so much time on her appearance that she was already late, so she ran out the back door, then back in to get the cupcakes from the refrigerator. By the time she made it to Jesse's office, it was five o'clock. She opened the front door and went straight into the reception area, only to find it empty. Hearing voices from Jesse's office, she tiptoed across the hall and was about to knock on the door when Violet appeared and placed a hand on her shoulder.

"Hello, Brooke." Violet squeezed her shoulder gently. "What a lovely Halloween queen you made on Saturday. I was hoping to get a chance to tell you. Your grandmother would have been proud."

"Thank you, Mrs. Finneran. That's so nice of you to say."

"Now, I know Jesse is waiting for you, so let's just tap on his door . . ." Violet did exactly that.

Jesse was standing in front of his desk, leaning back, talking to Liz about a property-damage case that they'd taken on. When he saw Brooke his face lit up, and Brooke was certain she wasn't the only one who'd noticed. Liz turned around to see what had put that light in his eyes.

"Brooke, you're right on time," he told her.

"Actually, I'm a bit late, but nice of you to cover for me," she said.

"Have you met Liz English?" he asked.

"We have met," Liz said. "I met you the first time at the regatta over the summer."

Brooke snapped her fingers. "I thought you looked familiar. Of course. You were sailing with Cameron O'Connor."

"My cousin. Sort of." Liz stood. "Nice to see you again."

"Liz, just send me a memo with your thoughts sometime tomorrow," Jesse told her.

"Will do." Liz was caught between Brooke and Violet in the narrow space, and appeared to be waiting for Violet to move so that she could leave.

"I've set up the conference room for you," Violet told Jesse. "I think you'll be more comfortable there. And I've ordered dinner to be delivered at six. I hope you like what I ordered for you." She looked from Brooke to Jesse. "You were on that conference call and you know that dinner orders have to be placed before five if you want delivery, so I had to play it by ear. Now, I'll stay a few more minutes if you like, in case you need anything."

"I think we're good, Violet. Thank you. I don't think you need to hang around."

"Well then, I hope you have a good meeting." Violet turned to leave. "Oh, I put Brooke's files on the conference room table for you. I made copies of everything I thought you both might want to write on or make notes on."

"Thanks, Violet. I appreciate it," Jesse said.

After Violet left the room, Liz mouthed, *Who was that woman and what happened to the real Violet?* as she, too, headed across the hall.

"Here, let me have that coat of yours." Jesse held the back of Brooke's coat as she slid out of it. He hung it on the coatrack in the corner.

"Thanks. It's nice and warm in here," Brooke noted. "Not so much outside."

"I know. I got blasted by the wind out there on the soccer field. Should have had the sense to wear a heavier jacket." He took her by the elbow. "The conference room is this way."

"You were playing soccer this afternoon?" she asked.

"Clay asked if I'd pitch in and co-coach his team. The other coach left without giving much warning, so it sort of left—"

"You were coaching Logan's team today?" Brooke frowned. And Clay hadn't bothered to mention it?

"It was fun." Jesse opened the door to the conference room and turned on the light. "Don't know how much of the fundamentals most of the kids are actually retaining, but it was fun. Eight is a funny age."

"Don't I know it." Then again, she reasoned, why would Clay have had any reason to think she'd be interested?

Jesse held the door for her and she stepped into the room. It was paneled halfway up the wall in cozy chestnut, with dark green wallpaper above the wainscot. There were portraits on the wall and a brick fireplace in the corner. The table could easily seat twelve and was surrounded by captain's chairs with green leather seats.

"Nice room," Brooke observed.

"I've only used it once or twice, and only with a large group." He held her chair for her. After she sat, he took his seat at the head of the table.

"Why's that?"

"Why have I only used it a few times?" He seemed to ask himself the same question. "I guess because I've only needed a larger space those few times. And, I guess, too, because it seems like it's my grandfather's room. I feel like an interloper when I'm sitting in his chair."

"I'm sure he doesn't feel that way."

When Jesse shrugged but made no comment, she said, "You and Mrs. Finneran seem to be getting along."

"I suspect my charm may have finally won her over," he said drily as he opened a file. "That and the fact that I asked her to help me plan my grandfather's birthday party. Remember I asked you about cup-cakes?"

Brooke nodded. "Did you decide on a date yet?"

"I'll have to look at a calendar, but probably the Saturday after next."

"Are you kidding? That's barely two weeks away."

He stared at her. "Right." After a moment he asked, "Is there something wrong with that date? Do you have a conflict?"

"No, but it usually takes awhile to plan a party."

"What's to plan? I thought we'd have it at Lola's since that's his favorite restaurant. They have that private room on the second floor."

"Invitations?"

"Violet is working on the guest list. She knows who his friends are. She'll know who to invite."

"You know that the shorter the amount of time between the invitations going out and the event, the more likely you'll have a lot of decliners, right?"

He still looked a little blank. He was, she realized, such a guy.

"I guess I should ask Violet about that list tomorrow." He frowned. It had obviously not occurred to him that people might have other plans.

"That would be wise." She suppressed a smile and added, "Let me know about those cupcakes as soon as you can."

"I'll do all that tomorrow." He ran a hand through his hair. "Sorry. I guess I haven't thought this through in those terms. I haven't thrown any parties."

"Ever?"

He shook his head. "I've been to a lot, but I've never given one."

"I'll help you. And Violet will help. It'll be fine."

"Thanks." He smiled and the worried expression left his face. She found she couldn't stop looking at his mouth. "So. Let's take a look at what we have here." He handed her a photocopy of her old will. "I guess the first thing we need to do is take Eric's name out." With a pen, he drew a line through Eric's name wherever it appeared on the first three pages.

She waited for the stab of pain in her heart, for the ache that would remind her of the finality of this action. But for the first time, she didn't feel as if Eric were watching from somewhere, accusing her of betraying him, of forgetting him too soon. She felt only that she was taking care of some necessary business, and that Eric would approve.

"Investments?" Jesse was asking.

"Still with the same broker as noted there."

"Real estate?"

"No."

"How 'bout the business that Eric started with his brother? Did they own a building or some land?" Jesse made notes as they went along.

"I don't know."

"So, I guess you haven't heard anything since our letter went out?" he asked. "I thought maybe he'd call you after her received it."

Brooke shook her head. "It really isn't like Jace to ignore a letter like the one you sent him. Did I tell you how much I appreciate that you made it so friendly?"

"There was no need not to be. We were just making an inquiry. Now, about a guardian in the event that something happens to you. Not that it's likely, but with Logan being so young, you really should have a plan."

"Of course. And it would be Clay," she told him.

"And if Clay were not available?"

The question caught her off guard. That something should happen to her and Clay both, after what had happened to Eric, was unthinkable. Yet she knew that in the real world, the unthinkable happened every day.

"I guess Dallas, but I've never discussed it with her. I should probably ask her first."

"How 'bout Eric's brother?"

She considered it for a moment, then shook her head. "I want Logan to grow up in St. Dennis. If I were gone—and Clay gone—well, my son's roots are here. I really hadn't thought about it all those years I lived away, but now that I'm back, I feel a very strong connection to the town and to the people I know and love here. I want him to have that, too."

Jesse nodded. "I understand. I wasn't born here, didn't grow up here, but I can understand what you mean. I think I'd like my kids to grow up here, too."

"You're planning on staying, then?" she asked a little too quickly, she thought, a little too eagerly. She felt her face flush red and tried to remember the last time she'd actually blushed. "What I mean is, there was some speculation that you were just filling in for Mike while Andrea was sick."

"In the long run, I suppose my granddad is going to have to decide what to do with the firm. But if it were up to me, yes, I'd stay and make a home here. I'm ready to settle down, I think, and this seems to be the right place for that."

Violet appeared in the doorway. "I had a few more things to finish, but I'll be taking off now unless you need me."

Jesse shook his head. "No, we're fine, Violet, thank you. Have a good night."

"Good night, Mrs. Finneran," Brooke said.

"Good night, dear." Violet disappeared for a moment, then reappeared. "Jesse, do you want me to lock the door?"

"No, I don't think you need to bother since the delivery guy is coming."

"He should be here in about forty-five minutes," she reminded him, her voice trailing off down the hall.

"Thanks again for putting the order in," Jesse called. "Now"—he turned back to Brooke—"where were we?"

"I think we were talking about a guardian for Logan."

He nodded. "Right. And that's taken care of, so now I think we need to talk about other provisions for Logan." He glanced at his notes. "You mentioned that you thought Clay had intended on reserving some of the farm for your son. If Clay is still planning on that, just make sure he has it written in his own will. If it isn't written down somewhere, have him call me and we can take care of that easily enough."

"I didn't ask him if he had a will, but if he does, it would be in this office. Either your grandfather or Mike would have done that. Mrs. Finneran would know."

They spent the next thirty minutes going over other changes and suggestions that Jesse made. At five after six the doorbell rang.

"Must be dinner." Jesse excused himself and went to the conference room door.

Brooke reached over to the folder with her name on it and picked up the will on which Jesse had been making notes in his small, neat, and precise handwriting. There was nothing there they hadn't talked about, and she slid the pages into the file and closed it, topping it with her copy. She was pretty sure they'd covered everything that needed discussing. As far as she was concerned, the business portion of the meeting was over. The rest of the evening—well, through dinner, at the very least—should be more casual, more social, but she felt slightly nervous and wasn't sure why. She took a deep breath and forced herself to relax. It was only dinner, right?

Jesse came into the room carrying two bags from which heavenly fragrances wafted.

"I don't know what Violet ordered, but it smells great." He placed the bags on the table and grinned when he saw that Brooke had folded up the files and cleared away the papers and pens. "Work time is over. I agree. Let me get a few plates . . ."

He disappeared down the hall as he talked, his voice fading out for a moment, then rising again as he returned to the conference room.

" . . . and we can take a few minutes to unwind. I don't know about you, but I've had a long day." He handed Brooke the plates. "What about you? How was your day?"

"Long," she agreed, and told him about the cupcakes she'd risen early to bake and deliver. Then, having been asked for more, she went back home and baked another three dozen cupcakes.

"So basically you baked all day." He started to unpack the bags.

"No, I had two classes, one this morning, one this afternoon."

"You're almost finished, though, right?"

She nodded. "I'll have my B.S. in December. Assuming, of course, that I don't screw up between now and then."

He shook his head. "Not gonna happen. You're focused and you're fierce in that. You do what you set out to do. That's one of the things I really like and admire about you. You're not afraid to work hard and you don't make excuses for yourself."

Before she could respond to the compliment, he'd opened a container. "Looks like brown rice." He opened another and sniffed. "And . . . beef in what smells like a wine sauce."

She opened the large Styrofoam box. "Salad. Looks like enough for both of us."

"Is this okay with you?" he asked.

"It's perfect. Thanks, Jesse. This was a nice idea."

"I'm glad you agreed. Otherwise, I'd be trolling for some fast food tonight." He handed her the containers so she could serve herself.

"Is that your way of reminding me that I promised you a cookbook?" She glanced up and caught his eye as he moved his chair just a little closer to hers.

"That wasn't subtle?"

"I'll do better than that." She spooned beef and rice onto her plate and handed the containers back to him. "I'll bring the cookbook and the ingredients for something terrific and I'll cook at your place."

"That's an offer I'd never refuse." He smiled and she noticed that the closer she got, the deeper his dimples appeared.

Who could resist a man whose smile went all the way to his eyes and who had dimples? Especially a man who looked at her the way he was looking at her right that moment.

So why, she couldn't help but wonder, hadn't he asked her out? For a moment she felt something in common with all those guys who'd been turned down when they'd called her, as if the tables had suddenly been turned and she was looking at the situation from an unfamiliar perspective. But unlike the guys who'd asked her out and taken no for an answer, she wasn't going to shrug her shoulders and walk away. There was something between her and Jesse, something electric that hung in the air of the conference room, that dared her to come a little closer and drew her in.

"How about Saturday night?" She licked her suddenly dry lips. "Unless, of course, you have other plans . . ."

"No plans. I'm all yours." His voice was casual, friendly even, but when his eyes met hers, there was a hint of something dark and sultry there.

Her breath caught in her throat and she shifted in her seat. When their knees touched under the table, it was all she could do not to kick off her shoes and run her toes along the side of his calf. How, she mused, would he react if she did just that?

The temptation was greater than she'd imagined it would be, and she wished the notion had never occurred to her. Suddenly she couldn't get the thought of touching him out of her mind.

"Brooke?" He waved a hand in front of her face slowly, slowly enough to hypnotize her.

"Oh. I'm sorry. I was just . . ."

He put his fork down and reached out for her, his hand at the nape of her neck, and drew her slowly to him. When his lips brushed against hers, she felt a jolt that shot all the way through her, and she knew she was in big trouble.

She dropped her fork and touched the side of his face, her hand lingering on his cheek. His mouth claimed her, his lips hungry on hers, his tongue tracing the corners of her mouth. She felt him in every fiber of her body, and when he pushed his chair back and pulled her onto his lap, she went willingly. His tongue met hers through parted lips and the zing she'd felt when he first kissed her intensified. She held his face in her hands and kissed him in a way she'd thought she'd forgotten how to kiss. She felt as if she'd caught fire, the heat that moved through her burning hotter and hotter. She turned so that her body pressed closer to his, unable to stop herself, drawn into him by a force more powerful than either of them. When his mouth made its way down the side of her throat, she was barely aware that the "Yes, yes . . ." she heard murmured was coming from her. His hand slid up her thigh and she knew that a few more inches and she'd explode right there and then.

She wasn't sure what to do next, it had been so long since she'd wanted so terribly, ached so deeply, for a man's touch. His thumb moved farther up under her skirt and found its way under the thin silk of her thong. When his fingers brushed against her core she saw stars.

"Oh my God, Jesse," she gasped as wave after wave of a pleasure close to pain coursed through her.

"Shhhh," he whispered, his breath hot against her ear. "Let it go, Brooke . . ."

As if she could stop the flood of sensation that rippled through her body. As if she could do anything but ride the rhythm of his fingers as they slipped inside her and threatened to bring her back to the brink again. What she most wanted was the feel of his hands on her skin. It had been so long since she'd been touched with such gentleness and such need. She met his eyes and started to unbutton her shirt, hoping that he would understand that this wasn't something she did every day, but that whatever had started between them as friendship had just ignited into something else, something she hadn't expected, but couldn't turn away from. His free hand closed over her breast and she fumbled with the buttons, pulling her bra strap down to free herself from it. His thumb and forefinger teased her flesh until she peaked again, this time arching her back until she thought she'd break in two.

"Oh my God, Jesse."

"That had a familiar ring to it," he gasped, and turned her to straddle him. She took his face in her hands and kissed him deeply. She had just reached for his belt buckle to undo it, when the front door slammed.

She sat up as if she'd been shot.

"You expecting someone?" she panted.

"No." He cleared his throat. "We had dinner, right?"

She nodded.

"Then it's not the delivery boy." He groaned and moved her off him. "This had better be good," he muttered. "Give me a minute to get rid of whoever it is."

"Hello? Is anyone here?" a voice called from the front hall.

"Hell." Jesse went to the door and gestured for Brooke to stay where she was. Rattled, she slipped back into her bra and buttoned her shirt. She stood and smoothed her skirt and looked under the table for her shoes, wondering when she'd taken them off.

"I'm looking for Jesse Enright." She heard the voice from the hall.

"You've found him. What can I do for you?"

"I have this letter . . ."

Brooke froze, one shoe on, the other dangling from the tips of her toes. She heard the sound of paper rustling, and squeezed her eyes tightly closed.

Oh, no . . . please, God, anyone but . . .

"I'm Jason Bowers. You represent my sister-in-law, Brooke Bowers, right?"

"That's correct. Mr. Bowers, come on into my office and we'll . . ."

There was the sound of more paper rattling.

"I know how lawyers work. I know that once someone is represented, the opposing party isn't allowed to talk to them. So I just want you—"

"Mr. Bowers, you've totally misunderstood the intent of my letter. Brooke was merely trying to—"

"—to find out if I was going to stiff my nephew. I got that."

"—determine if you were still in business, and if so, she just wanted to know—"

"—if she was ever going to see a penny of the money Eric loaned me. Right. I got that part, too."

"Please come into my office and sit down, Mr. Bowers. I can tell you're upset, and I know that's the last thing Brooke would want."

"At this point, I don't really care what Brooke would want. Here's a cashier's check made out to her for the full fifty thousand dollars. You tell her . . ."

Brooke couldn't take any more. She smoothed her hair and hoped she didn't look like she'd been doing what she and Jesse had been doing before Jason had let himself into the building. She stepped into the hall and walked toward the foyer.

"You can tell me yourself, Jace."

She couldn't remember Jason Bowers ever looking the way he looked at that moment when he saw her. He stared at her, then at Jesse.

"Oh, so that's how it is. You hook up with this law-yer, then the two of you decide to squeeze me into—" Jason took one too many steps toward Brooke, and Jesse reacted.

"Whoa, hold it, buddy." Jesse grabbed him by the arm.

"Get your hands off me." Jason's anger went clear to his eyes.

"Jace, could we please sit down and talk for a few minutes? Could you let me explain why I asked Jesse to write that letter?"

"I think it's pretty obvious."

"It isn't what you think." She lowered her voice. "Please. For Logan's sake, could we just talk about this and why I asked Jesse to send that letter?"

Jason glanced at Jesse, and Brooke could see that her brother-in-law figured he now had two reasons to want to deck him, and the letter wasn't the part that he was most objecting to.

"First of all, this firm has represented my family for well over one hundred years. Jesse is a member of the firm. When I needed legal counsel, I called on him. He's my lawyer, and he's my friend."

"I think I can figure out what he is, Brooke. I'm not blind."

"I had an appointment late this afternoon to have my will rewritten." That was true, but she couldn't bring herself to say more.

"You don't owe me any explanations, Brooke."

"You're right. I don't. But I can see you're upset,

and I don't want you to be. There isn't any reason to be. As far as the letter is concerned, I merely asked Jesse to help me find out what the status of the business is at this point."

"You could have called me and asked me yourself."

"I did that. Twice. You didn't return my calls."

"If you left messages, I never got them."

"Check with your garage, or wherever it is that you keep your equipment. That's the number you gave me. It's the only one I had."

He stared at her for a long moment. "The status of the business is 'sold.'"

"When did you sell it?" She frowned.

"The day after I got this letter. There's a guy who's been wanting to buy me out for the last couple of years. I called him and told him this was his chance. He met my price, and we signed the papers on Monday. I drove up here to pay back what I owed you."

"You sold your business?" She closed the distance between them slowly. "Why did you do that?"

"Because I couldn't pay you back any other way."

"I wasn't asking you to pay me back, you idiot. I was only asking *what was going on*. What part of that don't you get?" She poked him in the chest. He was six four but to her, he was still Eric's little brother. "You're asking me why I didn't call? Why didn't *you* call when you received the letter? If you didn't want to talk to me, you could have called Jesse."

"I thought—"

"You didn't think with anything but your Irish temper." She went to him and put her arms around him, and he let her. "Oh, Jason, I never intended for you to do something like that. I wasn't asking for money. I just wanted some information. I wasn't hounding you or asking you to pay back Eric's share. I just wanted to know."

"Well, now you do."

"So what are you going to do?" she asked.

He took a deep breath. "I hadn't thought that far ahead."

"You Bowers guys with your hot heads," she muttered. "I'm hoping that's one thing Logan didn't inherit from his father."

She poked him again. "And stop glaring at Jesse."

His eyes shifted from Jesse back to Brooke.

"Sorry," he said, though he clearly didn't mean it. "But you know, my brother hasn't even been gone for three years, Brooke. I can't help but wonder how long you waited before you—"

She felt as if she'd taken a sharp, swift punch to the gut.

"All right." Jesse stepped forward and put a hand on Brooke's shoulder. "I think that's enough. You don't know a thing about her, or about our relationship, and frankly, it's none of your business."

"I can tell by looking at both of you what your relationship is."

"So what you're saying is that after Eric died, Brooke should have become a nun?"

"Of course not. I'm just saying it hasn't been that long."

"You said it yourself. Almost three years. Have you gone three years without someone loving you?"

"We're not talking about my life. We're talking about Brooke's."

"Look, I don't know you, and I didn't know your

brother. And for what it's worth, I am sorry for what happened to him."

Jason smirked and it was becoming more and more apparent to Brooke that Jesse was using every bit of his self-control not to throw the first punch.

"From everything I've heard from everyone who's met him, Eric was a hell of a guy. I know Brooke's missed him terribly. I'm sure you do, too."

Jason's smirk began to fade slowly.

"But all that aside—you don't get to decide when it's time for Brooke to try to rebuild her life. And you don't get to decide who she builds it with. Whatever you think you know about her and this situation— you're probably wrong." Jesse's hand touched the small of her back.

As the two men stared at each other, Brooke could almost feel the steam begin to evaporate from the foyer, where only moments earlier, the emotions had built close to the combustion point.

"I didn't mean . . . hell, Brooke, I'm sorry." This time, it sounded as if Jason meant it. "Look, I'll give you a call when I figure out where I'm going to go—"

"No, you won't." She reached out to take his hand. "You're coming back to the farm with me."

"I think I'd be better off . . ."

She shook her head. "No. You're not leaving St. Dennis without seeing Logan and spending some time with him. He misses you, Jace."

"I miss him, too," Jason admitted. "All right. I'll stop out and say hello."

"That's a start." She patted his arm. "Do you have a car?"

Jason nodded. "It's parked around the corner."

"Why don't you get it and wait for me out front? You can follow me home."

He nodded again, looked back at Jesse, but didn't speak before leaving the office.

Brooke turned to Jesse. "I'm sorry. For everything. For Jason showing up and making a scene. And I'm sorry for . . ." She pointed in the direction of the conference room. "I don't usually act like that. I don't want you to think I . . ." She couldn't find the word she wanted. She wasn't sure what she felt other than confusion and embarrassment. Jason's unexpected arrival at the worst possible time had rattled her straight to her soul.

With his thumb Jesse brushed away tears she hadn't been aware had fallen.

"I think you're the woman I've waited for all my life, and I think we both know it," he said softly. "And please, don't break my heart by apologizing. I've been wanting to touch you since the first time I looked at you."

He put his arms around her and drew her close, rocked her gently, and all the conflicting feelings she'd had melted away. Being with Jesse hadn't felt anything but right.

"Brooke, the things Jason said, what he implied . . . you understand that he was surprised to find you here with me, right? That maybe for him, the years haven't been as long as they have been for you?"

"You're probably right. For years, Eric and Jason only had each other after their parents died." She sniffed back more tears and nodded slowly. Of course Jesse was right. What could have prepared Jason for seeing her with someone other than his brother? "What makes you so smart?"

"Hey, I've been a lawyer for more than a decade. I've spent a hell of a lot of time listening to what people say and figuring out what they really mean."

"The look he gave me when I first came out into the hall was so hateful." She shuddered at the memory of the way Jason's eyes had cut right through her.

"He was taken off guard. He thought he was just coming in to drop off a check and here you were. With me. He wasn't expecting to see you and he apparently never thought about you in a relationship with anyone other than Eric."

"Are we in a relationship?"

"You betcha." Jesse kissed the side of her face, and she felt all the anxiety of the past twenty minutes start to fade. "This is just the beginning, Brooke."

Headlights shined through the front window.

"I guess that's Jason. I should go." She glanced around. "Where did you put his check?"

He picked up the envelope he'd tossed onto his desk and handed it to her.

"Thanks," she said as she slipped it into her bag. "This goes right back to Jason. He can use it to start up again. The idiot."

"Want me to come with you?"

She shook her head. "No. I think you defused the situation but I need to take it from here. Thank you for sticking up for me, by the way. You didn't have to, but I appreciate that you did. So . . . well, thank you. I was afraid you two were going to go at it for a moment there."

"I really didn't want it to come to that. It wouldn't

have been a fair fight." He stepped into his office and got her coat, helped her to slip into it.

"Jason's a scrapper," she said.

"He was too emotional. He would have gone down hard. Besides, if we wrecked anything in here, Violet would have my head."

"And just when you and Mrs. Finneran were starting to get along so well." She leaned up and kissed him. "You were my hero tonight."

"Are we still on for Saturday night?"

She nodded. "I owe you one."

"Actually, you owe me two." He smiled and she felt its warmth all the way to her heart. "Not that I was counting . . ."

Chapter 14

H ANNAH was in the kitchen when Brooke arrived, Jason in tow.

"Mom, look who I found wandering around St. Dennis." Brooke knew that wasn't quite where she'd encountered him, but it would suffice for the moment.

"Jason! What a nice surprise." Hannah embraced him and gave him a long hug. "Why didn't you let us know you were coming?"

"He wanted to surprise us," Brooke said before Jason could respond.

Jason nodded. "Right."

"Well, sit, then. Have you had dinner?" Hannah went directly to the refrigerator and opened the door.

"No, I—"

"Let me fix you something. Let's see, we have—"

"No need to bother, Hannah," he told her. "I can stop somewhere on my way back to the motel."

"You have a room?" Hannah stood. "Where?"

"The small place out on the highway right past the first shopping center after the light on River Road."

Hannah made a face. "For heaven's sake, you can't stay there. Call them up and cancel the room. You'll stay here." She ducked into the refrigerator again. "Hamburger okay?"

"A hamburger would be great, but really, Hannah, you don't need to—"

She shushed him with a wave of her hand. "Sit."

Jason sat.

"Where's Clay?" Brooke asked.

"He's upstairs with Logan. Shower time." Hannah turned to Jason. "Say, why don't you go right on up and surprise him?"

"I'd love to see him, thank you." Jason stood. "Which way?"

"You can go right up the back steps here and it'll be the third door on the right."

Jason's footsteps echoed up the steps, and overhead they heard floorboards squeak.

"All right, now." Hannah turned to her daughter. "What's going on? Did you know Jason was coming? And why do you look so out of sorts? I thought you were finishing up your will at Jesse's office."

Brooke dropped into a chair.

"I didn't know Jason was coming. I was at Jesse's office when he arrived."

"Jason went to Jesse's office?" Hannah frowned. "Why would he have done that?"

"Remember I told you that Jesse wrote a letter to Jace, just asking about the state of the landscaping business because of the money that Eric pitched in as seed money?"

"Right." Hannah began to make a burger for Jason.

"Well, Jason took that to mean that I wanted him to pay back the money now." Brooke shook her head. "He was furious. It never occurred to me that he'd take it that way. I was only *asking* because I didn't even know if he was still in business. I thought I should know because of Logan . . ."

"Of course, you should know. No need to explain. And shame on Jason for not calling you to ask if that was what you wanted him to do."

"That's exactly what I told him. But he sold the business so he could pay me back. He came here to give me a check. Actually, he wasn't even going to do that. He was just going to leave it with Jesse without even calling me."

"Oh, dear lord. No wonder you're upset."

"That isn't all of it."

Hannah turned around. "So . . . ?"

"So Jesse and I were in the conference room when Jason arrived. We'd been . . . we were . . ." Brooke was trying to decide how best to word it.

"Oh. I see." Hannah took a small skillet from the rack overhead and placed it on the stove. "You and Jesse. Well."

"Well . . . ?"

"Well, it's about time."

"Mom . . ."

"Brooke, I know you've had a terrible time of things. Maybe I'm especially sensitive because I lost my husband, too. I know that after all the years I spent with your father, I won't be looking for someone else. But you're so young, sweetie—much too young to hang up your dancing shoes."

"Jesse and I weren't exactly dancing, Mom."

"I got that part, sweetie." Hannah turned back to the stove, a small smile on her lips. "It was a metaphor for . . . for whatever you were doing."

"It was . . . awkward, to say the least. Jason figured things out real fast and wasn't very nice. To either of us."

"Said things he shouldn't have?"

Brooke nodded. "He made me feel like . . . like . . ."

Hannah put her arms around her daughter's shoulders. "Don't let him do that, honey. Don't let anyone do that to you. There's still happiness in store for you with someone. I want you to find it. Embrace it."

"That's pretty much what I was doing when Jason arrived," Brooke muttered.

The kitchen was silent, Hannah looking for a spatula in an overstuffed drawer, Brooke trying to put everything that happened into perspective.

"I really like Jesse, Mom. There's something about him . . . I can't put my finger on it, but sometimes I feel as if I've known him forever. Which of course I haven't, but—"

"Funny. I said the same thing about your father when I first met him." Hannah found what she was looking for and closed the drawer, muttering, "Gotta clean that out before I move."

"I thought you always knew him, the way everyone knows everyone around here." Brooke turned in her chair to face her mother.

"Remember that your father was five years older than me. I knew who he was because I knew his family, but I didn't actually meet him until I was sixteen and he was already twenty-one and farming." Hannah stood at the window looking out.

"You met him at a hayride, right?" She'd heard the story before, but it was a good one, and it looked as if her mother was remembering it, too, just the way it happened all those years ago.

"The hayride was over on the Emmonses farm. I went with a couple of my girlfriends. Your dad was there with his brother, Everett, and his girlfriend." Hannah paused. "I wonder what ever happened to her. I don't think I saw her again after Everett died in Vietnam. Anyway, Dave climbed onto the hay wagon we were on, and sat next to me. I never looked at another boy after that. Couldn't wait until I was eighteen so he'd go out with me." She looked over her shoulder. "He thought my parents would think he was too old for me. Which they did. But I knew I was going to marry him. Even before I knew I was really in love with him, I knew that. It happens that way sometimes. I don't understand it myself, but there it is."

Logan bounded into to room. "Uncle Jason's here!"

"I know. I saw him!"

"Can I stay home from school tomorrow with him?"

"I must have water in my ears because for a minute there, it sounded like you asked if you could stay home from school tomorrow." Brooke slicked back his wet hair.

Logan made a face. "I figured you'd say that. But on Saturday he's going to come watch me play soccer and I told him I'd buy him an ice-cream cone at Scoop." Logan turned her face so that they were eye to eye. "You still have that little ticket Vanessa gave me on Halloween, right? The one for a free cone?"

Brooke nodded. "It's upstairs on my desk. I suggest you leave it there until you're ready to use it."

"Where is your uncle, Logan?" Hannah asked.

"He's upstairs, talking to Uncle Clay. They're talking about *beer*."

"Would you please go tell him that his hamburger is ready?"

"Sure, Gramma." Logan went to the foot of the steps and started to shout, "Uncle—"

"I could have done that myself." Hannah rolled her eyes. "Go upstairs and tell him, please."

When Logan had gone, Hannah asked, "Why do you suppose Jason overreacted to your letter the way he did?"

Brooke shook her head. "I don't know. I've been asking myself the same question. I mean, just selling out like that was extreme. I have to think that either he reacted from sheer blind anger, in which case he has to be regretting it—"

"Or he was looking for a reason to sell it and your letter provided one."

"We'll see, I guess, if he sticks around long enough. As for me"—Brooke stood and stretched—"all the drama aside, I still have a paper due in the morning and six dozen cupcakes to bake. Please make my excuses to Jason, but I have to get to work . . ."

She was almost to the door leading into the front hall when she stopped. "Mom," she said, "thanks."

Hannah turned off the burner under the skillet.

"It's time to let go of the past whether or not Jesse

turns out to be your future. And really, the only way to know for sure is to give him a chance. Don't turn your back on something that could be very right for you because you're afraid of what Jason or anyone else may think. It's your life, Brooke. Start living again."

Chapter 15

"HEY, Soccer Boy," Brooke greeted Logan as he ran off the field after his game on Saturday morning. "Nice goal."

"I just kicked the ball and it went in." Logan's beaming face told the story.

"Well, that sounds easy, and it looked easy, but I'll bet it wasn't all that easy when you were doing it, right?"

He nodded. "It was a lot of running on the field."

"So what you're saying is that running was the hardest part?" Jason walked up next to Brooke and he and Logan high-fived.

"Yup." Logan went to the cooler and found a bottle of water. He screwed off the lid and took a drink. "Somebody tried to trip me, but Cody tripped him instead."

"That dumb Matt from the other team." Cody joined Logan at the cooler. "He trips everybody."

"He doesn't play fair," Logan agreed, and the two boys scanned the cluster of players from the opposing team, looking, Brooke supposed, for the kid who liked to play dirty.

"Boys," Brooke called to them. "Handshake time."

"I'm not gonna shake Matt's hand, are you?" she heard Cody say as they ran to catch up with their teammates.

"Is that your . . . lawyer . . . your friend? He's coaching?" Jason stood with his hands in his pockets.

"Yes, he is. Clay asked him to." Brooke immediately went on the defensive, her hackles up.

Jason held up both hands. "I was only commenting. I wasn't sure it was the same guy. Don't read something into it that isn't there."

"The way you were only commenting on Thursday night at Jesse's office?"

Jason exhaled deeply. "I was out of line, Brooke. I apologize once again. I'll apologize to him, too, if you want. I had no right to say any of those things. Color me stupid."

"I already have. Mostly for selling your business at the drop of a hat like that."

He shrugged. "It's done. No point in talking about it now."

"Were you just tired of landscaping?"

"No, I love working with plants. I have to admit that working in a place like Florida limits what you can do, because of the climate. But no, I'm not tired of it." He seemed to think for a moment. "Maybe the challenge to do something different was missing. Like I said, you're pretty limited to working with tropicals there."

Logan and Cody were back, jostling each other and laughing.

"Uncle Jace, we're gonna go to Scoop now and I'm going to buy you an ice-cream cone." Logan looked up at his mother. "Did you bring the ice-cream ticket?"

"I did." She opened her wallet and took out the little gift certificate. "Here you go."

"Cool. Come on, Uncle Jace. The ice-cream place is just on the other side of those trees." Logan tugged at his sleeve.

"Great game, you two," Brooke called to Jesse and Clay, who were gathering the team together.

"The Rockets rule, right, guys?" Jesse said as he jogged over, and both boys nodded in agreement.

"We rock," Cody said as he, Logan, and Jason hurried to catch up with the others. They'd fallen into a sloppy line behind Clay, who was waving for Jesse to join them.

"You walking over to Steffie's to get ice cream with us?" Jesse asked Brooke. "Clay and I promised them all cones if they won today."

She shook her head. "I have another three dozen cupcakes to frost, decorate, and deliver by four."

"What kind?"

"Black Forest and pumpkin." She paused. "Are we still on for dinner?"

"Of course. Why would we not be?"

"Just checking. I'll be over around seven."

"Why so late?" He touched her arm, and trotted off in Scoop's direction. "Make it six."

Brooke walked up the path to Jesse's front door, her arms filled with groceries and her nerves on edge. She'd gone food shopping and had all the ingredients she needed, but she knew tonight wasn't going to be all about dinner.

Jesse was waiting for her at the door. He took the bags from her arms and she followed him into the kitchen.

"Is there anything here that needs to be refrigerated?" he asked.

"Well, yeah, you make crab cakes with crab and eggs and . . ." She watched him remove those items from the bags. Instead of placing them on the counter, he opened the refrigerator door and placed them on a shelf.

"Anything else?"

She shook her head, no.

"Good."

She was in his arms before she had time to blink, caught up in a rush that took her breath away. Jesse's mouth was on hers, his tongue teasing and tangling with hers, his lips owning hers. Brooke's arms slid around his neck and she pressed her body into his.

" . . . unfinished business," he whispered in her ear.

"Yes," she murmured, even though she hadn't heard anything except for those two words.

Jesse's hands slid over her body as she backed into the counter. She wanted him to touch her everywhere at once, wanted to touch him. She reached for the hem of her sweater and started to pull it over her head, but stopped when he said, "Upstairs."

"Yes," she replied.

He took her hand and led her to the stairwell, following close behind her, close enough that she could feel his breath on the back of her neck.

"First room on the right," he told her.

She pushed the door open and turned to him.

"Now," he told her, and she pulled off the sweater,

then removed her bra. She wiggled out of her skirt and thought she couldn't be free of her clothes fast enough. She backed onto the bed and Jesse was there, his clothes tossed somewhere, his arms next to her body on the mattress, following her across the bed, until he sank next to her with a soft groan.

She tried to remember the last time she'd felt this alive, the last time she'd wanted anything as much as she wanted him, but her thoughts were too jumbled to recall much of anything. Every inch of her seemed to be crying out for him to touch her, to taste her, to be inside her. She was floating on sensation, lost in an ancient rhythm, the beat of which she thought she'd forgotten. She wrapped her legs around his waist and pulled him in. His lips found her breast and she was lost. He thrust inside her and she arched her back and thought she heard someone calling his name before she recognized the voice as her own. She shattered into a thousand pieces and held on to him as they crashed together.

"Oh my God," she panted. "I think I saw stars."

"I saw stars." He nodded, his forehead against hers. "Stars definitely out tonight."

He slid to one side and nestled her in the crook of his arm.

"So what were you going to make for dinner, anyway?" His eyes were closed, but hers were open. He looked like she felt—relaxed, content, happy.

"Crab cakes and I'm still going to make them."

"Okay. Wake me when they're ready."

"As if." She forced one of his eyes open. "You snooze, you lose."

Jesse opened both eyes. "Kidding."

"I figured." She rested for a moment, her eyes scanning the room. It was a big square with a bay window in the front and three doors on the left wall. "Does one of those doors lead to a bathroom?"

"The one on the right."

She slipped out of his arms and walked across the wood floor to the bathroom. The door squeaked slightly when she opened it, and again when she closed it behind her. She turned on the light and looked in the mirror.

Her face was flushed and her lips puffy, her eyes bright. She looked alive, and the thought made her smile. She splashed water on her face to see if the glow would wash off. It didn't. When she went back to the bedroom a few minutes later, she was still smiling. She tripped over Jesse's shirt on her way toward the bed, so she picked it up and tossed it at him.

"What are you doing now?" he asked sleepily.

"Gathering up my clothes so I can get dressed." She found her skirt, inside out, and righted it. "I like company when I cook," she added pointedly.

"Got it." He sat up and pulled the shirt over his head. She tossed him his shorts and he laughed.

"I'll meet you in the kitchen," she told him.

"Five minutes," he promised.

It had been less than five, but not by much, before he slid up to her at the sink and wrapped his arms around her from behind. He kissed the tip of her ear, then went to the fridge.

"Do you like wine with your company while you cook?" he asked.

"I do."

"White or red?"

"White."

He took two glasses from the cupboard and filled them. He handed one to her and said, "To us. To new beginnings." He touched the rim of his glass to hers and winked.

"Jesse," she said, "there is something about you—"

"I'm irresistible, right?"

Brooke laughed. "In your own way, yes, you are."

"Good. Now, what can I do to help you?"

"You can find one of those yellow ware bowls for me."

"This one?" He held up the large bowl he'd used for Halloween candy.

"That'll do." She went through the grocery bags she'd brought with her, lining up celery, carrots, an onion, a plastic bag of bread crumbs, chives, a red pepper, a bottle of Worcestershire sauce, and an egg on the kitchen table.

"This is a neat table," she said.

"It's made from old reclaimed barn boards," he told her. "A guy in Pennsylvania makes them. I bought it when I was passing through on my way here in January."

"Maybe you can tell me how to find him. I think I'd like something like this for my new house." She opened the fridge and took out a package of crabmeat wrapped in brown paper.

"When do you think you'll be moving?"

"Not as soon as I'd like. My brother got an estimate for the basic, most necessary renovations from

Cam O'Connor—do you know him? Cameron? Tall blond guy?"

"I may have met him."

"Anyway, he's our local contractor. He gave Clay an estimate that was higher than I'd anticipated. But I figure with school being over, I'll have more time, so I can do some of the work myself. At least the interior painting."

"I can help with that," he told her. "I'm good at that."

"You don't have to."

"I know. But since I plan on spending a lot of time there, I figure I should carry my weight."

"You mean this wasn't a one-night stand?" She'd thought to make a joke of it, but it didn't come out that way.

"Not on your life." He leaned back in the chair at the kitchen table and made no move to touch her, but she *felt* touched, as if he'd run his hands down her arms. "You sleep with me, you have to keep me. You *own* me."

She laughed. "Knife?"

"Seriously?"

She laughed again. "I need to chop this stuff." She pointed to some of the vegetables.

"I'll chop. You do the rest."

He brought a knife and a cutting board to the table and picked up the red pepper. "How small?"

"Small," she told him. "Really small."

"Okay. So we need to talk about my grandfather's birthday party," he began as he was slicing up the pepper.

"How are the plans going?"

"Pretty good. Yesterday Violet made up some invitations and Liz printed them off in the office. They actually looked really good. She said that was the only way they'd get done in time. Then she emailed them to everyone whose email address she had, printed them out for those whose email addresses she didn't have. Didn't you get yours?"

"I haven't looked at email in a week. I'll check when I get home. Are you definitely having it at Lola's?"

"Yes. I called yesterday and spoke with Jimmy. He said they'd take care of everything, that they know what dishes he likes and they'll set up a buffet. All I have to do is give him a final count the day before."

"Are you doing the decorating yourself?" she asked.

"What decorating?" Jesse frowned.

"You know, in the room. At Lola's. For the party."

He had that deer-in-the-headlights look again.

"Like what?"

"Well, like flowers. And balloons," she suggested.

"He's going to be eighty-five. Do you think he'll want balloons?"

"Everyone wants balloons. Wouldn't you?"

He appeared to think it over. "I think I would." He nodded. "Yes, I would like balloons. Remember that if you ever give me a party. Helium balloons. Lots of them."

"That's exactly what I had in mind."

"Where do I get those?"

"Party store in the shopping center near the gas station," she told him as she broke an egg into the bowl and beat it with a fork. "I got the ones for Logan's birthday party there." She paused. "I wonder if Steffie would have time to make an ice-cream flavor just for him."

"Do you think she would?" Jesse grinned. "That would be so cool."

"We can ask. I don't know if she'll have time, but as my mom says, if you don't ask, the answer is always no." Brooke measured out what looked to be the right amount of mayonnaise and plopped it into the bowl. She followed it with mustard, hot sauce, and Worcestershire and mixed it all with a spoon before folding in the crabmeat. "How are you doing there with your chopping?"

"It's moving along." He glanced into the bowl. "I suppose your part of this operation is finished."

She folded her arms and nodded.

"Show-off," he muttered.

Brooke sat and waited for him to finish chopping the pepper into small pieces. "You can dump it right in here." She pointed to the bowl.

He tossed in the red pepper and started on the onion.

"I think I'm going to get a dog," she told him. "Logan is dying for one, but I didn't want to inconvenience Clay by getting one while we're still living with him."

"Doesn't Clay like dogs?"

"He loves dogs. But it's one thing to love your own dog, and something else entirely when someone moves into your house and then one day brings a dog home."

"Grant always has dogs at the shelter," he said. "I heard he has some really nice ones. I was thinking about getting a dog there myself."

"What kind?"

"Probably a pit bull. I heard him say he had a lot of rescued pit-bull puppies. They're not all mean and vicious, you know."

"I do know. One of my neighbors in Kentucky had a pit bull. She was all white and she was so soft, such a sweet thing. I wouldn't mind having one like her."

Jesse finished chopping the onion and he dumped that into the mix.

"Anything else?" he asked.

"The thyme needs to be chopped really small."

"I got it covered." He washed the thyme and cut it into tiny pieces. "Good enough?" he asked.

When she nodded, he scattered it into the bowl.

"That's everything?"

"Except for some lemon rind." She took a zester from the bag and ran a lemon over it until all the rind had been removed and the lemon was white.

"You brought your own tools?"

She nodded. "I didn't think you'd have one of these."

"You thought right."

She washed her hands, then gave the bowl one more mix with the spoon. "You wouldn't happen to have a cookie sheet, would you? If not, a plate will do."

"There's a flat thing in here that my sister made cookies on when she was here a few months ago." He knelt down and found it in a cabinet.

Jesse watched her spoon up the mix, then roll it into balls that she placed on the cookie sheet and flattened with the palm of her hand.

"That looks like fun." He stepped next to her. "Can I make a few?"

"Go wash your hands." She slanted a look in his direction. "You forget I know where those hands have been."

"Should have thought about that before you had me chop up all that other stuff."

She made a face, and he laughed.

They made eight crab cakes then set them in the refrigerator to rest while potatoes and asparagus roasted. They drank wine by the fire, then cooked the crab cakes in a skillet and ate at the kitchen table.

"So I suppose there will be cupcakes for dessert?" he asked after he cleared away the dishes and rinsed them.

"Are you getting tired of cupcakes?" Brooke frowned. Maybe she should have brought something else. "Are you over my cupcakes?"

"I will never get tired of your cupcakes," he said solemnly. "I'll never be over them."

"I meant the kind I bake."

"Them, too. If you baked it, I'll love it."

"You're very accommodating," she observed.

"Well, I do need you to stick around to bake for my grandfather's birthday."

"You're going to have to give me a head count when you have one. I have orders for a dinner party that same weekend and a list of customers who want cupcakes for Thanksgiving."

"Then you'll be rolling right into the Christmas season. I'll bet you get a lot of orders for December."

"I already have a lot lined up. Plus the big wedding on December tenth." She was grateful for a few minutes to just sit and watch him. She liked the way he moved, liked the way his hair fell across his forehead when he leaned over to stack the dishes in the dishwasher. "And since I'm one of the attendants as well as one of the bakers—both brides want spectacular cakes and spectacular cupcakes—I will be a busy girl that weekend."

"I guess the paparazzi will be following you all over town, since you'll be with Dallas."

"They'll be following Dallas all over town. Or not, maybe. She's not publicizing this, so unless someone she invites spills it to the press, she just might get away with a wedding without photographers swinging from the chandeliers." She couldn't stop watching him. It was as if she'd been hypnotized a few days ago and hadn't come out of the trance yet. "Want to go with me to the wedding?"

"As your date?" He paused, a plate in hand, and turned. "Did you just ask me out?"

"I asked you if you wanted to go to the wedding with me, so yeah, I guess that counts as a date. So yeah, I asked you out."

"And this dinner . . ." He gestured to the crab cakes left on the plate. "This was your idea."

"I suppose it was. So what?"

"So if I go to the wedding with you, it would be our second date," he said thoughtfully.

Brooke couldn't tell if he was talking to himself or trying to confuse her by stating the obvious.

"Does that mean something to you?" she asked.

"Depends. On whether or not you agree that the wedding would be our second date."

Brooke shrugged. "Okay. It's our second date."

"And both times you asked me, right?"

She narrowed her eyes. "Do you have a bet going with someone?"

Jesse laughed. "No."

"Then are you going to tell me what this is all about?"

"Someday."

"Are you sure you and Clay don't have some thing going on here?"

"I swear, no. No bets. Besides, Clay is too hung up on his own love life to worry about mine."

"What do you mean?"

"I mean Lucy Sinclair came into Cuppachino the other day and he embarrassed us both by drooling all over himself. It was sad, Brooke, to watch a grown man reduced to—"

"Are you sure? Lucy?" Her eyes widened at the thought.

Jesse nodded. "I sat right across the table from him, gave him CPR after she left."

"Well, the wedding should be interesting, since she's the wedding planner and he's going to be in the wedding." She grinned. "Should be fun."

"Wouldn't miss it."

Brooke's cell phone rang, and she reached into her pocket to check the caller ID. "My mother," she told him. "Hi, Mom . . ."

"Are you at home?"

"No, actually, I'm at Jesse's. We just had dinner. Why?"

"Because Clay called and asked if I'd pick up Logan from Tiffany's birthday party and drop him and Cody off at Berry's house. Clay and Wade are still at some brewery over in Rehoboth talking to the brewer. Dallas is out and Berry isn't driving at night these days. My car has a flat, and I'm waiting for—"

"What time does he have to be picked up?"

"Ten minutes ago."

"I'm on my way."

"I'm sorry that I had to disturb you."

"That's nice of you, but not to worry. I'll leave right now. Thanks, Mom."

She disconnected the call and tossed the phone into her bag. She explained the situation to Jesse.

"I'll go with you," he said. "We can drop off the boys at Dallas's, then come back here." He pulled her to him. "You could sleep over since Logan's not going to be home." He kissed the side of her face. "What do you say?"

She pretended to mull it over. "Your car or mine?"

Chapter 16

JESSE took his time approaching the house that oc-
cupied a full block at the very end of Old St. Mary's
Church Road. While not the oldest house in St. Dennis, it was certainly one of the largest and grandest.
It was said that the original owner had been a to-
bacco planter, and had styled the house after a mansion owned by a cousin of his somewhere in one
of the Carolinas before the Civil War. Jesse's great-
grandfather had bought it for his wife over one hundred years ago, and the house had remained in the
family ever since. Jesse had only been inside three times,
and hadn't seen much more than the front entry hall—
which he'd thought was cavernous—and his grandfather's study.

It was hard not to be impressed, Jesse conceded as
he rang the doorbell. The house and grounds had
been beautifully maintained over the years, and the
residence was even now quite the showplace. Why, he
wondered, would one person want to live alone in a
house that big?

A moment later, his grandfather appeared, greeting
him warmly and holding the door open for him.

"Right on time." Curtis nodded approvingly.

"Can't be late for our six o'clock reservation at Lola's," Jesse said.

"They'd hold our table but it's always best to be prompt. Besides, I'm starving. I got caught up in reading something this afternoon, never did stop for lunch. Now, let me just get my overcoat . . ." Curtis paused. "Do I need an overcoat?"

"I think you'll want it later," Jesse said. "It's cool out now and likely to be cooler by the time we finish dinner."

His grandfather's coat lay over the back of a chair in the living room, which was visible from the hall. Jesse retrieved it for him and helped him into it. His overall impression of the room was of dark antiques and too many portraits on the walls.

"Thank you, son. Now"—Curtis patted Jesse on the back—"shall I drive?"

Jesse couldn't help but smile. While a ride in the old Caddy was tempting, he thought maybe Curtis might like a spin around town in the two-seater.

"I'll drive, if you don't mind," Jesse told him.

"Fine with me." Curtis locked the front door behind them. "Always wondered what it would be like to drive one of these things. Should have bought one for myself when I was still young enough to enjoy it."

Jesse held the keys out to him. "Can you drive stick?"

Curtis shook his head. "Not these days."

They arrived at Lola's with several minutes to spare, so they sat in the bar and chatted over drinks until their table was ready. Curtis was surprisingly up-to-date as far as the firm was concerned—thanks, no doubt, to Violet. But while he appeared to know the status of most of the ongoing cases, he wanted the details, the more complete, the better.

"Now, tell me how you approached Harold Lansing on that property issue of his," Curtis would say, and Jesse would tell him, step-by-step.

"And the Macallister divorce. How did you ever get Peter to agree to share the Rehoboth house with Nancy?"

"That squabble among the Hillyer kids over Cyrus's will . . . how's that going?"

"Wish I'd been there to see the look on old Jack Winbry's face when the jury came back in favor of our client." Curtis had chuckled over Jesse's defeat of an old adversary.

By the time they'd ordered dessert, Jesse figured Curtis knew as much as he did about the cases that had come into the office over the past ten months.

"The last thing I should be thinking about is pumpkin pie," Curtis told him, "but I just can't resist. Your grandmother made one hell of a pumpkin pie. Never did find one that rivaled it." He looked across the table at Jesse, his voice lowered. "I'm sorry you didn't know her. I'm sorry she didn't know you."

"I'm sorry, too, Pop. I feel like I know her a little, though, through different things that Violet has said from time to time. I know it's not the same thing, but I have an idea of the type of person she was."

"She was one in a million, son." Curtis stirred cream into his coffee. "Only woman I ever loved, and I loved her the minute I laid eyes on her. Hate to even admit how many years ago that was."

He raised the cup to his mouth and took one sip, then set it back down in the saucer.

"You ever been in love, Jesse?" he asked, and Jesse shook his head, no.

"At least, I don't think I have. I've been in *like* a couple of times, in *lust* several more, but I don't think I've ever been in love." He thought of the way he was starting to feel about Brooke, which was definitely different from anything he'd ever felt for anyone. But was it love? How would he know? "I haven't given up, though."

"Well, I hope you find her here, and I hope you find her soon. You are getting up there, you know."

Jesse laughed. "I'm only thirty-six."

"Long past the time when you should have found the right girl, settled down, gotten married. Started a family."

"I'd like to think that's in my future." Jesse stirred cream into his coffee. "But you know, my parents' marriage wasn't very good, and my father . . ."

"Didn't set a very good example for you, did he?"

"Not when it came to relationships." Jesse thought for a moment. "Or much of anything else, I'm afraid."

"I've never been able to understand Craig. He was the boy who had everything. He was smart, he was athletic, he was good-looking, he had a magnetism about him . . . he could have been anything. He had the family firm waiting for him, he had a family that loved him and wanted him to succeed. And yet he chose to be, well, what he is."

"I'm sorry," Jesse found himself saying.

"Oh, son, no need for you to apologize. Believe me, your father started messing up his life long before you came along." He shook his head. "We could never figure out where we went wrong, and God knows, Rose and I tried everything we could think of to help him turn it around. But it was like standing on the sidewalk watching a car go out of control. There was nothing you could do about it unless you were the one behind the wheel. After a while we just stopped trying. It occurred to me one day that nothing was going to change Craig unless and until he wanted to change. I never saw any sign that he wanted to."

"He never did."

"That business at that last law firm he was working for, that whole embezzlement thing." Curtis shook his head sadly. "I suppose that was the last straw as far as your mother was concerned."

"They'd actually split up before that," Jesse told him. "We'll just say that he'd already picked out wife number three and we'll leave it at that."

"Your mother is a fine woman. Smart, lovely, charming. A good woman. I'll never understand what she saw in him. Her or Craig's first wife." He paused. "Did you ever meet her? Delia?"

"The famous mystery writer. No, we never met, but I've heard a lot about her, and I've seen her on TV a couple of times, read a few magazine articles. She seems like a nice lady."

"Terrific woman. Rose and I loved her. Never did find out what happened there. Craig wouldn't discuss it, and when we tried to get Delia to open up, she shut us out. I mean, literally, shut us out. Wouldn't let us anywhere near the kids, no real explanation behind that. That was back in the days before grandparents had any rights." Curtis glanced at Jesse. "You do know there were children from that marriage?"

"I know I have a half brother and two half sisters, but we've never met." Jesse nodded and thought about the invitations that had already gone out, and hoped he'd made the right decision. Violet seemed to think so, had encouraged him to invite all the Enright offspring, and she would certainly be the one to know.

"That's a shame. For all of you. That shouldn't have been allowed to happen." Curtis sighed deeply. "It's very disappointing to get to this stage in your life and to look back, only to find you have so many regrets, so many things you wish you'd done differently."

"You can't change the past, Pop. We both know that." Jesse patted his grandfather's arm reassuringly. "And the decisions that my dad made . . . those are all on him."

"I have something to say to you that's long overdue." Curtis sighed and put down his cup. "I'm sorry I ever let my feeling of anger and frustration with your father come between us. You and the others. I deeply regret that I haven't done right by any of you. Those times when your father wasn't there for you, I should have been. Same for Nick and the girls. I should have been there for all of you. I shouldn't have taken no for an answer from any of my former daughters-in-law. At least when you became adults, I should have—"

"It's okay, Pop." Jesse felt his throat tighten. "Water over the dam now."

"You're a fine young man, Jesse. You make me very

proud." It seemed Curtis, too, had a catch in his throat.

"Well, now, look," Jesse said, "we're here and we just had a great dinner together and everything is fine. No need to look back, Pop. Just look ahead. You have lots of time to get to know all your grandkids." He grinned. "It ain't over till it's over."

"God, Rose would have loved you." Curtis chuckled. "When did you say your sister would be coming back for another visit?"

"In a few weeks."

"Good, good. We'll plan dinner or something special while she's here."

"Sounds good. I know she'll look forward to that."

The waiter served their desserts, pumpkin pie for Curtis, a Black Forest cupcake for Jesse, who couldn't help but smile when he ordered it. Everything about Brooke seemed to make him smile. He hadn't stopped thinking about her from the minute the door had closed behind her that morning. The way she looked all tousled from sleep when he'd awakened, the way his heart had swelled when she opened her eyes and reached for him . . .

"That looks tasty," Curtis remarked as he eyed the two cupcakes that were set before Jesse.

"Oh, these are wonderful," the waiter confided. "Made right here in St. Dennis."

"Brooke made them, Pop," Jesse said, his smile still in place. "Brooke Bowers." When his grandfather appeared a little confused, he added, "Brooke Madison?"

"Ah, yes. Little Brooke. She's a baker now?" Curtis chuckled. "She must take after her aunt Francie. Now, there was a woman who could bake. Took the blue at the county fair for both her lemon pound cake and her rhubarb cake every year for . . . I don't even remember how many years."

Jesse took a bite. The flavor was rich and sweet, the chocolate dense and delicious. Remarkable, but he could almost taste her in her creation.

"That must be one pretty darn good cupcake," Curtis mused. "You've been grinning from ear to ear since the waiter brought it out."

"You tell me." Jesse cut off a wedge and passed it to his grandfather, who used his fork to take a bite.

"Yes." Curtis nodded. "It is quite good. You be sure to ask her if she got this recipe from Francie when you see her again, hear?"

"I'll do that."

Curtis snapped his fingers. "Of course, of course. Brooke was the Halloween queen. There was a picture of her on the front page of the *Gazette* the other day. Dancing with a tall, dark-haired fellow who looked an awful lot like you."

"Pop, it *was* me."

"Thought he looked familiar." Curtis went back to his pumpkin pie. "Lovely girl, Brooke."

The waiter returned to refill their coffee cups, and they made small talk. When Curtis appeared to be tiring, Jesse signaled the waiter for the check.

"How 'bout if I get that?"

Curtis reached for it, but Jesse reminded him, "I invited you, remember?"

"Yes, you did, and I appreciate the invitation." Curtis acquiesced, and sat back while Jesse paid the bill. "I can't remember the last time one of my grandchildren took me to dinner. Actually, I can't remember the last time one of them accepted a dinner invitation from me."

"We'll have to do it more often." Jesse slid his wallet back into his pants pocket.

"Thank you for not reminding me that most of my grandchildren have good reason *not* to want to have dinner with me."

"You can change that anytime you want, Pop. It's all in your hands. It always has been. Maybe you'll get the chance to do that soon."

They got up from the table and said their goodnights to the hostess on their way to the door.

"Where's Lola tonight?" Curtis asked the young woman.

"I'm Lola," she replied.

"If you're Lola, I'll have whatever it is you're having," Curtis quipped. "I know for a fact that Lola is ninety-six years old, and if you'll pardon me for saying so, you don't look a day over twenty." He leaned a little closer. "And Lola was never as lovely as you."

The woman flashed the smile pretty young girls reserve for old men who mean well.

"You mean my great-aunt Lola," the woman said. "She's off tonight."

"Well, you tell her Curtis Enright was asking for her, if you think of it."

"I'll do that." She held the door for them and flashed a bright smile at Jesse as she did so.

When they got outside, Curtis said, "She's a pretty thing, don't you think?"

"Yeah."

"You didn't really notice, did you." Curtis stopped

next to the passenger-side door of Jesse's car and waited while it was unlocked.

"Sure, I noticed."

"You're not a good liar." Curtis ducked his head and slid into the little sports car. After Jesse got in behind the wheel, Curtis said, "She may not be royalty, but she's still a pretty girl and she was looking to flirt with you."

"That part I did *not* notice. And what royalty?"

"Halloween queen. Cupcake princess." Curtis chuckled. "She comes from a long line of beauty queens, you know."

"You mean Lola?"

"You know damned well who I mean. A man could do a lot worse than to fall in love with a beauty queen."

Jesse didn't reply, but when he pulled up in front of Curtis's house and turned off the car, he said, "Earlier you told me I was nothing like my father."

"I did." Curtis nodded. "You're not."

"What if I am, Pop?" Jesse asked softly. "What if deep inside, I am?"

"I think you would have known by now, son." He reached over and patted Jesse's hand where it rested on the gearshift. "We all would have known."

Jesse wasn't so sure.

"You and Gramma Rose had a good life together, didn't you?"

"The best."

"It's safe to say you were a happy and loving family?"

"Always." Curtis hesitated. "Well, until your father got into his teens and turned into someone we didn't know and brought chaos into our home. What are you thinking, Jess?"

"I'm just wondering why, if my father had such good role models in his parents, I should have any reason to think I'd be better at being married and raising kids than he was, since I had no role model at all. I wouldn't want to have a family and end up doing to them what he did to us."

"You're not him, that's why. Whatever is in him that makes him seemingly unable to stay in one place, to understand what love and commitment are all about, I don't see any of that in you. If you want to know the truth, I see more of me in you than I do of him." There was silence for a moment, until Curtis said, "I don't think that Craig ever really felt love for anyone, son. Not his parents, not his siblings. Maybe not for any of his wives or his children. There are people like that, you know. They think they love— they try to love and maybe convince themselves that that's what they feel. But inside, there's nothing. Can you look me in the eye and tell me that you've never felt love for anyone?"

Jesse thought of his mother, his sister, and what he was beginning to feel for Brooke. Even his grandfather, whom he was just getting to know, and knew the answer. "No, Pop. That's not me."

"I didn't believe for a second that it was. And I don't believe that you haven't fallen in love because you can't. I think it's because you haven't met the right girl yet. When you do, when you feel that zing to your heart, you'll know it, and you'll do the right thing." Curtis released his seat belt and opened the car door. He swung his legs out and looked back over his shoulder. "But I suggest you move that all along. You aren't getting any younger, you know . . ."

Curtis stood in the doorway and watched his grandson drive away, his heart beating with thanks for the gift he'd been given in Jesse. He closed the door and locked it, took off his overcoat and hung it in the closet, tucked his gloves inside his hat, and left them on the console in the hall. He went into the living room and turned on a lamp, sat in his favorite chair, and picked up the book he'd been reading that afternoon. The crime novel by his favorite author had been delivered from the online bookstore he'd ordered it from—God, but he loved technology!—and he was almost to the end. It bothered him that so far, he'd been unable to identify the killer. In the old days, he'd always known before he got to the middle of the book who the bad guy was. These days, not so much.

He tried to read but his thoughts kept wandering back to dinner and all he and Jesse had talked about. Family relationships. Love. Commitment. Parents and children. Husbands and wives. He'd never been one to talk about such things at such length with anyone but Rose, and it surprised him that he found it so easy to talk to Jesse, whom he'd barely even thought about a year ago. At first he'd thought that it might have been because he spent so much time alone now, that any opportunity to converse had the potential to turn into a discussion, but he knew that wasn't the case. He used to see his son Mike every day at the office, and they'd rarely had such conversations, had almost never discussed their feelings. Perhaps it was because this younger generation of men was more open about sharing how they felt about things. Curtis preferred to believe it was because he and this grandson had a connection.

He picked up the current issue of the *St. Dennis Gazette* that he'd been looking at earlier, and gazed at the picture on the front page. The camera had caught the beautiful young woman and the handsome young man in a waltz's embrace, smiling and gazing into each other's eyes.

Curtis knew that look. He and his Rose had looked at each other in the same way, their smiles only for the other, their eyes never seeing anyone else.

"What do you think, Rose?" he said aloud.

He waited to hear the rustle of that silken robe she liked so much, to smell the scent of gardenias that always accompanied her. Would she come tonight? He sat quietly, the book unopened on his lap, longing for her presence for just a little while. Sometimes he felt her here, sometimes in the conservatory on the side of the house, where she'd once tended her orchids and her gloxinia and those big leafy things she'd loved, some of which had, over time, grown taller than she, who'd been such a tiny thing.

Perhaps she waited for him there tonight as she had in the past. He started to rise, then tilted his head slightly to one side.

"Rose?"

He felt her glide into the room on the whisper of silk. He could not see her—he'd never seen her after she passed—but he could sense her as surely as he had when she was still alive. Funny, he thought, that he, who had never believed in ghosts or spirits or any of what he'd once considered nonsense, now looked forward every waking moment to experiencing just such a presence.

"Funny how it all works out, isn't it, my love?"

He leaned back and closed his eyes, letting the scent of gardenias surround him and fill the room.

"I spent the evening with our boy, Rose. He's a good boy. A good man. You'd like him." He considered for a moment. "Actually, I believe you'd love him. I see so much of myself in him, and nothing of Craig. Funny how sometimes things seem to skip a generation, isn't it?"

Behind him, he heard the faint *shush* of her robe.

"I want him to stay, Rose." He sighed. "I want so very much for him to stay . . ."

Chapter 17

I'M assuming that by now, you've both seen the photos of the bridesmaid dresses Steffie and I picked out while we were in New York." Dallas opened her bag and pulled out a photo and held it up. "Just in case you haven't . . ."

"Ooooh, nice." Vanessa nodded enthusiastically.

"I agree," Brooke said. "I love it."

"Good, 'cause the bride—or in this case, the *brides*— get to choose and you have to wear it." Steffie placed a dish of ice cream in front of each of her friends. She'd closed Scoop at eight on Sunday night so the four of them—she, Dallas, Brooke, and Vanessa— could meet to go over the wedding plans and try out her newest flavors at the same time.

"Lucky for us you have good taste. I've heard some real horror stories about ugly bridesmaid dresses." Brooke dug with the plastic spoon Steffie handed her. "This is really delicious, Stef. What are we calling this?"

"This is Honeymoon Heaven." Steffie grinned. "Just all sweetness and love."

"And coconut, I see," Brooked noted. "What's that other flavor I'm tasting?"

"White chocolate chips and honey." Steffie joined them at the table. "What do you think?"

"I think it's heavenly," Brooke said.

"I agree." Dallas nodded.

"Ness?" Steffie asked. "Did you taste it? What do you think?"

"Oh. I think it's lovely, Stef," Vanessa replied.

"Great. It's unanimous, then. We're serving it at the wedding along with a wedding cake that's yet to be determined and some of Brooke's fantastic 'White Wedding' cupcakes." Steffie licked her spoon.

"Speaking of ice-cream flavors . . . Stef, is there any chance you could make up something special for Mr. Enright?" Brooke asked.

"When did you start calling Jesse 'Mr. Enright'?" Stef asked.

"Not Jesse. Old Mr. Enright. Curtis," Brooke explained. "He's going to be eighty-five in two weeks and Jesse wants to surprise him with a party, and we—that is, Jesse—thought it would be fun to have an ice cream made for him. Of course, we'll—that is, Jesse will understand if you don't have time, with the wedding coming up so soon and everything."

"Oh, I love old Mr. Enright! He's such a sweet old man," Stef said. "I'd love to do something special for him. Let me think, what would be appropriate . . . ?"

Brooke shook her head. "I don't know what he likes. I'll have to ask Jesse."

"I guess it didn't occur to you to ask him last night." Stef smiled and scooped some ice cream onto her spoon. "Or this morning."

Brooke flushed scarlet.

"What's that mean?" Vanessa turned to Brooke. "Are you dating the barrister?"

"I'd say dating is the least of what she's doing." Stef elbowed Brooke.

"Okay, so how do you know about last night?" Brooke stuck her spoon into the mound of ice cream and left it there.

"Brooke." Steffie rolled her eyes. "This is St. Dennis. Your car was parked in his driveway last night when Wade and I came back from Berry's after dinner, and it was there again when we went jogging this morning."

"Seriously? You and Jesse Enright?" Dallas wiped her mouth with a napkin.

"All right. Seriously. Yes. Me and Jesse Enright." Still blushing, Brooke dug into her ice cream.

"Wow. Not bad, Brooke." Vanessa nodded her approval. "Not bad at all."

"He *is* pretty hunky," Stef acknowledged.

"And smart," Dallas added. "We had a long conversation one night about entertainment law. I'm thinking about hiring him to handle some work for me personally and for my studio as I get things finalized."

"I love a smart hunky guy," Stef said.

"You're marrying my little brother," Dallas reminded her.

"Wade's smart and hunky," Stef said defensively. "He's also hot."

"If you say so."

"You're his sister, Dallas. I would hope you didn't

find him hot." Steffie stood up. "Anyone want something to drink? Milk shake? Root-beer float? Iced tea? Water?"

"I'll have water, thanks," Vanessa said.

"I'm good," both Dallas and Brooke replied.

"Speaking of hunky guys . . ." Dallas turned to Brooke. "Who was the cutie you were with at Logan's game on Saturday morning?"

"That was Eric's brother, Jason. He paid a surprise visit. To see Logan. He's sticking around for a few days to spend some time with him and go to a few games. Logan is Jace's only nephew, so he just wants to spend a few days getting to know him a little better."

Steffie returned to the room.

"So what else do we need to know about your wedding plans?" Brooke asked.

"That was a slick attempt to change the subject." Stef handed Vanessa the requested bottle of water. "However slick it may have been, it's been rejected. We're not done grilling you about you and Jesse." She looked around the table. "Anyone feel they've heard enough?"

Dallas and Vanessa both shook their heads.

"There you have it. It's unanimous. So spill." Steffie sat and waited. "What's going on?"

"I'm not even sure *I* know what's going on," Brooke admitted. "I went over to his office the other night and we were going over the changes I wanted in my will, and the next thing I knew, I was on his lap and . . . I don't know, something just came over me and—"

"It's called 'lust,'" Dallas told her. "You've been alone a long, long time, girl."

"I guess." Brooke nodded. "But it wasn't just that. There's something about him that I really like. Something about him that makes me . . ."

"Hot?" Stef suggested.

"No. I mean yes, but no, something more than physical." Brooke thought for a moment, then said softly, "When I'm with Jesse, I don't hurt anymore."

"Awww, honey." Stef got up and put her arm around Brooke. "I don't know what to say."

"There's a first," Vanessa quipped.

"Sounds like this could be serious." Dallas leaned both arms on the table.

"It might be. I'm almost afraid that it could be. When you've loved someone and they're taken from you, the way Eric was taken, you don't ever want to be that vulnerable again. You don't want to ever be in a position to feel that kind of pain again. At least, that's how I felt. But there's something about this guy . . ."

"Sounds to me like you're starting to fall for him," Vanessa said.

"I think maybe I already have."

"How does Jesse feel about you?" Dallas asked. "Do you know?"

Brooke nodded. "I'm pretty sure he feels the same way. He's up-front about things. If this were a fling, I think he'd say so. I think he'd be honest about that."

"No one 'flings' with the Halloween queen in my town," Stef told her. "Bring him to the wedding and we'll all observe."

"That should make for a fun night for all, with everyone watching my every move. Besides," Brooke added, "you're going to be too busy being The Bride to be worried about what I'm doing."

"Don't kid yourself. My capacity for such things is boundless." Steffie gathered the dishes, all of which were empty except for Vanessa's. "Okay, so what didn't you like about it, Ness?"

"What?" Vanessa looked down at the bowl where the ice cream had melted into a creamy soup. "Oh. I guess I'm still full from dinner. Sorry, Stef."

"It's okay. You can taste-test later, if you like. Or tomorrow." Steffie removed the bowls and disposed of them in the trash behind the counter. "Now, since we have so many fun things to celebrate, I think I'll open that bottle of wine I picked up yesterday."

She went into the back room and returned with a bottle and four plastic cups. "I'm glad you and Vanessa like the dresses we picked out, Brooke. We thought they'd go nicely with the overall color scheme, which is basically white. Although Dallas's dress is really silver, but a darker shade than yours."

"Because I've been married before," Dallas reminded them. "I didn't want to wear white. I do have an eight-year-old son."

"I think those old rules are being stretched all the time," Brooke told her. "I think any bride should wear whatever color or whatever dress she wants to wear."

"I agree." Dallas nodded. "And this dark silver is exactly what I wanted. It's all sequin-y and sparkly and I love it. It's just what I had in mind."

"It's spectacular and Dallas looks like . . . well, she looks just like a big Hollywood movie star in it," Steffie told the others.

"It is almost over-the-top," Dallas agreed, "but stops short of 'is she kidding.'"

"Anyway, I'm wearing white." Steffie put the bottle on the table. "I cannot believe that I am going to be wearing a gown designed by Teresa Kearney."

"Me either. Never in a million years did I ever think I'd have something of hers. Even the knockoffs are beyond my reach," Brooke said. "It was very cool of her to offer complimentary gowns for the attendants."

"She's going to be getting a gazillion dollars' worth of free publicity from doing Dallas's dress. She *should* do something special for the wedding party." Steffie opened the wine. "Anyway, for Dallas's wedding, we're wearing the silver dresses and carrying white bouquets that will be dusted with silver glitter. For my wedding, you all and Dallas—who will wear her silver wedding dress—will wear wide satin sashes."

"What color?" Brooke asked.

Steffie grinned. "The MacGregor tartan. On the sash and wrapped around the bouquets, which for me will be white and red. No glitter. Oh, and I found shoes that are made in the tartan plaid. I'll need your shoe size so I can order those, everyone. And that reminds me, I'm going to have to have Grant call his former wife and make sure that Paige can come to St. Dennis to have her dress fitted. Not that the child would mind. She'd rather be here with her father than in Ohio with her mother."

Dallas took a small notebook from her bag and started to write. "Paige will need two pairs of shoes, then, since she's in both ceremonies. I'll get her size for you, Stef, so that you can order a pair of the plaid ones for her." She looked up at her soon-to-be sister-in-law. "Do they have flats?"

"They do, but I think she can wear a small heel. She's thirteen now." Steffie began to pour wine into the plastic cups.

"You're right. I should have thought of that. Don't want to get off on the wrong foot with my future stepdaughter." Dallas made another note in her pad.

"Was that a sort of pun?" Brooke asked. "Shoes? Wrong foot?"

"A poor attempt at best." Dallas took the cup of wine that Steffie handed her and took a sip. "Oh, this is yummy. Where's it from?"

Brooke picked up the bottle and read the label. "Oh, Ballard Vineyards. I didn't know they were putting out such nice wine."

Steffie sat and picked up her glass. "Let's toast the upcoming wedding."

"And Brooke's new relationship." Dallas took a sip. "I think we need to celebrate that as well."

"Okay, and we should also . . ." Steffie paused and looked across the table at Vanessa. "Is there something wrong with the wine, Ness? You haven't touched it."

"I guess I'm just not in the mood for wine." Vanessa tapped her fingers on the side of the cup and looked everywhere except at one of her friends.

"You are always in the mood for wine." Stef put her own cup down. "Are you sick?"

"No."

"Are you . . . depressed?"

"No."

"Then are you—" Steffie stopped midsentence. "Vanessa Keaton, look me in the eye."

"No."

"Talk," demanded Steffie. "We're your best friends. If something's wrong, we can help you. Did someone say something that upset you? We'll . . . why, we'll . . ." She thought for a moment. "We'll beat them up for you, right?" She looked to Dallas and Brooke for confirmation and they both nodded.

Vanessa sighed. "It seems as if . . . that is, I got one of those little test things . . . and . . . and . . ."

"Oh my God." Stef reached across the table. "Are you pregnant?"

Vanessa's eyes filled and she nodded. "It appears as if I am."

"Why, that's wonderful! A little baby Nessie or Grady!" Steffie pulled Vanessa from her chair and hugged her. "Aren't you thrilled?"

"I don't know. I'm not sure how I feel," Vanessa said.

"What's wrong, sweetie?" Dallas asked.

"Well, for one thing, you guys might remember that Grady and I are not married."

"Have you told him?" Brooke reached out and took Vanessa's hand.

Vanessa nodded. "He's over the moon. He can't wait to get married and . . ."

"And . . . ?" Brooke coaxed her to finish.

"And what if he only wants to marry me because I'm pregnant?" Vanessa sniffed back tears.

"Are we talking about the same Grady Shields who's been talking marriage for the past six months?" Steffie tugged her friend back to her chair. "The same

Grady Shields who sold his house in Montana and moved his business here to be with you? The same guy who flies back and forth between here and the great American West a couple of times every month so that he can keep his business *and* live with you?"

Vanessa nodded.

"So when Grady asked you to marry him . . . when did that happen, anyway?" Steffie frowned.

"Thursday night." Vanessa sniffed back tears that Brooke thought she was awfully close to shedding.

"And you said what, sweetie?" Brooke asked.

"I didn't say anything. I just cried. He figured that meant yes, because he said something about talking to Beck and Hal . . . you know, ask for my hand or whatever it is guys do with the men in the woman's family."

"Awww, that's so sweet," Steffie cooed. "How could you not say yes to a man like that? How could you not say yes to Grady? You're totally head over heels in love with him."

"Could I remind you all that I was married before?" Vanessa looked from one to the other. "Not once, but twice? Neither of those turned out so good."

"Well, duh. Husband number one was an old man who you married to get away from a crazy home situation, and husband number two was an abusive psychopath you married to get away from husband number one. Neither of those relationships has anything in common with what you and Grady have," Steffie assured her. "Didn't you tell me that you're happier now than you've ever been in your life? That Grady is the best thing that ever happened to you?"

Vanessa nodded. "Yes, but—"

"There are no *buts* in love. You and Grady belong together. Sometimes you just have to trust, Ness. This is one of them."

"You're right. Of course you're right. You're all right," Vanessa said. "I'm being goofy, that's all." She pushed her chair back and stood up. "I think I'll go home now, if we're through here."

"Go home and make sure Grady knows the answer was yes." Brooke stood and hugged her.

"A resounding yes." Dallas waited her turn to give Vanessa a hug, too.

"Come on, I'll walk you out," Steffie told her.

"No need. I'm parked right out the back." Vanessa kissed Steffie on the cheek. "You really are the very best friend I've ever had."

"Of course I am." Steffie walked with her to the back door and unlocked it.

"I love you guys, too," Vanessa called to Dallas and Brooke.

"Love you, Ness," they both called back.

"Isn't that nice? Another wedding to look forward to." Steffie came back with a huge smile on her face. "And a baby. That's the first baby for our little group. It's exciting."

" 'There are no *buts* in love'?" Brooke deadpanned. "Seriously, Stef?"

"It was the first thing that popped into my head." Steffie looked sheepish. "Okay, I admit it wasn't my best."

There was silence for a moment, then Brooke and Dallas began to giggle. Steffie looked wounded for all of about five seconds before she joined in.

"All right, it was bad." Steffie picked up the wine bottle and refilled the three cups. When she finished, she raised her cup and said, "To happily-ever-afters for all of us. To beautiful weddings and beautiful new babies and beautiful new beginnings and for finding love when we least expect it." She grinned and because she just couldn't resist, added, "No *buts* about it."

The following evening, while Brooke was studying for one of her exams, her phone rang.

"Bing Cherry Barrister," the voice on the other end said.

"Excuse me?" Brooke asked. "Who is this?"

"It's Stef. The ice cream for Mr. Enright's birthday party is going to be Bing Cherry Barrister. I was trying to think of something really good, and I remembered that he always asks for chopped-up cherries on his ice cream when he comes in to Scoop."

"That's terrific, Stef. But are you sure you'll have time . . . ?"

"I'll make time for him. He was my mom's cousin Horace's attorney. You know, the Cousin Horace who left me his house in his will? So no, it won't be a problem. Just let me know how many people we can look forward to serving."

"As soon as I know, you'll know. The invitations only went out a few days ago, though."

"I've never met a guy yet who would think that's a problem." Steffie laughed and hung up.

Brooke sat for a moment with the phone in her hand. Finally, she dialed Jesse's number.

"Stef's on board to make a special flavor for your

grandfather's birthday," Brooke told him when he picked up. "Bing Cherry Barrister."

"That's great. Thanks for asking her. I was going to stop down earlier today, but the day got away from me and then I took my grandfather to dinner."

"Think he'll be surprised about the party?"

"Oh, yeah. There's no way he'd ever suspect. It's going to be very cool."

Brooke could sense him grinning, could almost see the dimples and the dancing light in his eyes. He was obviously tickled about the whole idea of surprising his grandfather.

"I guess you haven't had any RSVPs yet."

"Actually, I did have a few via return email." He paused. "I think there might be more than one surprise that night. I hope he's okay with it."

"What do you mean?"

"I invited a few . . . relatives he hasn't seen in a long time. I hope he's glad to see them, if they show up."

"Maybe you should have talked to Violet before you mailed them out. Or your uncle Mike."

"Mike's in Florida, but I'm not sure he would have been the best person to ask. I did speak with Violet, though, and she thought it was a good idea, so I'm trusting her. We'll see."

"Sounds mysterious," Brooke said.

"I'll tell you about it sometime." Jesse paused. "Actually, if you wanted to come over right now, I could tell you tonight."

"Are you trying to lure me over with the promise of revealing family secrets just to get me into your lair?"

"Yeah. Is it working?"

"Not tonight, I'm afraid. I have an exam tomorrow and another one on Thursday."

"Damn. That pretty much takes care of the week." Jesse sounded genuinely disappointed. "And I had such plans for us this week."

"Good plans?"

"You betcha."

"Will they still be good next week?"

"I have a trial that's supposed to begin next Monday," he said thoughtfully. "The prep might tie me up most of the weekend. But if there's a break, or if the trial is postponed, I'll let you know." He paused. "If nothing else, we can at least get together for dinner one night, okay?"

"Sure. After Thursday, though." Brooke thought of all she had to do this week. She could barely keep up with her cupcake orders. "Maybe Friday night."

"I'm writing you in for dinner at . . . where do you want to go?"

She thought it over. Maybe someplace out of town, away from the prying eyes of her neighbors. That Steffie had figured out that there was something going on between her and Jesse didn't bother Brooke. Stef was a friend, as were Vanessa and Dallas, and she probably would have ended up telling them on Sunday night anyway. But not everyone in St. Dennis needed to know.

"How about Stop Four over in Ballard? It's a beautiful old place with lots of fireplaces and everyone says it has wonderful food."

"I'll make reservations first thing in the morning. Is seven good for you?"

"Seven is perfect."

"I'll see you then."

"I can't wait," Jesse said.

She wanted to say, *Neither can I,* but she couldn't get the words out. Instead, she said, "Good night, Jesse," and hung up.

She tried to concentrate on the notes she'd taken all semester, but her mind insisted on wandering back to Saturday night and Sunday morning. She sighed and forced the images from her mind. Thinking too hard about Jesse right now would be a little like staring too long into the sun. She'd be blinded and unable to see anything else, unable to think about anything else. Best to focus on the task at hand, which was doing well on her exams this week, getting her degree, and all the cupcakes she'd have to bake between now and tomorrow morning. Of course, if he should slip into her dreams again tonight, the way he had the night before, well, she wasn't responsible if her subconscious wanted to replay their night together over and over. And if that same subconscious insisted on looking forward to other nights and other mornings, she had no control over that either, right?

And yet, as much as she tried to keep focused on her notes, she found her mind wandering to things he said and things they did, and she couldn't deny the longing that stirred inside her. Jesse had awakened emotions she'd stopped feeling, had come to believe she'd never feel again. She was painfully aware of the promises she'd made to herself, that she'd never let herself be devastated by love again. But for the first time, she wasn't sure it was a promise she'd be able to keep.

It wasn't just lust, she insisted. It wasn't just about sex, though that had been outstanding. It was more about heart—and the fact that Jesse had more than any man she knew. And wasn't that what every woman was looking for?

Brooke sighed. It certainly worked for her.

Chapter 18

"Wow." Jesse was standing in the living room of the Madison farm talking to Brooke's mother when Brooke came into the room. "Like the dress."

"Thanks. Ready?" Brooke flashed a smile she hoped would knock him out. It appeared to work.

"Sure. Yes." He turned to her mother. "Good talking to you, Mrs. Madison."

"It's Hannah, and it was nice talking to you as well, Jesse." Hannah nodded and went into the kitchen.

"Well, that was awkward," Brooke told Jesse after they'd gotten into the car. "I haven't had a guy come to pick me up at my parents' house since I was in high school."

"Tell me about it. How long do you think it's been since I had to make nice with my date's mother?" Jesse laughed. "You said you're moving into your house when?"

"Hopefully sooner rather than later." She fastened her seat belt. "Clay said Cam's coming out on Tuesday with his carpenters to start replacing the windows before it gets too cold, then they're going to move on to remodeling the kitchen and building the new first-floor powder room and the laundry room. Then they'll work on the new bath upstairs and they're going to build some closets. He's going to have the roofers working at the same time. Cam says the entire project won't take too long because his guys need the work right now and if he can keep them all busy for a while it's good for everyone."

"Like how long?"

"I guess a few months at the most."

"Can't you live there while the work is being done?"

Brooke laughed. "Maybe I should have picked you up at your place."

"We'll try that next time."

"Did you mind so terribly?" she asked. "My mother's really harmless."

"I didn't. Especially when you look like that."

Brooke smiled to herself. She'd realized last night that she didn't have anything to wear. Everything in her closet was either too dressy or too casual. She put the matter aside until after she finished her exam, then fled straight to Vanessa's shop.

"Something I can help you with?" Vanessa asked politely while writing up the sales for another customer, then winked at Brooke. "Anything in particular you're looking for today?"

"I need a dress," Brooke told her. "Something terrific, but not too dressy. Easy lines, but nothing too casual. A little bit low, a little fitted, but not slutty."

Vanessa had continued talking to her customers but pulled the black knit dress with the low cowl neckline off the rack and handed it to Brooke.

"I have it in green as well, but I think the black is what you're looking for."

Brooke went into the fitting room to try it on. A few moments later, she stepped out into the shop and peered around the corner.

"Let's see you. Oh, I love it, do you?" Vanessa was walking her customer to the door.

"I do." Brooke turned around in front of the mirror and caught Vanessa frowning. "What?"

"Stay there." Vanessa disappeared to the front of the store, then returned, a mustard-colored belt in her hands. She wrapped the belt loosely around Brooke's hips. "There you go. You needed a bit of color."

"Thanks." Brooke took a quick glance around the shop. "Your customers are all gone?"

Vanessa nodded.

"So how are you feeling?" Brooke asked.

"Good. Great. Everything's fine," Vanessa assured her.

"What does that mean, exactly?"

"It means that Grady and I will tie the knot very quietly so as not to draw attention from the other two happy brides in town." Vanessa unbelted the belt and slung it lower on Brooke's hips. "I think you want to wear it lower, like this."

"What does that mean?" Brooke frowned.

"It means you don't want to belt it so tightly."

"Not that. The part about you and Grady tying the knot quietly. What's quietly? And why?"

"I don't want to take even a second of the spotlight from anyone. Not that anyone could ever compete with Dallas, but there is Steffie to consider. You know she's waited for Wade her whole entire life . . . well, since she was something like thirteen, so I want her to have her day." Vanessa paused, but before Brooke could get a word in, she went on. "Of course, she's sharing that day with her brother and Dallas, but that's a little different because Dallas has been married before, so it isn't her first trip down the aisle. Not that it's any less special, but—"

"Vanessa." Brooke took her by the shoulders. "Stop. You're babbling."

"Sorry. Anyway, don't tell Steffie, okay?"

"You haven't told her yet? She's going to be so excited and happy for you," Brooke told her.

"She can be happy for me when it's over."

"You mean, you're not going to tell her before . . . ?" Vanessa shook her head, no.

"Are you crazy? Steffie will kill you if you get married behind her back."

"I'm not getting married behind her back. I'm just not going to tell her until later."

"Ness, she's your very best friend."

"I know that. That's why I don't want to take anything from her big day."

"I repeat. She's going to kill you."

"She'll get over it." Vanessa tried to make light.

"No, she won't. She loves you like a . . . like a sister."

"I love her like a sister, too." Vanessa bit her bottom lip and Brooke was pretty sure she was close to tears.

"So let her be part of your day. She's going to be absolutely crushed if she isn't."

"She's just so focused on herself right now—and should be," Vanessa added quickly. "I thought it would be better for everyone if Grady and I just went to the courthouse and got married there and told everyone after Wade and Steffie get back from their honeymoon."

"That idea stinks, Ness, and you know it."

"Oh, maybe." Vanessa plunked down in one of the velvet club chairs she had placed near the dressing rooms. "Grady didn't think it was so hot either."

"This is his first marriage, right? And he's from a big family?"

Vanessa nodded. "Very big family."

"They'll never forgive you either." Brooke took off the belt and placed it on the counter. "You will not only alienate your new in-laws, but you'll lose your best friend at the same time. Good thinking, Ness. Way to go."

"What would you do if you were me?" Vanessa asked. "Obviously I don't want to wait too long. Everyone will know . . ." She patted her abdomen.

"That's not quite as much of a scandal as it used to be." It was the only thing Brooke could think of to say.

"It isn't just that. My mother was pregnant with me when she left the man who fathered me. I was raised by stepfathers." Vanessa looked up. "Notice I said step*fathers*. A whole slew of them. I don't want to be like my mother."

"You will never be like your mother, Ness." Brooke smiled and pushed the hair back from her friend's face. "You forget, I've met your mother."

"So what would you do?" Vanessa repeated.

"I would wait until Steffie calms down a bit, then I'd tell her. I'd plan the wedding for two weeks after Stef's if you really want to give her the undivided spotlight, which is already divided because of Dallas."

"That's my point. Stef would have to share it two ways."

"She's not a four-year-old who demands that all the attention be on her, you know."

"That's why, this time, she should have it. She's waited a long time for this."

"So have you, sweetie," Brooke reminded her as she went back into the dressing room.

The dress and belt had come home with Brooke, who'd known the dress was just right the minute she tried it on. The look on Jesse's face was exactly what she'd wanted it to be. She was aware that she turned more than a few heads when she and Jesse were led through the restaurant to their table.

"One of our most requested tables," the fawning maître d' told them. "A lovely view of the Bay, and close enough to the fireplace to feel its glow. Enjoy."

"I should take you to dinner more often," Jesse said, "if only to get the best tables."

Brooke smiled at the waiter when he brought their menus and took their drink orders.

"So, have you had many responses to the invitations to the surprise party?" she asked.

"I have. People who had other plans have canceled them or are trying to cancel them. It seems everyone wants to be there to honor Pop. I think it will make him very happy if everyone shows up." His eyes clouded with doubt. "At least, I'm hoping he will be."

"You said that the other night on the phone. If you

thought there was someone he wouldn't be happy to see, why would you invite that person?"

Jesse appeared to be mulling that over when the waiter brought their drinks and offered to give them more time to look over their menus, which lay untouched on the table.

"It isn't that I think he won't be happy . . . it's just that I don't know for sure." He opened the menu, and began to scan it. "Did you say you'd been here before? Do you know what's good?"

"I'm sure the waiter will be more than happy to rattle off the specials when he comes back." Brooke looked up. "And here he comes . . ."

They both decided on an entrée of fried Chesapeake oysters and beef tenderloin. Jesse looked over the wine list and ordered a bottle of Merlot from a local vineyard.

"How many people do you think you'll have?" Brooke redirected the conversation. "I'll need to know for the cupcakes and Steffie will need to know for the ice cream. And of course, Lola's will have to know as well."

"Right now, I'm going to guess maybe eighty-five people."

"Does that upstairs room at Lola's even hold that many people?"

"I guess so." Jesse frowned. "They didn't give me a limit."

"Didn't they ask you?"

"I told Jimmy I'd get back to him. I guess he was thinking there wouldn't be that many who'd want to come. Frankly, I hadn't given it much thought at all."

"Give Jimmy a call in the morning and tell him how many have confirmed so far and how many more you're waiting to hear from," Brooke suggested.

"What if he says they don't have the room?"

"Then I guess you'll be calling around for a caterer who can throw together something fabulous at the last minute and sending out another email changing the venue from Lola's to your place."

He looked so pathetic that Brooke couldn't help but reach across the table to pat his hand. He curled his fingers around hers.

"I'll help you, don't worry," she assured him. "Mr. Enright deserves to have a happy eighty-fifth and he will. Regardless of where you have it, he'll be happy that you thought to do this for him and that so many people wanted to mark the occasion with him. You'll see."

"You're right." With his free hand, he took a sip of his wine. "At least, I hope you are."

He played with her fingers for a few moments, then said, "The first time I came to St. Dennis to meet him, he tried to scare me away."

"I'm confused. When did you meet him the first time? And why would he try to scare you away?"

"My dad was his oldest son. The one, apparently, he'd planned to turn over the firm to one day."

"Why didn't he?"

"Because my dad was . . . is . . . a screwup. He was asked to leave two colleges and only got into law school because my great-grandfather had given the school a lot of money. He's gone through three wives and he's going on his fourth. He has kids he rarely thinks about because he's too busy thinking about himself. He lost his license to practice law because he was accused of having embezzled funds from a client. There's more, but I think I made my point."

Brooke sat back against the chair, too shocked to form a quick response. Finally, she simply said, "Wow."

Jesse nodded grimly. "My grandparents were very fond of Dad's first wife. Delia Enright, you ever hear of her?"

"The mystery writer? Sure. Wait . . . she was married to your father?"

"Had three kids with him, but he walked out on them when they were really little. After that, she shut out my grandparents with no explanation, and they weren't allowed to see the kids again, which apparently hurt them both very much. So when my dad remarried and had my sister and me, they were very tentative about getting too close to us. When my dad left my mother, and my mom wasn't feeling particularly friendly to the Enrights, and my grandmother died, my grandfather just sort of wrote off Sophie and me."

"These other siblings of yours . . . have they ever reconciled with your grandfather?"

"No, but that could change very soon. Depending on how they respond to their invitations."

"You invited them?"

"Violet at first wasn't sure, but then, after she thought it over, said it was the right thing to do. I figure invite them and they come or they don't, it's up to them. If they decide to come, whatever happens is between them and my grandfather."

"But you've never met them."

He shook his head. "I just recently learned their names. I have a half brother named Nick who's a marine biologist, and two half sisters, Zoey and Georgia."

"Zoey Enright," Brooke murmured. "Why do I know that name?"

"She works for one of those televised shopping channels."

Brooke snapped her fingers. "That's it. The Home MarketPlace. I saw her on TV. She's gorgeous and funny . . . and she's your *sister*?"

"My *half* sister."

"Oh, wow. It never occurred to me to connect the last name. I wonder what she's like in person. She's adorable on TV."

"Well, I guess we'll find out soon enough." Jesse leaned back to allow the server to place their entrées on the table. "Or not."

"Will you be upset if they decline?"

"Not as upset as I'd be if they totally ignored the invitation. I think that would bother me."

"Why?" She picked up her fork and stabbed at one of the plump oysters on her plate.

"Because the invitation was from me, and theirs was a very personal invitation that I wrote specifically to them, telling them who I was and asking them to come."

After a moment she said, "So if they don't respond and they don't come, you'll feel it's a rejection of you as well as of him."

"Now who's the smarty pants?" He tried to make a

joke, but she could tell by the look in his eyes that he wasn't taking the situation lightly.

"You do understand that if they choose not to come, it will be their loss, not yours?"

His eyes met hers across the table, and he put down his fork. He got up from his chair and slid into the one next to her, took her hand, and kissed the inside of her wrist.

"How did I ever get so lucky," he said softly, "to have you in my life?"

"Right place, right time?"

Jesse shook his head. "It's more than that, like having been drawn to St. Dennis was as much about finding you as it was about finding myself."

"For the record, I'm very glad you're here." She spoke the words slowly, words she never thought she'd say to anyone. "I don't really know where this is going to lead, but I'm in for the journey."

"It's bound to be a long one," he cautioned her. "You still on board?"

Brooke nodded. "Still on board."

He kissed the palm of her hand. "Come home with me. Stay with me tonight."

She covered her face in her hands and groaned. "I can't. Logan is home and I have to make tomorrow's cupcakes because I didn't make them after school like I planned."

"What did you do instead?"

"I went to Bling and bought this dress."

"It may have been worth it."

"You're not the one who has eight dozen cupcakes to bake when you get home."

"I'll come home with you and help," he said. "It's

not the same as you coming home with me and staying over, but I'm not ready to say good night. I want to be with you, whether it's in my bed—which would be my first choice—or in your kitchen. I'll take whatever time I can get."

"Jesse, that's really sweet, but watching me bake will not be very interesting," she told him. "It's just measuring and mixing."

"I don't mind."

"All right." She gave his hand a squeeze. "I *am* sorry. About not being able to stay . . . I probably should have told you that when you asked me out."

"I didn't ask you out tonight so that you'd sleep with me," he said, and she wasn't sure there wasn't just a hint of rebuke in his tone. "I asked you out because I want to be with you, spend some time with you. I'd have been real happy if we'd ended up at my place tonight—I'm not going to lie—but I didn't ask you to dinner figuring that was a given. I missed seeing you this week, missed talking to you."

"I missed seeing you, too," she told him.

"Come on, let's go back to the farm and bake."

Brooke had turned on the oven to heat up to the temperature she needed, gotten out her mixing bowls and spoons, her flour and sugar and butter, and placed everything on the big kitchen table that had presided over the Madison kitchen for more years than anyone could remember, even Hannah, who claimed it was there when she moved in as a bride.

Jesse had taken off his sport jacket and hung it over the back of a chair.

"Here." Brooke handed him a measuring cup. "Measure three cups of flour into this bowl. I'm going to run upstairs and see Logan and change into something else."

"Do you have to? That dress really is something."

"It will be something very messy if I don't get out of it now. And I'll need a few minutes to tuck in Logan."

"No need to, dear." Hannah came into the kitchen through the back door. "I just dropped him off at Cody's. It seems some big producer friend of Dallas's sent them a preview video of some upcoming movie that all the kids are talking about. Cody called right after you left and wanted Logan to come over to watch it with him and stay over. Dallas said she'll get the boys to soccer in the morning, so he took his uniform with him." She paused in the doorway leading to the hall. "I didn't think you'd mind."

"Mind? No, of course I don't mind." Brooke smiled. "Thanks, Mom."

"I'm turning in early myself," Hannah continued. "I spent all day moving furniture around in my new house. I'm exhausted. Oh, and Clay and Jason went down to Captain Walt's. God only knows when they'll be back."

Hannah blew Brooke a kiss, then headed for the stairs.

Brooke turned and looked at Jesse.

"We could probably bake just as well at my house as we could here, don't you think?" he asked.

"We'd have to pack up a lot of stuff." She looked around the kitchen at everything she'd already pulled out.

"It would be worth it." He came up behind her and kissed her neck.

"What happened to 'Brooke, it's all right if you can't stay tonight. I'm happy just to be with you'?"

"Oh, that. I was rationalizing." He hastened to add, "Not that I wouldn't be happy to just stay here and bake. That would be fine, too. Really. It's up to you. Whatever you decide is all right with me. It's sort of either-or as far as I'm concerned."

"You are *so* not a good liar." Brooke laughed.

"Look, you have to do the baking, it's your job, right?"

"Right." She sighed. She had commitments to fill, some of which had to be dropped off before seven the next morning.

"So we'll do the baking here. We'll pack up the cupcakes and whatever you need for the frostings and we'll take it to my place. At which time we'll take a little break, maybe, oh, nap a little or something, and then we'll do the frosting thing." Jesse put his arms around her. "What do you say? Sound like a plan?"

"Sounds like win-win. I like it." She nodded. "I'm going to go upstairs and change and then we'll get to work."

She ran halfway up the steps, then stopped and turned back. "Thanks, Jesse. I do need to get this baking finished. There's no way tomorrow could come and I'd not be able to deliver what I promised to my customers."

Jesse walked to the bottom of the steps. "There's no way I'd want you to jeopardize what you're working so hard to build. It's all good, Brooke. Go on and change."

"Thanks, Jess." She started back up the steps.

"Bring clothes for tomorrow," he called up after her. "And tell Hannah not to wait up . . ."

Chapter 19

JESSE had liked the apple-maple-walnut cupcakes they'd made on Friday night so much that he requested that Brooke add those to the list of cupcakes she was making for his grandfather's birthday party.

"And maybe something pumpkin-y," he'd said. "I know he likes pumpkin. And pecans. Do you have a recipe for something with pecans and pumpkin?"

"I have recipes for just about every flavor you can think of and some you haven't," she'd told him.

"Great. Pop likes variety."

"Pop likes variety," Brooke muttered to herself as she looked over the final list on Thursday morning. Jesse's final count for the party was over one hundred guests. He still hadn't heard from his half siblings, but she didn't see any sign that he was any more worried about that than he had been the week before.

"If they come, they come," he'd told her when he called to give her what he thought might be the final head count. "And maybe if not this time, maybe some other time they'll want to get in touch. This time isn't about me. It's about our grandfather, and they'll either show up to honor him or they won't."

Brooke figured a guest list that size was good for two cupcakes per person, but she was throwing in an extra few dozen just in case. She would hate for the desserts to run out, although there would be ice cream, she reminded herself. In addition to the cupcakes, she planned to make her usual chocolate-covered strawberries and truffles. Some of the cupcakes would be on tall cake stands, some on wire cupcake displays, some on shorter cake plates, others on round or rectangular silver trays. Besides the strawberries and handmade truffles, she'd add some sugared fruit to decorate the trays. She worked all day Thursday and all day Friday and both nights as well, and took off only for Logan's Saturday-morning soccer game.

"How's it look?" Jesse asked her after the game.

"It's all coming together." She nodded.

"Want me to come over and help you transport the cupcakes?"

"My mom's going to be driving her own car, and Clay will probably bring his, too, so they can take some of the boxes. I think we'll be okay. Let me worry about the cupcakes. You have other things to do," she reminded him. "Olivia promised to have the flowers there by five. And don't forget about the balloons. They'll be ready for you to pick up anytime after two on Saturday afternoon."

"Remind me again what I'm doing with the balloons?"

"You're going to be tying them to the sandbags that will be in the room when you get there. When I placed the order, I told them to make sure that the strings attached to the balloons were really long. You want them to sort of float above the crowd. And you're going to save a bunch of them to tie onto the back of your grandfather's chair."

"Okay. Right. Float above the crowd. Tie to the back of a chair. Got it." He gave her a quick peck on the cheek and took off for the parking lot.

Brooke couldn't help but smile. She knew that Jesse was so into this party because he wanted everything to be just right for his grandfather. Especially since Violet had mentioned that Curtis hadn't really celebrated a birthday since his wife died. Rose had always made a big fuss over every family milestone, Violet had noted, but after she passed away, no one had stepped forward to pick up that torch.

"Nice of your boyfriend to invite me to his party." Jason sauntered over from the bench where he'd been helping Logan unknot the laces of his soccer shoes.

"Yeah, well, he's a pretty nice guy," Brooke replied.

"Everyone seems to think so."

"Everyone is right." Brooke picked up her bag where she'd tossed it onto the ground when Logan had made a run toward the goal.

"I'm sorry," she heard Jason say.

"Excuse me?" She turned around.

"I said, I'm sorry. For being such a jerk where"— Jason nodded in Jesse's direction—"he's concerned. I know I said it before, but it bears repeating. I was out of line."

"Thanks, Jason. I appreciate that."

"Besides, it's none of my business what you do with your life." He cleared his throat. "That is, you do have a life. You ought to be living it. With someone." He took a deep breath. "Maybe even him."

"I very much appreciate that. Let me tell you this about Jesse so you can maybe understand one of the reasons I think he's so special." She swung the bag over her shoulder and lowered her sunglasses onto her face. "He's the only guy I've gone out with since Eric died who seemed to understand that I'll always carry something of Eric inside me—and he doesn't feel threatened by it."

Jason nodded. "Like I said, I heard he was a nice guy."

"Hey, Uncle Jason!" Logan called. "We're going to Scoop! Come on!"

"Be right there, buddy." Jason took a few steps, then stopped and said, "I hope you don't mind that I'm still around. Logan's all the family I have now, and I want to get to know him a little more before I take off."

"No, he isn't your only family," Brooke corrected. "He may be your only blood relative, but you have me, and my mom and Clay. We're still your family, Jace. You might want to think about that when you're deciding what to do and where to go. You don't have to be a lone wolf, pal. You do have family here."

"Thanks, Brooke. That means a lot to me. I haven't decided yet where I'll go. I do want to stay in land-scaping, but—"

"Uncle Jason! They're leaving without us!" Logan was starting to panic at the thought of being left behind.

To Jason, Brooke said, "Better catch up." To Logan, she called, "Have fun, guys," and waved. She wanted to blow a kiss, but had been chastised before for such public displays of motherly affection, especially where one of her son's athletic teams was concerned.

Brooke turned up the collar of her jacket against the brisk November breeze and hurried to her car. She had a lot of cupcakes to frost and decorate between now and six o'clock when she'd promised Jesse she'd be at Lola's to help with any last minute details. It was important to him, and so, she realized, it was important to her.

By four thirty, the cupcakes were all frosted and decorated with chopped nuts, coconut, sparkly colored sugar, tiny fondant apples, or cornucopias from which spilled tinier pieces of fruit. Brooke took a shower, which revived her, and slipped into a dress she hadn't remembered she had but was just right for a party such as this one—a dark red sheath with long sleeves and a sweetheart neckline. She paused at her jewelry box before deciding on dangling silver earrings and a ruby ring that had been her grandmother's that she wore on her right ring finger. She'd eyed a string of pearls that Eric had given her on their first anniversary, but put them back into their box, not sure she'd ever wear them again. Maybe she'd keep them to pass on to Logan's bride someday.

Brooke pulled her hair back into a low ponytail and went into the bathroom to put on makeup. She usually didn't wear all that much, but tonight was special and she wanted to wow everyone as much as possible. Jesse's family would be there—his sister Sophie had planned to arrive that afternoon—and she wanted to look her best. She grabbed shoes out of the closet and slid into them as she hurried down the stairs. At Clay's suggestion and with his help, they loaded the cupcakes into the cupcake van and he drove it to Lola's back door. They carried boxes up the stairs, where they were unpacked and the cupcakes put on display before Clay returned to the farm to change and pick up Jason. Brooke fussed a bit with their presentation as the first guests started to arrive, Jesse and a pretty dark-haired young woman being the first to be led up the stairs by the hostess, whom Brooke was introduced to as Lola's grandniece, also named Lola.

"Olivia's flowers are gorgeous, and you did a fantastic job with the balloons, Jess," Brooke told him.

"It didn't look quite this good when I finished, but my sister was on hand to straighten it all out," he confided. "Come meet Sophie . . ."

Jesse took Brooke by the hand and introduced her to the pretty girl with the sharply angled dark hair.

"I've heard so much about you," Sophie told Brooke. "I could have picked you out in a crowd anywhere, I think. Jesse described you perfectly."

"Oh?" Brooke raised an eyebrow and glanced at Jesse.

"It was all good," he assured her.

"Absolutely all good." Sophie nodded. "Now, Jess tells me you're a phenomenal baker and a single mother and you're finishing up your bachelor's. Tell me how you balance everything because I swear, I have trouble looking after myself some weeks when my job gets crazy . . ."

Brooke and Sophie chatted until guests began to fill the room and Brooke found herself stopping every second sentence to introduce Sophie to another arrival.

"We'll finish our conversation later," Brooke promised Sophie. "I want to hear what it's like to be a criminal prosecutor . . ."

At six thirty, Jesse left to pick up Curtis, who had been led to believe he was having a nice quiet dinner with his grandson again this weekend.

By six forty-five, all the guests who'd accepted Jesse's invitation had filed into the room at the top of the stairs—all except for Jesse and Sophie's three half siblings. It was almost time for Curtis to arrive. Brooke noticed that Sophie couldn't stop checking her watch for the time.

"It's only about a minute past the last time you looked," she whispered in Sophie's ear. "Don't worry. Jesse will get him here on time. Besides, everyone's here, so you don't have to be concerned that your grandfather will run into anyone downstairs and have the surprise ruined."

"I'm not worried about Jesse getting Pop here. It's the others." Sophie frowned. "The other Enright kids. Jesse insisted on inviting them. I thought it was a bad idea from the get-go but he really wanted them to know it was Pop's birthday and that they were welcome. Now they're not going to show and he's going to be crushed."

"Jesse won't be crushed," Brooke assured her. "He'll be disappointed in them, but he won't be crushed. He knows this isn't about him. It's about your grandfather."

"He said that?"

Brooke nodded. "He'll be okay with whatever happens. I think the only thing he's worried about where they're concerned is how your grandfather will react if they do show."

"It could get interesting, either way," Sophie agreed. "I guess we'll know pretty soon how it's going to play out."

"Shhhh," someone said. "I think they're here."

The crowd went silent and gathered to the left of the stairs where they wouldn't be immediately noticed. From the stairwell they could hear the hostess explaining to Curtis why they had to be seated upstairs instead of on the first floor.

" . . . decided to open up the second floor for dining because there's such a beautiful view of the Bay from those big windows," young Lola was saying.

"It's dark out," Curtis was heard to remind her. "You can't see a damned thing."

Giggles were muffled as the three pairs of footsteps drew near.

"Well, you can see the lights from the marina," Lola was saying. "Besides, we have several large parties of diners tonight who reserved almost every table downstairs."

"Surprise!" a hundred voices yelled as Curtis appeared at the top of the steps.

Curtis looked around as if not quite understanding at first that the surprise was for him. When the lights finally went on, he placed a hand over his heart.

"Oh, my. For me?" He glanced from familiar face to familiar face. "Oh, my, what a surprise. Did you do this, son?" He grabbed Jesse by the arm.

"With much help from Violet," Jesse told him. "And Brooke helped to organize things here."

"What a wonderful surprise." Curtis hugged his grandson. "Thank you, Jess. This was very thoughtful of you. Very thoughtful." He pounded Jesse on the back several times before being engulfed by well-wishers.

"You pulled it off." Brooke stepped back from the crowd and elbowed Jesse. "He was really surprised."

"I'm not so sure," Jesse leaned over to confide. "He's been smiling a lot since I picked him up. Humming and smiling. Not his usual demeanor."

"How would he have known?"

"Someone could have spilled it to him." Jesse eyed Violet suspiciously. "There's my number one suspect. There, did you see that? They just winked at each other."

"That doesn't mean a thing." Brooke waved a dismissive hand. "They could be sharing a joke."

"I suppose. And I guess it doesn't really matter. What matters is that everyone came and he's happy with the whole thing."

"I agree." Brooke nodded. "Did you see your uncle Mike is here with his wife? Andrea looks pretty good, I think. Better than she did the last time I saw her, anyway."

"I'm going to go over and say hello. It's embarrassing, but I've never met her," Jesse said.

"Then go. You'll love her. Everyone loves her. Andrea is one of those peaceful people who seems to bring calm into every room she's in."

"I'll get Sophie. She'll want to meet her, too."

"She's being introduced to the MacGregor clan," Brooke pointed out, "and if the look on her face is any indication, she's flat-out dazzled at meeting not only Dallas, but Berry as well."

"I was flat-out dazzled the first time I met them, too. Dallas is one of the most beautiful women in Hollywood, and Berry is a big-screen legend. Her movies are classics."

"She was quite the thing in her day," Brooke agreed. "Jess, didn't you hire a string quartet for tonight?"

He looked around the room. "I did, but they're obviously not here."

"You go visit with your guests. I'll check with Lola and see if she's heard anything," she told him.

"Thanks." He leaned down and kissed the side of her face. "I could not have done this without you. I will be forever in your debt."

"Good." She smiled. "I'll be sure to think of some way for you to repay me."

"You could make me your sex slave," he offered. "It's probably going to take me years to pay off that debt, but I'm a man who believes in settling his accounts. So what do you say?"

"I think we can probably work something out."

He grinned and went off to get Sophie.

Brooke found Lola, who was just on her way into the room to let Jesse know that the musicians had called and were stuck in traffic because of an accident on Route 50 but would be here as soon as possible, most likely before dinner was served. Lola suggested they extend the cocktail hour by another thirty minutes to give the quartet time to arrive and set up. Brooke told her that she thought it was a good way to handle the situation but that Lola needed to check with Jesse.

"Who is that?" Jason appeared at Brooke's elbow. "The woman you were just talking to. Who is she?"

"Lola, grandniece of the original Lola who opened this restaurant long before either of us was born," Brooke told him. "Why?"

Jason shrugged. "Just wondering."

Clay wandered over and handed her a glass of wine. "You look like you could use a little refreshment."

"Thanks, but I only drink club soda while I'm working," she replied.

"You're working?" He frowned.

"Until the desserts are served, I consider myself at work."

"I'll get you a club soda from the bar," Jason told her. "I'll be right back."

"Thanks, Jace, I appre . . ." Brooke's attention was drawn to the top of the stairs, where a small crowd of late arrivals had stopped and appeared to be lost. A petite woman with long blond hair, a dark-eyed woman Brooke recognized from channel-surfing, and a tall dark-haired man who looked an awful lot like Jesse.

"Excuse me." Brooke patted her brother on the arm and started toward the stairwell.

"Who are those people?" Clay asked.

Brooke turned to him and said, "I believe they're long-lost relatives."

She made her way through the crowd to where the six newcomers stood. The half siblings and their spouses, she assumed.

"Hi, I'm Brooke," she greeted them. "I'm a friend of Jesse's. You are . . ."

"Late," the dark-haired man told her. "We were stuck in traffic."

"I heard there was an accident on Route 50," she replied, and he nodded.

"That was the one." He extended a hand. "I'm Nick Enright. This is my wife, India . . . my sister Georgia . . . her husband, Matt . . . my sister Zoey . . . and her husband, Ben."

Brooke tried to put the faces with the correct names.

"It's nice to meet you all," she said. "I know Jesse will be so happy to see you."

The three Enright siblings exchanged glances.

"We're looking forward to meeting him, too," Zoey said.

"Why don't you come in and get something from the bar," Brooke suggested. "I'll find Jesse and Sophie and let them know that you're here. Then I'm sure you'll want to say hello to your grandfather."

Brooke met Jesse halfway across the room.

"Jess, you have company."

"I see. I see that we do. Where's Sophie?" he said without taking his eyes from his brother and sisters.

"I'll find her. Now take a deep breath and go introduce yourself."

She watched him make his way through the crowd, his eyes on the bar. Brooke scanned the room for Sophie, and found her talking to Cameron O'Connor.

"Jesse wants you to meet him at the bar," Brooke told Sophie. "There are some people he wants you to meet."

Sophie turned and glanced over toward the bar, and her mouth dropped slightly. "Is that them?" she asked. "Is that . . ."

Brooke nodded. "That's them. Go say hello."

"Holy crap, I never thought for a second that they'd show up," Sophie muttered.

"Well, they did." Brooke laughed. "Go."

Sophie excused herself and made a beeline for the bar.

Cam, being taller than most people, had a clear view of the room. Brooke expected him to ask about the late arrivals. But instead his eyes followed Sophie.

You and just about every other single guy here. Brooke smiled to herself. She'd be surprised if every single guy there wasn't watching Sophie's every move. Cam hadn't taken his eyes off her.

"So you think you'll have enough of a crew to start work on the tenant house this week?" Brooke asked.

Cam continued to stare at the bar. Brooke waved a hand in front of his face.

"Cam. I asked you a question."

"What? Oh. Right. Yeah, business is going fine," he told her.

"That wasn't the question."

"Oh. What was it?"

Brooke laughed and repeated it for him.

"Oh, yeah. I'm having some materials delivered on Monday so we're all ready to go first thing Tuesday morning."

"Great. I'm anxious to move in."

"Must be tough living at home after living on your own."

"It hasn't been too bad. We all have our own agendas and try not to get in each other's way. Clay has been great, but Mom will be moved out by Thanksgiving and I'm hoping to follow her in the not-too-distant future." She poked him in the chest. "That depends on you, though, so keep to the schedule."

"I'll do my best." Brooke couldn't help but notice that his eyes drifted back toward the bar again.

"I'm going to excuse myself and go say hello to the guest of honor," she told him.

Curtis Enright sat in a club chair that was festooned in balloons. Jesse had tied so many onto the back of the chair that they almost formed a solid barricade behind his grandfather. Well, she had told him to tie a bunch of them on.

"Hello, Mr. Enright," she greeted him.

"There's the girl who made all this possible." He reached out and took her hands in his.

She bent down and kissed his cheek. "Are you having a happy day, Mr. Enright?"

"One of the happiest days I can remember," he replied. "I can't thank you enough for everything you did to make this happen. Jesse tells me you pretty much played field general in getting this off the ground."

"I've had a little more experience giving parties than Jesse has. He just needed a little direction."

"That's not how I heard it, but thank you for your part in making this such a fine evening, Brooke." He patted her hand, then looking beyond her, froze. Brooke didn't need to turn around to know what was going on.

"Pop, you have some visitors." Jesse placed a hand on the back of Brooke's neck.

"I see that I do." Curtis stood unsteadily, and Nick reached out a hand to help him up. Curtis attempted to clear his throat but failed. Tears formed in the corners of his eyes and he struggled for words that did not readily come.

"How are you, Pop?" Nick asked.

Curtis tried again to clear his throat. Finally, he said, "I'm overcome. I'm simply overcome . . ."

"Take a deep breath," Jesse told him, then teased, "It isn't like you to be at a loss for words."

"It's a first." Curtis looked from one to the other of his grandchildren from whom he'd been estranged for so long. "It's good to see you again. It's good to see you all."

Brooke backed away to give Curtis a few minutes with his grandchildren. She mingled with the crowd and stopped to talk with friends, but every once in a while she glanced back at the small group. *How strange to have a brother or a sister you never met before,* she thought. *How strange to have to meet your siblings for the first time as adults—and to have a grandparent you barely remembered and didn't know.*

All appeared to be going well, though, she thought, observing occasional laughter from the Enrights, a sure sign that if anyone had any hidden resentment, they weren't likely to air it right then and there, for which she was grateful. She hadn't wanted anything to mar the gift that Jesse was offering his grandfather, and was happy to see that so far, nothing had.

By ten o'clock, dinner had been served and the dessert table had been wheeled out. Brooke's cupcakes were a clear hit, and the leftovers were boxed up to go home with Curtis, who only halfheartedly protested. By eleven, the party had officially come to a conclusion, and there was a long line of well-wishers bidding good night to the host and the birthday boy.

"Pop invited us back to the house," Jesse told Brooke as the last guests were drifting out. "Nick, Georgia, Zoey, Sophie, me. Want to come?"

Brooke debated with herself, then said, "No, I think I'll pass. I think this is a night for you and your siblings to get acquainted." When Jesse started to protest, she added, "You don't know how this will go. At some point, there may be some discussion that isn't meant for anyone but family. I think I should bow out."

"Tomorrow, then?" He nuzzled the side of her face. "I've been looking forward to getting you alone tonight. Want to go back to my house and wait for me there?"

She shook her head, no. "You'll be thinking that I'm waiting and maybe leave before you should. I'll see you tomorrow. We can catch up then."

"All right." He kissed her. "Thanks."

She nodded and watched him help his grandfather down the steps.

"Brooke's not coming?" she heard Curtis ask.

"She's tired," Jesse explained. "She baked up a storm this week . . ."

"So, you need a lift?" Clay handed her coat to her.

"I do, thanks. Just give me a minute to gather all my trays and things."

"I'll help."

They set about packing up her cupcake stands and cake stands and Clay took everything down to the car.

"Where's the van?" she asked.

"After I dropped you off earlier, I drove it home

and picked up my car." Clay grinned. "Say whatever you want, but that thing is no chick magnet."

"And when it was rusty and mottled white it was?"

"A guy could hope."

"Where's Jason?" She looked around as they headed out.

"He's downstairs at the bar. I told him I'd drive you home and then come back."

They went out through the back way and packed everything into the trunk of Clay's car. On the way home, he asked, "Not that it's any of my business, but why aren't you off with Jesse tonight? You two having a disagreement?"

"Not at all. His grandfather invited all of the grand-kids over to his place after the party, and yes, I was invited to go."

"So why didn't you? Is the bloom off the rose? He getting too interested and you're shutting him out?"

"What are you talking about?"

"I'm reminding you of the conversation we had some weeks ago about how you don't give guys a chance, and how you dump anyone who shows any real interest in you."

"For your information, I'm not dumping Jesse. I just felt that since Curtis hadn't seen three of his grandchildren in many years, it was a time and place for just them. They're Jesse's half siblings from a marriage his dad had before he married Jess's mother. Neither he nor Sophie had ever met them before, though they knew they were out there somewhere. I'd have felt like an intruder. People might be wanting to say some things that should be said among family members only. I didn't feel I should go."

"That was nice of you, but you still—"

"And as for Jesse . . ." She hesitated.

"Yes, go on. As for Jesse . . . ?"

"The bloom is definitely not off the rose, and that's all I'm saying about that." She looked out the window as they pulled up the long lane leading to the farmhouse. "You were right about something, back then. When we talked. You said I only went out with guys who asked me so that I could say that I went, but that I didn't give anyone a chance. You were right, of course. I didn't want anyone to care. I didn't want to care about anyone, ever again."

"And . . ."

"It isn't an *and,*" she said, "it's a *but.* As in, but Jesse somehow got around me. Before I knew it, I was asking him out. Funny, isn't it?"

"Funny," Clay agreed.

She remembered a comment she'd made to Jesse. "You and he didn't have some kind of bet going, did you?"

"What kind of a bet would I have where my sister is concerned?" He turned off the car. "What kind of a guy do you think I am?"

"Well, you *have* become friends . . ."

"He's a nice guy. But no, I swear there was no bet. But I am curious. It looks like the two of you are . . . well, getting involved. Are you?"

"You could say that."

"You care about him?"

"More than I ever thought I'd care about anyone again."

"What happened to the girl who didn't want to fall

in love ever again because she couldn't face the possibility of losing someone again?"

"I never thought I'd meet someone who'd be worth the risk."

"And you think Jesse is?"

She nodded. "There's no question in my mind that he's worth it. But I don't remember saying I was falling in love with him."

"Are you?" Clay asked, his hand on the car door.

Brooke shook her head. "I don't know . . ."

She was still asking herself the same question the next morning, when she rang Jesse's doorbell, and again later after they'd made love. She was still wondering when they sat across from each other at the kitchen table, drinking coffee and rehashing the events of the night before.

"Your granddad was really happy to see everyone, wasn't he?" she asked. "Especially his other grandchildren."

"He was delighted. Surprised at first, but totally beside himself." Jesse leaned back in his chair. "I really didn't know what to expect from them. What if they were bitter toward Sophie and me for their dad walking out on them?"

"Were they?"

Jesse shook his head. "Georgia admitted that for a long time after they heard that Dad remarried, they assumed he'd left them and their mother for our mother. They couldn't imagine there'd be any other reason a man would leave his family like that. But they said they talked to their mother again after the invitations arrived and she admitted that Dad's leaving them had nothing to do with my mom. That it was because of something that she'd—their mother—done long before she'd met their father."

"That's intriguing." Brooke sat up. "Did they say what it was?"

Jesse shook his head. "Whatever it was, it's between them and their mother. Who also admitted that she'd been responsible for them not seeing their grandparents. Nick said that her entire attitude has changed now that she's a grandparent herself, that she's apologized to all of them. She even wrote a letter to Pop that she had Nick deliver last night."

"Did he read it?"

"He said he'd take a look at it later, that he didn't want to get distracted from his grandkids. They apologized for just showing up, but by the time they'd all agreed to come, it was too late to RSVP."

"So it was a great reunion."

"And it's still going on." Jesse drained his cup and told her, "Drink up. We're meeting them for brunch at one at that place on Charles Street that does the great brunches."

"Let's Do Brunch?" she asked.

"That's the place. Come on." He got up, took her by the hand, and pulled her from her chair.

"I can't go like this." Brooke frowned.

"Why not?"

"Because I'm rumpled and I don't have any makeup on and my hair's a mess and I didn't plan on going out, so I didn't bring any clothes with me."

"How long will it take you to go home, change, and whatever other stuff you said?"

"Maybe thirty minutes." She calculated. "Includes drive time."

"You have plenty of time. I'll pick you up at twelve forty-five."

"I can meet you there. It would save you time."

"I'd like us to go together," he told her. "Last night was a party for everyone. Today is meet-the-family day for you. I want to see what you think of everyone."

"All right. I'll go with you." She walked into the foyer with him and picked up her bag that she'd dropped to the floor when he'd opened the door a few hours ago. "It should be interesting."

And it had been that, Brooke later reflected. Interesting if not a bit overwhelming, with pictures of this child or that new baby being passed around. She lost track of whose baby was whose, who was the mother of Alexa and who was the mother of Summer, whose son was Charlie and whose was Cole. All in all, though, Brooke had had to admit that she was happy to have been included, happy to have met such interesting people. Jesse had been right. They were all very nice and fun and it was gratifying to see Curtis enjoying himself so much.

It seemed, Brooke thought, that having made the decision to be part of this family again, Jesse's siblings had gone all out to blend. India, Nick's wife, was also an assistant district attorney, so she and Sophie had lots to talk about and stories to trade. Matt, Georgia's husband, shared a love for Sherlock Holmes with Jesse, and Brooke and Zoey bonded over food.

"Have you ever thought about putting together a cookbook of your cupcakes?" Zoey leaned behind her husband at the table to ask Brooke.

"No, never," Brooke replied.

"You should do that. Really. We have food from everywhere come through the studio," Zoey said, "but I swear I've never tasted cupcakes as good as yours. Maybe you could even make them for us. We sell a lot of food, and—"

"Whoa." Brooke laughed. "I'm just getting around to baking for a local caterer. I can't think of anything beyond filling those orders."

"After the holidays, give it some thought." Zoey took a business card from her bag and wrote on the back. "That's my cell number and my email address. Call me in January and we'll talk more." She turned to Jesse. "Make sure she doesn't forget, Jesse. This girl could go places with those cupcakes of hers . . ."

By the time brunch had ended, everyone had traded email addresses and cell numbers and had promised to be in touch over the holidays.

"Brooke," India said as she buttoned up her coat, "Jesse tells me you have an eight-year-old son."

"That's right," Brooke replied.

"We have an eight-year-old boy, too. Maybe we can get them together next year. Nick and I would love to have you and Jesse and your son come for a visit. We live on the Delaware Bay and there's no end to the places they could explore."

"Here, too," Brooke said. "Lots of stuff going on in St. Dennis since the town was 'discovered.'"

"And you can all stay at my place," Curtis told them. "Anytime. All of you. The door will always be open."

"We all know the way now. It really wasn't so far." Georgia stood on her tiptoes to kiss her grandfather's cheek, and it was obvious that the old man was moved.

Jesse had offered to drive Curtis home, since he'd arrived with Nick and India. When Jesse pulled up at the sidewalk in front of his grandfather's home, Curtis said, "Thank you again for everything, son—for the party, for gathering my friends together for me, but most of all for bringing my family back together. That was the greatest gift anyone ever gave me, and I will never be able to thank you enough. I only wish your grandmother had lived to see this day."

Jesse got out of the car to walk his grandfather to the door.

"It's not necessary," Curtis protested, but Jesse insisted.

Brooke sat in the car and watched the two of them—the tall handsome guy with the normally brisk step who'd slowed his pace so that the old white-haired gentleman could keep up—as they made their way up the long brick path, and felt her heart flip in her chest. For someone who'd been certain she'd never fall, she was dangerously close to tumbling headfirst.

Chapter 20

JESSE dropped off Brooke so that she could get busy with the orders she had lined up for the following day, then made a detour on his way home to the stone jetty that jutted out into the Bay off Cannonball Island. He walked out onto the rocks and stood watching a sailboat being driven by the wind into a few sharp turns. He'd never sailed, though he'd thought about taking lessons last summer. He'd been tempted, but had decided against it because he figured it would be one more thing he'd be leaving behind if his grandfather decided not to keep him on.

The thought of having that happen—of having Curtis decide he'd rather close the firm that had represented so many local families for well over a hundred and fifty years than turn it over to Jesse—made Jesse physically ill. The humiliation of having an entire town know that your own flesh and blood thought you were unworthy to carry on the family name would have been too much, and Jesse had promised himself that if that happened, he'd just pack up and leave St. Dennis and forget that the entire place existed. Curtis had given him one year, and he'd taken a one-year lease on the house on Hudson Street.

But then Jesse met Brooke, and he knew it would take more than professional embarrassment to make him leave and not look back. He'd spoken the truth when he told his grandfather that he didn't think he'd ever been in love. There had been any number of women he'd liked and whose company he'd enjoyed throughout his life. Some he had definitely been in lust with. But love was something he hadn't planned on, something he'd wanted none of. To Jesse, love was a stepping-stone that led to a lot of pain. His mother was living proof of that. She'd loved his father a great deal, and look where that had gotten her. The last thing Jesse ever wanted was to do to a woman what his father had done to his mother. Not that Jesse would set out to hurt someone, he'd certainly never plan on it, but how did he know he really wasn't a chip off the old block?

But that was before Brooke.

There was no denying he'd fallen hard and fast for her, and he knew in his heart that he could never be what his father had been. He'd proven professionally that he was a good lawyer, good enough to carry on the family name here in this town where *Enright* meant so much.

That was important to him—there was no way around it, living up to Curtis's high expectations meant the world to Jesse. Knowing that he'd made the grade had lifted an enormous burden from his shoulders.

Finding the siblings that had been lost to him over the years, finding that they had open hearts and open arms, had lifted an old sorrow from his heart. He'd be forever grateful that they'd taken the chance, and after what had apparently been a long debate, had accepted his invitation.

But finding Brooke had filled him with a joy that he could never have anticipated. He'd played it just the way Clay had told him to, played it cool for as long as he could, but there was no way he could pretend that she wasn't the center of his life. He was head over heels and didn't think he could hide that from her much longer, if in fact he'd hidden it at all.

Did she know? He wasn't sure.

The only thing he was sure of was how he felt, and that the days of playing it cool were past. As soon as the wedding was over and Brooke had more than a minute to focus on something other than her business, he was going to lay it all on the line. Staying in St. Dennis now meant more than staying at Enright and Enright. It meant staying with Brooke, and building a life with her and Logan right here in her hometown.

St. Dennis was now Jesse's home, too, and he had no intention of leaving.

Curtis turned on the lights in the conservatory and proceeded to water his wife's orchids and ferns. He'd made a point of tending her plants, those she'd cultivated and pampered, and it was a source of pride to him that over the years, he'd lost very few. He'd repotted and divided the way he'd seen her do, and as a result, had more orchids than he knew what to do with. But tending them had kept him close to her, and when he was here, doing what she would have done herself, he knew she approved and silently applauded and appreciated his efforts.

The night before, when all of their grandchildren had gathered in the big formal living room, the scent of gardenia had been so strong that at one point, Zoey had asked if there was a plant nearby. Mike's daughter, Elizabeth, had mentioned that she used a gardenia soap because their grandmother had been fond of it, and that had satisfied everyone. But Curtis knew it had been more than soap that had perfumed the air.

"Weren't they lovely, the lot of them?" He spoke aloud as he watered the ferns. "Mike's boys and Elizabeth were wonderful, made everyone feel at home. It did my heart good, I swear, to see them all together, talking and laughing like old friends." He put the watering can down on the bench and rubbed a hand over his face. "I'd have given whatever years I may have left to have had you here for that, Rose." He paused. "But of course, you were here, in your way, and I'm grateful for that."

The only one who'd been missing had been Craig, and for all the chaos his son had caused in so many lives, some small part of Curtis wished he'd been there as well.

"Not the real Craig, though," he told Rose. "The *should-have-been* Craig. The real Craig would have brought along too much pain to too many people." He sighed deeply. It was terrible to want so badly to love your son, when your son insisted on being so unlovable. How, Curtis wondered, had such a man fathered five such wonderful children?

It was one of those mysteries he'd never solve.

Curtis walked to the glass wall that overlooked the gardens that he now had to pay someone else to care for. His days of weeding and planting—the things he'd taken up after she was gone—had ended. These days, it was all he could do to walk the entire length of the property in the back and pull out the occasional dried and dead plant.

Like I'll be soon enough, he thought. Not for the first time, he wondered if he and Rose would be able to come back and look in on their progeny, much as Rose looked in on him. Curtis had no fear of dying, no intention of praying for another day or a little more time. He felt he'd died a little every morning he'd had to wake without her by his side and was more than ready to be with her again in whatever form that next world allowed. But he would like to make a final decision on what to do with this place. There were eight grandchildren. How to decide? How to choose one over the other?

The thought occurred to talk it over with Violet, and he was pretty sure that thought had been planted by Rose.

"All right," Curtis said aloud. "I'll give her a call in the morning, see if she has any thoughts on the matter. Between now and then, perhaps you'll slip an idea to one of us."

He picked up the watering can and shuffled to the door, pausing to turn off the light. He locked the front door and started slowly up the steps, but paused as her scent surrounded him. He smiled and turned off the hall light at the top of the stairs, and followed his wife into their silent room.

Chapter 21

INVITATIONS to the wedding of Dallas MacGregor to Grant Wyler, and that of Steffie Wyler to Wade MacGregor, were the hottest tickets in town. Even though scheduled for the same date at the same venue, separate invitations were mailed out. Guests were requested to keep the information to themselves to cut down on the invasion of paparazzi who vied to take the first photos of Dallas on her wedding day.

Things had been kept under wraps for the most part, but late in the week word had leaked out somehow and St. Dennis was overrun by photographers and reporters from every celebrity and entertainment magazine, TV show, and Internet social website. The good people of St. Dennis, however, did their best to ignore their requests for information about times and dates and addresses.

Lucy Sinclair arrived five days before the wedding, and when Brooke met with her at Scoop to test Steffie's wedding-day ice cream and Brooke's cupcakes, she looked as if she'd been hit by a truck.

"When did you last sleep?" Brooke asked Lucy.

"I don't know," Lucy replied wearily. "What day is it now?"

"It's Wednesday and the bags under your eyes have bags. You can't be working twenty-four hours a day, Lucy."

"For some reason, I just can't seem to sleep at the inn," Lucy confided. "It's crazy, right? I grew up there. People come from all over the country to stay there. But I don't get a wink of sleep when I'm home."

"You're going to be dead before Saturday if this keeps up. Can't you stay somewhere else?" Brooke opened the box of cupcakes and offered Lucy her choice.

"Gorgeous. I love them. If they taste as good as they look . . ." She picked up a white frosted cake covered with iridescent edible glitter and took a bite. "Heaven. Who needs wedding cake when you can have one of these little lovelies?"

"Thanks." Brooke cut one that had a silvery-lavender frosting and handed Lucy half. "Luce, you're going to have to sleep between now and Saturday. If you can't sleep at the inn, you're going to have to sleep somewhere else."

"How do you think my mother and brother would react if I told them I was staying at one of the other inns or B and Bs in town instead of at home with them?" Lucy covered a yawn with her hand. "Besides, everyone in town would be wondering why I wasn't staying there."

"Why would you want to stay at another inn since your family owns the best on the Eastern Shore?" Steffie carried a tray to the table and placed dishes of creamy white ice cream in front of Lucy and Brooke and saved the last one for herself. "Something going on at the inn that I don't know about?"

Lucy turned to Brooke. "See what I mean?"

"Lucy hasn't been able to sleep at the inn," Brooke told Steffie.

"Why do you suppose that is?" Steffie asked.

"I don't know." Lucy shook her head. "I never can sleep when I'm there."

Steffie took a spoonful of ice cream and grinned. "Perfection." She dipped the spoon in for a second bite. "Maybe the inn has ghosts." She put the spoon down in the dish. "I'll bet it does. I read in the brochure that the house was built in the 1800s. I'll bet there are lots of ghosts there. I'll bet that's what's keeping you awake, especially since you're descended from the original Sinclairs who built the place."

Lucy glanced at Brooke. "Is she always like this?"

Brooke nodded. "I'm afraid so."

"Stop it, you two." Steffie laughed. "This town is full of ghosts, everyone knows that." She turned to Lucy. "I'll bet your mother could find out who it is. She has this Ouija board, and she could probably contact whoever it is."

"My mother has a Ouija board and contacts ghosts," Lucy said flatly. "You have got to be kidding me. *My* mother?"

Steffie nodded. "She helped me to contact Horace, my grandmother's cousin who left his house to me?" She leaned forward and lowered her voice as several customers entered the shop. "We found out that Horace and Alice Ridgeway—her family built Vanessa's house and Alice lived there for ninety-some years and Ness bought it from Alice's estate—they were lovers."

"Vanessa and Alice were lovers?" Lucy deadpanned.

"Alice and Horace. No one knew, all those years." Steffie got up to wait on the two women who were looking over the selections in the freezer cases. "Ask your mom. Think about it."

"Steffie always was a fanciful girl with imagination to spare," Brooke said as she scooped up some ice cream onto her spoon and tasted it. "This is fabulous. I wonder what's in it?"

"I don't know, but I definitely agree." Lucy nodded.

"I taste coconut," Brooke said. "And maybe something fruity."

"You taste coconut and white peaches. There's also white chocolate, but the flavor isn't as pronounced." Steffie told them from the counter.

"It's delicious." Lucy waited until Steffie's customers had paid for their ice cream and seated themselves. "You know, you could sell this. There are a lot of ice creams on the market, but nothing as good as this. And I'm not saying that just because you're paying me a gajillion dollars to do your wedding."

"Dallas is paying you a gajillion dollars," Steffie reminded her. "Our affair is a lot more modest."

"Whatever. The point is that your ice cream is amazing. I would love to be able to offer this to my L.A. clients," Lucy said.

Steffie shook her head. "I'd have to do things differently if I expanded. I'd have to buy bigger machines and I wouldn't be able to fit them into the back room, so I'd have to move at least part of my business. I'd have to hire more people to run the machines and quality control would become an issue for me. I'd have to travel to meet accounts and do PR and talk up my ice cream. I wouldn't have time to do the things I like to do, like play around with different flavor combinations in between customers. You're not the first person to suggest that I expand and try to become the next Ben and Jerry, but I don't want to do that. I'm happy just the way things are. I have total control over every aspect of my business, every day. I know my customers and love chatting with them. Now, if you can think of a way that I could make Scoop better, I'd love to hear it. But bigger?" She shook her head again. "Not interested in bigger."

Lucy held up her spoon. "This stuff could make you rich, Stef."

"I'm already rich. I own this business lock, stock, and freezer. I make enough money during the tourist season to keep me happy and in shoes all year long. I set my hours and make whatever kind of ice cream I feel like making on any particular day. The only orders I have to fill are the ones I decide to take. I have my evenings with my honey and my girlfriends and a very good life. I wouldn't change a thing."

The bell over the door rang and Steffie smiled. "Hey, Barbara. What's up?"

"Just wanted to drop off a little something for you and Wade." Barbara Noonan, who owned the bookstore on Charles Street, paused on her way into the shop. "Is that Lucy Sinclair I see?"

"It is." Lucy touched her napkin to the corners of her mouth and got up from her seat to give Barbara a hug. "How's my favorite bookseller these days?"

"She's seen better days," Barbara returned the hug. "A lot of us independent bookstores have had ups and downs these past few years, but we're holding our own. Especially during the summer when all the tourists and the day-trippers come into town. But enough about me. How are plans for the big wedding going?"

"Fabulously well," Steffie responded before Lucy could. "Lucy is a genius. Wait till you see the inn. That's all I'm saying. Just wait till you see what she's got planned."

"I can't wait." Barbara handed a beautifully wrapped package to Steffie. "Much happiness to you and Wade."

"Aw, thank you, Barb." Steffie kissed the woman on the cheek.

"You're very welcome, dear."

"Do you have time to sit for a few minutes . . . ?" Steffie gestured toward the table where Brooke sat.

"I really don't, but thank you. I have to get back to the shop." Barbara waved to Brooke. "I'll see you all on Saturday. Can't wait!"

Steffie walked Barbara to the door and closed it behind her. She turned to Lucy and said, "Why would I ever want to leave here?"

"Forget I mentioned it," Lucy said as she sat down at the table again.

Steffie walked over and leaned on the back of the chair she'd earlier been sitting in. "You know, I'll bet your mother could get those ghosts to leave."

Lucy rolled her eyes. "If I'd known you were this into the otherworld, I'd have planned a different theme for the wedding." She pretended to be thinking. "I wonder if it's too late to put some gauzy things in the trees to look like floating spirits."

"Scoff if you must," Steffie said loftily. "You're the one who isn't getting any sleep."

"Sorry, Stef. I just don't believe in spirits," Lucy told her. "I really believe that once you're gone, you're gone, and you don't come back."

"That's a debate for another time." Steffie finished her ice cream. "The real issue right now is getting you some sleep so that you can turn the ballroom into my fantasy winter-wedding wonderland."

"Why don't you stay out at the farm with us?" Brooke suggested. "It's Clay's farm now, but my son and I are staying there until we're able to get the old tenant house renovated, and my mom is staying there until her new house is ready for her to move in, so you'll be well chaperoned." She grinned. "So you wouldn't have to worry about gossip going around about you and Clay."

"There are worse things that could be said about a woman than that she's tangled up with your brother." Steffie tapped Brooke on the head and tossed her dish, spoon, and napkin toward the trash can near the door.

Brooke thought she saw a bit of a flush creep up Lucy's neck, but she wouldn't have sworn to it.

"No way could I get away with that," Lucy said. "What excuse would I give my mother and Daniel for not staying at the inn?"

"I know." Steffie snapped her fingers. "You can stay at my place. We just finished fixing up the guest room and it's really sweet. I made Wade move back to Berry's for the week before the wedding, so it would be nice to have the company."

"Stef, that's really nice, but again, what do I tell Mom?"

"You tell her . . ." Steffie paused. "You tell her that you can't sleep at the inn because you keep thinking about the wedding and getting up to go down to the ballroom to check on this or that and you need to get away from it for a few hours at night. And you can tell her we're . . . we're working on the wedding favors."

"Someone else is doing that," Lucy reminded her.

"Does your mother know that?" Brooke asked.

"Probably." Lucy appeared to think it over. "I think she'll understand the can't-sleep-'cause-I-keep-running-downstairs-all-night excuse, though. She knows how particular I am about details." She nodded. "I think that's believable. Thanks, Stef. I really appreciate it."

"I close up here at seven," Steffie told her. "Come by and follow me home."

"I'll do it, thanks."

"Can't have my wedding planner slipping into some sort of sleep-deprived psychosis the day before the wedding." Steffie gathered up the empty bowls. "Anyone want seconds?"

Brooke and Lucy both shook their heads. "Thanks but no thanks," Brooke told her. "Any more and I'll never get that dress zipped on Saturday."

She turned to Lucy. "So we're set, right?"

"I think so." Lucy opened a notebook that lay on the table and turned a page so that Brooke could see the diagram. "After the cake is cut, we'll have the cupcakes and ice cream served from this table."

"You mean cakes, right? Two different cakes?" Brooke asked.

"Dallas decided at the last minute that there should only be one cake and it should be Stef and Wade's. She said she's happy with cupcakes. The display will be amazing, by the way. Just leave it all to me."

"If you need help setting them up . . ." Brooke began to offer, but Lucy waved her away.

"Your job on Saturday is to be a gorgeous brides-maid in all those photos that we know are going to surface from here to Beijing by Sunday morning. My job is to make sure everything is arranged perfectly in the ballroom."

"Then you'd better get some sleep between now and then." Brooke grabbed her bag from the back of her chair. "We're done for now?"

"We're done till Saturday." Lucy nodded.

"Great. I'm going to run. I have another eight million cupcakes to frost." Brooke waved to Steffie, who was waiting on a customer, and took off for the farm and the work waiting for her in the kitchen.

The Day was seasonably cold with clear blue cloud-less skies. Guests arrived at the Inn at Sinclair's Point for the first wedding, which was scheduled for one in the afternoon. There were whitecaps on the Bay, and over the inn's vast lawns, dozens of gulls swooped low. One of Dallas's West Coast guests noted that they looked like flying confetti, and wondered how they trained the birds to fly around the inn at the precise moment the guests were arriving.

Brooke stood in an anteroom with Dallas and the other attendants, adjusting the flowers in one another's hair and retying the glittery sashes that circled their waists. The last wedding she'd been in—her own— weighed heavily on her mind. On that day, she'd been the one crowned with roses, in a long satiny gown, and she'd marched into the church on the arm of her father. Eric's smile had lit up the room when he saw her walking down the aisle.

Brooke was painfully aware that both Eric and her dad were no longer with them. It saddened her. Since that day, her life had seen many changes, some good, some not so welcome. She'd made her peace with it all, and today, wished only to celebrate the new beginnings of her friends.

Funny, though, she mused, *that I'd be a bridesmaid for Dallas MacGregor in her wedding to Grant, since Dallas and I spent our high school years vying for his attention.* Dallas, of course, had always won, and if Brooke had hated her with all the might of a scorned teenager back then, these days, she'd grown to love Dallas like a sister. No one, Brooke had told Jesse, was happier for Dallas and Grant than she herself was.

Strings played softly in the smaller of the two ballrooms, where rows of chairs had been set up to form a center aisle covered with a white cloth runner that led to a wooden arch covered with white roses, orchids, hydrangea, and stephanotis. The ends of the rows were draped with white tulle gathered in waves and held together with huge bunches of lavender roses and white baby's breath. The Hollywood elite sat elbow to elbow with the local guests, and everyone stood when the strings announced the arrival of the bridal party and the back doors opened.

Berry Eberle, the bride's great-aunt, walked down the aisle proudly on the arm of her beau, Archer Callahan. They were followed by the groomsmen: the best man, Gabriel Beck, the town's chief of police and the groom's best friend; Clay Madison; Cameron O'Connor; and the bride's son, Cody. The bride's two-year-old nephew, Wade's son Austin, toddled along behind Cody and waved to everyone he knew.

Then came the bride's attendants: Laura Fielding, whose comeback as a star had been orchestrated by Dallas when she selected Laura to star in the debut film of Dallas's film company, served her old friend as maid of honor. The bridesmaids followed, all dressed in shiny silver satin and carrying lavender and white roses: Steffie, Vanessa, and Paige Wyler, daughter of the groom, headed up the aisle in front of Brooke. Her eye caught Jesse's in the crowd, and his wink brought a smile to her face.

Then the music changed, and the bride stood in the doorway wearing a long fitted dress of silver sequins with a high neck and low back that shimmered with her every move. In her arms she carried a bouquet of white flowers and trailing ivy. She walked up the aisle on the arm of her brother, who would soon celebrate his own wedding in this very room—after a suitable change of decor at the instruction of the wedding planner, of course.

The ceremony was performed by Archer Callahan, who was a justice of the peace as well as a retired judge, and was short and very sweet, both the bride and the groom promising to love, honor, and cherish—

though not to obey—every day of their lives, in this world and in the next.

Next came a cocktail hour in the inn's solarium, which was decked out in more roses and orchids and clouds of white tulle. Brooke shared a glass of champagne with Jesse and nibbled on a few excellent hors d'oeuvres before having to disappear upstairs to change the accessories that would outfit her for Steffie's wedding.

She marveled at the transformation Lucy had orchestrated, turning the small ballroom from white sophistication to a celebration in red in a very short amount of time. The white runner remained, but was strewn with red rose petals. Gone were the yards of white tulle and the white-and-lavender bouquets at the ends of the rows. In their place were cone-shaped vessels covered in red, green, and white tartan fabric that held the red-and-white bouquets of roses, ivy, and branches of holly. The arch that previously had sparkled in silver and white was now festooned with red and white flowers and streams of tartan ribbon. Everything was bright and cheery and smacked of the holiday season, just as Steffie had wanted.

Grant escorted his mother, Shirley—the mother of the bride—to her seat, then joined the groom and his groomsmen at the right side of the arch. Next to Wade stood Grant, the best man, Beck, Clay, Cameron, and Cody. A trumpet sounded to alert the guests to rise and the bridesmaids—Brooke, Dallas, Paige, and the bride's married cousin Kristin, with Vanessa as maid of honor—began their march. They wore the same silver satin gowns with a difference: the wide

sashes at their waists, their high heels, and the rib-
bons wrapping their bouquets were all done in the
red, green, and white of the MacGregor tartan. Even
Dallas had added the tartan accessories to her wedding attire. They looked, Brooke had quipped, like an
advertisement for Scottish shortbread.

The bride, dressed in a white silk dress with a wide
skirt that was gathered on one side, entered on the
arm of her father, George Wyler. The same wide sash
of tartan plaid circled her waist and her shoes matched
those of her attendants. She carried white roses inter-
spersed with red holly berries and trails of ivy. On her
head she wore a short veil held back with a crown of
white rosebuds. She was breathtaking, and as Brooke
had told her moments before the doors opened, Steffie needn't be worried about walking in the shadow
of her famous sister-in-law.

Judge Callahan performed the second ceremony as
well, this one slightly longer than the first. When the
judge pronounced Wade and Steffie husband and
wife, the bride raised her bouquet over her head and
hooted to the applause of their guests.

A second cocktail hour not being needed, the guests
followed the wedding party into the large ballroom,
where the decor wowed everyone. Tall leafless trees in
silvery planters lined the room, their branches draped
with tulle and tiny white twinkling lights—Steffie's
"fairy lights." The tables were covered alternately in
red or white with the opposing color overlay, and
centered with tall vases of curly willow spray painted
with a glittery silver paint. From the branches hung
tiny lanterns that flickered like fireflies, and around

the bottoms of the vases were smaller vases filled with white orchids and red roses.

"I can't believe Lucy was able to pull this off," Brooke said to no one in particular as the wedding parties stood in the receiving line.

"Neither can I." Vanessa slid into line next to her. "It's mind-blowing. No mortal could have arranged this. Let's start a rumor that Lucy's an alien."

"She'd have to be to have done all that," agreed Kristin. "I've never seen anything like this." She pointed around the ballroom. "It's spectacular."

"Have you talked to Stef yet about . . . you know," Brooke whispered to Vanessa.

"Uh-uh. Grady and I agreed to wait until she and Wade get back from their honeymoon. He totally agreed with you, just so you know," Vanessa told her in the same low, confidential tone. "He thinks we need to do the wedding thing." She looked around the room. "It sure won't be anything like this one, though."

"Doesn't have to be," Brooke assured her. "Whatever you decide to do, just make sure that all the people you most love are there with you, then you'll never have regrets when you look back on the day."

"You're right, of course." Vanessa nodded.

"What are you two whispering about?" Steffie leaned behind Wade to ask.

"I just asked Brooke if she thought this dress made my butt look big," Vanessa told her solemnly.

Steffie rolled her eyes and turned to greet the first of the guests to come through the line.

It seemed to Brooke that the line was endless, as if everyone in St. Dennis were there.

Close enough, she thought as she glanced down the line. Every face was familiar, from Grace Sinclair to Violet Finneran to Steffie's two part-time workers and the veterinary assistants from Grant's animal hospital. Jesse stood next to his grandfather, and Nita Perry, who owned the antique shop on Charles Street, chatted with Luke Haldeman, who'd just bought the boat sales showroom and marina from the estate of the previous owner. Brooke's mother was deep in conversation with the new librarian and Mr. Clausen, who'd taught American history to both Grant and Steffie in high school and was somehow related to Berry.

We're all somehow related to one another here, Brooke mused, *if not by blood, then by marriage, and if not by marriage, then by friendship.* She was glad she'd followed her heart and come home when she did.

And while I'm on the subject of my heart . . .

Jesse leaned forward to kiss her.

"You look . . . spectacular," he told her.

"You're supposed to say that to the bride," Brooke whispered.

"I did that, but you look spectacular, too." He leaned closer to her ear and whispered, "I can't wait to get you alone."

"Ditto. Now move along so we can keep the line moving. I'm starving."

"How can you be starving?" Vanessa frowned. "You ate all that shrimp an hour ago." Vanessa covered her mouth with her hand. "I shouldn't have said the S-word. The very thought of seafood makes me want to—"

"I get it. Hang strong for about fifteen more minutes. Want Jesse to get you some club soda?"

Vanessa shook her head and smiled at Hal Garrity, the closest thing she had to a father, as he came through the line with her mother, Maggie, on his arm.

Brooke's mother was next, and so on down the line, until Brooke was convinced that she'd been right earlier: all of St. Dennis had been invited.

The reception went by mostly in a blur. Brooke danced with Jesse and Curtis, with Clay and with Grady and Grant and Wade and who knew who else, until she was dizzy. Between the band's sets, she grabbed Jesse by the arm.

"Air," she told him. "I need air."

"It's pretty cool out," he told her. "You should bring whatever wrap you brought with you."

"It's upstairs," she told him. "I'd pass out before I got it. Let's just go out on the terrace for a minute."

She took him by the hand and led him through the lobby to the inn's bar and beyond to the terrace.

"Wow, look at all those stars," was the first thing she said when they'd walked outside. The second was, "You were right. It really is pretty chilly."

He took off his suit coat and draped it over her shoulders.

"Now you'll be cold," she protested.

He wrapped his arms around her and drew her in. "Nah," he said. "I've got a hot date tonight."

"It was a beautiful day, wasn't it?"

"Amazing that they were able to pull that off," he said. "Switching everything around that fast, having the reception incorporate the colors and the flowers from both weddings."

"That was Lucy's doing. That's why Dallas and Steffie wanted her to do their weddings."

"Ah, Lucy. The redhead who made your brother drool."

"I wish I'd seen that." Brooke laughed. "I've never seen Clay look foolish over anyone."

"The right girl can do that to a guy." He rested his chin lightly on the top of her head. "The right girl can make a guy not care how foolish he looks. Take me, for instance."

"There's nothing foolish about you, Jess."

"If things had gone differently, there could have been."

"What do you mean?"

"If my grandfather had found me lacking and fired me from the firm, I'd have looked very foolish." He rocked her slowly, side to side. "But I'd have stayed here and faced it, if it meant having a chance with you."

She leaned back and looked up into his eyes.

"You are the woman of my dreams," he told her. "The woman I've been looking for all my life. I'd stay and face down anything to be with you."

"Jess . . ." She was so touched she hardly knew what to say.

"All my life, I was afraid I'd wake up one day and find out I'd turned into my father," he said. "I've always felt him looking over my shoulder, as if he were waiting for me to be like him."

"From what you've told me about him, and from knowing you, I don't see that happening." She shivered inside his coat but didn't want to go inside. There were things they needed to say to each other, and she knew this was the right time and the right place. "You're not him. Your grandfather knows it and your brother and sisters know it and I know it. You're a man that a woman can trust with her heart. A man a woman can trust with her future."

"You trust me with yours?"

"I do. I never thought I'd say that again, but I do. I never wanted to take a chance again, but I will."

"You'll never be sorry," Jesse promised. "I swear, you'll never be sorry . . ."

In her heart, Brooke already knew that. She smiled and drew him closer, and made promises of her own.

Diary ~

Well, it's done—The Wedding Day has come and gone. I can't even begin to tell how proud I am of our Lucy! What a day she planned! Two distinct weddings blended into one perfect reception. Sigh. Everyone in town was there and no one left without making a point of telling me what a bang-up job she'd done. Lucy says that the sign of a good wedding planner is when none of the guests even think about who put it together, but I told her that was impossible around here because everyone has known her since she was just a wee one, and everyone was so happy that she was such a huge success. I know that both brides were delighted with everything— the food was exquisite from soup to nuts, literally, the dessert course being the most popular, but the new chef Daniel hired is the best we've ever had. Truly first class.

But I digress . . . I'd invited Trula for the wedding weekend because I know that someone near and dear to her has a very special wedding coming up and she wants it to be here. So she came armed with her camera and took a million pictures at the reception. I told her to just stroll around and snap away, and if anyone asked, she was one of the photographer's assistants, although, well, as she rightly pointed out, most wedding photographers have assistants who are in their twenties, not their seventies, but she pulled it off all right.

Other than having someone accuse her of selling her photos to one of those sleazy publications you see in the supermarkets. Ha! I said. Trula Comfort—Paparazzi!

In any event, Trula is definitely going to push her Robert to have his wedding here next year, but only if Lucy will come back to do it. Now, I ask you: what event planner would turn down Robert Magellan? Yes, of course, the wedding of Dallas MacGregor was a huge coup, and will certainly give Lucy's business a huge celebrity bump. But Robert Magellan is one of the wealthiest men in the hemisphere, and had been bordering on becoming a recluse for a while. He never gives parties and is almost never seen out and about socially, never frequents those fancy places that other wealthy folks favor. He could have his wedding anywhere in the world—literally—but if he chooses the Inn at Sinclair's Point . . . well, do I have to spell out what that would do for our reputation?

Not to mention that it would bring Lucy back for another few weeks. I keep hoping she'll find whatever it is she's looking for right here at home, but I'm beginning to wonder if even she knows what she wants.

It's just awful when you know what's right for your kids but you can't make them see it. I've always believed that Lucy's destiny was in St. Dennis, but I can't convince her of that. Why, even dear Alice is in agreement. No, of course, I didn't pull out the herbs and the spell book, though I'd be sore tempted if I knew for sure it would work. Anyway, Alice tells me—through the Ouija board—that Lucy's future is here. "Well," I said, "Alice, this is going to be a test of how much you really know." Alice, of course, went silent after that, but I know she'll be back. She does so love to chat . . .

Here I am prattling along about the wedding as if there were nothing else going on in St. Dennis! Old Curtis Enright got a big surprise on his eighty-fifth birthday when grandson Jesse threw a big party to celebrate at Lola's. I heard that almost everyone who was invited attended, which was nice, since Curtis is such a gentleman. The biggest surprise of the evening, though, was the appearance of the children from his son Craig's first marriage. No one in St. Dennis had seen them—two girls and a boy—in, oh, dear, since before Rose died. I heard it said that Jesse had never met any of his half siblings before, so it was especially nice of him to have invited them. It looked like there was a happy reunion, which I was glad to see. Jesse's sister Sophie came for the party—lovely, lovely girl. All the young men in the room seemed to think so, too.

Of course, there's the Holiday House Tour next

weekend—my favorite event of the year. I just love to see this little town of ours dressed up, the old houses decorated from rooftop to front door. Call me nosy if you must, but I just love going inside to see how everyone decorates for the season. I love decorating the inn, though every year it seems to be just a little more difficult for me to do all the downstairs rooms by myself. Lucy said this year I should have asked for help from the local historical society. Perhaps next year . . . Anyway, it's fun to think that this time next week we'll be leading the weekenders and the day-trippers from room to room and talking about the history of the inn. The Holiday House Tour has become such a huge fund-raiser for the town, not to mention a boon to the merchants.

There was one sad note at the wedding, and it took me back so many years. During the toasts, both Steffie and Grant made mention of their sister, Natalie, who died when she was four. She and Lucy had been the closest of friends from the first day of nursery school when they discovered they shared the same birthday. They'd been inseparable, those two. Why, sometimes when I look out the back windows of the inn, I can almost see them playing on the swings or in the sandbox. Natalie was such a darling girl, and when she fell ill . . . well, it hit everyone in the community hard. Lucy was despondent when Natalie died, and for a few years, she refused to celebrate her birthday without her friend. It was a poignant moment on a beautiful and memorable day. Lucy later said that if for no other reason, she was glad to have been at the weddings to remember Natalie.

And one interesting note: while Lucy tried her darnedest to fade into the background, it seemed she hadn't faded quite far enough that her old friend Clay Madison wasn't able to find her and talk her into a dance or two. I know she'd just about kill me if she knew I said so, but they do make a lovely couple ~

~ Grace ~

Read on for previews of books two and three
from the Chesapeake Diaries series

Available from Ballantine Books

Book Two

Home Again

AT the precise moment Dallas MacGregor was picking up her son, Cody, from his pricey summer day camp out near Topanga State Park, the home video starring her soon-to-be-ex-husband and two of the female production assistants from his latest film had already been uploaded to the Internet. By the time she arrived at her Malibu home—she'd stopped once on the way from the set of her latest movie promo shoot to pick up dinner—the one-thousandth viewing had already been downloaded.

The phone was on overdrive, ringing like mad, when she walked into her kitchen.

"Miss MacGregor, you have many messages. Two from your aunt Beryl." Elena, her housekeeper, cast a wary glance at Cody and handed her employer a stack of pink slips as the phone continued to ring. "About Mr. Emilio . . ."

"Would you mind answering that?" Dallas slid the heavy paper bag onto the counter. "And why are you still here? I thought you wanted to leave today by four?"

"Yes, miss, I . . ." Elena lifted the receiver. "Miss MacGregor's . . . oh, hello, Miss Townsend. Yes, she's home now, she just arrived. Yes, I gave her the message but . . . of course, Miss Townsend . . ."

Elena held the phone out to Dallas.

"It's your great-aunt," she whispered.

"I figured that out." Dallas smiled and took the cordless receiver from Elena. "Hello, Berry. I was just thinking about—"

"Dallas." Her aunt cut her off sharply. "What the hell is going on out there?"

"Not much." Dallas paused. "What's supposed to be going on?"

"That numbskull you were married to." Berry's breath came in ragged puffs.

She was obviously in a lather over something. Not unusual, Dallas thought. At eighty-one, it didn't take much to rile Berry these days.

"What's he done now?" Dallas began emptying the bag, lining up the contents on the counter.

"Not *what* as much as *who*." Berry was becoming increasingly agitated.

"Mommy." Cody tugged at her sleeve. "Why are all those cars out there?"

"Berry, hold on for just a moment, please." Dallas glanced out the side window where cars were lined up on the other side of the fence that completely encircled the gated property, cars that had not been there five minutes ago when they drove through the gates. It wasn't unusual for paparazzi to follow her home, but she hadn't noticed any cars tailing her today. She raised the blinds just a little, and saw more cars were arriving even as she watched.

"I don't know, Cody. Maybe the studio put out something about Mommy's new movie. Maybe we should turn on the television and see."

"No!" Elena and Berry both shouted at the same time.

"What?" Dallas frowned and turned to her housekeeper, who stood behind Cody. She pointed to the child, then raised her index finger to her lips, their silent code for "not in front of Cody."

Keeping a curious eye on Elena, Dallas asked, "Berry, why don't you tell me . . . ?"

"Are you saying you don't know? Seriously? You haven't heard?"

"Heard what?"

"That idiot ex of yours—"

"Not ex yet, but soon, please God . . . ," Dallas muttered. "And it's long been established that he's an idiot, so anything he's done should be viewed with that in mind."

"—managed to get himself filmed doing . . . all sorts of things that you will not want Cody to see . . ." Berry was almost gasping. "And with more than one person. It was disgusting. Perverted."

"You mean . . ." Dallas's knees went weak and she sat in the chair that Elena wisely pulled out for her.

"Yes. A sex tape. Not one, but *two* young women. I was shocked. Appalled!"

"Wait! You actually *saw* it?"

"Three times!" Dallas could almost see Berry fanning herself. "It was vile, just vile! You know, Dallas, that I never liked that man. I told you when you first brought him home that I—"

"Berry, where did you see this?"

"On my computer. There was a link to a site—"

"Hold on for a moment, Berry." Dallas put her hand over the mouthpiece and turned to Elena. "Would you mind cutting up an apple for Cody? Cody, go wash your hands so you can have your snack."

After her son left the room, Dallas took the phone outside and sat at one of the tables on her shaded patio.

"Dear God, Berry, let me get this straight. Emilio made a sex tape and it was put on the Internet? Is that what you're telling me?"

"Yes, and not just any sex tape. This one had—"

"Wait a minute; they allowed you to download the whole thing?"

"No, no, not all of it, just a little peek. You had to pay to see the whole thing."

"And you did? You paid to watch . . ." Dallas didn't know whether to laugh or cry. The thought of her elderly aunt watching Emilio and his latest conquests burning up the sheets—and paying for the privilege—was horrifying and crazy funny at the same time. "Wait—did you say *three times*?"

"Yes, and it was—"

"Berry, why did you watch it three times?"

"Well," Berry sniffed. "I had to make sure it was really him."

The rest of the evening went downhill from there.

Dallas made every attempt to remain calm lest Cody pick up on the fact that she was almost blind with anger at the man she'd been married to for seven years.

Seven years, she repeated to herself. *Seven years out*

of my life, wasted on that reprobate. The only good thing to come out of those years was Cody—and Dallas had to admit that she would have weathered a lifetime of Emilio's amorous flings and general foolishness if she'd had to in order to have her son. When she filed for divorce eight months ago, following the latest in his long line of infidelities, Emilio hadn't even bothered to beg her to reconsider: they'd done that dance so often over the years that even he was tired of it.

She managed to have a normal evening with Cody and ignored the cars that parked beyond the protective fence. They had a nice dinner and watched a video together, then Cody had his bath and Dallas read a bedtime story before she tucked him in and turned off the light.

It wasn't until she went back downstairs, alone, that she permitted herself to fall apart.

There was no love lost between her and Emilio. She'd long since accepted the fact that he'd married her strictly to further his own career as a director. For a time, she'd remained stubbornly blind, insisting that her husband be signed to direct her movies, and for a time, she'd been equally blind to his affairs. Lately it occurred to her that she might well be the last person in the entire state of California to catch on to the extent of Emilio's indiscretions.

For the past five years, she and Emilio had battled over the same ground, over and over until Dallas no longer cared who he slept with, as long as it wasn't her. Looking back now, she realized she should have left him the first time he'd cheated on her, when the tabloids had leaked those photos of Emilio frolicking with a pretty up-and-coming Latina actress on a sunny, sandy beach in Guatemala when he'd told Dallas he was going to scout some locations for a film he was thinking about making, but it had been so much easier to stay than to leave. There was Cody to consider: Emilio had never wanted the child, but Dallas had hoped—for Cody's sake—that he'd come around. Besides, Dallas's schedule had been so hectic for the past three years that she'd barely had time to read the tabloids. She'd had the blessing—or the curse—of having had wonderful roles offered to her, roles that she'd really wanted, so she'd signed on for all of them, and had gone from one set right onto the next, leaving her time for nothing and no one other than her son. It had only been recently that Dallas admitted to herself that perhaps she'd been deliberately overworking herself to avoid having to deal with her home situation.

Well, avoid no more, she told herself as she dialed her attorney's number. This time, Emilio had gone too far. When the call went directly to voice mail, Dallas left the message that she wanted her lawyer to do whatever had to be done to speed up the divorce.

"And oh," she'd added, "we need to talk about that custody arrangement we'd worked out . . ."

While she waited for the return call, Dallas logged on to the computer in her home office. She searched the Web for what she was looking for. The link to the video appeared almost instantaneously, along with a running tally of how many times the video had been watched—all thirteen thousand, four hundred, and thirty-one viewings. Her stomach churning, she clicked on the link and was asked first to confirm that she was over eighteen, then for her credit card number.

"Great," she murmured. "For the low, low price of nineteen ninety-five, I can watch my husband . . . that is, my soon-to-be-ex-husband, perform daring feats with his production assistants."

The video began abruptly—"What, no music?"—and while the lighting could have been better, there was no question who was the filling in the middle of that fleshy sandwich. As difficult as it was to watch, she forced herself to sit through it, commenting to herself from time to time. ("Emilio, Emilio, didn't anyone ever tell you to always keep your best side to the camera? And, babe, that is decidedly not your best side.")

When the phone rang before it was over, Dallas turned off her computer and answered the call.

"Hey, Dallas, it's Norma."

"Thanks for getting back to me right away." Dallas leaned back in her chair and exhaled. Just hearing her attorney's always cool and even voice relaxed her.

"I just got in and I was going to call you as soon as I kicked off my shoes." Norma Bradshaw was not only Dallas's lawyer, she was also her friend.

"So you heard . . ."

"Is there anyone in this town who has not? So sorry, Dallas. We knew he was a colossal shithead, but this latest stunt even beats his own personal best." Before Dallas could respond, Norma said, "So we're going to want to see if we can move the divorce along a little faster. We'll file a motion to revise those custody arrangements we'd previously agreed to."

"You read my mind."

"I'll file first thing in the morning. If nothing else, I think we should ask for sole custody for a period of at least six months, given the circumstances, which of course we'll spell out for the judge in very specific terms."

"Would it help to know that that little forty-two-minute production was filmed in his house? The same one Cody and I moved out of just eleven months ago because he refused to leave?"

"Really?" Norma made a "huh" sound. "Are you positive?"

"I picked out that furniture," Dallas replied. "Along with the carpets and the tile in the bath and the towels that were dropped around the hot tub."

"That was really stupid on his part. Now you can say you don't want Emilio to have unsupervised custody because you don't know who will be in the house or what they'll be doing. Or who might be filming it." Norma paused. "How are you doing?"

"On the one hand, I feel devastated. Humiliated. Nauseated. On the other, I feel like calling every reporter who chastised me for being so mean and unforgiving to poor Emilio when our separation was announced and yelling, '*See? I told you he was a jerk!*' "

"Anyone you want me to call for you?"

"No. I'm not making any statements to anyone. This is strictly a no-comment situation if ever there was one."

"You know you can always refer people to me."

"I'll have Elena start doing that tomorrow. Thanks."

"How did Cody react?"

"He hasn't. He doesn't know what's going on."

"You didn't tell him?"

"Of course not. Why would I tell him about something like that?"

"Do you really think you can keep him from finding out? Isn't he in camp this summer?"

"He just turned six. He's only in kindergarten." Dallas frowned. "How many of the kids at his camp do you think caught Emilio's act?"

"They could hear their parents talking, they could see the story on TV. It made the news, Dallas."

"I don't think it's going to be a problem." Dallas bit a fingernail. "At least, I hope it won't be. But if he hears about it, I'll have to tell him . . . something."

"Well, good luck with that. In the meantime, if you think of anything else I can do for you, you know how to reach me." Norma's calls always ended the same way, with the same closing sentence. She never bothered to wait until Dallas said good-bye. She just hung up, leaving Dallas to wonder just what she would tell Cody if he should hear something.

She didn't have long to wait to find out. When she arrived at camp the following afternoon, the Cody who got into the car was a very different child from the one she'd dropped off earlier that morning.

"How was camp, buddy?" she asked when he got into the car.

He looked out the window and muttered something.

"What did you say?" She turned in her seat to face him.

"I didn't say anything."

"Well, how *was* camp? Did you have your riding lesson today?"

He shook his head but did not look at her.

Uh-oh, she thought as she drove from the curb. *This doesn't bode well . . .*

"So what did you do today?" she asked.

"I don't want to talk."

"Why not, baby?"

"Because I don't and I'm not a baby," he yelled. He still hadn't looked at her.

Oh, God. Her hands began to shake and she clutched the wheel in an effort to make them stop.

She did not try to engage him in conversation the rest of the way home, and once they arrived, she drove in through the service entrance at the back of the property to avoid the crowd that was still stalking the front gate.

"Those cars out there, they're all there because . . ." Cody said accusingly. "Because . . ."

It was then that Dallas realized he was crying. She stopped the car and turned off the ignition, then got out and opened his door. She unbuckled his seat belt but he made no move toward her.

"Cody, what happened today?" When he didn't respond, she asked, "Does it have something to do with your dad?"

"They said he did things . . . with other ladies. Justin's big brother said his dad saw it on the computer and he heard his dad tell his mom." Huge, fat drops ran down Cody's face and Dallas's heart began to break in half. "Justin's daddy said my daddy was a very, very bad man. The big kids said he . . . they said he . . ." He began to sob.

Dallas had never felt so helpless in her life. She got into the backseat and rubbed Cody's shoulders, then coaxed him into her arms. How could she have been so naive as to think he wouldn't hear something from the older kids at camp? And how could she possibly explain his father's actions to her son?

"I'm never going back to camp, Mommy. Not ever. Nobody can make me." He hiccuped loudly. "Not even you. I'll run away if you try."

"All right, sweetie." Silently cursing Emilio for his stupidity and his carelessness, Dallas held her son tight, and let him cry it out. "It's going to be all right . . ."

But even as she promised, Dallas wondered if, for Cody, anything would ever be right again.

Book Three

Almost Home

"THAT'S it, right there, ace. The house where I spent my happiest years. Number Twelve River Road."

Wade MacGregor hoisted the squirming child onto his shoulders. Delighted to be released from the car seat where he'd spent way too much time over the past few days, the little boy kicked his feet in the air, wanting *down* more than he wanted *up*. "Hasn't changed a whole heck of a lot since then."

Wade studied the exterior of the house for a long moment. "Looks like there have been a few changes in some of the trim color there around the porch. Aunt Berry always likes to keep up with the latest trends. Must always be on the cutting edge, you know?"

He paused momentarily to stare at the fence that ran across the front of the property. He wondered when the fence had been installed, and why. No one had mentioned it in recent phone calls.

Then again, there were things he hadn't mentioned, either.

"Let's go check out the river. See the water?" Wade crossed the broad lawn to the wooden pier in long strides, fully aware that he was procrastinating. "Right down here is where I learned to fish and canoe and row and crab and do all kinds of fun things."

He looked up into the face of the dark-haired cherub whose heels kicked gleefully into his chest.

"Yeah, I suspect you'll be wanting to do those things one day, too. I'll teach you whenever you're ready," Wade told him. "I promised your mama that I'd raise you the best I could. I can't think of any better place for you to spend your summers than right here in St. Dennis, just like I did."

A sleek boat passed by, kicking up some wake as it headed toward the mouth of the New River, where it met the Chesapeake Bay.

"Someday soon, we'll go sailing out there. You'll like that. We'll have to get you a little life jacket first, though." Wade thought for a moment. "Your mama loved the water. That's one thing you'll want to know about her when you get older. She loved to swim and water-ski and dive. Maybe one day you'll want to do those things, too. She wanted to teach you herself, but that's not going to happen now." Wade swallowed the lump that threatened to close his throat. "I know you miss her, buddy. I miss her, too . . ."

Overhead a gull drifted, and attracted by something on the dock, dropped down onto one of the pilings to get a better look. It hopped to the deck, pecked at something solid for a moment, then took flight, the unexpected prize held in its beak. The bird changed direction, and angled back toward the Bay. Wade followed it with his eyes until it disappeared.

"Ring-billed gull," Wade said aloud. "Not to be confused with the herring gull. Someday you'll know the difference. Someday you'll know all the shorebirds."

Figuring he'd gotten about all he was going to get out of his efforts to put off the inevitable, he glanced over his shoulder at the house.

"Well, I guess it's time to face the music." He started back across the lawn. "You ready to meet your aunt Dallas and your cousin Cody and your great-great-aunt Berry?"

The back door opened and a golden retriever sped out, a fluffy white dog on its heels, both barking wildly at the intruders.

"Fleur!" A little boy of six or seven raced after the dogs. "Ally! Stop! Come back!"

The dogs continued to run toward Wade.

"See doggie!" The toddler demanded and struggled to get down. "Wanna see doggie!"

Wade stood stock-still, waiting to see just how close the dogs would come, if they'd continue to bark, and if they'd show signs of real aggression.

"Ally! Fleur!" The boy ran after them and caught up with them when they stopped about ten feet from Wade.

"Hi, Cody," Wade said. "Do you remember me?"

Cody narrowed his eyes and searched Wade's face momentarily before a smile appeared.

"You're my uncle Wade," he said. "You live in Texas."

"Not anymore." Wade gestured to the dogs, who had calmed down a little. "They don't bite, do they?"

"Nah." The boy shook his head. "They just act tough. Mom says they think they're Dobermans or rottweilers or something."

Wade laughed. "Where is your mom?"

"She's in the house. She didn't say you were coming

today." Cody pointed to Austin, who was trying to wiggle out of Wade's grasp to get to the ground. "Who's that?"

"Cody, this is Austin." Wade lifted the toddler in an arc over his head and placed him on his feet on the grass. "He's your cousin."

"Hi, Austin." Cody knelt down in front of Austin, who pointed a chubby finger at the dogs, who approached cautiously, wagging their tales. "Austin, this is Ally. She's Aunt Berry's dog. And this one"—he pointed to the white dog—"is Fleur. She's mine."

"Here, doggie!" Austin chortled as the golden retriever drew closer.

Cody glanced up at Wade. "My mom didn't tell me I had a little cousin."

"Your mom doesn't know."

"Boy, will she be surprised." Cody commanded the dogs to sit, then led Austin to them.

"Boy, will she ever," Wade muttered.

A woman started around the side of the house, her pale blond hair pulled back in a ponytail, her dark glasses obscuring half her face.

"Cody, who are you talking—" she began, then stopped in her tracks. "Wade?"

"Hey, Dallas." Wade walked to meet his sister as she started toward him. "We were just on our way up to the house when Cody and his furry friends came out to greet us."

"You stinker! You didn't tell us you were coming home this week!" Dallas MacGregor wrapped her arms around him and hugged tightly. "You're looking good, kiddo."

"You're looking even better." Wade hugged her in

return and spun her halfway around before setting her down. "St. Dennis agrees with you."

"Why didn't you let us know you were coming? And what's with the trailer?" She pointed to the drive, where Wade's Jeep sat with a trailer hooked up to the back. "You hauling your beer in there? Expanding your business to the Chesapeake?"

"Actually, I closed the business. I sold the equipment and the building."

Dallas's jaw dropped. When she recovered, she asked, "What happened? Your brewery was doing so well. All those awards you won . . . I thought you were really solid."

"We were. It's a long story, Dallas."

Wade looked away. He'd been dreading this conversation for weeks. He'd been so proud of KenneMac, the brewery he'd started from scratch with his best friend from college. He'd hated closing it down, but hated the idea of selling it even more. The company name—that had been his and Robin's. His brewing secrets had taken him years to perfect. KenneMac Brews had been the best part of his life for the past eight years. Giving it up was one thing. Selling it—allowing someone else to become KenneMac Brews—well, that just wasn't going to happen.

But then again, even giving up the brewery wasn't the worst thing that had happened over the past few months.

The back door opened and a woman of indeterminable age stepped out onto the porch.

"Dallas, who's that you're talking to? And what's that thing parked in my driveway?" Hands on her hips, Beryl Eberle—once known internationally as screen star Beryl Townsend—paused, appearing to study the scene. "Is that Wade?"

"Yes, Aunt Berry. It's me." Wade's smile was genuine. He adored his great-aunt. She'd been the indulgent grandmother he hadn't known and Auntie Mame all in one. He counted the years he'd lived with her as some of the best of his life.

She came down the porch steps, holding on, he noticed, to the railing all the way. She was always so spry, so clever and lively, he often forgot that she'd turned eighty-one on her last birthday and had another approaching. He quickened his step so that she wouldn't have to walk across the entire yard to greet him.

"You are a sight for these old eyes, Wade MacGregor." She hugged him fiercely. "How dare you stay away for so long."

"What was I thinking?" He embraced her gently.

"I'll be damned if I know." She stood back and held him at arm's length. "You look more and more like your father every year. And I don't mind saying that Ned was the best-looking young man I ever—"

"Stop feeding his ego with that stuff," Dallas admonished. "He's already got a big head."

"What is that thing in the driveway?" Berry asked again.

"It's a trailer," he explained. "Holds all my worldly goods."

"Does this mean you've come home? That you're staying?" Berry, clearly joyful at the very thought, grabbed Wade's hand and gave it a squeeze.

"I'm not staying, Aunt Berry," he said softly. "I'm just passing through St. Dennis on my way to Connecticut. I'm going to be working for another brewery."

"What happened to your brewery?" she demanded.

"We were just starting to talk about that, Berry," Dallas told her.

"Well, he's going to have to start from the beginning, because I want—" A squeal of laughter erupted from the lawn. "What on earth . . . ?"

Berry's eyes narrowed. "Is that a small child I see down there with Cody and the dogs?" She stretched out her arm, her thin finger pointing to the tangle of fur and human on the ground. "There. There's a little boy. Where did that child come from?"

"Ah, Berry, actually, he's mine." Wade's eyes glanced from his aunt's startled face to his sister's. "That's Austin."

"Did you say . . . he's yours?" Dallas's eyes widened, as if she wasn't quite sure she'd heard correctly.

"Yeah." Wade nodded again.

"Well, who . . . I mean, when . . ." Dallas sputtered.

"You've had a *child* and you didn't think to let us know about him?" Berry's face was deadly with accusation.

Wade started to mount a defense, then stopped. Of course he owed them an explanation. What had he been thinking, not telling them as soon as the whole thing started? It wasn't so much that he'd wanted to keep Austin a secret. It was simply that every time he thought about calling and telling them, he'd get cold feet. There were so many questions, and after the past six months, he was so depleted emotionally, it had been too difficult to think about having that conversation on the phone.

Wade sighed. "It's really complicated."

"Assume for a moment that your sister and I possess a certain degree of intelligence. Perhaps even enough to understand." Berry raised one eyebrow, her favored expression to convey sarcasm. "Provided you speak slowly and use only very small words, of course."

Feeling like a chastised twelve-year-old, Wade went to his son and picked him up.

"No!" Austin protested loudly. "Play doggie."

"The dogs are going to come with us, right, Cody?"

"Right." Cody ran ahead and both dogs followed. "They're following us, Austin. See?"

"Down." Austin continued to struggle all the way across the lawn.

"Austin, meet your aunt Dallas and your great-great-aunt Berry." Wade held the child in both arms.

Austin's attention momentarily distracted from Ally and Fleur, he giggled and pointed to Berry and proclaimed, "Berry!"

"You coached him to do that so I'd melt right here on this very spot," Berry accused. "And it worked. Hello, Austin."

Berry held out her hand and Austin giggled again.

"Let me have him." Dallas reached for the child, and Wade passed him over. "He is a darling little thing, isn't he?" She met her brother's eyes. "Who's his mother, Wade? And where is she?"

"That's the complicated part," he told her softly. "It's a really long story."

"I've got all day. Berry? You have plans for this afternoon?" Dallas shifted a squirming Austin in her arms, then let him get down.

"I do now. Into the house. All of you—kids, dogs, everyone." Berry turned and started up the steps. "I can't have this conversation standing out in the hot sun without a cold glass of iced tea. It isn't civilized."

"She says march, we march." Dallas shrugged and followed in Berry's footsteps. She paused partway up and turned to Wade. "Wade, are you married to Austin's mother?"

"I was."

"When?"

"For almost three weeks, in July."

"Three weeks?" Dallas frowned. "You were only married for three weeks? Jeez, Wade, why bother?"

"Because she was dying," he said softly, "and I wanted her to die in peace."

For the second time in less than ten minutes, Dallas was momentarily stunned. When she recovered, she raised her hand and gently touched his face. "Oh, sweetie. What happened to you in Texas?"

"Like I said, it's a long story."

"Like I said, I have all day." Dallas took him by the hand and walked the rest of the way up the steps in silence. When they got to the deck, she paused and asked, "Is Austin your son?"

"He is now."

He opened the door for his sister, and waited while she entered the house, a million questions on her face and in her eyes.

He waited for the boys and the two dogs at the top of the stairs, and wondered where to begin to tell the story he should have told them months ago.